3/14

A WOUNDED NAME

A WOUNDED NAME

BY DOT HUTCHISON

✿ carolrhoda LAB
MINNEAPOLIS

To my family—
Those of blood and those of choice

Carolrhoda Lab™
An imprint of Carolrhoda Books
A division of Lerner Publishing Group, Inc.
241 First Avenue North
Minneapolis, MN 55401 U.S.A.

Website address: www.lernerbooks.com

The images in this book are used with the permission of:
© istockphoto.com/Selahattin Bayram (paper background).
Front cover: © Brooke Shaden.

Main body text set in Janson Text LT Std 10/14.
Typeface provided by Linotype AG.

Library of Congress Cataloging-in-Publication Data

Hutchison, Dot.
    A wounded name / by Dot Hutchison.
        pages   cm
    Summary: A reimagining of the world and story of Hamlet—from Ophelia's perspective and set in an American boarding school.
    ISBN 978–1–4677–0887–6 (trade hard cover : alk. paper)
    ISBN 978–1–4677–1618–5 (eBook)
    [1. Revenge—Fiction. 2. Ghosts—Fiction. 3. Emotional problems—Fiction. 4. Boarding schools—Fiction. 5. Schools—Fiction.] I. Title.
PZ7.H96448Wo 2013
    [Fic]—dc23   2012043424

Manufactured in the United States of America
1 – BP – 7/15/13

To this very day, travelers can hear the bells of the churches of Ys sounding the hours, deep in the shadowed bay.

—Alberto Manguel and Gianni Guadalupi,
The Dictionary of Imaginary Places

Away, come away.
Empty your heart of its mortal dream.
The winds awaken, the leaves whirl round,
Our cheeks are pale, our hair is unbound,
Our breasts are heaving, our eyes are a-gleam,
Our arms are waving, our lips are apart;
And if any gaze on our rushing band,
We come between him and the deed of his hand,
We come between him and the hope of his heart.

—W. B. Yeats

And let me speak to th' yet-unknowing world how these things came about. So shall you hear of carnal, bloody, and unnatural acts, of accidental judgments, casual slaughters, of deaths put on by cunning and for no cause, and, in this upshot, purposes mistook fallen on th' inventors' heads.

—*Hamlet*, act V, scene 2, lines 355–361

PART I

CHAPTER 1

The sky is blue today.

Blue like glacier ice, like hidden springs. Blue like jays' wings, peacock feathers. Blue like my mother's skin.

It isn't right. Today the sky should be black or deep, roiling grey, a vast, mottled purple bruise overhead. The air should weep, the Heavens pound in anguish and loss, for today we bury the King of Elsinore.

But it isn't. And they don't.

The sky is blue today, lovely and innocent and callous, too bright to reflect the sorrow of the bean sidhe keening beyond the cemetery fence. They cannot step foot on consecrated ground, yet they wail still for the man who will lie forever in the holy earth's cold, unfeeling embrace. They rend their clothes and tear their hair, impossibly lovely voices rising and falling in an unearthly madrigal of death and mourning, all the grief the sky can't be bothered to show.

The Headmaster will be buried today, and the bean sidhe keen.

I watch and listen for as long as possible, framed by the window that looks down the hill to the chapel and the graveyard beyond. There is madness in their grief to those with the ears to hear it, and to listen too long invites a resonance. They are sorrow, but through the woods behind them rides rage, in the lake whispers seduction. All around the church and its yard, beyond the reach of its unthinking blessings, the madness holds sway.

The song wraps around me, incomprehensible syllables a balm to the grief within me, but there is pain there too, an agony born of guilt that I listen to them at all. That I hear the sorrow that resonates within mine. Father will see the wildness in my eyes, if he sees anything at all, but my brother will see far more than the wildness. In the clever way in which he sees almost everything around him, he will see the way my body sways to the bean sidhe song, the way my head cocks to listen to the feral cries of the Hunt as it rides. And in the way he always does, he will tell Father, who will look at me with such disappointment.

And such fear.

He trembles to give it voice, as though voicing it will make it real, but always the truth is there in his eyes: I am too much my mother's daughter.

The pain is fleeting, consumed by the wanting. I cannot abide the thought of standing beside that hole in the ground, not when the death songs are so lovely. It would be easy to cross to them instead of the unassuming grey stone church, to weave and dance beyond the reach of the wrought iron fence and add my voice to theirs. So easy.

Only then do I turn from the window, reach for the box of pills beside the bed. Every Saturday, Father splits the pills into different days so I can't forget the little round blue, the oblong yellow, the tiny white and the horse-pill white, and all but seven days each month the pink oval like a Tic Tac. Every day the pills, every week the accounting with Father to reassure him I've taken them all. I pry open Tuesday's box and choke them down dry. Nausea races up from my empty stomach, and too late, I remember the warning label on the orange bottles locked in Father's study: *take with food.* I can choke down the pills, but I couldn't deal with the toast or the eggs, only the coffee, heavily sugared and creamed, that nonetheless burned a trail to my stomach.

I empty the pills from Sunday and Monday and slip them into the plastic baggie hidden between my mattresses. There are too many pills there, too many days I forget or else just can't make

2

myself turn away all the sights and sounds of that other world that weaves so closely through ours, but I can't let Father see the forgets. He'd send me to the cold place again, like he did after Mama died, and though he'd miss me while I was gone, he wouldn't bring me home until he thought I was stable again.

The nausea rises, more forceful this time, harder to swallow back. I clench my teeth on the need to gag. If my body rejects the pills now, I'll have to wait to take a new dose with food after the funeral, and my father and brother will know. Even now, after three missed days, the dose won't do enough to chase away the wildness before I must see them.

On my vanity, a small basket of violets sits waiting for me. Every morning, Jack leaves a small basket of flowers just outside my door, as he's done for years, as he did for my mother. From the first bloom of early spring to the last bloom of late summer, there are violets. Sometimes other flowers as well but always violets, soft petals ranging from their namesake color through shades of indigo, blue, and heavy cream.

The Headmaster loves violets.

Loved violets.

He laughed and laughed when I told him of their elusive scent, how smelling them actually makes it impossible to smell anything for a little while, and he knotted a flower into my hair and told me the most beautiful things will always be the most elusive. I was nine years old, my first day back after the cold place, and he'd come to welcome me home with flowers that Jack gave him.

Sitting carefully in the delicate white chair, I knot the violets into my hair, a flower crown that pulls my night-dark hair back from a too-pale face. A handful remains when the crown is complete, but I knot those in as well, soft jewels of color through the length of my hair.

The door opens without a knock, and I know without looking that it's my brother. He never knocks. Father will at least give a cursory tap in case I'm changing clothes, but the pause between sound and entrance is never more than a fraction of a second. I am too much my mother's daughter to be afforded real privacy. Sometimes I think my brother, who grew up on Mama's stories just as I did, understands better than Father what that means.

"Ophelia, it's time to go down."

"I know." I knot the second-to-last violet several inches from the ends of my hair, not wanting to sit on it when we get to the chapel. I stand and smooth the black dress. The fabric is lightweight for summer, but the color smothers me. Sometimes I wonder if they really did revive me all those years ago or if I'm just a ghost, a trick of shadows and light that both Father and Laertes think they see.

His eyes are on the violets, a vertical line between his eyebrows as he studies their arrangement. "Father won't like this."

"I'm not doing it for Father."

We will never be seen as anything but siblings, Laertes and I; we both look like Mama. The same moonlight skin, the same purple-black hair. His eyes are more blue than mine, deep blue like the water at night, but mine are our mother's exactly, a bruise-colored indigo the same shade as the shadows beneath them. He at least inherited her height, the graceful build that helps him dance so smoothly in the boxing ring. Father must have chosen Laertes' suit this morning; even the shirt is black, the edges of jacket, tie, and shirt all indistinct as they layer against each other.

"He still won't approve," he says eventually. "You might as well take them out now and save us all the hassle."

"I'm not doing it for Father." There's one violet left in the woven basket, bruise-colored with a heart of cream. I pick it up and cradle it in my hand, lift it so I can breathe in deep. The scent is gone before I can even identify it, but if I'm patient, in a few minutes when my nerves recover, I'll be able to breathe it in and know it for what it is: the elusive scent of a violet. "And I'm not taking them out. The Headmaster loved violets."

"Ophelia . . ." Before I can lower my hands, he's crossed the room and yanked at my chin, forcing my face up so he can see my eyes. He sighs. He'll ask the question because he sometimes believes in being fair, but it doesn't matter what I say; he's already decided he knows the answer. "Goddamn it. This—of all mornings—why couldn't you just take your pills?"

And even though it doesn't matter, I tell him the truth anyway, because that is the dance we repeat so often. "I did take them."

"You can't lie when you have that look in your eye. You didn't take them, and we both know it. You're practically dancing to that damn banshee song you hear."

Bean sidhe. He used to give the words our mother's voice, a lilting sound as much music as the laments they sing. But that was before, before he grew into our father's son, before he was afraid.

"Think of what this will do to Father; you know he doesn't need more distractions today."

Father never needs distractions; he exists in a cacophony of them. Distractions from memory, from fear, from the loneliness he doesn't know how to let us fill. He never needs more of them, but he looks for them anyway because that is what he does in the name of making everything run smoothly. I don't say any of this. I never do. Laertes and I understand Father in very different ways, I think, and I never can decide who has the more right of it.

My black wrap sits on the foot of the bed, and I push Laertes away to pick it up. Even in high summer, the church is always cold. It clings to the stone, to the silence. I switch the violet to my left hand and drape the wrap over that arm to hide it from view. This final flower will be a gift, the last one I can give to a dear friend now gone. That sort of gift must always be a private thing. "It's time," I remind him. "We should go."

He shakes his head but holds the door open for me. The absence of a scent—a ghost, an echo of violets—follows us into the hall. This is the day Hamlet Danemark V, Headmaster of Elsinore Academy, is laid to rest, and the world mourns.

CHAPTER 2

The house is a flurry of activity, black-clad servants racing through the lower floors to ensure that everything will be ready for the reception after the burial. Though it's officially called the Headmaster's House, others live here as well: Father is the Dean of Curriculum, so his family has a place here. And the scholarship students who may or may not be able to return home for the summer often have rooms here.

In the entryway, a grand place of gleaming crystal and polished black marble, Gertrude Danemark supervises everything with a strained calm. She has always been the ideal headmaster's wife, a woman of poise and grace and the utmost propriety. Though her eyes are red with the weeping she has done, she sheds no tears now. Her makeup is flawless, natural, and her black suit is both elegant and flattering. Under her watchful eye, the funeral meats are arranged on the long, black-draped tables in the banquet hall, the casseroles and other selections settled into chafing dishes.

Nearby, her brother-in-law Claudius stands deep in discussion with Father. Claudius has a diamond tiepin that winks and flashes from the chandelier overhead, a glittering fracture against the heart of his black suit. Father's suit is plainer and has already succumbed to the slight rumple that always envelops him. It isn't dishevelment, nothing so drastic nor so improper, just the tiny touches, like the way his tie is just a little lopsided at the knot, the way he has cuff links from two different sets, the way one of his glossy black dress shoes is double knotted at the laces while the other has only one knot. So aware of elements at odd in others, but never conscious of his own rumple, and it always makes me smile to see it.

At the bottom of the stairs, before he can bring me to Father's attention, I break away from Laertes to find Dane. I already know where he will be: where he has spent the past three days of the wake, hidden as best as can be from the steady stream of condolences and well-wishes and never-ending tears, some real and some forced. Deep in the shadows under the stairs, he sprawls over a velvet-covered bench, one arm thrown across his eyes as though he could shut the world out.

My heels click on the tiles, and he tenses, his entire body taut with grief and anger and fear. I stop, let him decide if he wants me to come closer or not. Slowly, he turns his head just enough for me to see his eyes through the crook of his elbow. He's always pale, but now he looks sickly, half dead himself, his tear-ravaged eyes lined with painful reds and pinks. "Ophelia?" he whispers.

I take that as permission and enter the hidden alcove, sit next to his head on the very end of the bench. Today I bury a friend, a mentor, a beloved headmaster. Dane buries his father. As much as I want to comfort him, I have nothing to offer. I don't know this feeling. My mother is dead, but I never buried her; I was in the hospital, plugged in to machines that struggled to keep me breathing, and so I have never had to face the casket with the still figure within. I have nothing to offer. My fingers stroke his shower-damp sable hair and trace the edges of the water stain on the velvet. The hand not over his eyes clutches a silver crucifix, the back dull from years of rubbing against skin and fabric. His father gave it to him for his First Communion; he hasn't been without it since. He clings to it as though this piece of his father could bring the man back. Bruises still linger on his knuckles and cheek from his last spar.

"Ophelia, I don't think I can do this." His arm drops to his side, and he looks up at me, his face so naked I should be ashamed to see it.

But Dane is my friend, my oldest friend, my sometimes-brother. This emotional baring is somehow more intimate than any physical nakedness could be, but I don't turn away. I just stroke his hair, with nothing to say, and so I say nothing.

"Will you sit with me during the—the . . . ?"

"The service?" I finish gently. The word *funeral* is ash in my mouth, as it must also be in his, and he looks grateful for a different name, a different term.

He nods, swallowing hard. "And . . . and after."

For the burial. For the reception. For the tide of people that must be faced in the name of propriety and the good of the school. My place is with Father or with Laertes, behind the Danemarks but not part of them. "I'll stay with you. I promise."

He gropes for my hand and squeezes it too tightly, but I let him. I can accept the small pains if they will help him bear this greater one. "My uncle has already applied to the Board of Governors to be the new headmaster," he mumbles.

"It's not really something that can wait. The school year will come quickly."

"Father's not even buried, and already someone wants to take his place."

"Dane, your family has run this school since its founding," says a voice from beyond the shadows. The tall shape ducks under the bottom of the stairs and sits on the edge of another bench. "Your father was proud of that legacy; your uncle wants to keep that pride intact." Horatio gives me a nod of greeting, his hands clasped between his knees and his eyes on Dane.

Now we need only Laertes for our quartet to be complete, but my brother is minded too much of our father today. He will not be seen lurking in shadows. He will stay near Father, even when his friend needs him, because that is where he is supposed to be. Sometimes I wonder if that sort of certainty brings with it its own kind of comfort. Then I wonder if it should. Like so many things, I never find an answer.

Gertrude comes to retrieve her son and his dismal company.

She watches our silence for a moment, an almost smile a subtle curve on her painted lips. She is too young to be a widow, I think suddenly, too lovely to be left alone. "Dane," she says softly, "it is time for us to go."

He slowly stands, allows Horatio and me to adjust his clothing, but he can't look at his mother, can't share this grief even with her. He jerks his head in what might be a nod, to acknowledge her presence or her words I'm not sure, and walks past her.

Her smile deepens when I step out of the shadows and she can see me more clearly. "You look lovely, Ophelia." Her fingers brush gently against one of the violets, too light a touch to dislodge it. "Hamlet always loved seeing you with flowers in your hair, like you'd stepped right out of a fairy tale."

I cringe inwardly, grateful that neither Laertes nor Father followed her to the alcove.

"Thank you for doing this, for him. And . . ." Her voice trembles, the strength crumbling to reveal the grief beneath. Then she clears her throat, and the moment has passed. "And for Dane. This is especially hard for him." She links my arm through hers. "I'm glad he has his friends to help him through this." We join the others in the entryway.

Father's eyes show his concern when he sees the flowers in my hair, but no surprise; Laertes must have told him already. Whatever he might say, though, is unknowingly cut off by Gertrude, who again brushes her fingertips across the silky petals.

"It does me good to see this," she murmurs. "Hamlet would have liked to see this."

Dane's jaw clenches, as it does whenever he hears his father put into past or conditional tenses. Strange, how words can be so precise and yet have so many shades of meaning. Words, words, words, it's a wonder that they mean anything at all, when so often they don't.

But that is the last said of the violets in my hair. Even in the midst of his worry, Father won't go against Gertrude in this. At his shoulder, Laertes shakes his head. He is more and more like our father, losing those pieces of him that made him like our mother, like me. Soon enough I shall lose my brother entirely, and I don't want to be alone in our mother's memories.

Claudius offers his arm to Gertrude for the walk to the church. Dane should fall in behind them, but he hesitates, glances back at me, and shakily extends his hand. Ignoring my father's startled look, I take it. My fingers ache in his grip, but soon enough the feeling leaves them entirely, so it doesn't hurt anymore. Father and Laertes walk behind us, Horatio bringing up the rear by himself, always slightly out of place but never taking offense at it.

Sometimes I think Horatio is the best of us, and I never feel disloyal for it. Sometimes love is naming the faults so they can't be forgotten.

CHAPTER 3

We're the last to enter the grey stone church, the polished wooden pews packed with current and former students, with administrators from other schools. There are senators there and business executives and diplomats and all manner of successful men who have come from the halls of Elsinore Academy, many with their perfect trophy wives on their arms. That is what this school teaches us to be. For the male students, success is measured by money and power. For the female students, success is measured by the success of our husbands and how our accomplishments may serve to aid them. The boys progress and advance, and the girls cling to a time that was never ours.

All turn to watch us as we pace down the long center aisle to the front pews on the right side. There is nothing so tacky as a sign to mark those spaces apart; it is proper, so it is left empty.

Dane still has my right hand in a crushing grip so I end up between him and Gertrude, much to Father's dismay. His fingers tighten spasmodically on mine, so hard one of the knuckles pops with an unnaturally loud sound in the quiet church. I don't have to look at him to know what he sees, because I see it too.

The casket.

It's an elegant construction of polished mahogany and silver upon the altar, the inside lined with ice blue, the color of the sky, of death. It is one of Elsinore Academy's colors, but I cannot see it without remembering my mother's lips, the skin around her eyes. The lid stands open, and before we sit I can see just a glimpse of the figure within, the waxy skin smooth and serene, the expression shaped into the stern smile he wore so often. Over his crisp, midnight-blue suit and ice-blue tie, the undertakers have dressed him in his open navy professorial robes and mortarboard, the ceremonial attire of the Headmaster. His hands are folded gently over his chest, a pale stripe on his left hand where his wedding ring sat for nineteen years.

The plain gold band sits now on Dane's finger, the metal cold and bruising against my skin.

The priest begins the service with a prayer. There will be no friends to give eulogy, for Hamlet was so well respected and admired, how could one ever choose who to speak? Gertrude wishes to offend no one, and so she has placed the service squarely within the priest's hands, her trust in him absolute to commend her husband's soul to God.

I like the death the priest speaks of, a quiet place of rest and ease and warmth, so unlike the cold ground that lies waiting to receive the body. He speaks not of pain but of light, the healing of the soul sundered from Heaven so it could walk its time on Earth. He speaks of death as coming home. There is no judgment in his words, no fear of sin or Purgatory. I wonder if this is how he spoke at my mother's service.

One of the graduates, a rare one who made a name for herself outside of a husband by becoming one of the leading sopranos of opera, leads us in a hymn, but almost no one sings along. Her song shakes the dust motes in the light that streams from the plain glass windows, beautiful and strong and perfectly human. Within the church, I can't hear the feral wails of the bean sidhe.

I wish I could. Even with the wildness they bring to my eyes, even with the pain it causes my father and brother, their songs are more suited to death than this voice that stirs life.

My fingers are white within Dane's. Tears track steady paths down his cheeks, silent and dignified, glistening scars that may never fade. I have tissues tucked in the hidden pocket of my wrap but no way to reach them, and little enough will to try. I cannot find anything unnatural in a son grieving for a beloved father, whatever propriety may say of public shows of emotion. A full chorus of sniffles and soft weeping ripples behind me. The women sob softly into tissues or lacy handkerchiefs, but even the men have recourse to them, their jaws set against the grief even as their moist eyes betray their intentions.

Then it's time. It's been time so often today, but it's time again, this time to close the lid and forever place Hamlet in darkness. The priest places a hand on the sectioned lid, then glances at the line of ravens in the front pew and asks if we'd like to pay our respects. The violet waits patiently in my palm, its fan-shaped petals a little wilted but the colors still true.

Claudius goes up first, his face impassive as he studies his elder brother. His face shows nothing, but then, it so rarely does. Claudius is not one to let others know his thoughts or plans if he can avoid it. He doesn't touch the body, doesn't even rest his hand on the edge of the casket but, instead, clasps his hands at the small of his back in a vaguely military stance that keeps his spine stiff and straight.

Dignity.

Propriety.

Gertrude joins him there, and one of Claudius' hands floats away to rest on her back. His fingers curve over the small of her back, his palm against the swell of her hip. It's an intimate stance. I've had much occasion over the past three days to study how people touch each other in support: a grip on the shoulder, the forearm, a hand placed gently against one of the shoulder blades, all things as though they could help the grief stand on its own. It's too close for brother and sister, as they have been for nearly two decades, and yet there his hand rests, and she doesn't step away.

Her blue eyes glisten, and tears tremble on her lashes but do not fall. She touches her husband's cheek, leans down to press a soft kiss against his cold lips. Her hand shakes.

Dane stands abruptly, yanking me gracelessly to my feet beside him. He stalks up the steps to the altar, jerky as a badly controlled marionette. We pass his mother and uncle on their way back to the pew, and Gertrude's hand brushes across my cheek in passing. The shiver crawls under my skin. Was it the same hand? From dead flesh to living flesh, could her hand tell the difference?

There's something profoundly unnatural in seeing the Headmaster lie so still within the ice-blue satin, a lace-edged pillow under his neck to prop his head. There was always a sharply contained energy within him, a strength even in stillness that said he was just waiting for his next movement. Now that is gone and he is only still, never to move again. More of my knuckles pop within Dane's grip; his own joints creak and protest in his other hand where it squeezes the edge of the casket in a desperate search for strength. He stares at his father, at the mirror he'll see when he's older, and a low, growling keen builds deep in his chest, nearly inaudible.

I uncurl the fingers of my left hand to reveal the cream-throated violet. Hamlet's fingers are cold, the texture of the skin strange with the preservations, but I tuck the short stem against the pale stripe left by his wedding band to make a purple spill against his hand.

Ever since the hospital, ever since the cold place, since that first homecoming and his quiet welcome back, I went to his study every night before I went to bed. No matter what he was doing, who he was talking with, he set it aside just long enough to kiss my cheek and receive a kiss in return against his bearded cheek. I lean down now to kiss the neatly trimmed whiskers, my lips tingling, and whisper as I have so many times before "Good night, sir; sleep well."

And every night, he would say back "Good night, child; sleep well." Now I'll never hear that again.

"Sleep," Dane echoes beside me, his voice little more than breath. "As if he just sleeps through death." He cups his hand over his father's, fingers curved over the flower to protect it, and says nothing more.

I flinch at the sound of the casket closing, both sections coming together with the rest of the wood to drown Hamlet in darkness. On the surface, where the two sections meet, the school crest is carved into the polished wood. His entire life was about the school; so his death will be too.

The pallbearers step forward: two senators, a governor, two Fortune 500 CEOs, and Horatio. I wonder if Horatio's presence is for Hamlet or for Dane, for the one who gave him the scholarship to change his life or the one who decided the scholarship didn't matter. Horatio rests his hand against the wood over Hamlet's chest, and tears course down his cheeks without any attempt to hide them. When the governor nods, he lifts his portion with the rest of them, the wood digging into his shoulder.

We filter out behind them, and somehow this is worse, this trek to the graveyard in the wake of a closed box that holds what used to be a man. Dane does not let go of my hand, even when my father tries to draw me away, but Dane finally sees the mottled colors of my fingers and eases his grip. His other hand smoothes over mine, easing the painful return of sensation.

As soon as we step out into the mocking sunlight of clear skies, the keening sweeps over me again, and I sway against Dane. Laertes makes a sound, but I shade my eyes as though it is only the departure from the dim interior of the church that unsteadies me. Father lightly touches my shoulder, avoiding the violets, but says nothing.

It is a small gathering against the square-edged hole in the ground. The rest have gone on to the Headmaster's House, to wait for us at the reception and give this small pretense of privacy, as if there was anything private about a funeral and burial. In a maneuver so smooth they must have practiced it, the pallbearers pass strands of thick webbing beneath the casket and shift their grip to these, slowly easing the casket down into the grave. A blanket of plastic grass covers the mound of earth that waits to bury him. Just beyond the fence, surrounded by the faerie women he cannot see, Jack Barrows waits with a spade to replace the soil. He never steps foot in the church, and he's uncomfortable in the consecrated ground, but he tends the graves because that is the debt the living owe the dead. He gives me a small nod when I see him, a bare smile on his wrinkled, dirt-smeared face when he sees the violets in my hair.

Farther away, straddling the line between sacred and unconsecrated ground, fresh flowers deck my mother's grave. Just as he did when she was alive, Jack brings her flowers every day.

We are not meant to watch the burial, just this charade of placing a body in a hole we dare to call its home, but when Gertrude touches her son's shoulder, he shakes his head and remains where he is. She moves the touch to me, one finger resting on the strand of my mother's pearls. "You'll stay with him?" she asks quietly, and despite Father's clearing throat, I lay my free hand over hers.

"I'll stay with him."

As the others follow the pallbearers up the hill, Horatio hesitates, one hand outstretched. "Dane?"

"We'll be along," he says shortly. "I need to see this."

"Do you want me to stay?"

I can feel the part of him that wants to say yes; that is not the part that wins out. The tension in his arm, in his face, that is what wins, and so he gives our friend the fraction of a smile he can muster and tells him to join the others, because there is just enough of him that can't stand the potential to break down in front of someone even so close as Horatio.

Horatio just nods, as if he expected this answer, and walks to the house by himself.

The decorative gate squeals as Jack lets himself in, his ordinary shovel gripped in one hand. Without a word to either of us, he jerks aside the false grass and starts spading the dark soil into the hole.

Dane cries out with the first thump of impact against the coffin, and breaks down with the second. Sobs wrack his entire body. He pulls me to him, his hands crushing the flowers in my hair, and buries his face against the crown of violets. I can't breathe, but neither can he, and without air even an elusive scent can never be found. Silk rubs against my cheek, sticks damply to my palms as I slide my arms around to his back. I'm not even sure he can feel it, but I squeeze back just as hard.

It doesn't take long for Jack to fill it in completely and smooth the blade of the shovel over the curved mound. There's no headstone yet, but he retreats beyond the fence and pushes in an enormous wheelbarrow full of blossoms from both gardens and greenhouses. Roses of many shades, violets, star-of-Bethlehem, Narcissi, love-lies-bleeding, hydrangea globes, stalks of freesia like chiming bells, and so many more. He lays them out across the earth until the soil can't even be seen.

Dane hiccups through the end of the tears, and I twist in his arms until I can see the ghost of a smile on his face. "Thank you, Mr. Barrows," he manages, and Jack gives him a deep bow, the kind no one gives each other anymore, and vanishes with his shovel and wheelbarrow back into the woods.

Now that he's buried, the song of the bean sidhe softens. They don't keen or wail, but they mourn. The faerie women sing for the deaths in the great families, for the deaths of great or holy men. They will sing the mourning for Hamlet until they feel they have honored him his due.

They may sing forever.

"Does it get better, Ophelia?"

I glance over to my mother's grave. Though all the headstones have small bouquets or wreaths, hers is the only one decked in flowers like Hamlet's. "I don't know," I confess. "I suppose I'm still waiting to find out myself."

"I can't go back there. I can't see all those people, hear them talk about him."

"Your mother needs you."

He straightens, mops uselessly at his face with one hand. "He would want me to take care of her," he murmurs.

I take a few steps away from the grave, arm stretched between us, to see if he'll follow. He does without complaint or protest, and I lead him back into the silent church. Even the priest has gone up to the house, to give his breed of comfort where he may. Dane walks with me into the single stall bathroom, watches passively as I take his handkerchief and dampen it at the sink.

His eyes study my face as I gently wipe the evidence of his grief from his skin, the cloth cool against swollen eyes. The uneven color of his cheeks gradually recedes. Except for the pink wash over his dark grey eyes and the lines of red that rim them, he looks as he did before. Not before the death or before the funeral, just before this fresh bout of tears. It will take time, a long time, I think, for him to look as he did before everything.

His hand rises to my face, the fingertips tracing a path similar to the patterns I've wiped across his skin. He studies me as though I'm something rare and precious and wonderful, a gift in the midst of his pain. I've never seen this in him before, and my pulse races beneath his gentle touch. "How," he whispers, "are you the only one who can make this feel real without it being overwhelming?"

It *is* overwhelming—he *is* overwhelmed, but before I can find a way to say this, his lips brush against mine and my eyes flutter closed. His thumb still traces patterns against my cheekbone, the corner of my eye, but his fingers slide against my neck, twine through strands of hair, to pull me closer against him. No longer a brush of butterfly wings, he kisses me again, deeper, mouth moving against mine as though he would consume me.

Panic steals my breath, but in the airless void, in each flex of his fingers against my scalp, each wordless murmur against my lips, seeds of fire bloom to push away the lingering cold of death. This is new and terrifying, but there's also joy, a wildness that belongs with the songs outside the churchyard, with the feral cries of the Hunt as it rides endlessly through the woods.

He pulls away, presses another soft, tentative kiss against my temple. "Thank you," he whispers. "Thank you for staying with me."

My lips shape the word I have no voice to give sound. *Always*.

CHAPTER 4

A thundercloud of black clothing, interspersed with flashes of deep jewel tones, drifts between the entryway and the banquet hall of the Headmaster's House, small china plates and crystal punch glasses in their hands as they speak in hushed tones. Infrequent bursts of laughter fall too harsh, too loud against the sepulchral atmosphere.

As soon as we walk in, Father pulls me from Dane under the guise of introducing me to someone. Then he hands me an empty plate and tells me to occupy myself in some manner that will neither disgrace myself and my family nor burden the Danemarks. Part of me wants to ask why he doesn't just pat me on the head like a five-year-old while he's at it, but I know he didn't mean it the way it came out. Father can be awkward and consumed by his tasks, but he is never intentionally cruel. Mama was, sometimes—especially to Father—but he's never taken her example.

I can't stand the crush of people, too many that I've never seen before. Some of them share stories of Hamlet; too many speak of business or politics.

After the sixth time I get stopped by some woman who wants to cluck over my empty plate, I finally drift by the banquet tables and load a few things onto it, enough that people will leave me alone. There are chairs lined against the walls, and some have moved them into tight little knots, pockets and clusters of people all talking over each other and barely making a dent in the silence.

Laertes watches me. I don't know if he's under orders from our father or if it's simply something he's taken upon himself, but his eyes follow my progress about the room. Perhaps it's both. I doubt he believed that I was struck by the light when the keening rose.

I wait until a portly man in a too-loud tie engages him in conversation and then leave the hall in a cluster of black-clad people who join the line to speak to the Danemarks. Easing past them, I slip up the stairs to the second floor. The servants have turned off all the lights on the upper levels to discourage guests from exploring the living areas, so the reading nook is pleasantly shadowed. Despite the comfortable chairs, I sink down onto the rug and press my cheek against the wooden banister.

I'm invisible here. Even those below who examine the entryway with curious, nervous, or acquisitive eyes miss me in the shadows. I wonder what kind of compromises and sacrifices had to be made to let so many people come here on such short notice. There are jobs and families, travel arrangements and accommodations, so many details to maneuver in only three days.

Dane stands at the bottom of the stairs, his hips against the elaborate rail post. Even from here I can see the muscle jumping in his jaw. He stares past the well-wishers, the strangers who want to shake his hand, the former students who think that loss of the Headmaster is equal to the loss of Father, even those who were here long before Hamlet was a student, much less the Headmaster. They try to touch this piece of his father, but he says nothing, offers nothing. He stares off into space as though he would force the air into the shape of his father and breathe life into it again.

Beside him, Gertrude is more gracious. She accepts all the words with murmured thanks and gives a name to every single person who approaches. She has smiles for them, nothing too broad or inappropriate, but small gestures of strength and elegance even in the face of grief. I can hear her weeping at night; she's never been alone—she doesn't know what it means—but a social event is something she knows. It gives her poise.

A hand floats, pale and assuming, at the small of her back. Claudius is Hamlet's brother, his blood. It's natural and right for him to be in this line of condolence, but he takes a strange place in it. Dane said his uncle had already made his bid to become Headmaster, but he acts as though it already is his. His gestures and words take on a propriety air, not just in the way he greets the guests but in the hand at Gertrude's back, the way his thumb rubs small circles into the layered silk and linen.

His face changes with every word, shifting from restrained grief to welcome to curiosity, whatever it is that's silently asked of him by those he speaks with. The muscles move, the expression shifts, but his eyes never change their calculating expression even as people offer their sympathies for his loss.

His eyes are like the hand at Gertrude's back: they have lost nothing.

Part of me waits for Gertrude to move away from his overfamiliar touch, to remind him of the impropriety, but she is like my father in some ways, or perhaps my father is like her. She is not going to create a Scene.

Laertes escapes from the fat man in the suit of poor taste; I can see him stalk through the gathering in search of me. He even checks the alcove beneath the stairs and rakes a hand through his ear-length hair when he cannot find me.

Father flits between the door and the banquet hall, his tasks split between managing the line of mourners and the catering staff. There's a crash of crystal and china, followed by the piercing wail of a small child, and he rushes away from the door. Like little puppets on their miniature stage, everyone moves about, using the rest of the gathering as an audience. My hands will never hold their strings, but from above I can see the patterns that their audiences can't.

Here the women who hated each other in school loudly exclaim over pictures of children, words like *cute* and *adorable* floating in a haze around them even as each is convinced that her brood is far superior to anyone else's. Here are the men making business deals and hoping no one sees it. Most of the current students clump together in uncomfortable pockets, wearing their uniforms in honor of the Headmaster, ill at ease amidst so many strangers. Others stand at their parents' shoulders, bored or ambitious as they're introduced to Invaluable Contacts.

"Ophelia." A hand lightly touches my shoulder and I flinch. Horatio smiles down at me and with his other hand offers me a plain, sturdy mug of milky coffee. When I accept it, he digs a few packets of raw sugar from his pocket and stacks them neatly on my abandoned plate.

He's the only person I know with my talent, the ability to disappear right in a crowd of people, and he uses it much the same way. Watch, observe, don't bring attention to yourself, or they might remember all those other things they think they know about you. He wears his uniform not because it shows support for his school but because it's the nicest thing he owns.

He isn't like the rest of us, who've grown up with unthinking wealth. His family put every penny they had into getting him here. While others talk of vacations and shopping, he just listens with this half smile on his face and gives them no reason to notice that he isn't part of their world. Of our world, I suppose, though Laertes and I often stand outside it as well.

He folds his long legs against his body so he can sit with me on the floor of the nook, his back pressed against the rails right on the edge of the stairs. The edge of his polished dress shoe, still with bits of grass and soil clinging to it, nudges my plate closer to my knee. "At least eat the roll," he whispers. "That coffee will burn a hole in your stomach otherwise."

"I ate breakfast."

"No, you attended breakfast." He smiles and shakes his head. "You don't eat when you're nervous, Ophelia, because you can't keep it down."

I should be irritated, but it's different than the way my father or brother would say it. Horatio isn't accusing me of anything; he doesn't think me incapable of taking care of myself. Because of his smile, the same smile he's always given me, I take the airy roll from the plate, pinch off a piece, and drop it on my tongue. It melts there, more breath than substance, but suddenly—painfully—I'm *hungry*. I slowly eat the rest of the roll to make my stomach think there's more of it because the rest of my plate is filled with raspberry and blackberry tartlets. The catering service handles all special events for the school, and the tartlets are always so sweet they make my teeth ache. I only put them on the plate because they're pretty and they take up room.

There's nothing to stir the sugar into the coffee, but I sprinkle it in anyway and watch the clear brown crystals dissolve in the steaming, milky liquid. Horatio looks washed out in the shadows, the way I or Dane or Laertes look out in sunlight. He spends the summer outdoors swimming and rowing in the lake, sometimes helping Jack in the gardens, so where we're pale, he's deeply tanned, his chestnut hair bright with blondish sun streaks. Even his eyes belong outside, a dappled hazel of deep earthy browns and forest greens.

He twirls his silver class ring on his finger, the oval sapphire flanked by rectangular chips of aquamarine. He never would have had it on his own; the cost of it could have paid his family's rent for at least a month. It was a gift from Hamlet, done as quietly and with as much of an eye towards dignity as everything the man did. The upcoming seniors received their rings the week before classes let out, and none of them have been seen without them since. Even Dane wears his, though now on his right hand to balance out his father's wedding band on his left. It'll be another two years before I see mine.

Two years younger and yet always a part of their group. I know it started as protectiveness; when I got back from the cold place, Laertes didn't want to let me out of his sight, even snuck into my room at night and slept on an air mattress on the floor. As soon as his classes were done and my tutor released me from my lessons, he took responsibility for me. First, Dane, then Horatio when he came, joined in looking out for me, but they didn't smother me as Laertes in his fear so often did.

"I took my pills this morning."

As soon as the words spill from my mouth I want to take them back. They don't mean anything, can't mean anything, and I've never liked useless words.

But Horatio simply takes one of the tartlets, bites into it, and chews with a slight grimace. "I believe you."

"Laertes doesn't."

"He's scared." He swallows and considers the rest of the sweet, then eats it anyway. "If you're taking your pills and still seeing things, he has to face the possibility that maybe you really are just seeing more than the rest of us can."

"Or I've more madness than the pills can handle."

"Or that," he agrees readily enough. "There are good days and bad days; you've said that before. Besides . . ." He picks up another tartlet but turns it over in his hands, the sugar crumbling against his fingers. "You said you hear the bean sidhe, right?" He stumbles only slightly over the unfamiliar pronunciation. I love him a little for that. "That they mourn for the dead?" I nod and he gives me a small smile. "I like the idea of Nature mourning for the Headmaster. He was a good man."

I sip the coffee and rest my cheek against the wooden post. The line of people wanting to talk to the Danemarks is as long as ever, but Dane isn't holding up. It's harder for him to stare off into space, harder to grit his teeth against the inanities, against the apologies that are as inadequate as they are inaccurate.

"He's going to bite someone's head off in a minute," says Horatio, following my line of sight.

"His mother will send him to get her something to drink before he has the opportunity," I murmur.

"I don't know how to help him."

I study him from the corner of my eye, all his attention on our friend at the bottom of the stairs. "Nor do I."

"So what do we do?"

I shake my head, the polished wood rough against my cheek, because I don't have an answer. We sit in easy silence, tucked away from the rest of the world as we so often are and watch with the relentless fascination of outsiders.

Laertes leans against the wall by the door, the vertical line back between his eyes. His gaze darts through the gathering, his left hand twisting the class ring on his right. I sip my coffee and watch him search for me. A kinder person—a better sister—would go down and reassure him, allow herself to be shepherded around the rooms with an iron grip on her arm.

I am not always a kinder person, or a better sister, and that iron grip too often bruises.

A harsh, unnatural fit of laughter bursts from the space below us, followed by an embarrassed hush. Laertes glances at the source of the outburst, then tracks up towards the ceiling. I know the moment he sees me because his entire body stiffens. He gives the Danemarks on the other side of the stair base a wide berth and stalks up the carpeted steps to tower over us.

Horatio gives him a lazy, two-fingered salute. "Laertes."

"Horatio, would you excuse us? I need to talk to my sister."

He glances at me, and while I'm grateful for the silent offer of support, I shrug. Laertes has a difficult time scolding without working up to yelling, and he can't yell without creating a Scene. Unfolding his legs, Horatio picks up the plate and shoves gracefully to his feet. "I'll bring you back something more to your taste," he promises.

"Ophelia—"

"Father told me to stay out of the way," I tell him. "I don't do well with crowds. Laertes, you know that. Up here, there's very little chance for me to embarrass us."

"It isn't . . . *appropriate* for you to hide in dark corners with boys, especially not at a funeral."

I can't help but smile at that. "It's Horatio, and it isn't a dark corner, it's a reading nook in full view of the people below. And there was at least two feet of space between us. Save your scoldings for when you can mean them."

He sighs and sinks down on one of the chairs a few feet away, his hands buried in his hair. "I need something to do," he admits quietly. "I can't stand down there and listen to everyone talk about the Headmaster and not have something to do."

"Then stay here with me, and with Horatio when he comes back with food, and keep us company and out of trouble. We'll be Dane's silent cheering section."

As if he could somehow hear, or perhaps he simply followed Laertes' progress up the stairs, Dane turns and looks straight at us, his face sickly pale from the strain of keeping it together. I raise my mug in salute, and he almost smiles, gives an imperceptible nod, and straightens his shoulders. When he turns back, he actually manages to give a polite response to one of the endless well-wishers.

That's enough for Laertes to drop down beside me on the floor and tug at the knot in his tie. Now when Father asks him where he was, he wasn't just keeping an eye on me, he was also keeping Dane from making a Scene without being obtrusive. Laertes needs a reason to do things, just as he needs things to do.

So maybe, in giving him that, I can be a good sister after all.

When Horatio rejoins us, fingers of one hand threaded through the handles of three mugs and three plates balanced along the other arm, Dane can look up as often as he needs to and see the three of us supporting him. Maybe it's enough for now.

CHAPTER 5

The reception drags on but finally ends, and the last of the stragglers bid farewell to the exhausted Danemarks and make their way out of the Headmaster's House. As soon as the door closes on the last person, Gertrude sighs and sinks down into a chair for the first time since the hard wooden pew of the stone church. I've lived with her all my life and never seen her slouch, but now she folds in on herself, her face buried in her hands as she ignores her brother-in-law's hand at her shoulder.

Dane sits beside her before his uncle can and drapes an arm across her back, returning some of the strength she fed into him all through the long day. She leans against him, grateful. I have always been so used to thinking of Dane as Hamlet's son—his namesake though we never call him by that name—but he is Gertrude's son as well. Sable and strawberry blonde, their heads hover close together against the endless buffeting of grief.

Claudius flinches from his nephew's touch. His hands snap behind his back, return to that vaguely military stance he always has despite never having served. He steps away from Gertrude and Dane, pulls my father from his tasks with the caterers for another of the hushed conversations that have become a common sight these days past. Father will be a formidable ally in Claudius' quest to be the new headmaster. Father makes all the day-to-day decisions for the school, manages all the numerous, smaller tasks that keep him working long hours in his study. He doesn't actually get a vote in the matter, but the Board will listen if the Dean of Curriculum gives his support to a candidate.

What kind of man can think of such things when his brother has been dead barely three days?

But then, Gertrude has attended to every detail of the funeral despite her grief; I should not judge Claudius too harshly for what may be no more than an occupation to keep him from dwelling on his loss.

I don't know Claudius the way I know the rest of the Danemarks. He is only these few months past returned to the school from his business ventures, and so I have only ever seen him in passing when he joined his brother's family for scattered holidays or birthdays. It is easy to suspect the worst of him when I know almost nothing of him. It is unkind of me, but I find that I don't want to know this cold-eyed man, this stranger who stands in his brother's place.

We hesitate at the top of the stairs, reluctant to disturb the Danemarks' hard-won moment of peace, but the caterers need their plates and mugs returned and there's really no call anymore to hide in the reading nook. Horatio and I ease down the stairs like shadows, unnoticed against the silence, but Laertes' steps fall loud and harsh upon the polished wood, and those at the bottom look up at the sound.

Gertrude reaches out to me and I step forward, let her take my hand and draw me even closer until she can press the back of my hand to her powdered cheek. "Thank you, Ophelia."

"If I could be of any help, that's thanks enough," I answer quietly, and she smiles through her exhaustion.

"Goodness, look at us, all crows in our fine feathers." She shakes her head and stands with both Dane and me to steady her. "We should change. And perhaps . . . will anyone mind too much if supper is a bit . . . informal tonight?"

We all shake our heads, and Dane even manages a shaky laugh. "I'm not even sure I could think of eating," he admits.

His mother kisses his cheek, passes a hand along his dark hair in a soothing gesture.

The house is silent, but my room is not. The keening cry of the bean sidhe pierces the glass of the window, curls in the heavy pockets of warm air the air-conditioning can't move. It's softer now that Hamlet is buried, full of a deep mourning rather than a razor-sharp grief. I close my eyes and just listen. Can Hamlet, at rest now within the earth, hear them?

When I cross to the window, I can see them clustered just beyond the iron fence of the graveyard, five unearthly beauties with long silver-white hair that falls past their feet to puddle like quicksilver in the grass. They wear robes like spun moonlight, glowing gently against the deepening twilight, every feature of their faces sharp and defined despite the distance, carved in such a way no human hand could ever capture. They are faerie woman, the singers of death.

As the sun sinks into the lake, the bean sidhe are joined by other forms within the cemetery itself, flickering like candles as they slowly gain definition. Mostly to one side of the cemetery though, the side built on unconsecrated ground where the body may gain eternal rest but the soul may not. Tears burn my eyes, and the blue-white shapes waver like flame.

A knock on the door makes me dash my hand across my eyes even as I turn, expecting it to swing open with no further warning.

It stays closed.

There's a smear of mascara and eyeliner on the back of my hand, but the closed door so puzzles me that I ignore the mess and cross the room to answer the door. Dane stands just outside, one arm against the frame as though it's the only thing keeping him standing. He's changed his clothes already, abandoned the suit in favor of jeans and a long-sleeved shirt, both black. The angry red that washes his eyes provides his only color.

One eyebrow arches, and he reaches out with his other hand to trace the lines of black across my cheeks. "You've been crying?"

"I think I was about to," I admit.

Hesitantly, as if he's unsure of the comfort, he folds me into his arms. I can't help but marvel at it, his heartbeat racing against my cheek. His arms crush the wilted carcasses of the violets in my hair, and they release a last, ghostly scent that's gone before my body can even register that it was there. There isn't anything left but an echo of the perfume. All day I have sought to give him comfort, and now he would comfort me. The tears damp my cheeks, his shirt, and I know when he feels them because his grip tightens almost painfully against my back, and I don't even care because I finally have hope that Dane might recover from this.

He pulls a folded handkerchief from his back pocket and gravely wipes my face, using the moisture of the tears to clean away the makeup. "You haven't even changed yet."

I glance down at the black dress. In the bleeding light from the hallway, my pale skin nearly glows against the void of color, blue veins close to the surface in my hands and wrists. "I couldn't decide how."

A smile flickers across his face, the ghost of the Dane I knew only a few days ago, the Dane who would seize on the words and play with them, carve them down to every possible meaning until they mean nothing in their ambiguity. But this Dane smiles, and that's enough for now. The rest will recover with time.

"I was hoping we could do something tonight," he tells me. "The four of us. For . . . for my father."

Part of me wants to tell him that this whole day has been for his father, but of course it wasn't. Funerals are for the living, not the dead. "How should I change?"

The smile again, and this time his fingers against my face, tracing the sharp line of my cheekbone. "Never change," he whispers. "Stay exactly like this, exactly you, forever." He brushes a soft kiss against my lips, his body hunched to close the space between us, and I sway into him, my hand at his hip. Heat swamps me, followed by a fierce shiver until goose bumps race along my skin despite the fire that blazes within. "Never change," he murmurs again. "But if you could manage to wear something suitable for sitting on the ground while staying exactly as you are, that might be best."

I promise to meet him downstairs in a few minutes, and he gently closes the door. My hands wrestle with the fastenings of my dress, but my thoughts are flying everywhere—anywhere—else. Before this day, I have never been kissed, but now Dane has kissed me more than once, and I don't know if it's because he craves the simple contact or if it's actually me he sees.

A knife slides between my ribs, a white-hot agony aimed unerringly at my heart. I want it to be me, want it to be real, but even if it isn't, I'll let him kiss me because it almost makes him smile. Because it eases his pain. There's something profoundly wrong with that, something that shrieks in my mother's voice that I should let no one take such things from me, but I don't think my mother ever loved anyone deeply enough that they even could hurt her, much less loved them enough to let them. I am my mother's daughter, but I don't have her selfishness.

I love and I hurt, inescapable and intertwined.

If Dane didn't love his father so much, his death wouldn't have hurt as badly as it does. To love is to hurt, either in giving pain or in suffering it. Which helps more with grief: feeling the pain or sharing it?

CHAPTER 6

Eventually my hands cooperate enough that I can drape the dress across the laundry hamper for the maids, but with Gertrude in charge of my wardrobe, I have nothing truly suitable for sitting on the ground. I'm half naked and shivering for several minutes before I finally find a black skirt and pair it with a black blouse. I hate black, but Dane seems to need it around him just now. Peeling away the nylons, I slip my feet into sandals and open the door to reveal Laertes, his hand curved as if reaching for the doorknob.

He eyes me suspiciously. "Dane asked to see us."

"I know; he told me."

"When?"

"A few minutes ago."

"He came to your room." Laertes' gaze is locked on the dress and underthings lying in the open.

Ah. I let out a slow breath and look him in the eyes. "He knocked on the door and never came farther than the frame. He didn't enter the room, and he did not see, say, or do anything *inappropriate*. Laertes, at some point, you really do have to trust me."

His expression says that day will never come. Only then does it occur to me to wonder if my lips are kiss-swollen. I have seen it in other girls as they rush slightly late to class or when they emerge from the gardens with their boyfriends—or with Laertes—but I have always supposed it takes many kisses before such a thing can happen.

I cannot raise a hand to check without making him wonder at the gesture, so I simply close the door behind me and content myself with the observation that the high collar of his shirt doesn't quite hide the fading hickey on the side of his neck.

Horatio meets us at the bottom of the stairs, unashamed of his worn jeans with the threadbare knees and faded shirt that used to be black before too many washings. He stands with a hand in one of the back pockets; in the other, denim bulges around a pack of cigarettes. "Dane's getting something; he'll be right back," he says in greeting.

When Dane joins us a moment later, a black jacket open over his shirt, his hands are empty. He immediately takes my hand, fingers lacing through mine, and ignores Laertes' scowl. "Thank you," he tells us, and even my brother is not immune to the simple sincerity—to the need—that resonates within those words. The scowl fades, and if he does not look at our joined hands, at least he doesn't speak against them either.

Dane leads us outside, down the path to the church and the graveyard beside it. I flinch, his hand squeezing mine in response, and I shake my head slightly at the implicit question. I don't want to speak of it where Laertes can hear.

But oh, the ghosts!

They hover above their graves in unhallowed ground, suicides and vocal unbelievers, those who have crossed the laws of Heaven so openly that their souls remain tied to these mounds of earth and decay. As the night deepens, they gain solidity and the flickering blue-white light becomes individual bodies, faces, people, some of whom I've known.

There are others, so many others over the century and a half the school has been open, but the ones I knew are always the hardest to see, their faces so familiar. They always look somewhat baffled to appear in the graveyard, tied to their unblessed graves rather than the afterlife or oblivion. Then, when the initial moments have passed, when they realize they'll spend another night watching the world they've left behind, some of them weep, some of them rage, and some of them look so lost I wonder if they'll ever find a way beyond this.

I try to stay away from the graveyard at night, watching the ghosts through my window so they never know that I can see them, hear them, when the medications are forgotten or not working. I tear my eyes away from them as I follow Dane through the fence into hallowed ground. I don't want them to know. I don't want them to find someone who can hear them but not help them, and I don't want anyone to see me interacting with them.

I don't want to go back to the cold place.

Dane stops beside his father's grave and drops gracelessly to the ground, his long legs folded beneath him. My hand still in his, I have no choice but to follow him to the freshly packed earth on one side of the flower-decked mound. After a brief hesitation, Horatio and Laertes sit on the other side of the grave. We nearly glow in the moonlight, in the ghostlight, except for Horatio, whose tan skin blends with the shadows of the night.

From the pockets of his jacket, Dane produces two flasks, a pack of cigarettes, and a lighter. He tosses one flask across to Laertes, unscrews the cap of the other, and takes a long slug. He offers me both the pack and the flask; I take the flask, ignoring Laertes' habitual growl of disapproval, and let the liquid burn down my throat. Alcohol interferes with the pills, but they've become next to useless anyway. The boys light up; the sour smell of tobacco floats through the sickly sweet scent of the wilting flowers, and soon a thin wreath of smoke hovers between us.

On the other side of the fence, two of the bean sidhe watch us curiously, brushing their long hair with silver-backed combs as the other three continue to sing.

How many times have we gathered like this, the boys smoking, the flasks being passed back and forth? I've never thought to count it and can't now that I try. So many times we've sat like this in the gardens, in the fringe of the woods, or even somewhere in town. The place is new, the grave is new, but the rest of it is familiar and comforting, even as my skin prickles under the bean sidhe's sight.

A candle flickers at the head of the grave where the heavy stone will one day stand. It's a simple thing, a cheap blackout candle in a dented tin cup, but its flame slides over the gold of the band on Dane's left hand, the silver class rings, the steel flasks. I know that Jack put it there, Jack who's pagan to the soles of his feet and believes that the dead need a light to guide them home. He'll keep a candle lit at the head of the grave for the next seven nights, so whenever Hamlet's soul leaves his body, the candle will take his spirit and fling it homeward on a wisp of smoke.

I asked Jack once what he meant by home, but all he said was "whatever comes after." I suppose he doesn't believe in Heaven or doesn't want to presume what the afterlife may be, but he's always called it home, as if nothing living has a home or if home changes with death.

"He's really gone, isn't he?" Dane asks suddenly, and the way the silence shatters makes us all flinch.

Even the ghosts look over, woken from their own pain to wonder at someone else's. They see the four of us gathered, the newer spirits recognize us, and they watch us to see who has died. There are a handful of ghosts scattered across the sanctified ground, murdered or unfinished, but those ghosts are always selfish, with no concern for the living except what touches them. Our grief never disturbs them from their own reflections.

Horatio flicks the ash from the glowing end of his cigarette onto a small mound of bare earth, where nothing lives to catch the fire. Neither Dane nor Laertes pause to consider where the ashes will land, but Horatio always takes this care. "He is gone," he answers, "but his legacy remains."

"His legacy." Dane laughs, a humorless sound, and swigs from the flask. "And what will that be, I wonder?"

"We are, I suppose." Horatio flexes his hand, studies the glint of his class ring in the light of the single candle. "The first time I ever saw your father, I had just come home from delivering papers, and he was sitting at our kitchen table. I'd never seen a suit so nice. Mom was frantic, terrified that whatever she gave him wouldn't be good enough. But the Headmaster—*your father*—smiled and said that tap water was just fine. He seemed delighted to meet my brothers and sisters. They were all in awe of him. And then he offered me a scholarship to come here, said all of my expenses would be paid, said as long as I worked hard and behaved as I should, I'd be guaranteed a free ride into a good college, and I could do whatever I wanted in the world."

I knew the Headmaster always went out to offer the scholarships in person once the selection process was finished, but it had never occurred to me that Horatio had once met him in such a way. I'd known Hamlet all my life, familiar before I even knew what familiar was, but Horatio could remember the first time, only six years ago.

"He took me back with him the next day. I left most of my clothing there for my brothers because he said uniforms were part of the scholarship, but he took me out and bought me clothing and a suitcase so I could walk into the school and not feel . . . less. I'd never flown before, never even seen a limo, much less ridden in one, never seen anything like my first sight of Elsinore Academy, and I kept expecting him to take it all away, to tell me there'd been a mistake and this was all much too fine for me.

"And then he brought me into the house," he continued, his words accompanied by thin threads of smoke. "He introduced me to you, Dane, and said I was a new student and would need help to learn my way before classes started. Then you introduced me to Laertes, and between the two of you, you made sure that I knew the school and grounds better than most returning students. I kept waiting for the catch. For you to mock me because I was poor and in over my head, but you never did. If that's not your father's legacy, what is?"

The ghosts murmur amongst themselves, and one of them suddenly wails an off-key counterpoint to the soft, steady keening of the faerie women. "The Headmaster's dead!" she cries. The others join her cry, but their voices are human, grating against the beauty of the bean sidhe, and I wish I could close my ears to them and still hear the death songs of the keeners.

Dane hands the flask back to me, and I take another sip, the metal warm where his lips have been.

Across from me, my brother lights another cigarette from the old one and crushes the now-dead butt against the heel of his shoe, then tucks it behind his ear to dispose of later. "I was unbelievably nervous before my first bout," he offers, a new contribution to this impromptu tribute. "I spent the entire day before pacing myself into a sick frenzy—couldn't eat, couldn't sleep, snapped at everyone and everything. After dinner, the Headmaster took me to the gym and handed me my gloves and started working me through simple warm-ups. He held the heavy bag or sparred with the punching mitts, and the longer we worked, the more I put my body through the steps I knew so well, the less nervous I felt. Finally, he put his hand on my shoulder and told me to remember that moment, that place where everything felt right and made sense, and the rest would work itself out.

"When I won the next day, I thought I would burst when he said he was proud of me, not just because I was one of his students or because he looked at me as a . . . a nephew of sorts but because he actually was proud of me, just as me."

He leaves the rest of it unsaid, why that feeling was so foreign and new: our father's pride is hard to come by, his attention hard to win from his tasks when we want it rather than when we'd prefer to avoid it.

Dane shifts next to me, and I know he's waiting to see if I'll add a story, a memory, some reminiscence that makes the feeling of Hamlet strong between us, but how do I separate out a single thread from everything that is and was Hamlet? And how can I say what I loved best about him when that statement will bring my brother such pain, such anger?

How can I say, as I sit with the wails of the ghosts and the bean sidhe ringing in my ears, that his greatest kindness was in not treating me like I'm mad?

Dane briefly lets go of my hand to light a second cigarette, breathing deep to let the flame catch, then reclaims my hand. "I don't know how to do this," he confesses.

Laertes stiffens, and even as he fights the urge, I can see his head turn and his eyes glance over his shoulder to where our mother's grave sits bathed in moonlight. There is no ghost there, not that he could see it if there were. "No one knows how to do this," he says eventually. "We do it anyway."

"Why?"

We all turn to look at him, but Dane has eyes only for the dying blossoms that hide his father's grave with decaying beauty.

"Why do we do it, why do we blindly march alongside death and act as though it won't claim us as well? Why do we put up with it? Why do we work so hard to get through it when all we can do is experience it again and again?"

"Because the alternative isn't any better," Horatio tells him.

"Isn't it?"

Horatio takes a long look around the cemetery. To him, it's silent but for the sound of our breathing and the breeze that rattles and whistles through holes in the statuary. "If this is where it ends, no, I don't think it's better."

"What if this isn't where it ends?"

"You mean Heaven?" asks Laertes.

"Or Hell or Purgatory or any sort of after. How do we even know that something does come after? What if this is all it is?"

"Then we should be in even less of a hurry to discard it," points out Horatio.

"We fear death because we don't know what secrets it holds, but isn't that exactly what we do with life?" Dane argues. "How can we define them differently if in action we treat them the same?"

"You can work through fear of living, even the fear of dying, but the fear of being dead or whatever comes after . . . there's nothing you can do against that. They're not the same."

The song has shifted. I recognize this one, remember it wrapping around and pulling me down as I drowned all those years ago. I'd never realized that the bean sidhe have different death songs, always thought of it as one endless song that shifts to embrace the one it mourns, but it's genuinely different from the song they give Hamlet, even as threads weave through them to keep the honor of the Headmaster.

I close my eyes and lean against Dane's shoulder, lost in the memory of water in my lungs and bells ringing in my ears. He releases my hand to drape his arm across my back and arrange me comfortably against his side. His fingers idly twine through my hair to unknot the violets that soon fall in a limp circle around me.

The boys keep arguing, and somehow the words become lyrics to the alien language of the song, death and dying and living in death, until I wonder if they've forgotten the original questions. There's Laertes' voice, a light tenor that skips across the words even when anger gives them an edge, always looking for the next word before the previous is even done. Beside him is Horatio's baritone, earth-rich and smooth, a voice that carries on the breeze and wraps through the keening, never angry, never cruel. I can feel Dane's voice as much as hear it, between the other two in pitch but knife-sharp with pain, with longing. The words are quick, but the meaning is not, and the others miss a great deal by trying to answer rather than absorb.

Dane presses the rim of the flask against my lips, the burning edge of his cigarette so close to my skin I can feel the heat, and I wonder if he'll let it burn me even as I obediently swallow the vodka. His thumb rolls across my lower lip to catch a stray drop.

A sudden shout of cloth against cloth and I know Laertes has jumped to his feet. "Ophelia, it's time for us to go. Father will be worried."

"Let her be for once, Castellan, can't you?" sighs Horatio.

I almost want to open my eyes, to see Horatio's expression at this unexpected defense, but my eyes remember the darkness of the lake within the death songs and so won't allow me light.

"This isn't your business, Tennant," Laertes growls. "Ophelia, come on."

But he isn't brave enough to grab at me with Dane's arm around me, and I don't move away. I can hear Dane's heartbeat, the way I heard my own until the water stopped it, and his doesn't falter, doesn't stop. Slowly, the cold waters of the lake recede and let me feel the warmth of his body against mine.

"If you're that worried about your father, go tell him where we are then." Dane's words, his tone, challenge my brother as they have so many times before, friends who compete against each other constantly in school, in temperament and, I think, for Hamlet's affection, Dane who needed that pride from his father and Laertes who can only find a very different sort of pride in his own, a pride that stumbles over awkwardly expressed affection. "Perhaps you could refill the flasks while you're at it."

I open my eyes in time to see Laertes stalk away, both flasks left behind. He may come back in a while with new flasks or a bottle. He may not come back at all. It's impossible to tell how the pieces of him will war and win against the others. He is more and more our father's son. He will drink and smoke and take girls to his room, but he won't let himself think even for a moment that little Ophelia can make her own choices and decide who she wants to be with or that she wants to be with someone. I think if he comes back tonight, it will be to drag me home to a lecture from Father, some new way to call me a liar when I've not lied.

I took my pills, but the pills are like words, they don't always mean anything even when they should.

The discussion ends with his departure, and the three of us sit in a silence that should be far less comfortable than it is. In the end though, it's always been Laertes who's needed to talk, to fill the space with sound because he's our father's son. When silence is a living thing, it can be a friend, sometimes even a comfort. The flasks are empty now, and neither boy moves to light another cigarette. The moonlight pours down on us, makes the weak flame of the candle tremble and shake in a fitful breeze.

Dane's hand drifts down my back, my side, smoothes my hair over the curve of my hip until my entire awareness follows the paths of his fingers against my skirt, the fabric slowly inching up until he can trace patterns on the skin above my knee.

Horatio smiles slightly, meets my eyes, and the smile grows. With a push against his knees, he unfolds and stands, one of the flasks in hand. "I'll be back," he says quietly, his voice somehow part of the silence rather than an intrusion. Dane says nothing, simply hands him the other flask and watches him walk away.

"Will you promise me something, Ophelia?"

He hesitates, but I wait, knowing he'll continue when he's arranged the words the way he wants them, the way that will mean something real.

"Will you help me?" he whispers and turns so his breath stirs strands of hair across my temple. "Help me remember, help me forget? Help me get through this?" He tilts my face towards his, and the muscles in my neck scream in protest, but then he's kissing me and I can taste the vodka and the bitter sourness of the cigarettes and I know I'd promise him the moon if he asked for it.

He gathers me even closer, shifts me against him so I'm nearly in his lap, but the awkward pain in my neck eases and I hesitantly kiss him back, my fingertips trembling against the line of his jaw, a touch as light and insubstantial as the ghost I sometimes am. One of his hands twines through my hair, his short nails pricking against my scalp, and the other rests on my thigh beneath the skirt.

He asked for my help, and I don't know if this is helping, but I don't know how to pull away. I don't know how to walk away from this boy who needs me so much. Still alive when I should be dead, Father and Laertes need to protect me, but they don't actually need me. There are others who could give Dane comfort, perhaps even this comfort, but he's asked for my help, for my promise. He needs me, and I've never been needed before, something as terrifying and wonderful as the kisses that leave me dizzy and clinging to him.

"Promise me," he whispers against my lips, and I answer in kind.

At the head of the grave, the candle pops with a sudden strength, the flame tall and wide. For just a moment from the corner of my eye, I think I see a flicker of blue-white, like the beginning of the

41

ghosts that have long since ceased to find us interesting, but even before another kiss closes my eyes, the thought is gone in a trick of moonlight.

And sometime in the dark hour before Horatio returns, I tell him of the man I knew, the man who greeted me with violets and made time each night to chase the nightmares away with a kiss and a blessing, the man who was never afraid of me when my own father can never hide the fear in his eyes, the man who sleeps beneath the earth beside us and will never wake again. I kiss away the tears that tremble down Dane's cheeks with every word and let my own fall to splash against my blouse, and when the words surrender to the meaning that goes beyond words, we let the silence speak the meaning.

To Hamlet Danemark VI, who I have only ever known as Dane except when he was in trouble, I give the best I have of his father, and he marvels at the gift even as he weeps that such a gift could ever be. So perhaps this is healing, and perhaps this is helping.

I remember death. I remember the silence and the stillness, the absolute serenity. I remember that there was no fear. It was only after, when they brought me back to life, when they plugged me into machines and gave me pills and left me alone in the cold place, that I felt fear. Fear is only ever for the living, and Dane bears enough fear for us both, so I will be his bravery.

I'll be whatever he needs me to be.

I promise.

CHAPTER 7

It's been a week since the funeral, but the strangeness doesn't fade. I still expect Hamlet to join us for dinner, to see him walking through the gardens in the afternoons. I still wake up expecting to smell coffee permeating the house, to walk down to breakfast and see him refilling his mug at the sideboard. He went through five cups before noon, and now the kitchen stocks instant singles that are as unpalatable as watery mud.

I find myself waiting for him in the gardens, where we'd sometimes spend quiet summer afternoons reading, surrounded by the blooms and the soft breezes that dance off the lake. Dane comes to me there now, his black clothing a wound against the bright days, after mornings spent assisting his mother with thank-you cards and letters and all the things a woman of good breeding must do even in the midst of grief. He shows no interest in what I'm reading but sprawls out on the grass beside me, his head in my lap.

Sometimes he sleeps. Sometimes he just stares at the clouds that drift in feathery wisps across the unfeeling sky. And sometimes he takes the book from my hand, closes it, and asks me to talk to him. Never about anything, never words of consequence or meaning but just words, words to take off the edge, words to make him remember, words to make him forget.

Just words.

We spend the afternoons this way, then separate to change for dinner, a meal marked by the empty chair at the head of the table. Claudius tried to sit there the day after the funeral, and Dane became so hysterical he threw half the contents of the table at his uncle. None of us ate that night. It was impossible not to overhear the screaming fit between Claudius and Dane about respect. I'm not really sure who won. Claudius hasn't tried to sit at the head of the table since, but he has been firmly ensconced next to Gertrude, where his hand finds its way too frequently to her arm and, I suspect, her knee under the table.

Neither of them has the thing he truly wants, so they both glower at each other from opposite ends of the table.

Father sits next to Claudius. When Claudius doesn't have his head bent towards Gertrude, he speaks with Father about the school and the Board of Governors. He's been accepted onto the short list of applicants for the vacant position, but it will be a few weeks before any kind of decision is made. In the meantime, he seems intent on learning as much as possible about how the school is run. Father prefers Laertes to sit near him so he can hear the discussions as well. He hasn't said anything about it yet, at least not to my knowledge, but I think he wants my brother to take his place one day.

That notion is as entertaining as it is disconcerting. More and more Laertes is becoming the kind of man who is at home behind a desk—becoming our father—but I remember the little boy who sat wide-eyed against our mother's side and listened to the stories of a city that drowned in a storm at high tide, of the King and his men who ride endlessly through the fierce winds in the desperate hope that one day they can dismount without turning to dust. That little boy would never belong behind a desk.

When dinner is done, Dane stands from his place between me and Horatio and walks away. Sometimes Horatio follows him, to keep him company for as long as he'll allow.

I don't follow.

Because as the evening draws to a close, as the sun starts to set into the lake, and the ghosts start to flicker in the cemetery, Dane drifts to my open doorway, his lanky body propped against the frame, and holds out his hand. He never says a word then. He doesn't have to.

Because I take his hand, every evening, and let him lead me away. Sometimes he wanders for hours in search of some tiny place on the grounds that doesn't remind him in any way of his father. Sometimes he wants to go where those memories are strongest.

Tonight he leads me to the lake, to the small crescent stretch of grass half buried beneath the drooping branches of the willows that line the water. My heart skips a beat, then another, and my steps falter next to his, but he tugs me forward with a curious look and I force myself to remember that I've come to the lake many times since that day.

But it's different, because now Hamlet's dead. He was the one to pull me out, the one to bruise my chest and mouth with the desperate need to make me breathe, make me live. No one was there to do the same for him.

"Ophelia?"

I swallow hard and look up at Dane's face, the pale skin marred less and less by fits of weeping as the days go by.

"Are you all right?"

Am I? "I will be," I answer after a moment. "I just . . . don't come to the lake that often."

"We won't go near the water," he promises. He looks so pleased with himself that I can't help but smile. Suddenly the world makes sense again, because Dane is able to protect me, when I've spent so much of the past week trying to protect him.

"I'll hold you to that."

"I always keep my promises."

That too is Hamlet's legacy to those who called him family: you keep your promises, and if you have cause to regret that, you should be more careful in making those promises.

We sit down within the tangled roots of the willows, a safe distance back from the grassy lip that curls over the edge. I start to sit beside him, but he tugs me into his lap, one leg bent at the knee to provide more of a cushion between my thin dress and the

45

roots below us. He tugs me back against his chest, his hands curled around mine against my thighs.

Through the curtain of thin branches and leaves, we can see the colors streak against the surface of the lake. From this angle, the sun itself is invisible behind the island in the center of the lake, a roughly circular stand with a shock of willows that keep the center hidden. Jack tends the flowers there, his personal shrine to my mother, who loved that place above all others. How much time did we spend within the shelter of the willows, braiding flower crowns as she told me stories she said were truths? And through her stories rang the bells of the drowned city, the church bells that rang and rang and rang long after there was anyone to ring them.

Pale shapes rise from the waters around the island, an echo of laughter floating across the lake. I close my eyes. I took my pills.

I *took* my pills.

When I open my eyes again, the shapes are gone. I'm not sure if I miss them or not.

I turn our hands and flatten them against my thighs. His hands, with long slender fingers and large knuckles, completely cover my own. On his left hand, his father's wedding band gleams gold against the pale skin, brassy and cheap against his complexion. On his right, the cool silver, dark sapphire, and ice-blue aquamarine of his class ring look more natural, more real. More right.

"What are you thinking?" he whispers in my ear. "Your face never says."

"Gold washes you out," I answer honestly.

He laughs, a sudden, startled sound that makes my heart flutter in my chest. It's been almost two weeks since I've heard him laugh. The sound fades too quickly. Just one more loss to mourn. "It was Father's."

"I know."

"I just . . . it makes me feel . . ."

"Close."

He considers the word, turning it over on his tongue, and finally nods. "I suppose." He stretches one finger across from the other hand to trace the plain gold band. "Mother stopped wearing hers."

The day after the funeral, in fact. She came down to breakfast, her hand strange and unfamiliar without the tasteful band of gold-set diamonds. When Claudius took her hand to help her sit, his thumb rubbed against the pale skin where it had been. She took her hand away but didn't scold him for it, and I still don't understand why.

The sunset is a bloody one that speaks to a clear night. We need the rain. The grass is still green, but it's crisp and stiff, and the lake is lower than usual. We haven't had rain since before Hamlet died. Even as I think it I tell myself it's ridiculous, but it's starting to feel like it never will.

As the lavenders and reds deepen to the shifting blues, purples, and blacks of night, Dane pulls his class ring off and slides it down each of my fingers, one by one. It doesn't fit any of them. Even on my thumb, the ring slides around so much that I have to make a fist to keep it from falling off.

"Mine will be smaller," I remind him. "The girls' rings are more delicate."

"I like my ring on you."

"If it's on me like this, I'll lose it." My skin shivers at his words. I know he didn't mean it. It still makes me wonder. Not even about the uncertain future, the far-off days when a ring might actually mean something, but about what happens when school starts again and the halls flood with girls who are far more in Dane's sphere than I could ever be.

He takes the ring back, twirls it on a fingertip, and I watch the gleam in the dying light. It flashes through the sapphire, dark and deep. "I think I have it."

"Have what?"

"The solution."

"To what?" I ask on a laugh. "You're talking in riddles, Dane."

"But I am so very good at it." He lifts my heavy mass of hair and drapes it over one shoulder, takes individual stray strands and places them with others. I tremble under his gentle touch, his fingertips soft and scratchy against the back of my neck, and with a flick of his hand, the clasp of my necklace releases. The thin silver chain drops from the weight of the pendant, but I'm not fast enough to catch it before it disappears down the top of my dress.

He laughs again, a low and wicked sound that should be unfamiliar, but I remember this Dane, the Dane of mood swings and mischief before they took him to the doctor for his own pills. His voice caresses the curve of my ear. "I'll retrieve it if you let me."

My face flames. His hand sweeps around to trace my collarbone, my sternum, flirt at the edge of the fabric, and finally I clap my hand against his to keep it in place. "Don't," I whisper.

"Why not?"

Because it's not real yet. Because I'm scared I may be my mother's daughter. "Just . . . don't."

"Then get the chain back, Ophelia, or I will."

I shudder, but it doesn't even occur to me not to obey that low voice with just a hint of a threat. Or perhaps a promise. I'm not sure which it is. My blush spreads down my chest as I move my hand over his, down into my dress where the heavy knot pendant has caught against my bra. I lift it out, and his fingers twine through the chain before I even have it above the line of fabric. In his grip, the pendant slides down the length of silver until it rests in his other palm. He hands it to me, then strings his class ring on the chain, and reclasps it around my neck.

His ring hangs just above the hollow of my breasts, half hidden by the top of the dress. He presses a hand against it, concealing it even as he pushes it closer against my skin. His lips brush my ear. "Promise me you'll wear it."

"Dane—"

"Please."

"Why are you doing this?"

He tugs at my legs to turn me sideways in his lap, his dark grey eyes trained on my face. He doesn't even answer at first, just knots the silver pendant into my hair until it can brush against my shoulder. He taps at it to make it swing. "You're the one thing that's real," he tells me finally. "The one thing that makes all of this real, that makes me feel real. I need you, Ophelia. I need to know that you won't walk away."

I've never been the one to walk away. I'm always the one waiting for the others to come back, because I don't have anyone else to walk towards.

His hands are moving again, teasing beneath my skirt at my knee, the soft skin above it. His other arm supports my back, keeps me against his chest, the length of his fingers uncurled against the side of my breast through the dress. I try to remind myself that he's done this with other girls and that he only clings to me because I'm the one here, but his ring is cold against my flesh.

His mouth claims mine, tender but urgent, and I shatter. All the protests, the words of refusal that a good girl should have on her lips, the concern and the thoughts and the things that make sense, they all splinter off into nothingness, shards of unreality that sink into the lake and drown. "There is no word for you, Ophelia," he murmurs between kisses. "You're everything. Just . . . everything."

I can hear laughter from the waters, but I can't remember if I took my pills. I'm almost certain I did, scared that Father would check after breakfast the way he sometimes does, but I can't . . . The memory is there, but it's lost within Dane's kisses, trapped with every reasonable thing until only this moment exists.

But every moment ends.

We're both breathless when he pulls away, our eyes caught in a kind of horrified fascination. He breaks the line of sight and cradles me against his chest, and somewhere the gasps for air become sobs that wrack his entire frame. There are good days and bad days, as Horatio reminded me. Sometimes everything seems fine, and then the world explodes so suddenly, so drastically, that you can't even recognize it in the fragments that remain.

I hold Dane through his tears, comb my fingers through his dark hair just as my mother used to do to me when I woke from nightmares of the fury and despair that ride on ageless steeds through the forest. Just as I did during those long nights, he slowly calms under the repetition. Finally, he captures my hand and presses a scorching kiss against my palm.

"You're everything," he says again, and this time I believe him.

We stay at the lake until full dark makes it impossible to see. We're halfway back to the house when he stops on the path and hesitates. "Do you mind if we . . ."

I'm used to his silences now, used to the way he trails off as if the words have suddenly lost purpose. "You want to say good night to your father."

He nods.

I shyly reach for his hand, and he lets me take it, lets me weave my fingers through his and give a light squeeze. "Then let's go."

His gratitude is no less for staying silent, and despite the darkness, we turn off the path to cross the yard to the plain stone church. Lamps mounted on either side of the wooden double doors act as a beacon, but we curve to the right, to the cemetery that has become such a familiar sight. The light from the door doesn't reach far, does little to alleviate the darkness over the graves, but where Dane is blind, I can see the ghostly light of the spirits chained to the unhallowed ground.

I lead him to Hamlet's grave. The flowers have died and been replaced with new ones through the week, the freshly cut blooms over the dead ones, but in the right light you can see the decaying remnants through the gaps of the blossoms.

A blue-white flicker rivets my gaze to the head of the grave. The breath rips from my throat in a hoarse gasp.

"Ophelia?"

I shake my head, terror clawing through my skin in a violent wave of goose bumps. It's indistinct as yet, a vague form of light that could almost be man-shaped. There is nothing there to scare me.

Except . . . oh, except . . .

"Ophelia, what's wrong?" Now Dane sounds scared, his voice higher, more like Laertes, and I realize how tightly I'm gripping his hand, almost as hard as he held mine through the funeral.

I scramble for an answer, a word without meaning because I can't stand to tell him the truth. "I . . . Jack!"

His eyes scan the darkness around us. "He isn't here, Ophelia, now what's wrong?"

"He . . . he stopped lighting the candle." My entire arm trembles as I point to where the candle burned every night for a week. "I knew he'd stop after a week, but I thought . . ."

"It seems impossible that so much time has passed," he murmurs.

He says good night to his father's grave and leads me away from the cemetery, but I hesitate at the gate and turn to look over my shoulder at the blue-white flicker in the moonlight. There's nothing there that should scare me.

Except that the fledgling ghost is born from Hamlet's grave.

I don't know if Jack's candle didn't work or if there's something more sinister that keeps him tied to the dead flesh beneath the earth, but Hamlet is still here.

With Dane's hand warm against mine, his kisses still bruising my lips, it's all I can do not to weep.

CHAPTER 8

Each night, Dane and I end our evening in the graveyard so he can say good night to his father's grave.

Each night, he thinks it's futile, thinks there's nothing he can say that his father will ever hear.

Each night, I watch the ghost gather strength and definition, and I say nothing. It's clearer now, the features visible beneath the amorphous blue-white light. The light is always there, but it's pulling in under the skin until it's just a halo around him. I can see the strong features, the dark hair with its dignified sweeps of grey, the close-trimmed beard with the silver ribbons near the corners of his mouth.

Some nights he watches us, his face lost to an expression of such infinite sorrow that I drown in a storm of tears as soon as I'm safely back in my room.

Some nights he rages, his face marred by a paroxysm of such fury that I can't breathe, can't think of anything but running away.

And I say nothing to Dane, standing beside me thinking his father is on his way to Heaven, because I can't bear to give him this fresh pain. Dane can't see the ghosts; there's no way for him to ever know.

In the daylight, when the fear and the sorrow recede, curiosity invades. I tell myself not to ask questions because no good can come of knowing, so perhaps there is something of my father in me after all.

It takes me almost a fortnight to make a decision on it, but finally I have to know. Why is Hamlet tied to earth? It cannot simply be that he died without confession and absolution or all the world would be awash with the ghosts of good and bad alike.

After lunch, I retrieve my book from my room and head out into the gardens, but rather than seek out a comfortable bench, I look for Jack.

Jack Barrows is as much a part of this school as the Danemarks, a descendant of the original caretakers, as tied to the soil as any of the plants he tends. The gardens are extensive even before the greenhouses, but somehow he cares for them all, order within the shock of life. Every day, no matter the weather, he spends his time in the gardens, soil streaked up his arms and across his face, and every night he retreats to his tiny cabin deep in the woods. He comes up to the house to eat with the servants and leave a basket of flowers outside my door each morning and always seems uncomfortable within walls. Some nights I can see the thin trail of smoke from his chimney when he needs more light than the candles can give him in a single-room building with no electricity.

Hamlet offered to run power out there for him, but Jack refused.

He isn't easy to find, but everywhere I walk I can see the careful tending that says he's been through recently. The roses are pruned back, some of them tied to the delicate trellises that separate the paths; the weeds have been pulled, the soil loose where their roots clung.

He worships my mother, and I've never been sure why. Even now, over seven years after her death, he tends the flowers on her grave and on the island in the center of the lake, continues to bring me flowers every morning as he did when she was alive. I asked Mama once if he was in love with her, and she laughed so brightly, I almost felt ashamed of the question, but then she gathered me close and buried her face in my hair and told me there were all kinds of love. It wasn't really an answer, but then, what could I expect when I'd asked the wrong question?

I finally find him in a sunny alcove, on his knees in the grass to transplant violets in a great ring about the space. The stone bench is more a chaise, a low stone couch with one high curved end for support. This was Hamlet's favorite spot in the gardens, with a view of both the house and the lake, and his afternoon reading often turned into a nap in the sunlight.

And it was where he died, where Jack found him lifeless and warm. Gertrude didn't want an autopsy or blood tests, didn't want the doctors cutting into her husband's body. As ever, the local authorities were deferential to a fault where the Academy was concerned, so the coroners examined him as best they could and said it must have been a heart attack despite there being no warnings of it in his last physical. Such things can happen, they said, especially in stressful jobs, even though Hamlet was perhaps young for such spontaneous failure.

Jack grunts a greeting as he lowers a plant into the waiting hole, the roots carefully cupped in his gnarled fingers. He doesn't look away or pause, intent on his task.

I sit down on the very edge of the bench, my skin crawling with memory, and wait.

He isn't one for talking. I was almost five before he ever said anything to me, and that was just a warning not to play in the lake until I knew how to swim. When Mama was gone on her frequent flights, her escapes from the gilded cage of the Academy grounds, I followed Jack around the gardens with an endless stream of chatter, parroting Mama's stories of the Wild Hunt and the faeries that danced in the stone rings and the bells that rang in the lake.

Then one day, he sat back on his heels, studied me for so long I wanted to fidget and squirm, and then handed me a trowel and showed me how to gently dig around the roots of a plant that needed to be moved. He'd always tolerated my presence before that, as he tolerated Laertes, but from that day on, I was truly my mother's daughter in his eyes, something that pleases him as much as it terrifies my father.

Sometimes I wonder if there will ever be a time when I'm not defined by my mother, but I do it as much to myself as anyone else.

Finally, all the violets have moved from the pots to the beds that ring the clearing and Jack's blue eyes flick to me as he paces the perimeter with a dented, battered watering can. "Penny, Miss Ophelia."

"I've been thinking of the Headmaster," I answer, and the wealth of lines around his eyes deepen.

"I suspect most of us have."

"Tell me about when you found him?"

He shakes his head in time with the gentle shakes of the watering can that ensures no plant is hit too hard with the falling liquid. "Can't be any good in that."

I watch him sprinkle the last of the water, the can stacked neatly beside his other tools when he's done. Jack always knows more than he says. I don't even remember when I learned that, if it was something I realized over time or if my mother told me once, but he always knows more than he says. Jack sees more than most people, even if he can't see the faeries he believes in so fervently.

It takes more effort for him to kneel than it used to. He must be eighty if he's a day, and he can barely move when the rain is gathering, but he refuses to retire. The most help he'll accept is letting others clip the hedges and mow the lawns. He sinks his knees into the damp soil and leans over the violets to search the blooms beyond for invading weeds.

He isn't going to say anything else without a reason.

I open the book in my lap, run my fingers across the shape of the letters without seeing them. Like Jack, I always know more than I say, but I think of the sorrow in Hamlet's glowing eyes some nights, and other nights the rage, and I know it's worth whatever momentary pain I have to pay.

"He's a ghost, you know."

He sits up so quickly that his back seizes, and the next few minutes are lost to a grimace of pain and slow, deep breaths to relax the muscles. Finally, he looks back at me over his shoulder, his thin white ponytail streaked with dirt and bits of plant matter. "You've seen him?"

"Every night," I whisper. "He'll find his voice soon; I think he has something he needs very badly to say."

"Knowledge is a dangerous thing, Miss Ophelia. Knowledge cast us from the garden that was to the mercy of the demons and the fair folk. All the sins of the world, just from knowing for the first time what sin was."

"I thought you didn't believe in sin."

"No, but I believe in Nature, and in the acts that go against it."

"Meaning?"

He doesn't answer right away, and once again, I wait. He'll either say it or he won't. I think he will, because the conversation has already come this far, but he just as clearly doesn't want to say it. "I hear the funeral home did a good job of presenting him for the funeral," he says eventually. "Made his face smooth and stern."

"That's right."

"Wasn't how it was when he died."

I remember death, peaceful and serene, but I know that's not how death always is. "Is a heart attack painful?"

"Fearful painful, until you can't feel it anymore," he answers absently, and he should know, having had several of them over the past two decades. "But his face was contorted past that level of pain. Whatever he was feeling had to be worse."

"So he didn't die of a heart attack."

"I stripped his shirt to try CPR. Knew it was too late, still needed to try. He had a rash that spread across the skin, rough like oak bark. Never heard of a heart attack causing that." With a deep sigh, he digs in the chest pocket of his stained overalls and withdraws a small syringe, like the kind doctors use to take blood samples. A large bead of potter's clay covers the needle's point. Only a trace of liquid remains, milky but mostly clear, too thick to be water. Dirty fingerprints cloud the surface of the glass, grains of soil caught in the ridges of the handle. He hands it across to me, the glass cool despite the sunlight that beats against us. "Found that half buried in the flowers. Fingerprints are mine, weren't any on it when I pulled it from the ground."

"Poison?"

"Most like." He scratches at his bald pate, leaving smears of earth on his leathery skin. "Don't know what kind, don't want to. Even if he had a reason to, he couldn't have taken it himself and buried it in the flowers; he didn't have any gloves on him, no dirt either except his shoes."

I know I should be more shocked, more appalled, but ghosts always come back for a reason. Something had to work against the blessings of the priest and the sanctified ground. I roll the syringe across my palm, careful not to touch the needle or handle.

"Miss Ophelia."

I look away from the syringe to see Jack watching me expectantly.

"I was the one to find him, but do you remember the first here?"

I was reading on a blanket by the tiny field of lavender that struggles to survive when I heard Jack's shout. I left the book, left the blanket, because I'd never heard such a sound from him, and raced to the alcove as fast as I could run.

Claudius was there before I was. He was the one who called the ambulance, the one who held Gertrude when the noise brought her from the house, the one who ordered us to keep Dane away when he would have come to look as well.

"What could make a man kill his own brother?" I whisper, the thoughts too dark for the bright day.

"Why did Cain kill Abel?"

"He was jealous," I answer automatically, words before comprehension. My eyes widen as I realize the meaning. "He was jealous . . ."

"Been here a long time, Miss Ophelia. I remember those boys at school. Never a thing the elder had the younger didn't want, never a privilege or an honor earned by the elder that the younger didn't expect a share in. Back when the Fourth was losing to the sickness, when he went to choose between his boys to succeed him, how quick the younger came running back, when the elder had been here working for the school all along."

"He's already submitted for the position," I tell him quietly. "The Board is doing the final interviews this week and next."

"That's one way of it," he agrees, his tone so mild I know to turn the idea over again to look for what I'm missing.

I think of the way Claudius tried to sit at the head of the table, the way he greeted mourners at the funeral as if welcoming them to his home, the way his hand— "Gertrude."

"Beautiful woman. Both boys courted her here at school."

"But she chose Hamlet."

"Which is when the younger one left, off to make a fortune in dealings he never did speak of. Off to Europe and Asia to wager other men's money in businesses I would rather not understand. Only back when summoned for family occasions, and never a letter in between." Jack scowls down at his tools. "Never seen a man run so far from a good family."

"A prestigious position and a beautiful wife," I murmur. "I suppose men have killed for less. But a brother . . ." I flinch at the touch of cool metal on my other hand and realize I'm clutching Dane's class ring, like I'm trying to protect any piece of him from this terrible conversation. "You know Claudius better than I do."

"I don't suppose anyone could know that man. His words don't give much of himself."

True enough. "Will there be proof?"

Jack shakes his head and indicates the syringe. "That's as much as we'll find, I'd wager, and that's careless enough to make me wonder, unless he just couldn't get far enough away and still be close enough to hear the discovery."

"You'd think he'd want to be far away when the discovery was made."

"But then who would comfort Mrs. Danemark from the terrible sight? Who would be seen doing his best to rescue both her husband and her son?"

"Hamlet was strong. How could Claudius have injected the poison without there being a fight of some sort? Some kind of cry?"

"Poison to sleep, poison to die. One's much like another, and the Headmaster was sleeping very heavy that day."

I stare at the syringe, at the remnants of the cloudy liquid that smear the inside of the glass. "Jack . . . what do I do?"

"What do you think you should do?"

It's the question my mother would have asked. Father would give me a lecture on rules and regulations, on duty, but Mama would just turn the question back so there's no easy answer. Mama thought easy answers were the worst kind of self-deception, of foolishness.

Mama thought Father was the biggest kind of fool.

I take a deep breath, the carvings on the ring band pressing into my skin. "There's no proof."

"None whatsoever."

"Dane and Gertrude would be hurt if I accused without proof."

"Undoubtedly."

"There's Father."

He doesn't even say anything to that; doesn't have to. Even if I did have proof, Father would send me back to the cold place until the medications are adjusted and working properly again. For my own good, ostensibly, and yet how much would he suffer for it as well, bearing the guilt of locking me away? Hamlet greeted my return with violets, but Father always brought me home with palpable relief—and to an emptier liquor cabinet.

"I'm the only one who can see his ghost."

"Choose your debts carefully, Miss Ophelia. A debt's as good as a promise."

To whom do we owe the greater debt, the living or the dead?

To the memory of the man who taught me integrity, who prized honor and truth and strength of character, I owe the courage to make this known, whatever the consequences, whatever the price I have to pay to ensure that a murderer doesn't get away with his unnatural deeds.

But what about the things I owe Dane—the promises I made—as his friend, as his maybe something more? What about what I owe

Gertrude, who shows such grace even in her grief and treats me like a daughter? What do I owe Father and Laertes? How do the debts balance until one is greater than the others?

Jack's advice about being careful may be too late.

"There's no proof," I whisper.

Jack just shakes his head.

I slowly place the syringe in the pocket of my sundress. "I'll regret this."

"Can't escape that no matter what you choose," he tells me, not unkindly. From the sagging tool belt around his hips, he pulls out a pair of hand snips and delicately shears away a violet blossom from the main branch of its plant. He places the indigo flower in my palm, where the syringe so recently rested. "Regret follows any decision where there isn't a good choice to make. Be careful, Miss Ophelia. Knowledge got us exiled from the garden that was; that wasn't the worst thing it's done to us."

I curl my fingers around the violet. It would be so easy to clench my fist, to crush the flower until the clear sap stings my skin and the bruised petals rip apart like silk. It's so easy to destroy.

Jack stands with an effort and touches my shoulder, a faint smear of dirt left behind. Without another word, he tugs me to my feet and walks me to another alcove, a different bench, and leaves me there in the sunlight and the bright blue sky with its shredded wisps of white cloud.

When Dane finds me there, the violet is still safe in my palm. He doesn't see it though, and when he takes my hand, the blossom is crushed between us.

I don't tell him about the poison.

CHAPTER 9

The syringe is hidden in my room, buried in the cedar chest at the foot of the bed between all the layers of my mother's gowns. I can make it disappear from sight, but I can't forget it, can't help but think of it whenever I look at Claudius walking around the Head-master's House, when I see his hand at the base of Gertrude's back, the way he leans in too close to whisper in her ear.

Dane is mostly civil to him, though. I don't know if Gertrude has spoken to him or if he has truly come to believe in the Dane-mark legacy, but he seems resigned to the general expectation that Claudius will be the next headmaster. The other applicants have been ruled against, one by one, until only Claudius and one other remain.

The Fortins have been involved with Elsinore Academy nearly as long as the Danemarks and have always held a position on the Board of Governors. Their children have attended the school as long as it has been open, until just recently. For the past forty years or so, the Fortins and the Danemarks have stood on opposite sides of a fierce debate over the education the students receive. The For-tins argue that the girls should be held to the same standard as the boys, given the same opportunities, rather than grow up into gen-eration after generation of trophy wives.

I see the virtue in it, see the appeal, but the Danemarks stand by tradition, and most of the Board stands with them. After all, most of the Board attended the school, most of them have wives who attended the school. They have no reason to see anything wrong with the traditions that make us as we are. Even Dane and Laertes see nothing wrong, and Horatio has stopped trying to make them understand.

Reggie Fortin was the first Fortin not to attend Elsinore Academy. While his uncle remains on the Board of Governors and continues the debate at every opportunity, young Fortin attended a different prestigious institution and joined the faculty there in turn.

I know Hamlet respected the younger Fortin, even admired his passion for education, but he also was adamant about not changing the curriculum.

One afternoon Father sends word through the servants that we are going out to eat in town with the Danemarks, and that we should dress appropriately. We always dress for dinner, and there is no restaurant in town so grand that extra care is ever actually appropriate, but just as we have our traditions, there is something of reputation to consider as well.

Gertrude knocks on my door as I stand in front of my closet. Her knock is distinctive, light and soft, almost impossible to hear because it's more a tap of fingernails against wood than any true knock. When I open the door for her, I see she is already dressed, elegant in a sheath of red satin with an understated ruby and diamond design at her throat and ears. Her blonde hair, just a hint of strawberry to it, frames her face and leaves her slender neck bare except for the gold chain for the pendant.

"I thought I might help, if that's all right?" she says with a smile.

I step aside to let her enter. "You look lovely."

"Thank you." She kisses my cheek as she walks past, scarlet heels sinking into the thick carpet, but she doesn't so much as wobble.

I'm glad she's here; seeing her, I know I would have been woefully underdressed. We don't often eat in town, so there must be some occasion to celebrate. I decide Claudius must have been selected as the Headmaster. She's dressed too finely for any of the restaurants in town, dressed for the city and the establishments without menus or prices, but somehow she won't look out of place.

She skips past the array of clothing meant for usual dinners and sorts through the dresses and gowns I have for more formal occasions. Some of them are patently unsuitable even as finely dressed as she is, but after a few minutes she selects a dusky rose that almost contrives to bring color to my face. Father dislikes that dress because it comes off my shoulders, shows too clearly that I'm not a little girl anymore, but I've always loved the deep neckline and the lace-edged crinoline that gives shape to the calf-length skirt.

She helps me with the long row of cloth-covered buttons up the back, using a short metal hook to drag the satin cord loops over the fastenings. As I sit at the vanity to adjust my light makeup to better suit the dress, she stands behind me and brushes the day's tangles from my hair. For dinner and nicer events, I generally wear it down with an Alice band or a bit of ribbon to keep it out of my face, a youthful style that seems to reassure Father, but Gertrude pulls my small container of pins to the edge of the table and sorts through them with a thoughtful look on her face.

She smiles at my reflection in the mirror, kissing my temple. She presses our cheeks together so she can meet the reflection of my eyes. "You're not a little girl anymore, Ophelia. Polonius needs to see the young woman you're becoming."

A child can be controlled; he's afraid the woman cannot be. But I don't say this, because Gertrude has never really understood the complicated relationship between Laertes, Father, and me. We revolve around my dead mother and the space she left behind, revolve around the fear and uncertainty and sense of loss, each of us having lost something very different. Instead, I just watch as she pins my hair into an elegant, heavy twist on the back of my head. This morning's basket of flowers included a mass of delicate white star-of-Bethlehem. She pins these in as well along one side.

I'm a different creature under her ministrations. I'm no longer the sylph that disappears in the shadows, overlooked and forgotten. I'm someone to be seen, noticed.

I'm not sure I like the change. I like being able to disappear in plain sight, like knowing who will see me no matter how I disappear.

Horatio always sees me. Dane always sees me. I dislike when people notice me only because someone else has brought attention to me.

Gertrude's hands rest on my bare shoulders, her fingertips light against my collarbones, and I see the glint of a blocky diamond on one finger. "You look more like your mother every day," she tells me.

It occurs to me that she must not know Father as well as I thought she did if she believes this to be a good thing.

She frowns slightly at the thin silver chain at my throat, the ring tucked in the hollow of my breasts. She can't see the ring, but the chain is clearly not the best choice for the dress. I press one hand against the neckline, keep the ring hidden from sight, and she gives me this small preference.

We're the last ones downstairs. Horatio isn't there, but Dane wears a heavy leather jacket over his suit coat, the black plastic handle of a comb sticking out from one pocket. The sight, ridiculous as it, cheers me; if he's riding his motorcycle again, his general mood must be improving. He enjoys the thrill too much to ride it when he's depressed. He still wears all black, down to the tie that's too loosely knotted against his silk shirt, but he smiles when he sees me, and his dark grey eyes light up. He doesn't say anything, but he doesn't have to; his eyes show me a clearer reflection than the mirror upstairs.

Laertes scowls. He should look more comfortable, his blue shirt open at the throat—he hates ties and only wears them when he has a hickey to conceal—but he hunches into his jacket and quickly steps between me and Dane. "You're overdressed," he growls under his breath.

"Gertrude selected it."

There's nothing he can say to that, but it's clear he's distressed over it. He keeps himself between me and Dane, unable to see the mocking gleam in our friend's eyes. Dane knows exactly what my brother is doing, and it amuses him in a way that isn't entirely kind. He winks at me when Laertes can't see him, even blows me a teasing kiss.

Gertrude must have told Father of her wish to help me dress because he tells me only that I look quite presentable. Memories of Mama darken his eyes as he says it, though, and he keeps his gaze on my face. Claudius helps Gertrude into a light summer jacket that precisely matches her dress and leads us outside to the limousine that waits on the long circular drive. Just behind it stands Dane's motorcycle, the helmet balanced on the seat. As much as his mother hates the bike and the dangers it presents, I think she's too relieved to see him take an interest in anything to tell him to ride with the rest of us in the car.

It's not a long drive into town, but it's done in silence. I stare out the window so I can't see the way Claudius has Gertrude's hand clasped against his knee. I think of the syringe, of Cain and Abel, and I just can't bear to see it.

Dane reaches the restaurant before us; when the limo pulls in to release us, he stands at the doors combing his hair into some semblance of order. He offers his hand to help me from the car and, when Laertes and Father can't see, brushes a hand against the silver chain where it disappears under the fabric, where his ring rests. He says nothing, but I can see the pleasure in his expression that I wear it.

The other patrons of the restaurant stare at us as we pass through to a private room. Town and school have little to do with each other, even when the older students come down on the weekends for a chance to escape the grounds. They think us arrogant, and perhaps we are, invading this place in our too-fine clothing.

Laertes manages to seat me between him and Father; Dane actually laughs when he sees it and promptly sits across from me. His good humor is such a change from the grieving boy of the past month. It's a joy to see, even if my brother bears the sting of it. Then again, I don't think Laertes realizes our friend is laughing at him. My brother doesn't always realize when he's being mocked.

A waiter hovers in one corner of the room. He's young enough that this is probably his first summer working; he's clearly nervous. As he pours water and wine into our glasses, his hands shake so much it's a wonder he doesn't tip anything over. He blushes every time he looks at me, his eyes snapping away from my neckline or face.

Dane watches him closely as he leans over my shoulder to take away the half-eaten plate of fruit I had in place of a salad. "Didn't you like the melons?" Dane asks innocently, his timing impeccable.

The waiter looks at the plate directly in front of my chest, his eyes widening at the view straight down my dress, and backs away so suddenly the plate bangs against my shoulder. A piece of cantaloupe slides off the plate with the violent motion, dropping into the dress. I'm not sure who's blushing more fiercely, me or the poor waiter, but Dane leans forward in his seat.

"Do you need some help?"

Father glances over and frowns, distracted from Claudius and Gertrude's conversation. "Help with what? Do you need some help, Ophelia?"

Dane grins at me. Or at my scowling brother. It's hard to be certain.

"No, Father, I don't need help, but may I be excused to the restroom?" I'm actually proud of how evenly my voice emerges. It's hard to play at having dignity when you have fruit lodged between your breasts.

"Yes, of course." He squeezes my hand briefly, then turns his attention back to the other end of the table.

As I scoot my chair back to stand, the mortified waiter pulls it out so quickly I have to grab the edge of the table to stay standing. The waiter isn't so lucky, and he drops to one knee to keep both the plate and the chair from hitting the carpet.

His smile growing, Dane shifts into my father's line of sight. "Doesn't Ophelia look lovely tonight, sir? Soon all the boys will be falling at her feet."

"Yes, yes, of course," Father replies absently. Then he sees the waiter, still on the floor with his eyes screwed shut to keep from looking up my skirts. "Are you ill, boy?"

"N-n-no, s-sir, I j-just—"

"The chair overbalanced as he was helping me," I say quickly. "He was just going to show me the way to the restroom."

Dane's eyes dance even as he pulls his smile into a semblance of a pout. This is the Dane who plays and laughs, the Dane I've missed even as I marvel at the Dane who needs me. "Do you need a chaperone?"

"Do you think you qualify?"

His laugh makes warmth pool in my chest, radiating outwards from the silver band of his ring. I follow the speechless, shaking boy to the restrooms, and he blushes when I thank him. I retrieve the bit of fruit and throw it away, then wet a paper towel to wash away the stickiness of the juice. The mirror shows me Gertrude's creature, a young woman dressed with more assurance than she feels. I can't help but wonder what makes the boy blush. I look like Mama, but my mother's beauty was a feral thing, a beauty as like to cut as captivate. I don't have my mother's wildness, don't have that hard-to-define piece that draws the eye. Who looks at the shadows when they can see the light?

When I leave the restroom, Dane is waiting in the short hallway, leaning against the wall, between the doors to the men's room and an employee area. "You do look lovely," he says softly. He reaches out to trace one finger along the chain that holds his ring. "It isn't you I mean to mock."

"No," I agree with a small smile. "It's the whole world."

He tugs me gently against him and kisses me, barely a whisper of his mouth against mine. Pearly pink gloss gleams on his lips when he pulls away. For a moment I wonder if he'll leave it there for Laertes to see, but he winks and disappears into the men's room.

With a deep breath, I make my way back to the private dining room, all too aware of the eyes that track my progress. I don't think I like being Gertrude's creature. I miss my shadows, miss being unseen. This isn't real, like Cinderella at the ball. It has to end, and what happens then? Father nods absently when I reclaim my seat, Laertes studying me with narrowed eyes, and when Dane returns several minutes later, the waiter comes in with reinforcements and the main course.

When the desserts are delivered, the waiter nearly runs from the room. He won't be needed again, and I suspect he's not so secretly grateful for the chance to escape.

Claudius stands, his glass of wine in his hand. It's his third or fourth of the evening, his cheeks flushed, and his cold green eyes are bright. "You may have been wondering the reason for this celebration," he says grandly, as if he speaks to a room full of people rather than a mere five others.

Dane smirks and rests his cheek on one fist. "Not really," he mutters.

I raise my glass to hide my smile.

"Our cause for joy is twofold," Claudius continues. Either he didn't hear his nephew or he's choosing to ignore him. "The Board of Governors has made its final decision: the Danemark legacy will continue to be the guiding force of Elsinore Academy. They have selected me to uphold the traditions my brother held so dear to his heart."

He pauses, clearly expecting applause as would be suitable for a larger gathering, and Gertrude and Father are quick to oblige him. Laertes follows suit, his elbow digging into my ribs when he feels me too slow to join in. We're expected to congratulate him for murdering his brother to take his place. But of course they don't know that, and even Dane manages a bored-looking golf clap.

And they don't know what's coming. They've already forgotten that he said there were two reasons to celebrate. They haven't noticed the blocky diamond on Gertrude's left hand. I fold my hands in my lap, stare at the veins that trace through the thin skin of my wrists. A shoe nudges my ankle, and I look up to see Dane's curious, half-concerned expression.

He has no idea what's coming.

Claudius reaches down for Gertrude's hand; she blushes as she places it in his palm, the diamond bright and gaudy in the candlelight from the table. He lifts her hand to kiss the ring. "And Gertrude, whom I have loved since we were but children, has consented to be my wife."

A stunned silence follows his words. Even Father stares, blindsided by this information. He'll never say it, especially now that Claudius is the new headmaster, but I think a part of him is appalled. He never remarried after Mama's death, never even considered dating. For Gertrude to consent to an engagement barely a month after her husband's death . . .

"Uncle, if that is a joke, it is in very poor taste," Dane says quietly, his dark grey eyes riveted on the blond man at the head of the table.

"This is no joke, son."

Wrong word.

Dane explodes into motion, dishes rattling and glasses toppling as his movement shakes the table. Water and wine splash violently against the pristine cloth, a rapidly spreading stain. "So it's not enough that you take his position in the school; now you must take his position in bed?"

"Dane," Gertrude reproves. Her eyes flick anxiously to the doorway that separates us from the rest of the restaurant.

"Father's been dead barely a month! What the hell is wrong with you? Barely in the ground but you need to replace him? Christ, and with his *brother*!"

"Dane—"

"Did you even wait for him to die? Did you even wait for his body to be—to be in the ground before you took that thing into your bed?" He kicks at the table. One of the legs cracks, groans, and then fractures in an avalanche of splinters and shattering dishes. Laertes hauls me out of my chair barely in time to avoid the candelabra that crashes down where my head would have been; the wicks land in a puddle of water on the floor and sputter out in a hiss of weak smoke. "How could you?"

An ugly flush rises in Claudius' face as he takes in the destruction. "Hamlet Danemark, you will restrain yourself this instant!"

I lower my head into my hands and laugh silently, much to Laertes' dismay.

"You're not my father! You are—" Dane bellows. He closes his eyes, forces himself to take a deep breath. When he opens them again, his voice trembles with a terrible intensity. "You are nothing but a pale shadow who has to steal what my father left behind because you could never earn it in your own right. And my dear, sweet mother is apparently the filthy *whore* who lets you." He rips open the door and stalks out; as it swings awkwardly on its hinges, I can see the entire restaurant staring at our private room.

The blood drains from Gertrude's face, leaving her ashen beneath her makeup, and one hand flutters weakly in my direction. "Ophelia . . . he listens to you."

What does she expect me to say to him? It's all right, Dane, at least the incest is better than the murder? This is not a grief that I can wash from his eyes.

But I can see the tears she won't let fall in public as she reaches for my hand, the faint lines around her tightly held mouth. I'm not sure which has wounded her more, her son's words or his pain.

Father grabs my arm, his fingers digging into my skin, and yanks me towards the doorway. "For the love of God, calm him down, Ophelia," he pleads. Real fear—a father's fear for a son unhinged—fills his eyes. "Do not let him hurt himself."

He closes the door behind me as though that will return some sense of dignity to the proceedings. Fire burns in my cheeks as the other diners stare at me. I am the one who goes unseen, who disappears into the shadows, but now every eye is on me. I try to walk gracefully, try to remember the poise that Gertrude has spent so long teaching me, but after only a few steps, my courage deserts me and I run through the restaurant and out the front door.

Dane stands at his motorcycle, one arm shoved into the bulky leather jacket as his other struggles behind him. He growls when he sees me. "Did they send you out to calm me? Make me see reason?"

His voice stabs me, because it's exactly why they sent me out. "That's what they expect," I whisper.

He stares at my hand, and I realize that once again I've clutched the ring without thought, like a prayer for strength. "Is it what you'll do?"

"No."

Three quick steps and he's close enough to pull me against him, the jacket draped off one shoulder. His fingers slide into my hair, yank out the pins that keep it contained and toss them to the asphalt. "Put the helmet on," he snaps.

"Dane—"

"If you're coming with me, then put the helmet on. Otherwise, stay here with the other idiots."

I reach for his jacket and silently hold it up for him to slide his other arm through. He gives me a fleeting smile, as much grimace as smirk, and puts the helmet on me himself. It's heavy and awkward, and the padding reeks of mildewed shampoo, but as soon as it's securely fastened, he lifts me by the waist and drops me onto the back of the motorcycle.

He mounts in front of me and grabs my knees to pull me flush against his back. He wraps my arms around his waist; I can barely hear his warning through the helmet. "Hold on tight."

The motorcycle starts with a snarl. He doesn't even bother to pull out of the space but just goes over the grassy divide that separates the lot from the main road. He cuts off one car, nearly runs into the back bumper of another, then starts weaving through the evening traffic. Even through the helmet I can hear him laughing, a manic sound that tugs at my heart and makes me weep. Car horns blare around us; sometimes through an open window I can hear a muffled curse before we tear away.

I don't think this is what Father intended.

CHAPTER 10

As we leave the lights of the town behind us, I bury my head as best I can against his back and hold on for dear life, something I suspect Dane no longer finds all that dear.

We streak past the school guards at the gate and up the long circular drive. Dane jerks us aside onto the cobblestone pathways, then off any path at all as he aims across the manicured lawns and down the slope. For a heart-stopping moment, I think he intends to drive us straight into the lake, but at the last possible second, he yanks us into a tight spin and we skid across the grass.

The wheels stop half a foot from the water.

I can't move, can't breathe, can't do anything but cling to him.

He just laughs.

Thunder, bone-deep and menacing, rolls across the sky. We've been promised rain all week, but nothing's happened. Clouds have drifted in all afternoon, impossible to see now that night has fallen. There are no stars. Even in the gaps where stars might be, there is nothing, no stars, no moon, nothing but a darkness swelled with rain that refuses to fall.

With shaking hands, I loosen the helmet and pull it off; some of my hair tries to follow it. Dane snatches the helmet and hurls it away as far as he can. It lands in the lake with a dismal splash.

We sit there in silence, our hearts racing frantically. Just as I start to think the storm might be over, he dismounts and hauls me from the seat, his grip on my upper arms punishingly strong. He yanks me across the grass to the stand of willows and shoves me up against one of the trunks. His entire body presses flush against mine; my feet can't even touch the tangled roots below me.

"You knew," he whispers fiercely. I can't hear my Dane in his voice.

"No."

"You weren't surprised, Ophelia. Everyone else, even your damn father, was stunned, but you knew!" He shakes me a little. Pain blossoms where his fingers press into my skin.

"I wondered!" I cry, startled by the pain. "I saw how he watched her, how he touched her, how she . . . how she let him! I didn't think this would actually happen!"

"What would happen? That she would betray everything my father stood for? That she would whore herself out to the first man that came sniffing around, even her own brother-in-law? My father loved her with everything in him, and this is how she repays him? His own brother?"

He shakes me again, harder, and my head knocks back against the tree. Stars bloom in front of my eyes, and I can't help but smile. The night has stars now. How can a night with stars be frightening?

"What woman who claims to love a man could do such a thing?"

"A woman who's afraid." I whisper.

Curses spill from his lips, dark and sour and knife-sharp, but with each splintered word, his grip lessens slightly and my feet come a little closer to the tangle of roots. He doesn't actually let go of me, doesn't let me step away from the tree, but I can finally stand on my own. "Afraid of what?"

"If she isn't the Headmaster's wife, who is she?" I try to piece together things Jack has told me, things Gertrude herself has told me, even things Father and Mama have said over the years. "It's the only thing she's ever known, ever been. If she had to leave, where would she go? What would she do? Dane, you were the primary beneficiary of your father's will; what he left her is comfortable but not what she's used to. She's never been alone, never had to support herself."

"She could have stayed as his hostess," he snarls, but his head drops to rest against my hair. "The school rules allow for an unmarried headmaster to have a family member act as his official hostess—even I know that—so she could have stayed in that respect. But they've called each other brother and sister for twenty years! How can they be brother and sister and suddenly become husband and wife?"

"I don't know."

"How, Ophelia, tell me how!" He slams me into the tree again.

"I don't know!" Tears burn in my eyes. An ear-shattering crack of thunder shakes us, and the salt spills down my cheeks. "I'm sorry. I'm so sorry. But I don't know."

"It's unnatural."

"Yes."

"It's horrific."

"Yes."

"It's . . . it's . . ."

"Yes," I say anyway, because he'll never find the word he needs. I can't even touch him, my arms pinned at my sides by his grip, by the weight of his body slamming against me.

With a violent explosion of lightning, the rain finally falls. It batters the lake, the trees, and the willows provide little shelter against the stinging slap of each drop. A rain like this will shred the gardens, churn the soil until the roots are exposed and broken, tear the petals away and leave only ugliness in its wake. I shiver and try to turn my face against Dane's chest for shelter. The water soaks through my hair, weighs down the lovely rose dress that can probably never be saved. The buttons dig into my spine.

I'm not sure Dane even notices the rain.

One hand finally releases my arm, and I can't help the hiss that slides between my teeth as blood rushes back to the area. He lifts his head away to see my face, rain dripping from his hair to splash against my chest. His fingers trace the angry red lines left behind on my biceps. "I did this to you," he whispers, voice soft with horror. "Ophelia, I . . . I . . ."

"Shh."

He steps away from me, drops to his knees at the sight of my other arm equally adorned with the promise of future bruises. "I'm not this person. I swear I'm not. My father didn't raise me to be this person." He clutches his hair, his entire body folded in under an incomprehensible weight. "You're the only thing that's real. It's like breaking you will make it all a dream."

Still on his knees, he comes forward again and presses his face against my stomach, his arms sliding around my hips to pull me from the tree. "Ophelia, forgive me. I'm so sorry."

"There's nothing to forgive."

Except there is. But I can't ask him to forgive me for the secrets I keep, can't form an apology without giving away the truths that will only cause him more pain. I run my fingers through his soaked hair, stroke away the strands plastered to his pale face.

"Ophelia, why can't this all be a terrible dream? Why can't I wake up?"

How many ways can a heart break?

I suspect, because of Dane, I will discover them all.

But I sink down onto his lap, sitting across his thighs so we're nearly the same height, and kiss his cheek. "Just for tonight," I murmur. "Just for tonight, it can all be a dream. In the morning you'll have to wake up, and the terrible things will still be there, but tonight can be a dream."

He almost laughs. One finger brushes against the slender chain at my throat. "I need . . . Ophelia, I need . . . Ophelia, please."

I don't even know what he's asking, but I nod, and his hands tear at the buttons at the back of my dress. He fumbles with the tiny loops of cord. He yanks at them in frustration, and they come away in his hands, drop to the ground to float in small puddles like rose petals. The fabric clings to my skin, but he peels it away until it pools at my elbows and waist.

I know I should protest, know I should voice the fear that stabs through me, but the way he looks at me . . . His hand shakes as he traces the chain down to the silver ring between my breasts. His palms smooth across lace, and he lowers his head to place a soft kiss against the skin where the ring rests.

Every time, he asks a little bit more of me, needs a bit more of me, and I know I should say no.

And yet, the word can never form, never find breath or impulse or even origin. I should tell him no, but I can't, not when I drown in his kisses, not when I tense under the unfamiliar touch that tightens everything within me to a single, terrifying point. Not when he says my name that way, like I'm the only beauty in a dark world, like I'm the only thing that keeps him whole.

His hands, his lips fall still, and he cradles me back against the tree, his ear pressed to my racing heartbeat. Thunder rolls through us. Goose bumps ripple along my skin with each new wave of rain, each cold wind off the lake that blows more water at us.

Headlights flash up the drive, the limousine returning from the carnage at the restaurant, and Dane sits up with an unfathomable expression. He says nothing as he fixes my bra, pulls the dress back up where it belongs. The buttons are a lost cause, so he shrugs out of his leather jacket and drapes it over my shoulders with a burning kiss that leaves me feeling selfish for wanting more of him.

"Dane . . ."

"Why can't the dream be real?"

"Then what would we dream?"

"Tell them we fell," he says abruptly. "To explain the mud. Just tell them we fell. It won't really be a lie." He walks back to the motorcycle and starts it with a wild spray of mud from the spinning tires. He leaves me there at the edge of the lake.

I should follow him, should say something to Gertrude or Father, should at least get warm and dry and clean, but I sit down at the edge of the lake, take off my heels, and let my feet dangle into the rising water. Fear sparks up my spine, an unexpected warmth. Dane says he can't bear to think that I'll walk away from him, but I'm never the one who walks away. Never the one that could.

Two pale shapes rise from the dark waters of the lake. One of them glitters silver like fish scales in the flashes of lightning, diamonds glinting like stars in the pale gold hair that floats around her on the rippling surface. The other is a bruise against the night, purple-black hair clinging to moonlight pale skin like a teasing gown that displays more than it conceals. Wine-stained lips curve in a secretive smile beneath large indigo eyes.

"That's my girl," greets the second one. "Self-preservation is not our first impulse, is it?"

My mother.

I close my eyes and remind myself again that I've taken my pills every day. When I open them, she's still there. "I know," I whisper.

"It scares you, doesn't it? Being my daughter?"

"Shouldn't it?"

She shrugs and her damp curtain of hair shifts across her breasts. "I left fear behind a long time ago, Ophelia." She curls around my leg and I tense, wondering if she'll pull me in. She has before. I only drowned the once, when she drowned too, but since then she sometimes finds it amusing to pull me in and remind me of the promises she made.

Because down deep at the bottom of the lake, she says the City of Ys waits to rise again. It was a great city once, until a spoiled king's daughter opened the gates that held back the tide. The storm-swollen waters rushed in, and the princess was lost to the sea.

The princess smoothes a hand over her jewel-strewn hair and looks back at me with an indifferent gaze. Dahut became a morgen, a sea spirit who lures men to their deaths in the waters. She and Mama have been friends of a sort ever since Mama came to the school, or perhaps just kindred spirits. My mother has promised for years, ever since I can remember, to take me deep beneath the lake to where the church bells of the city still ring the hours.

"It's different," Mama says suddenly. I look down at the face that will never change. "You love him. That makes it different."

"Does it?"

"Passion is different when there's more than just hunger to feed it." She takes my hand, tugs me down towards her, but only kisses my cheek. "I keep my promises, Ophelia. As rarely as I make them, I always keep them."

"I've been taking my pills. Every day, I take them."

"Oh, sweetheart." She moves as though to sit beside me, but my mother can never fully leave the lake. None of the morgens can, but she and Dahut are the only ones who come so near the shore. "The pills are meant to strip away what isn't real. They can't take away what actually exists."

"But they usually take you away. Always before, I would take them, and your world would just go away, like it doesn't exist at all. Just stories that you used to tell us that I believed too much."

"But things are changing, Ophelia. Can't you feel it?" Her bruise-colored eyes nearly glow with excitement, and her cold hands clutch my arm around the deepening marks. "The bean sidhe feel it. The washerwomen ready their tubs. The Hunt senses the rage that stirs. Even the board of that absurd school you cling to cannot help but feel what is coming. Things are changing, and you, my dear daughter, my mirror, are a part of it. What could pills possibly do against that?"

I struggle to my feet, legs tangled in the mud-heavy skirts, and race back towards the safety of Headmaster's House and the bedroom with the curtains I close to keep the other world out of sight. Mama's laughter follows me through the rain, punctuated by the deep toll of church bells from beneath the waters of the lake.

CHAPTER 11

Despite Dane's furious protests, despite even Father's cautiously worded concerns, the plans for the wedding have gone forward unabated. Try as I might, I cannot understand why it isn't delayed until a more appropriate time, when mourning has run its course and they might attempt such a venture without censure. To remarry only six weeks after Hamlet's death . . . it smacks of everything unnatural—and it will surely cause tongues to wag. Gossip is never a friend to those who must maintain a reputation, and Gertrude knows this as well as anyone.

She at least tries to mitigate the damage. It's to be a very small affair, one with witnesses instead of guests, and no honeymoon. She and Claudius have shared a name these two decades past, and so there will be no eyebrows raised on that score, but Claudius seems oblivious to the consequences of their engagement. He calls her Sweetheart and Love and Angel, no matter the company, and whenever they share proximity, his hand seeks a way to touch her in some way. It might be sweet were it less possessive, less like a trophy clutched to the chest in equal parts shock and triumph.

Whatever progress Dane had made in recovering from his father's death is gone now, shattered in the face of his mother's betrayal. His black clothing—he has worn nothing else since that day—is less a sign of grief than a weapon, an accusation to make Gertrude flush and pale in a tight sequence of pain and mortification.

She fears he's gone off his medication, and I think she must be right, because his mood swings become truly terrifying. He rages and weeps and sulks with little warning or transition between them.

I try to be there for him, but Gertrude pulls me into the preparations for the ceremony and the formal, private dinner afterwards. She seems to think I need to learn the skills of a proper hostess, or perhaps she simply needs the additional distraction to overcome the insults her son hurls at her so frequently. I learn more than I have ever wanted to know about flower arrangements and centerpieces and how to pair wines with foods. She orders me a dress for the wedding but keeps it in her closet "as a surprise" as if I have any reason to look forward to it, as if anticipation is a feeling that should even be applied to the circumstances.

She takes a simple pleasure in the arrangements that's both sweet and painful. She doesn't know how to be a widow; she knows how to be a hostess. As she experiments with the placement of flowers in different vases, she smiles and hums.

Until Dane walks in. Where he goes these days, pain frequently follows.

One afternoon, he joins Gertrude and me in a small workroom attached to the greenhouse. We sit in silence as his mother talks about the meanings of the different flowers, as she twines different ribbons into bows and smiles or frowns at the results. My eyes glaze over as she meditates on the advantages and disadvantages of wire-edged ribbon.

Dane leans forward and pulls an untrimmed stalk of lavender from the scarred wooden surface. "The Victorians, wasn't it?"

"What?"

"They're the ones who came up with the language of flowers, right?" He reaches out to roll the lavender across my cheek, the scent filling my nose with each breath. "Every flower has a meaning?"

I think that was somewhere in the lesson. Gertrude's given me this lesson so many times over the years, and I've never given it the attention I should.

"Shall we make a bouquet for my mother?"

"Dane . . ."

"Now, let's see if I remember my lessons. Lavender, that's for . . . distrust. Yes! An excellent flower for my mother!" He places it in my hand and turns to rummage over the surface of the table. Gertrude clipped one of everything in the greenhouse, so the table is a riot of color and different kinds of petals. He holds up a slender stem with deep pink flowers edged in white, like starbursts. "What's this one?"

"Love-lies-bleeding," I answer automatically. "Amaranth."

"Amaranth, right. 'Immortal love.' No, that doesn't quite work for Mother, does it? Out with it!" He grinds the plant underfoot. "Hyacinth? No, no sincerity here. Pansy? Not a bit. Jasmine? Yes, grace and elegance she has, if not the sense that should accompany them." He scoops the pink-tinted blossoms into my lap.

Gertrude watches him with tears in her eyes, her hands clutched around a vase with sapphire ribbon twined about her fingers. But Dane ignores her, intent on rooting through the flowers. He sorts through them with ruthless efficiency until the floor resembles a botanical slaughterhouse. When he's done, he finds a bit of coarse twine and knots it around the flowers in my lap.

It's an ugly bouquet of ugly meanings, and one by one I touch the blooms to name their meaning. Lavender and jasmine, yes, but also marigold—desire for riches—and stargazer lily—for ambition—and clumps of rue and fennel for regret and flattery and deceit. He hurls the arrangement at his mother and it smacks her in the chest. She catches it before it can drop and, cradling the bouquet against her breast, walks quickly from the room.

Not quickly enough to hide the tears.

I can't remonstrate Dane for his mother's pain, can't censure him in any way that won't provoke one of his rages. Instead, I nudge a shredded globe of hydrangea—perseverance—and keep my eyes on the floor. "I don't think the flowers did anything to hurt you."

"No," he agrees pensively, "the flowers were quite innocent, as flowers usually are. Sometimes the innocent are the first to suffer, and I'm not sure if that's a mercy. But then there's you." He pulls his hand out of his pocket and uncurls the fingers, revealing a solitary blossom sheltered from the carnage.

A violet.

He knots it into my hair, arranges it so it falls over my heart. "Do you know what violets stand for, Ophelia?" Before I can answer, he kisses me deeply and walks away.

I finger the silky petals over my heart. Hamlet used to greet me with a basket of violets every time I returned from the cold place, and as I shared the secret of their scent, he shared the secret of their meaning.

Faithfulness.

Oh, Dane.

Claudius has learned from the debacle of the restaurant, from the shouting match over the chair at the head of the table. He doesn't try to remonstrate with Dane, even when his behavior is at its worst. He doesn't try to be stern, doesn't try to discipline, offers no sign that he considers himself in any way an authority figure over him. He's unfailingly mild and polite against even the worst insults. Dane's pain is very real, but Claudius' serene countenance makes his nephew look somewhat ridiculous in his vehemence.

It forces me to revise my opinion of Claudius. He isn't just ambitious; he's clever. He knows very well that the appearance of a thing is far more understood than the thing itself, and so he gives the best appearance possible. When visitors see uncle and nephew interacting, they don't remember the nagging feeling of distaste that Claudius is so quickly marrying his brother's widow; they remember the awkward ugliness of Dane's uncontrolled anger—righteous though it may be. They leave in sympathy for Claudius, having completely forgotten the moral outrage that brought them to the school in the first place.

With Father consumed with educating Claudius in his new official role as the Headmaster, Laertes has taken it upon himself to watch me like a hawk. He bursts into my room whenever he feels like it, wants to watch me take my pills each morning because he thinks I'll seize on any excuse not to take them. There isn't a way to tell him that I actually want to take them, because that would involve telling him what happens when I don't.

Those first few days after speaking with Mama at the lake, I purposefully didn't take the pills. I wanted to see if she was right, if they really were useless. The first day, even the second day, were fine, or as fine as they ever are when I can hear the Wild Hunt riding through the woods and see the ghosts flicker like blue flame in the graveyard at night. By the third day, though, as always happens when I don't take my meds for any stretch of time, my thoughts splintered and the fear crawled up my spine. I tried to stay away from everyone that day because words fell from my lips, nonsensical and too honest, too full of meaning to mean anything.

Horatio stayed with me through that evening, kept me walking through the gardens with him so no one could go to one place and expect to find me there. He listened patiently to the fractured sentences, answered them when he could, and never looked at me with pity or disgust. Or fear. He gave me the gift that Father and Laertes can never give me, that Dane is too wounded now to give anyone.

He made me feel real.

I took my pills the next morning, but it wasn't until the next day that my brother began his morning raids, as ever too late.

The morning of the wedding arrives, and I'm supposed to be making my way to Gertrude's room for hours of female indulgence before the late afternoon ceremony. Instead, I sit on my bed, my hands in my lap as I contemplate the dark rings of bruises around my upper arms. They're finally starting to fade, but the marks were deep, and I bruise so easily. My body lets go of its wounds reluctantly, as if the physical injuries could excuse the mental fragility. No one but Dane has seen them; since the night he gave them to me, he's asked to see them only once, and upon sight his face was etched over by the deepest expression of loathing, and he stalked away to ignore me altogether for two days.

I lift a hand to trace the lines, the purple edged in sickly green and yellow as it heals. I can actually see where his fingers were, remember the feeling of his grip. As much as he despises the pain he gave me, I think there's a part of him that would enjoy seeing the bruises ruin his mother's perfect day. It's the first time I've wished to see the dress Gertrude has selected for me. It's still summer, still hot despite the cool breezes that whisper in over the lake, and the air is thick with humidity and promised rain. If the dress is sleeveless, the bruises will show, and there's really nothing to disguise them for what they are. One arm I could perhaps blame on Father, for how strongly he grabbed and yanked at the restaurant that night, but there is no excuse for the other that does not shine a foul light directly on Dane.

"Ophelia?" Fingernails tap against the door in a perfunctory knock. "The car's ready to take us into town."

There's nothing to be done; the bruises will either be seen or they won't. With a deep sigh, I pull on a light cardigan and go to meet Gertrude at the door.

We spend the morning at the salon in town. Gertrude says nothing of the wedding, but she shows the women swatches of fabric I'm not allowed to see and lets them think this is some sort of occasion for my honor. Perhaps a debut or a cotillion or whatever it is the young women of society have that I will never truly be part of.

Obedient to Gertrude's wishes, I keep my eyes closed almost the entire morning as women bustle around me. They hiss when they see the bruises. I manage some story of falling off the motorcycle, of Dane grabbing me to keep me from injury. It must be believable because their voices turn to what a fine young man he is, of how proud his father would be, and the part of me that's petty hopes it causes Gertrude pain to hear about Hamlet's legacy in their son.

They file and buff and polish my nails, massage lotions into my hands and feet, paint my face with something thick that stings and strips away layers of dead skin like an acid wash. They shampoo my hair and trim the ends, then arrange it into some heavy confection that makes my neck ache from the strain of keeping it all upright. Even my makeup is seen to under their talented hands. They render me into Gertrude's creature, a china doll meant to be displayed.

I have no idea why Gertrude even bothers. This evening will only be the Danemarks, the Castellans, Horatio, and the priest. There is no one to amaze, no one to awe, no one who needs to see me as anything other than I am.

She undergoes the same treatments, and before she tells me to close my eyes again, I can see that she's a picture of soft pinks and muted golds, a natural beauty accentuated by the powders that hide the faint lines at her eyes and mouth. She can't blindfold me without smudging my makeup or ruining my hair, so she bids me keep my eyes closed, and I let her lead me around blind.

She doesn't talk about Dane as we sip smoothies for lunch. She doesn't talk about her soon-to-be-husband either. She chatters about gossip from the city or reminisces about places around the world she's seen that she wants to show me someday. They're places I've always been curious about but never felt any particular drive to see. The school is home. It's safe, even when it isn't. It's where I can disappear.

Finally, we return to the school, and she walks me carefully up the stairs to her rooms, the private suite she had even while married to Hamlet. I asked her about it once, when I was too young to know about tact, but she just smiled and said that even married women need space sometimes, a place to call only her own.

She still doesn't let me open my eyes, tells me she wants everything to be complete so I can see the whole picture. Is that what I am? A painting? Will I be framed and displayed somewhere, admired for my silence and the colors across my face?

One of the maids helps me step blindly into a dress of slithering satin that whispers against my skin with every movement. Even without seeing it, I know my father will have a heart attack when he sees the strapless dress and the light boning that makes my waist seem smaller than it is. Then the maid slides a lace bolero jacket up my arms and tugs the back to make it sit correctly, and Gertrude laughs at my relief.

"I'm out to educate your father, sweetheart, not shock him." Her fingers brush against my neck and something cold settles between the ridges of my collarbone. "Open your eyes, Ophelia."

It takes everything in me not to shriek and tear the dress from my body. Gertrude's insensibility is shocking.

Ice blue, cold blue, the color of drowned skin and Hamlet's coffin lining.

So might I have looked had Hamlet not pulled me from the lake that day, if he and Father had let my mother take me the rest of the way down to the City of Ys to see the morgens that live among the drowned towers and keep time not by day and night but by the cathedral bells that toll with no one to ring them.

I can't look at the dress or the pale azure and white makeup that makes my eyes huge bruises against my face, nor the icy silk flowers in the heavy crown of braids and dripping curls that's too sophisticated for me. I can't look at the drowned creature in the mirror, so I look at the necklace she's put on me, a silver-set double heart. The larger sweep of the outer heart glitters with tiny diamonds; the other side glints with aquamarine. Nestled within the outer design, a heart-shaped sapphire draws the eye, dark against the flashier brightness of the other two types of stones.

Gertrude has dressed me in the school colors, making her wedding about the school even when there's no one to see her statement—no one to be convinced that this travesty of a marriage is actually a perverse loyalty. Of fear.

For the first time, I think Gertrude might not be quite bright. Clever, perhaps, in the way a society wife must always be clever, but not quite bright, and even as I feel guilty for thinking it, I know the idea will always be there now. She looks so pleased with herself, pleased with her creation.

I swallow hard and force a wan smile to my face. "It's a lovely dress."

"And you look beautiful in it, Ophelia. I knew you would."

She's dressed as well now, a simple but elegant gown of rose silk that brings a healthy glow to her skin. She bends close to the mirror to adjust the way her hair frames her face, and I take the moment to study the elbow-length sleeves of the dyed lace. The bruises are still there, if one knows to look for them, but they look like shadows of the pattern. Neither Father nor Laertes will see them.

Dane will.

If he shows up. I don't know why it hasn't occurred to me before, but he has no reason to want to be there this evening. I know Gertrude expects him to be there, in the way a mother expects her son to be there for important events, in the way a hostess expects her progeny to do their duty, but what could possibly compel him to witness an occasion he detests with every fiber of his being?

We walk to the stone church in silence. The men are already there, waiting for us. A basket sits in the nave with two small bouquets entirely of white. Gertrude hands me the one twined through with pale blue ribbon. It's smaller, but not by much; neither of the arrangements is large or ostentatious.

"Walk before me, Ophelia."

There's no music, nothing to tell me how fast to walk, and Father's shaking head makes me decide I must be going too quickly.

Laughter, sharp and derisive, fills the small gathering at the altar, and I glance to one side to see Dane sprawled across a pew, an unlit cigarette in one hand. "Eager, Ophelia?" he asks. "Or just desperate to get it done with?"

There's no safe answer with my father there, and Dane knows it, but he still seems to expect some response. I pull one of the white roses from the bouquet and hand it to him, watch his fingers curl into a fist around it, crushing it.

Claudius beams as Gertrude walks down the aisle. His hard eyes seem almost human as he watches her. It makes me wonder if, somewhere in wanting whatever his older brother had, he might actually love her, might have loved her all these years that she was his brother's wife. It still makes my skin crawl.

Even the priest seems disconcerted. He doesn't look at either of them as he speaks but keeps his eyes on the open book in his hands. When the time comes to exchange rings, Claudius slides a gaudy eyesore onto Gertrude's finger, a flashing, bulky thing of diamond and gold.

Ambitious and clever, but not subtle.

It looks like it should bruise her skin with its weight. The ring he gives her to place on his own hand is nearly as bad, bright and tacky in the candlelight.

I look away when he leans forward to kiss her, stare resolutely out one of the plain glass windows. Sap stings my hands, and I know I'm squeezing the stems too tightly, but if I drop the bouquet I'll just punish my hands some other way to keep from saying anything, to keep from walking away.

A blue-white flicker in the window slowly resolves into a face as the evening turns to night. A dignified face, full of strength and pride and love. And sorrow. An infinite, nameless sorrow. Hamlet is here to watch his wife and brother marry. Captivated by the weight of his grief, I stare too intently, until Laertes grabs my elbow with a scowl to jolt my attention back to the now-married couple.

What God has joined, let no man rent asunder.

No man save Claudius, who sundered a marriage, sundered a life, so he could claim the woman at his side.

While Claudius and Gertrude pose at the altar for the hired photographer, I mumble something to my father about hair spray and needing air. He nods abstractedly, his eyes on the photographer, and I walk silently and quickly through the nave and out the door, the bouquet left behind on the stone floor. I'm only vaguely aware of Dane following me, too intent on just getting out, getting away. On the front steps, I gulp in shaky breaths.

"You hate this, don't you?" I look at Dane, his face soft in spite of the frown that furrows between his eyes. For the first time since the engagement was announced, he accuses me of nothing. "Anyone sensible to true feeling must," I whisper, stunned by my own honesty.

"I'm drowning, Ophelia."

I remember drowning. The pain goes away when you die. It only comes back when you try to live. I offer him my hand because I have nothing else to offer. He considers it for a long moment, then reaches out and takes it. He doesn't step any closer and neither do I, our joined hands between us like a promise.

The ghost walks away from the window and returns to his grave, sits down on the elaborate marble headstone only two days planted.

But he's not alone.

At the foot of the grave, a second blue-white shadow coalesces into an identical form, but where its twin is sorrow, this one is rage.

A hand closes around my heart and squeezes. It's impossible to breathe, impossible to think. There's only fear and a gasping, painful shock. I've grown up with the ghosts that play hide-and-seek through the gaps in my medications, but I've never seen two ghosts for a single man, never seen a split like this. How is such a thing even possible?

I'm sorry, Hamlet. I'm so sorry.

I'm sorry I can't speak against your murder.

I'm sorry I can't protect your son.

I'm sorry I can't fix this.

As if he can hear me, the ghost on the headstone gives a slow, sad smile and a solemn nod.

The other throws back his head and gives a feral, silent scream that contorts his face, makes his fisted hands shake.

And even though the lake is out of sight, I can hear my mother laughing.

PART II

CHAPTER 12

The lake has become a strange sort of refuge of late. My mother and I died here, but somehow that holds less pain than the gardens where Hamlet was murdered, the graveyard where the fractured pieces of his soul find different forms, the house where his wife and murderer share a bed. In the lake, the pain went away, didn't return until they dragged me from the water and bruised my chest and mouth with their desperate need to make me live.

I'm not brave enough to go to the island yet. Mama taught me how to swim when I was young, and I suppose it's not truly possible to forget, but I haven't actually done so since the drowning. I wave to Horatio, swimming laps in front of the island, and he waves back with his next front stroke. I sit on the edge of the dock, where the students sometimes launch canoes on the weekends, and dangle my legs over the edge. The water is still lower than usual, the ever-present promise of rain in the thick air an oft-repeated taunt against our expectations. My feet barely touch the surface, a slight coolness against my skin that almost makes me think I could walk across it like glass.

I don't try.

Once, I might have, and Mama would have laughed and encouraged me in the attempt, but I know better now.

I know better than to trust what my mother finds delightful.

Even in life, my mother was a strange, beautiful creature who never belonged in a mundane world. Her marriage vows, the fact of Laertes, of me, were ties that brought her back to the school time and time again, but she always ran away, as if just once she might sever those bindings and be truly free. Always she came back. Always she ran away again.

Father doesn't speak of it, and I'm not sure how much Laertes knows, but Mama never stopped to consider what was appropriate to tell her daughter, and when you disappear in public no one ever watches what they say. My mother seduced and betrayed; she threw herself at men to make herself feel alive because within her there was such a terrible emptiness that the lake waited patiently to fill.

That is what I fear when I think of what it means to be mother's daughter. The madness my father and brother see . . . it only scares me when I see the reflection of it in their eyes. It's too natural, too much a part of me, to scare me on its own.

Before Dane's kisses, before his needy touch that set my skin on fire, I never knew to fear the rest of my mother's legacy, the part that seduces and is seduced in equal measure.

The morgens play at the island, not just Mama and Dahut but a number of them, their laughter like music over the water. Ignoring Horatio, who can't see them anyway, they dare each other as far as possible up the small stretch of land to gather flowers and weave them into coronets. The ones who manage to get all but a foot out of the lake tease their friends by hanging the garlands from the willows that line the island. The others dive deep and push off, slicing through the water and up, up into the air as high as they can in a fountain of droplets that glitter like diamonds in the afternoon sun, and reach for the flower crowns.

They left fear behind a long time ago when they left behind life to become morgens. They'll spend forever this way, young and beautiful, waiting for the chance to lure men to their deaths, men who are foolish and starstruck. It doesn't matter if the man is good or not, simply that he is male and therefore capable of betrayal. They never try to lure Horatio or Dane because Mama calls them mine.

I could be one of them, if I wanted.

Mama promised.

As rarely as she makes her promises, she always keeps them.

I wouldn't know fear, wouldn't know pain. No one would be scared of me because no one would see me.

When I think of such things, it isn't the thought of Laertes that keeps me from calling out to my mother and asking her to keep her promise. It's partially Father, who needs so badly for me to be a better daughter than my mother was a wife. Mostly, it's Dane. Because he needs me as much as Father does. Because I'm never the one to walk away. Even when everyone else leaves, I never do.

I lift the chains at my throat until I can hold both the pendant and the ring in my cupped palms. Gertrude shows such obvious pleasure in seeing that I continue to wear it. Silver and ice blue and sapphire, her unintentional match to her son's class ring. The school's colors, the colors of death and funerals and weddings, all tied together so I can't think of one without recalling the others.

"Ophelia, what are you doing here?" A sharp voice, taut with fear and accusation.

Laertes.

I don't turn around, my eyes still on Horatio and the laughing morgens. I can hear him stomp down the length of the dock, feel him stop behind me. He doesn't touch me, but it isn't hard to imagine his hands clenched into fists at his sides. "It's a beautiful day," I answer neutrally. "I'm enjoying it."

"What is that in your hand?"

I let the ring drop so only the double-heart pendant shows, even as I know he's already seen it. "The necklace Gertrude gave me."

"The other." He doesn't wait for an answer but drops down beside me, his hand yanking at the longer chain to expose the ring. "Whose is this?"

"Mine."

The answer makes him scowl. "Ophelia, don't make me bring this to Father."

Don't make me bring this to Father. Don't make me tell Father. As if I could make him do anything he didn't want to do. I sometimes wonder what would happen if I returned the threat, if I offered to tell Father of the cigarettes and liquor, of the steady stream of girls that find their way into his bed when Father's locked away in his office. All the small defiances that don't mean anything because he never makes them known.

He squints at the interior of the ring, the smooth silver marred by a slender inscription. "This is Dane's."

Wordlessly, I take the ring from his grasp and replace it within my shirt

"Christ. Why do you have Dane's ring?"

"Because he gave it to me."

"Why did he give it to you?"

Why do you ask so many questions and never make them the right ones?

"You two have been close since the funeral," he says slowly.

I shrug. "We've always been close."

"Not close like this."

"Like what?"

His scowl deepens. He doesn't like it when I ask the questions, doesn't like realizing that he doesn't have all the answers. "You know he'll never be serious about you. He never is."

Does he realize he's looking at a mirror rather than a window? Dane's no blushing virgin, but he hasn't made nearly the dent in the female student body as Laertes. In the past several years, I can only think of four or five girls whose names have been tied in any way to Dane's.

Seeing her children together, Mama detaches herself from the other morgens and glides towards us. Barely a ripple follows her progress through the water.

"Ophelia."

I watch Mama instead of Laertes. Mama smiles, not at all a nice smile, and the cruelty there is aimed at the son who refuses to see her.

"Ophelia, are you even listening to me? He's only taking advantage of you!"

"He's done nothing, Laertes," I tell him. "We talk, or we sit together. That's all."

"That's not the way he looks at you."

"You would know, I'm sure."

He flinches and hunches his shoulders against some invisible blow. When he loses a boxing match, that's almost always the reason why: he always flinches from the blow. He cracks his knuckles out of reflex, then winces as his swollen, discolored finger pops back into place. "He's just going to hurt you. No one can reason with him right now, so you need to be the one to break off whatever this is. It's my job to protect you, Ophelia."

"It isn't."

He hisses and opens his mouth to argue, but a sudden splash makes his shirt cling to him, plasters a few strands of hair across his face. He looks out across the lake for a breeze, ripples, anything to explain this, but Horatio is much too far away. He doesn't see Mama floating in the water, doesn't hear her laughing.

I turn away so he can't see my smile.

Once upon a time he saw the same things I did, heard the same things I heard, and always felt guilty because Father gently—sometimes brusquely—told us they were only stories. One night Mama took us deep into the woods and told us to watch for the Wild Hunt as it rode past. She said humans who listened to the Hunt could be driven mad.

I watched them in wonder, the horses and the greyhounds and the men with their ageless rage and fatigue, and clasped my hands in front of me at the terrible beauty of their passage.

Laertes clapped his hands to his ears and knelt down in the grass and autumn leaves, buried his face against his knees so he couldn't see anything. After that, he never did. He never again saw the faeries that dance along the garden paths on moon-soaked nights, never heard the bean sidhe keen for those who died at the school. He convinced himself they weren't real.

The last time he saw Mama, she was in a box like the Headmaster's, lowered into a hole on the boundary of the hallowed ground, a delicate compromise with the priest who couldn't decide if it was an accident or suicide.

His cell phone rings in his pocket, and he pulls it out, but he doesn't answer it right away. He grabs at my chin, forces my face towards his, and studies me as though something would tell him the answers he seeks. "Stay away from Dane, Ophelia. Stay far, far away from him."

"Answer your phone."

He swears but does, and as he walks away, I can hear him greeting the female voice that emerges, faint and tinny, from the speaker. In theory, it's *our* phone, to be shared between us. I've never carried it. Who would I call?

"It's always a sad day to discover that one's son is a hypercritical prick," Mama says with a mock sigh. She lays back against the water, her dark hair floating around her on the surface like an oil slick.

"You don't feel sad anymore. No sorrow, no fear, no anger, no pain."

"That's certainly true. But I imagine I might be sad to discover such a thing." She watches me from half-closed eyes. "Are you going to do as he says?"

"No."

Her laughter makes me question the wisdom of that decision, but it's the only decision I know how to make. Dane needs me. "That's my girl."

"That's the problem."

"Always is."

She leaves soon after, returns to the morgens and their easy play.

I stay on the dock until my skin stings from the sun. I feel like I've reclaimed the lake from my nightmares, or at least begun to. Standing, I wave again to Horatio and point to the house so he won't worry when he sees me gone. I walk barefoot up the paths and through the gardens, avoiding the alcove where Hamlet died.

Jack waters the plants as they need it, but some of them show signs of the wait for rain, their leaves curled at the edges, the grass spiky and crisp despite the sprinklers. There are pockets of shade across the garden paths, trees that grow overhead or the sudden height of a hedge, but the sun and lack of water gradually make me light-headed, and I know it's time to head in.

I enter the house through the kitchen to ask for some lemonade and a snack. I'm perfectly capable of carrying it up the stairs myself, but the cook tells me she'll send a maid with it once the current batch of cookies is out of the oven. I don't argue with her.

Instead, I poke my head into Father's study on the first floor. His flyaway hair is barely visible over stacks of folders and papers. I clear my throat to get his attention.

He looks up with a scowl at being interrupted, an expression that quickly changes to concern when he sees who it is. "Ophelia? Are you ill?"

"No. I just wanted to let you know I'm going to lie down for a while."

His eyes flick across my pink cheeks. For a moment he actually smiles, and it transforms his entire face into something softer. "There's a marvelous invention called sunscreen, or a hat if you want to be old-fashioned. You might try them next time."

I smile back, leaning against the doorway. "I'll try to remember."

"Get some rest then," he instructs. "Just remember to be up and dressed in time for dinner."

Then it's back to work, even though I haven't left yet. As I gently close the door, I can hear him muttering about immunizations for the new students.

The Danemarks and the male scholarship students live on the second floor; the female scholarship students, none of whom have stayed for the summer, share the third floor with us Castellans. This level should be silent, and at first I think it is, until I pass my brother's door and hear the muffled sounds within. There's a towel pushed under the door.

I wonder what her name is, if it's the same girl he spoke with on the phone, if it's someone I know. He sometimes brings up girls from town, I suppose to impress them with the school and the house, something no boyfriend in town could ever equal.

It's petty. I know that as soon as the thought comes into my head, but it doesn't stop me from crouching down and carefully tugging the towel from under the door. The doors are cut high for the carpet but they misjudged and cut too high, so even the thickest carpet leaves a gap for sound to emerge. Without the towel there, the sounds are more obvious, unquestionable.

I twist the knob and let the door drift open in the currents from the air conditioning.

My room, sandwiched between Father and Laertes', doesn't allow for the privacy I'd like at times like these. Even if I'd left the door closed and the towel in place, I'd still hear the sounds of my brother having sex in the next room. The walls conceal nothing, and while Laertes is usually pretty quiet—up to a point—whatever girl he has in there is anything but. I don't know if she's loud enough to bring anyone running up from the first floor, but just the fact that they could be discovered through the open doorway amuses me.

All of Laertes' warnings about Dane are the warnings he should be giving about himself. He won't be serious, he'll hurt you. He'll take advantage of you. He'll take what he wants from you and then move on to someone else.

Dane hurts himself by hurting me. It doesn't mean he won't do it again, but I saw his face when he saw the bruises.

I bury my head under my pillows to try to filter out the sounds from the next room. I can hear Laertes grunting, which he only does when he's close to finished. The pillows are useless.

Then there's a crash in the hallway and a strangled gasp, and I remember the maid that was going to bring my snack.

Still buried in the pillows, I laugh until my sides ache. The maids won't tell Father; the maids don't tell anyone anything except when gossiping amongst themselves, but Laertes doesn't know that.

Through the wall, I can hear the girl start sobbing, hear Laertes' frantic apologies—to the maid or the girl, I'm not sure.

When my door opens, I'm still laughing, but the maid just touches my elbow with a warm smile and tells me it'll be a few more minutes before my snack is ready. She knows I opened the door. She'll tell the other maids as they gather in the kitchen between duties, and they'll all have a good laugh that little Ophelia was able to pull one over on her overprotective brother.

I close my hand around the class ring and wonder if I should tell Dane. In the right mood, he'll find it hilarious. In the wrong mood, I'll have to explain why the hypocrisy is so funny, have to tell him that his friend doesn't trust him with me.

And suddenly the laughter is gone, and tears sting my eyes as I lay back and stare at the ceiling.

Because I trust him.

Even knowing that Laertes is just a little bit right.

CHAPTER 13

Every year, two or three weeks before school starts, Gertrude takes me into the city for a weekend of shopping. She calls it a girls' weekend out, time to spoil ourselves silly. I don't think it ever occurs to her that I don't enjoy these outings. I enjoy the city on the rare occasions I get to see a concert or a play, or spend a day or two lost in the museums, but with Gertrude I only ever see the shops and the employees that trail around us holding our selections and the purchases from other stores.

I don't like being her living doll, the human toy to dress up however she wants, but I always let her do it. I let her because it gives her pleasure, because it pleases Father.

Dane teases me about it the night before we leave. We sit out on the dock with Horatio. The flasks make no appearance, but both boys have cigarettes aglow in their hands. He tells me I should make outrageous suggestions, find clothing to make his mother blush and gasp, say rude things to the shopkeepers to see if I can get us thrown out. We all know I'd never do any of it, but he has us laughing ourselves breathless anyway just trying to imagine it.

When I finally say good night and head back inside, he follows me to my door and kisses me softly, gently, a kiss with no anger or grief in it. For once he doesn't push, doesn't ask for anything more. I see this Dane too rarely anymore, so I treasure his brief appearance.

It's a long ride into the city, one I intend to only be half awake for, but Gertrude has the car stop to get us real coffee like we haven't had since Hamlet died rather than the muddy instant singles. She has a stack of glossy magazines beside her that acts as an impromptu table for the box of Danishes, and every now and then she hands me the current selection folded back on a page and asks my opinion about it.

Most of my opinion is taken up in wishing I'd sat on the right side instead of the left, so at least her new wedding ring wouldn't intrude quite so much, but I manage mostly reasonable responses until she turns the page and looks for something else.

Against a chorus of blaring car horns, our driver rolls the center window down to tell us we'll be late in arriving; an accident has brought the freeway to a dead stop until it can be cleared away.

"He's still angry, isn't he?"

At her soft words, I stop trying to see the distant wreck and turn back in my seat to face her. Her eyes are downcast, focused on a picture of an evening gown, but I don't think she actually sees it.

"He doesn't even speak to me anymore, not since the wedding. Sometimes he even leaves the room when I walk in." The large diamonds in her ring flash in the morning sun through the window. "How can he hate me so?"

Because you betrayed his father. Because you didn't wait.

Too often I don't say what I really think; how many opportunities do I miss because of that?

"He's hurt," I answer finally.

"He's never been lonely."

"He is now."

She smiles at that and lightly touches my cheek. "How can he possibly be lonely when he has you, dear child?"

The idea intrudes as it has too often since the wedding: Gertrude is not quite bright. Loneliness isn't the absence of other people, has nothing to do with who is or is not around you. Loneliness is something harder to define. But Gertrude doesn't understand that. She thinks loneliness is the simple act of being alone; she marries a man when her husband is barely in the ground so that she doesn't have to be alone.

"He misses his father."

She sighs at that, returns her gaze to the evening gown as though it will offer her an answer. "They were always close, but this excessive grief cannot bring Hamlet back from the grave."

Perhaps excessive grief cannot, but murder and incest apparently can. I've almost grown used to Hamlet's two ghosts. One sits with lowered head and sad eyes on the gravestone, never wanders, never interacts even with the other ghosts. The other prowls the boundary of the iron fence with furious steps, tests the limits, and each night he comes a little farther away, stretches his tether a little bit more.

She lifts a hand to her hair, and the sun sparkles violently on the ring. "Had circumstances been slightly different twenty years ago, Dane would have had Claudius, rather than Hamlet, for a father."

He wouldn't have become Dane. Dane is very much a product of his father's teachings, combined with his mother's anxieties. The product of Claudius and Gertrude would have been someone very different.

But she's given me an opening, a chance to assuage the curiosity that's been nagging me even as I knew I would never broach the topic myself. As casually as I can, I shift in the seat to better see her expressions. "Jack told me you used to date both brothers."

She laughs at that, like it means nothing. "He would remember that, I suppose. How many times did he chase us from the hedge maze with bits of leaves in our hair?"

There's a limit to what I need to know; that . . . no. Just no.

But she smiles and leans forward like she's sharing a secret, and perhaps she is; perhaps this is something most others have forgotten over the years. "I was honest with them, Ophelia, which is the only way a woman may ever honorably be courted by more than one man. Hamlet laughed when I told him, said he would do his best and respect my choice. Claudius vowed to win me. They were so different, even then."

"Different how?"

"I suppose they wanted very different things," she says slowly. She isn't sure of the answer; she tests the words as they come out and doesn't seem satisfied by them, but she doesn't know another answer to give. "Even then, Hamlet was always full of ideas for the school. He used to talk all the time about instituting a scholarship program; his father finally gave in on the condition that Hamlet run it himself, and the way he threw himself into it, you'd think someone had given him a prize beyond measure. He always knew he'd come back to the school as soon as he could. He was proud of the Danemark legacy, proud to be a part of it. He was the Headmaster's son, wealthy, influential, very handsome . . . all the girls spoke of him in that kind of voice, hushed, like they were afraid he'd hear how much they admired him. I don't know that he ever realized it; it was just such a part of who he was."

"And Claudius?"

She hesitates. Her right hand twitches to cover the gaudy ring on her left. "Claudius as a boy was . . . driven, I suppose. The younger son. Things are very different for younger sons, even now when we think they shouldn't be. Hamlet was always guaranteed a certain measure of success by virtue of being the elder. Claudius always felt he had to work twice as hard to get half as far. He was . . . oh, fierce, I suppose, in pursuing what he wanted. Being with Hamlet felt like being treasured; being with Claudius felt like being won."

"But you made a choice. Eventually."

"Of a sort. I couldn't decide between them no matter how often I sat and tried, so I finally decided I would marry the one who asked me first. It seemed the fairest way I could think of. They were both in college when I graduated, both focused on their studies, so I attended a women's college, and then when Hamlet graduated with his first degree, he took me out to dinner and proposed. Said he hadn't felt right about offering marriage if he couldn't support me on his own without recourse to his parents."

I glance away so she can't see my wince. She didn't make a decision at all, simply left it up to their characters. How could any man on the wrong side of that ever be content with it, knowing it was a question of timing and not of affection that denied him the chance to ever be with the woman he loved?

"After the wedding, we lived in a small house while he pursued his other degrees, and I spent time with the faculty wives when he taught the lower classes, and then, of course, we came back to the school. Claudius finished his first degree a year after the wedding, and he just left. Went off to England first, though he spoke occasionally of traveling elsewhere as well. It was hard for him to see us together, especially once Dane was born. It pained me that he never married, never tried to have children of his own. He would have made a very good father. Now, of course . . ." She turns the page too quickly and tears the thin, glossy paper near the spine. She frowns and smoothes a finger across it like that will somehow mend the rip. "Claudius has waited all his life to be recognized for his skills; now he finally has the chance. And when he asked me . . ."

I swirl the last of the coffee, long since cold, in the bottom of the cup. I recognize this from Dane, the type of thing that's easier to say when no one is looking at you. When no one can see your face to judge your motives. I watch her from the corner of my eye, though. She has no idea why she said yes when he asked her to marry him.

All the pain the answer has caused, will continue to cause, and she doesn't even know why she gave it.

"Love is a funny thing, Ophelia," she murmurs eventually. "I suppose it makes fools of even the best of us. I've loved both of them since we were little more than children." She laughs suddenly, thrusts the entire question from her mind with a careless wave of her hand. "If anyone knows that better than I, it would be your father."

"Father?"

Mama thinks he's the biggest kind of fool; being a fool for love can only be a piece of that.

"Have you never heard how your parents came together?" she asks with surprise.

104

I shake my head. Father never speaks of Mama, and Mama doesn't speak of what used to cause her pain. Whatever brought my parents, so dissimilar in every way, to marriage isn't the kind of story they would fondly tell their children. It's on the tip of my tongue to ask if she's ever told Dane of her love for both brothers, but the question can't be anything but cruel, so it stays silent, unasked.

"When I was a student, your father came back to the school as assistant to the Headmaster, Hamlet IV at that point. There was a girl a few years younger than me, Morgen Bishop, a wild child such as the school had never seen. She truly seemed sometimes half feral. She was beautiful, Ophelia, I'm sure you remember that. There was something about her that drew the eye, something wild and untamed that made almost every boy in school want to be the one to tame her. But she set her sights on Polonius."

I'd known there was a significant age difference between my parents; I'd never learned why.

"I don't know if it was just a challenge for her or if there was a bet or perhaps there really was something about him that drew her, but Polonius never really had a chance once Morgen put her mind to it. He was mortified by it; he came straight to my father-in-law and offered his resignation, but Morgen was eighteen, barely, and Polonius wasn't her teacher, so the Headmaster simply told him to be sure it never happened again."

"Did it?"

"A few times more, I should imagine. Morgen was never so entranced by a thing until she was told she couldn't have it. Then, near the end of the school year, she fainted in class and the nurse discovered she was pregnant. You must understand, Ophelia, and I mean no pain to you in this, your mother was . . . well . . ."

"Promiscuous?"

She looks relieved at not having to choose a word, or perhaps it's simply that I've said it for her. "Yes, precisely. There was no guarantee that the child was even Polonius', but he said if there was even the chance, he was going to do right by her and the child, so he went to the Bishops and confessed what had happened and offered to marry her. To be honest, I think they were relieved. Here was someone willing to take their wayward girl off their hands. Morgen actually ran away in protest, but she didn't have anyone to run to, so after a month or so she returned and they were married."

She studies my face, but I think it's my mother she sees. "Despite everything, I truly believe Polonius came to love her and hoped that she would feel the same for him. I don't know that she ever did, though. He tried to make her happy, tried to give her what she wanted. It didn't ever seem to be enough."

Only the lake was enough to make her happy, to take away the emptiness that made her restless and lonely and scared.

"When Laertes was born, we all tried to see something of Polonius in him, but he looked so very much like Morgen, and then you . . . you lack her height but could otherwise be her twin, so little of Polonius in either of you, but he never hesitated to call you his. It's easier to see it now that you're older, especially in Laertes. He is very much his father's son, I believe, and the school will be the better for having someone of such competence to continue your father's work."

She doesn't stop to consider whether or not Laertes would want to continue Father's tasks. It simply makes sense to her, like the way generations of Danemarks take up the tasks of those before them to continue to lead the school.

"I think he still loves her, Ophelia. He's never gone out on dates, never expressed any interest in another woman, doesn't even speak of her for the pain it causes him to know that she's gone."

That she left.

"Things are never so terrifying as when love is involved." Her voice is soft, almost a whisper, like she's forgotten I'm in the car with her. "What we do for love . . . it can be wonderful, the best of all that man has to offer. But sometimes . . . sometimes it isn't. Sometimes what we see is far from the best it could be."

There's a syringe hidden in a chest of my mother's clothes, a small tube of glass with poison still clinging to the smooth surfaces. There's a body in the graveyard, a pair of ghosts that show the best and worst of the Headmaster that was, and a boy shredding himself and everyone else in the face of emotions he doesn't know how to define or control.

For the first time, I wonder if Gertrude knows—or suspects—about that syringe, about what her new husband did to gain his titles. There are some men for whom love—love of position, love of power, love of a woman—can be a whip to murder, and she's married one of those men.

Does she know that?

And a more terrible idea, one that pricks needles along my spine and makes my head swim: is she all right with that?

Was she part of it?

She crosses her legs at the knee, her hands resting atop it with her right hand covering her left. She hides the ring so often, like she's ashamed of it, like it doesn't—or shouldn't—exist. This is the woman who decided to marry the first man who asked her so she wouldn't have to make the more difficult choice between them.

I don't think she knows.

I don't think she'd allow herself to.

Horns blare all around us, and the car moves forward a few yards, that much farther from the school and her son and her husbands, away from my parents. Still, memory sits heavy between us.

Which is worse, to struggle to fly against the tether that always snaps you back? Or to accept the tether with such blind contentment that you don't even mind when your wings are clipped?

CHAPTER 14

I know I should tell Father that the pills aren't working as they were so he can make me an appointment with the doctor for different medications. It's happened before, and the doctor said that was perfectly natural, that the body develops immunities or that it can change as it goes through puberty. Different pills might prove my mother wrong, might take away the sights and sounds, might restore the barrier between myth and reality. They might make me blind to the changes coming. They might leave me deaf and unbalanced in a world that's suddenly so small and limited.

But I don't want to go back to the cold place. Every time we've had to adjust the medications, they lock me in the cold place until they're sure the new chemicals are working, so I can't accidentally speak the truth before the pills are strong enough to stop me. Then I'm surrounded by machines and cameras and strangers with needles and I can't . . .

I don't want to go back to the cold place again.

There's another storm building outside, fierce and shrieking even though it hasn't broken yet. Winds race through the gardens and the woods, rattle branches into a murderous thunder against the sides of the house. The song of the bean sidhe is soft now, almost done, just a whisper, an echo. The death they might grieve forever, but they mourn only the ghost that is sorrow.

Behind that though, woven through the winds, are the hoofbeats and feral cries of the Wild Hunt in the woods. They always ride when the winds are fiercest. Sometimes I think the wind hurts them, burns their skin and strikes tears to their eyes with the speed of their chase, and that they use this as distraction from the greater pains. They've been riding for so long already, countless centuries, and they must ride still or turn to dust as they dismount.

I wonder if any of them choose that death, choose to suddenly age and crumble into dust and ash when the endless Hunt becomes too much.

Such a price do men pay when they would visit with the kings of faerie. There is always a price to see their private world.

I lie awake in my bed, the blankets pushed back and my knee-length nightgown bunched against my thighs. There is no ceiling fan in my room, only the painted-over holes to show where one used to be, so the air sits in heavy pockets wherever the weak push of the air-conditioning vents can't reach. Through the walls to my right I can hear Father snoring as he does whenever the weather changes, a deep, stuttering sound that seems more like he's choking than simply breathing wrong.

Laertes isn't in his room. He was for a while, but then his phone rang and I heard him sneak out. He's probably in town now, charming the pants off some girl who hasn't listened to her friends and doesn't realize that he isn't making her any promises. They'll have sex and maybe he'll call her again, but it'll only ever be for something physical, something with no ties and no demands, nothing he ever has to keep track of or give himself to.

It should disgust me, but in this one way, Laertes is our mother's son. In every other way, he's Father's, but he still has this one piece of Mama. He doesn't think of it that way because he's never known how she was, but it comforts me even as it probably shouldn't.

A bell tolls through the dead night, clear and poignant, one rich note for each hour. Three o'clock in the morning, and I have yet to sleep.

At this point, I might as well give up and concede that I won't. Not this night, at least.

The house is still. Not silent but still. I can hear Father's snores on the third level, and on the second I can just barely hear the music Horatio plays to help him sleep. On the bottom level, a light glows from the Headmaster's study. I can hear Claudius' voice but no other; he must be on the phone. It should startle me, but I suppose he has many contacts over the world from his traveling days. What is absurdly early here must be quite reasonable for whoever he's talking to.

Did he get the poison from one of those people? Some way that would be harder to trace to him? Or did he manage it all himself so there wasn't even the potential of a trail?

Sweat pearls on my skin as soon as I step outside, the humidity a deep weight in my lungs. Almost it makes me think of drowning. Strands of hair stick unpleasantly to my face, neck, and back. I'm on the wrong side of the house for the winds that whip through the trees.

As I walk around to the back, to the gardens, I can see a light on in Dane's room. Not the main light, but something smaller, softer. A desk light, perhaps? I've never been in his room, never even stood in the doorway, but it seems right. He's just a shadow from here. I think about going to him, about asking if he wants to walk with me, but I need this moment for myself.

He's going away.

Or at least trying to, which really amounts to the same thing. For days he's done nothing but read over the study abroad information, seizing on it as a way to run from his father's death and mother's betrayal, a way he won't have to see his uncle officially take his father's place. He could run away, hide himself for months in some foreign country. Maybe he could be someone new there, someone who doesn't have the weight of Elsinore Academy's legacy, someone who isn't lost.

He's got Laertes excited about it too. My brother has nagged our father endlessly over the past few days and seems very likely to continue. Father isn't pleased; he worries what would befall one of his children so far away, so far from his immediate supervision and influence. He tries to brush it aside, tells Laertes that he'll forget about it soon enough, but Laertes can be stubborn, far more so than Father has any reason to suspect.

Even Horatio looks through the papers. His scholarship doesn't cover options like study abroad, but Gertrude—seeing Dane's interest in it—has offered to pay for it herself should he decide to pursue it.

They're all leaving or trying to leave. They all want to walk away.

I stay and I stay and I never walk away and I watch everyone else walk away from me.

The wind snaps suddenly, whirls my hair around me in a purple-black flurry, and I slap a hand to my thigh to keep my nightgown down. Either Claudius or Dane could see me through their windows, perhaps even Father should he awaken.

I can see flashes of the Wild Hunt as it moves through the deep woods, lean greyhounds draped across the saddles. Centuries ago, a human king and his men visited a faerie king in his own lands and emerged to find three hundred years had passed in the space of an evening. The first man to dismount aged and crumbled to dust and ash before his fellows' eyes. But faeries aren't entirely without mercy; their host gave them a pack of fae hounds to carry with them. The dogs will know when the men can safely dismount, and they'll jump down from the saddles. Until then, the men ride and ride and ride through the centuries, waiting for that sign.

They've been waiting so long. Sometimes I wonder if the dogs will ever jump down.

I stop when my feet touch something wet. Without realizing it, I've come to the edge of the lake. Not the dock, nor the stretch of willows where Dane lit a fire inside me that won't abate, but the midpoint. The property line of Elsinore Academy ends halfway through the lake; the rest of the lake belongs to a reclusive couple who insisted on some sort of boundary being erected to keep students off their side of the water. They mounted tall posts deep into the lake bed and strung a chain between them to keep the boats from crossing. There's nothing to be done against those who swim—it's a rite of passage to swim to the far side and leave something on the couple's back porch—but it clears the school of responsibility.

It's also the way to the island.

Mama showed it to me, taught me the trick. I haven't done it in years, haven't been to the island since I drowned, but I step forward onto the first post despite the fear that crawls under my skin.

They're all going to leave.

Maybe this can finally be the time I walk away. The time I leave.

I step carefully onto the links of the chain, remembering what Mama said. The chain will sway; it always does. If you tense up, you'll fall. Sway with it. Don't sway so hard you make it sway more, but let your body move with the chain so you can keep your balance.

It would be easier to just go into the water and pull myself along the chain, but there's something about walking across the water that appeals to me, that appealed to Mama. My feet remember the journey. It's a drunken, unsteady progress to the second post but easier to the third, to the fourth, until I feel as though I could walk a tightrope without fearing the fall. Not even the wind scares me. It tugs and pushes in equal measure, stirs my hair about me like a cloak of silk rags, licks away the sweat from my skin.

The last post stands a little more than a foot from the edge of the island, from the tangled roots that creep out into the water. I lurch back and jump, land clumsily on the thick grass that grows between the surrounding willow trees. The center of the island is a thick profusion of flowers, carefully tended every day by Jack. He comes out here in a little canoe, every morning and every evening. My mother's grave may be in the cemetery, but this is her shrine.

The wind teases the flower crowns tangled in the drooping willow branches. Some of them are old, dried in place, but others are so fresh I know the morgens have been playing at the edge of the water again. Jack never says anything when he sees the flowers in the trees. Jack always knows more than he says.

We used to dance here, Mama and I, to the music that no one else could hear. Our feet crushed the thick grass in a circle between the flowers and the trees, hidden from the school by the curtains of the willows. And she'd laugh—oh, how she'd laugh. We spun through the night, our pale skin aglow in the moonlight, our dark hair like shadows.

I take one step, then another, and spin on the ball of my foot and feel my hair spin with me. My nightgown tugs at my legs, narrow and confining, and I shrug out of it and drape it over one of the branches. My underwear follows. Now there's nothing but moonlight, nothing but the pale gleam of silver and white and lifeless veins of blue under the skin. Just as my feet remember how to cross the chain, they remember how to dance, and I spin around the shock of flowers with my arms spread wide.

So many steps but always in a circle, always coming back to the same point again and again. Never going anywhere. Never leaving, never walking away, always coming back.

The wind murmurs through the leaves and kisses away the sweat as soon as it forms on my skin. Thunder rumbles softly overhead, drums to dance to, to sway to.

We dance in the circles, and the rest of the world goes away. There are no bruises, no poisons, no foreign places. There is no marriage, no death. Colors fade away, lost to the deepest shadows and moonlight. There is no ice blue, no drowned skin or coffin linings or attendant dresses. Dane belongs here, in the shadows of the night dance, his dark grey eyes and sable hair and moonlight skin. He belongs here, but he doesn't know how to dance, because the dance isn't a word to play with and dissect and destroy. He can't understand the dance, can't make it less than it is by finding every meaning.

My mother's laugh fills the circle.

It's only later that I realize it's coming from me.

CHAPTER 15

Two nights before the students return, Claudius decides to hold a formal dinner to celebrate. I'm not even sure what he intends to honor with this gathering; he has held so many celebrations through the past two months, so many gatherings with little more outward point than to talk and drink too much wine. Gertrude doesn't stop him, doesn't tactfully suggest that such festivities make him less than dignified.

She simply asks me to assist her and doesn't look directly at her son.

Any more tension and Dane will snap, but this is not something either Gertrude or Claudius chooses to see. He, Horatio, and Laertes have all formally submitted their requests for the study abroad programs; Laertes has set his sights on France, while the other two aim for Germany. They all promise to write me long letters in place of the e-mails Father would surely read, sending them by way of Jack, but they're promises that will most likely be forgotten as soon as they step foot off the planes. I try to be happy for them, but it's hard.

They're my only friends.

I don't know if it came from growing up at the school, if it's from the fact that I died, or it's just something to do with me, but I've never been able to make friends with the other students. I try sometimes, in an awkward and thoroughly self-conscious way, but such conversations never last long. The only girls who willingly talk to me are the ones who are trying to get to my brother and think cozying up to his sister is a sure way of achieving that.

If they spread their legs, that's a very sure way of getting my brother's attention.

Sometimes I even tell them that.

They never seem to appreciate it.

The Board of Governors will be here tonight, along with a handful of influential donors, people Claudius desperately needs to keep happy through this first year. No one says the word *probation*, but it's understood. If, at the end of his first year as the Headmaster, the Board is unhappy with his performance, they will seek to replace him.

Reggie Fortin won't be here, though he has the right to attend. He's at his school preparing for the year ahead. His uncle, whose health is poor, has sent representatives to speak for them. Rumor says that they want to institute an exchange program for the students. They don't mention the girls specifically, but I think we all understand what isn't said: they want the girls from Elsinore Academy to see what a true education should be, to get the students behind their push for reform.

I think they'll be the only ones surprised when Claudius refuses. The trophy wife traditions of Elsinore Academy have given Claudius a wife so docile she'll marry her brother-in-law only six weeks after her husband's death and support him wholeheartedly in every endeavor. It's not in his interest to change that. If he has his way, which seems likely, future versions of himself will still have the opportunity to cull obedient, charming wives from the graduates of this school.

I lack the assurance a good society wife must have, but in so many ways I am Elsinore's ideal female graduate. I don't speak unless spoken to; I never venture an opinion; I almost never show an inclination but for what my father—who is, after all, the Dean of Curriculum—instructs. If I weren't a ghost tied to my dead mother in the lake—if I had things I wanted to do and a person I wanted to be—I think I would hate it here. We have separate classes that teach us nothing of the world beyond our boundaries, and sometimes I wonder how many of my classmates would leap to exactly the chance Reggie Fortin wants to offer.

When we have everything arranged to her satisfaction, Gertrude shoos me upstairs to dress. She mentions the ice-blue dress, but I pretend not to hear. I'll never wear that dress again, not only because of the purpose it was put to but because it's the color of death and drowning and all cold things. I don't have a choice of wearing the color given the accents on the school uniforms, but that dress I can banish to the depths of the closet.

Upon my return to the first floor, Father fusses over the low, square neckline of my simple lavender dress and the height of the heels, his mostly grey and white hair just slightly untidy. More than ever, with Laertes so desperate to get away to someplace new, Father needs me to be the biddable little girl with nothing more than flowers on my mind. He needs me to be a good daughter. Gertrude chides him for it, a delicate dance of tact and friendship that says nothing of my mother. He lets it drop, but he watches me; his worried eyes track me whenever Dane and I cross paths.

Dane, for his part, takes care to make sure this happens as frequently as possible. There's a part of me that delights in the possibility that he just wants that much to be around me, but I know Dane too well: he's doing it because my father's concern amuses him. It's less than kind, but at least it means he's not sulking in the corner.

Nothing can make him polite to the guests.

Perhaps she realizes this, because after a time, Gertrude gives her permission for us to hide in the alcove under the stairs. Laertes keeps to Father's shoulder, a taller shadow with barely concealed impatience. The rest of us retreat immediately. Though the guests are invisible from our places on the velvet-covered benches, the sounds float on the air, contained bursts of too-light laughter and the low rumble of grave conversations.

Sheltered from sight, Dane tucks an orchid into my hair and laughs as Horatio and I try to remember its meaning. Finally, he leans forward, lips moving against my ear, and tells us it stands for delicate beauty, and Horatio smiles at the soft kiss that follows.

Eventually, however, all the guests are gathered, and Father's assistant Reynaldo retrieves us for the first stage of festivities. We all gather in the parlor, flutes of sparkling champagne in our hands, and watch the new headmaster mount the small platform against one wall. It's little more than two steps, but it gives him the advantage of height, drags the eye to him as something to be noticed. Gertrude stands on the step below him, beautiful and elegant in a sapphire silk sheath.

"My brother's death is still a fresh wound on our hearts," he begins, his voice carefully modulated to carry through the room but not appear overloud, "a grief that will renew as the students return and mourn his loss for the first time as fact. His loss must be a constant memory, his legacy our only concern. This hallowed institution formed the foundation of his life, its excellence his greatest passion, and I will dedicate myself to that in his name, to keep this academy as he has always wished it to be.

"To that end, though I hope it causes no offense, I have decided not to bind us to the Monticello Academy through its offered exchange program, a decision I have great faith in the Board of Governors to uphold. Our traditions must guide us through these changing times and this period of uncertainty, and the education of our students must be foremost in our thoughts. Our curriculum has done us much good in every venue, our graduates among the most prestigious that can be named. To change that now, when we have seen so clearly the success of it, is to invite a lesser standard that will go against everything this school has held dear for so many generations."

"Such pretty words," mutters Dane, heard only by Horatio and me. "How long do you think it took him to come up with them?"

"Though our hearts are made sore by loss, our lives must, and do, continue. The beautiful Gertrude, whose grace and poise have been an ideal example for our charges these years past, has become my wife, and I am grateful beyond speech can convey for her love and affection." He lifts her hand and presses a kiss against the glittering ring. A charming blush gives her face warmth and color beneath the powders. "In even the deepest loss there is something of hope and life, and I find it in the woman I have dearly loved since childhood."

I doubt his audience cares much for his personal happiness; their concern is for the school and their children, not his incestuous bliss.

"Ladies and gentlemen, a toast if you will, to the continued greatness of Elsinore Academy, to the strong legacy of the Danemark traditions, and to the excellent school year ahead."

Nearly everyone lifts their glasses with his. The light from the chandelier bounces off the pale liquid as from chocolate diamonds, a fierce glitter half lost to shadow. "To Elsinore" drips from two score mouths, not quite in unison, and they all take small sips of the sparkling wine to seal the toast.

Dane's knuckle pops around the stem of his glass, his dark grey eyes riveted on his uncle-stepfather and mother. Then, with a convulsive, jerky gesture, he lifts the flute to his lips and drains it all at once. "Such pretty words," he says again, "and no one insufficiently dazzled to look beyond them to the ugliness beneath."

"They like the glitter," Horatio tells him quietly. "If they look past the glitter, they have to see everything else, and no one wants to do that. No one wants to see the ugliness of a thing."

"Unless it's the ugliness they can rally against, the ugliness of something outside their realm."

"But that's a very different thing, isn't it?" Horatio takes a cautious sip of his champagne, the sweet wine such a change from the harsh burn of the vodka we pass in flasks. "After all, your uncle is one of them, born and raised in this world. Whatever his ugliness, they're nearly obliged to overlook it."

"Closing ranks?"

"Pretty much."

In a gesture of goodwill, Claudius shakes hands with Messrs. Cornelius and Voltemand, the ambassadors from Monticello Academy, and gives them more pretty words to take back to the Fortins. With Polonius and Laertes nearly on his heels and Gertrude's hand light on his elbow, Claudius makes his way through the gathering to join us against the far wall. He smiles at the sight of Dane's empty glass. "A true toast, Dane. I'm pleased to see it."

His jaw tight, Dane turns his head to one side and says nothing.

I catch his eye and touch the longer silver chain at my throat. His gaze tracks down to where the chain disappears under the neckline, to the hollow of my breasts where he knows his class ring resides. His face softens, not into a smile but at least to something almost neutral.

"Laertes, your father hinted that you wished to ask me something?"

My brother clears his throat, unwontedly nervous. Of Hamlet we would never have hesitated to ask anything, but none of us knows Claudius enough to make us comfortable in his presence. "Yes, sir. I . . . I had hoped, that is, I very much wish, to go to France on the study abroad program. It is a wonderful opportunity, one I would like to take advantage of, with your permission, sir."

Claudius already knows this, of course, given the three applications that sit on his desk, but I think it pleases him to be asked in this way. Like a king granting audience. "And what does your father say to this? I know, Laertes, that your father is in every way the backbone of this school—utterly invaluable. I would not act against his wishes as concerns his family."

Father smiles slightly and shakes his head. "By virtue of much argument, he has gradually swayed me to his thinking," he answers, effortlessly matching Claudius' carefully structured formality. "He has my blessing to go, to see the greater world before he returns to take his place, and I would join my voice to his in asking your permission for the venture."

"Then by all means, that permission is granted. France is a beautiful country with much to offer to an enterprising young man; I hope you will take full advantage of it and return to us afire with your experiences."

"If not afire from syphilis," Dane mutters.

I choke on my sip of champagne. With a frown, Father takes the glass from my hands, as if the wine had anything to do with the reaction. But then, he didn't hear Dane's commentary, so I suppose he has nothing else to blame for it.

"Mr. Tennant."

Horatio stands straighter against the wall at Claudius' address. He looks uncomfortable in his suit, bought by Gertrude for the wedding and worn again now where the uniform would be inappropriate. "Sir?"

"I seem to remember your name being on a study abroad application as well. Germany, was it?"

"Ah, yes, sir. Wittenberg, to be precise. The university there sponsors an excellent philosophy program for the exchange students." He glances beside him at Dane, whose interest has sharpened at this mention.

"I am told you are an amiable, hardworking young man with a great deal of potential. Certainly your records reflect that, and my brother saw much in you to be sponsored. My dear Gertrude tells me she wishes to grant you this opportunity, should you wish to accept it."

Another glance at Dane, more uncertain this time. "Thank you, sir. I'm very grateful."

Two of them gone and surely three, for why would Gertrude finance Horatio if she doesn't intend her son to go? I close my eyes to identify the knife-sharp pain in my chest. Get used to this pain, Ophelia; it will be your constant companion these next months when they've all gone away.

"And Dane, I had a chance to see your application there as well." Those green eyes study the young man next to me. There's affection of a sort there on the surface, but it doesn't go very deep, doesn't offer any warmth to the emeralds in his face. "After discussing it a great deal with your mother, we would ask you to stay here with us this year."

We all stare at him, even Laertes. Even Father, whose slight frown is such a habitual part of his expression that it's hard to decide if it's even real anymore.

Gertrude reaches out to touch Dane's face, her touch light and loving, elegance in every graceful motion. "It's only a year until you go off to college, darling, and the great wide world with all its opportunities." Her words sound rehearsed. At her side, Claudius looks pleased with the delivery. "I know it's selfish of me, but having lost your father, being so soon to lose you to everything else life has to offer, it's hard for me to watch you leave when I have so little time left with you."

He visibly swallows whatever argument he'd been about to make. Against Claudius he would argue and fight until both were flushed and breathless, but against his mother . . . he'll hurt her for her disloyalty to his father, but he can't do it for his own sake. The need to take care of her was enough to take him from his father's graveside. It will be enough to keep him from Germany, however much he might chafe at it.

"I would not cause you pain," is all he says, and his mother's face creases into a gentle smile.

The pain doesn't go away though. It actually expands, a white-hot sun in the center of my chest that burns away all the air until only searing heat remains. I press a hand against my sternum, try to force air back inside, but find only the flickering points of light that dance before my eyes.

Horatio reaches behind Dane to hand me his glass. I take a sip and feel it ease the star that burns inside my skin. I take another sip and another, until I can almost breathe, and return the glass to him. He studies it for a moment against his tanned hands, then drains it. His eyes are dark with pain, but I can't read the thoughts behind them.

Claudius claps Dane on the shoulder, hard enough to knock

him off balance, and turns to the rest of the room. "Let us now to dinner, to our celebration! We have a wonderful year ahead of us!"

He and Gertrude lead the way without seeing if the rest of us follow. Father and Laertes do so without hesitation, good little boys with their lines written into their tongues. The others of the gathering drift after them in pairs and clusters, off across the entrance hall to the banquet hall with tables groaning under the weight of china and silver and fine linens.

One of the maids gives us a knowing look and gently closes the parlor doors. A moment later, Dane's empty glass sails through the air to shatter against the wall. "God, that a bullet in the head wouldn't consign me here forever!" he snarls. He snatches at Horatio's glass, and it too shatters in a rain of glass against the wall, a gleaming spread against the dark carpet. "Thank God my father is dead so he can't see the whore he married. And his stupid brother, like he's half the man he's replaced! That whore!" His fist slams into the door, and both Horatio and I jump. "That whore, that filthy whore!" Another punch to the heavy wood. This time, blood clings to the varnish from split knuckles. "That bastard! How can . . . how can he keep me here to gloat?" Another punch, another bloody stamp.

Poison and pain fill the air, pour against the closed doors. Dane rages, the mockery gone in a blaze of fury. This is why there's a sun burning where my heart should be, because Dane's fury is too great for his body to hold. The words spill from him, quick and sharp as though the shapes singe his tongue, and they scald the air in the room until there's nothing left to breathe.

He turns to me suddenly, and I brace myself for a bruising grip, but his hands tremble against my face, touching it only by virtue of that fine quaking. "There is nothing good to this, nothing that can be good of this," he whispers. "Neither in silence nor in speech can good come of it, but how the heart must break not to speak of it!"

And we, who love him, break our hearts as well. The same pain in Dane's face echoes through my bones, darkens Horatio's eyes until they're nearly black against his skin, but there is no word for this, no silence profound enough.

His silence will poison us as surely as speech, and all that stands between us and a verbal slaughter is the fragile thought that he must take care of his mother. How long can such a thing last against the pain that eats away everything else?

CHAPTER 16

Horatio studies the knuckle prints on the closed doors because it's easier to look at them than to watch the pacing Dane. We should all be in the banquet hall, scattered around the great tables and picking at our food as people chatter around us, watching Claudius and Gertrude hold court at opposite ends. I don't think any of us can stomach going in there.

After the meal, they'll return to the parlor for sweets and coffee and try to guess which teams will vie for championships this year, how many Ivy League acceptances there will be among the senior class, or perhaps they'll talk about some of the recent graduates and how wonderful their prospects are. Anything to keep the glory of Elsinore Academy as a whole the topic of conversation, so the ugly details never have to be even thought of.

We shouldn't be here when they come back.

I turn to Horatio, and he nods before I even say anything, like the need to protect Dane somehow makes us identical in thought and deed. Perhaps not identical; I'm not sure what Horatio would have done with the syringe. He's the best of us, in nearly every way, his integrity a bright flame within him.

"Dane?"

He looks over at us, his eyes tear-bright even in his rage.

"Let's go."

"Go where?"

"Somewhere else." Horatio shrugs and his coat moves with him, the shoulders too broad against the expectation that he'll continue to grow. "Anywhere else. Just . . . away."

"To the gardens then."

"We can go to the gardens." His voice is mild, soft, the way we're told to speak to wild animals or touchy people with more power and alacrity to insult than good sense. Like Dane is something dangerous.

We leave the parlor, the house, and there's no one there to notice, no one to scold us for deserting our duty as representatives of the school or the student body or the Danemark legacy or whatever it is we've been dressed up and trotted out to stand for.

I don't think any of us are surprised when he leads us to the alcove with the low stone couch where his father napped in the afternoons. Where he died. Dane never saw him that last afternoon, didn't see him dead in the grass as paramedics swarmed over him.

What is surprising is that someone's already there: Jack, with a battered watering can full of ice and bottles of beer, a candle in a tin cup at his hip that makes light and shadows dance across his wrinkled face. He doesn't seem startled to see us. Jack rarely seems surprised by anything. He nods a greeting and continues his slow perusal of the dark flower beds.

He can't see the brilliant, tiny pinpricks of light, the sweeping trail of sparkling dust that marks the passage of the pixies that prowl each night through the blossoms and seek stray petals for their gowns. Their wings flutter almost silently, gossamer veined with slender threads of dark light, tiny flashes of neon jewels. What little can be heard sounds more like crickets as their clumsy flight makes them bump into each other, gossamer against gossamer. He can't see the pixies, but sometimes, when the morning dew collects in the shallow impressions their footsteps leave behind, he can marvel at them.

They make the air shimmer all around us, like living inside a snow globe. Everything is shaken up, and the glitter rains around us. It's almost a different world, one that's never heard of death or despair or rage.

125

Dane sinks down onto the grass and tugs me into his lap, his arms wrapped around me as if he thinks I might try to move away. As if I could. Horatio sits carefully next to Jack on the bench. This is his only suit. Dane and I can afford not to care about our clothing or what may ruin it. Horatio will never be that thoughtless, even if he one day has an entire closet full of suits.

Jack hands us each a bottle from the watering can, the glass slick with condensation. The champagne was for a special occasion, a single-glass concession against the law that says we shouldn't drink, a decision that had to be brought up and deliberated. Jack just doesn't care. The beer is thin and sour with an unpleasant aftertaste, but it chases away the sweetness of the champagne, helps ease the sun inside my chest.

We drink in silence fraught with tension. There's something to be said, but I have no idea what or who's supposed to say it. The very air waits for it.

After a moment, I decide the words must lie on Horatio's tongue. He hunches over, rolling the bottle back and forth against his palms. He doesn't normally fidget. Fidgeting draws attention, catches the eye, and he has too much of my talent for disappearing into the shadows.

"Marc Elliot called me in a panic two nights ago," he says suddenly.

The pixies hiss and vanish. For a heartbeat, two, the darkness still dances with the memory of glitter and dust, but even that disappears too quickly.

"Isn't Marc always in a panic?" Dane asks. There's an edge to his voice, a tautness to his muscles. I nearly expect him to vibrate like a plucked string.

"This is a new one. He said he saw a ghost."

Jack's gaze suddenly sharpens on the empty flower beds, the only indication that he's even listening.

I think I know what Horatio would have done with the syringe.

"I figured he was drunk, but I went up to the widow's walk anyway, and he said it was gone. Stone cold sober, though. We both went back last night to see if whatever it was he saw would repeat itself."

"Did it?"

"It did." Horatio's eyes flick between me and Dane, ceaseless and restless and anxious, things I've always associated with Dane rather than Horatio. "Right around midnight we saw it, bright blue-white along the walk."

"Hell, we've always known there were ghosts here." Dane's hand strokes my hair, twines through the fine strands at the nape of the neck. I tell myself it's this that sends the shivers down my spine, and not fear.

I know it's the fear.

I've never been good at lying to myself.

"Ophelia's seen them."

And now I know why I was included in that nervous dance of attention: Horatio knows that. He's afraid I've seen this too. It's not hard to guess which ghost he's seen.

But why?

Every now and then, one of the students claims to see one and perhaps it's even the truth, but only ever in flickers. Can a ghost make itself be seen? Can they choose to be visible?

"Dane . . . this wasn't just any ghost. I recognized him."

Dane still doesn't understand, isn't paying attention. He's too caught up in teasing my neck with his fingers, flimsy patterns traced against the skin.

"It was your father."

Everything in him snaps to a sudden point; his hand clenches painfully in my hair. He stares at Horatio, his friend, the one who's never been uncertain about him, and all the blood leaves his face. "Horatio . . ."

"He walked along the rail like he was looking for something," Horatio continues, his voice low and grim. "I asked if there was any message we could deliver, anything he needed, but he didn't answer. He didn't say anything, but sometimes his mouth would open like there was something he needed to say. Even had his robes and mortar on, like at the funeral. He paced and paced and paced, and then, when it was almost dawn, he just disappeared." He gives me a quick, cautious look. "I've never seen a ghost before. I know you see them, Ophelia, but I never have, never thought to, and here he was."

"A ghost . . ." Dane's hand curls into a fist so tight his knuckles pop. Caught between his fingers, my hair tugs away from my scalp, stings tears into my eyes. "How can he be a ghost? He had a heart attack, he was blessed by the priest, and he was buried in sanctified ground. It isn't possible that he's a ghost."

"The priest tells us of demons who take on a loved one's form," I murmur. Please, let this be enough, let this idea take root so he doesn't look too closely for the truth. "It's a cruel trick."

"And you believe in demons?"

"If we believe in Heaven, in Hell, don't we have to? If there are angels to watch over us, there must be demons to plague our steps."

Jack shakes his head and lifts his eyes to the lake. The bells carry over the surface of the water where the moonlight gleams off the pearl-white bodies of the morgens come to soak in the light. They float in clouds of hair, unashamed of breasts and bellies and thighs. "No good can come of spirits," he mumbles in his weary, cracked voice. "Never a good thing to come of them, no matter their origin."

"Maybe not, but I'll find out anyway." Dane takes a deep breath. He stares at the bench, at Jack and Horatio on the curved stone, but I know it's his father he sees, dead in the warm afternoon sun. "If there's even the chance that it's him . . . maybe . . ."

Maybe he'll tell his son to put aside his grief, to remember what it is to be alive and cling to that rather than to what is lost and ir-retrievable.

And maybe the City of Ys will rise from the lake in a flood of gleaming towers and bronze walls.

Because even though I haven't asked, even though I won't, I know which ghost Horatio has seen. It is not the echo of dignity and grace and love, not the form with a head bowed from sorrow. That ghost sits atop the headstone and waits patiently for the nights to end. The ghost that walks, that challenges, is the fury that murmurs through his son.

There are only so many ways a heart can break before it shatters to dust that cannot be mended into something whole once more.

Fiercely, passionately, with a strength that surprises me, I wish Horatio hadn't said anything.

"There are too many people on the grounds tonight," Dane continues in a more even tone. "Tomorrow, around midnight. We'll go up to the walk and see for ourselves if it will reappear. If it doesn't, then it's just a trick. Moonlight off the lake or a shred of fog."

"And if it isn't?" Horatio asks softly. "If it's real?"

Dane shakes his head, and finally his hand eases in my hair. "I don't know. I guess we'll find out."

The whole world will find out if anyone does. The sun explodes within my heart, and I can't breathe, can't make sense of the words that flow over my head, all around me.

A rough, callused hand takes mine, and a silken soft flower is pressed against my palm before the hand drops away. I curl my fingers and feel the sting of death as the flower is crushed.

There is nothing of life in this endeavor.

CHAPTER 17

Laertes' chagrin at finding out that Father and Claudius staged the entire "favor" last night is nothing to his panic at finding out that he must pack and leave for the airport by five o'clock. The maids spend the morning washing nearly all of his clothing so he can decide what to bring, and I spend the afternoon sitting on his bed with the clothing in a mountain on one side and his vast suitcase open on the other. As he selects each item, he hands it to me to fold and pack into the case because he can't fold a shirt to save his life.

"Thanks, Ophelia," he says as I fold yet another button-down shirt. The gratitude is so unlike him that I know he's freaking out.

But I tell him that he's welcome and make no mention of how grateful I am for the distraction. Mindless folding keeps me from remembering that at midnight tonight, we go to see if Hamlet has rediscovered his voice.

Eventually, with all the clothing sorted, folded, and wedged into the suitcase, he turns to all the other things he'll need for four months away. For lack of anything more productive to do, I curl up against his headboard and watch. He'll never fit half of what he's dragging out, but it should be fun to watch him try.

I don't realize I'm turning Dane's ring through my fingers until I notice Laertes' eyes riveted on the silver band. "Something?"

"You're still wearing that?"

"I don't have any particular reason to take it off, do I?"

He sighs and sits down next to me on the bed, tosses the toiletry bag into the suitcase, and immediately regrets it when he has nothing to fidget with. "Look, I know you think he loves you, and for right now, maybe he does. Maybe he loves you while he needs your help to deal with grief, while there's no one else here, and maybe he'll even love you for a little bit longer, but Ophelia—please listen to me this time—it's not going to last. Even if he wanted it to, it couldn't. He'll almost definitely be Headmaster one day; the woman he marries will be the official hostess, will have to be someone who can ably deal with all of the arrangements and gatherings, not someone who disappears into reading alcoves or haunts the edges of crowds."

So I'm not the only one who thinks I'm sometimes a ghost.

"Whatever he wants to give you now, he won't be able to give you forever. He won't be able to marry you, Ophelia, and you need to remember that. You're . . . you're so innocent, and Dane's . . . well, Dane. He has a lot more experience than you, and you need to stay away from that. From him. This isn't a bad novel; he isn't going to marry you simply because you let him seduce you into bed and you wind up pregnant."

Like Mama did to Father, only marriage was never what she wanted. She hated it, hated him sometimes, but Laertes has never heard this about them, perhaps never even wondered why there was such a difference between them in so many ways.

"You know what this school is like, and you know how gossip spreads. Your reputation has to be everything, and it would repay Father and Gertrude very poorly for you to throw that away. You owe it to the family, to the Danemarks, to use better sense."

That he believes what he says I have no doubt.

That what he says makes him a hypocritical prig I am equally sure.

But I don't want to start an argument right before he leaves for four months, so I give him a small smile even as I drop the ring back into my blouse. "I promise to keep your words close to heart, Laertes, on one condition."

"A condition?"

"Do not preach to me that chastity and virginity are the steep path to Heaven while you debauch your way through Paris."

"Ophelia!"

"What? You do it here when Father is only two doors away and the risk is great of getting caught; why wouldn't you do it an ocean away? Oh, and . . ." I peel away the lining of the suitcase to show the many condoms he thinks he's so cleverly hidden there. "You'll want to find a better way to hide these before Father has Reynaldo go through your things."

"He wouldn't."

"Who, Father? Or Reynaldo?"

He doesn't answer, probably because there's no true answer he can give without losing face. Father gives our rooms a cursory search once a week, and Reynaldo—technically his assistant, realistically his bent-backed evil minion—never hesitates to invade our privacy at whim, hoping to find some small detail that will further ingratiate him with Father. Reynaldo's been gone much of the summer for family concerns, but he's back now and no doubt eager to continue pawing through my lingerie drawer.

"You could just buy them over there, you know. Unless you think it's that certain that you'll join the mile high club, in which case you could just put one or two in your wallet."

"Ophelia, can you please spare me the pain of having this conversation with my little sister?" God, he's actually blushing. I think he'd give anything to get out of this.

"You were very eager to have this conversation when it was about me."

"About you *not* having sex," he corrects with a pained grimace, "which is an entirely different conversation."

"And yet, you still haven't agreed to my condition."

A ring scrapes against the outside of the door, and he yanks away the condoms in a panic, shoves them between the pillows and the headboard in the time it takes Father to open the door. He smiles to see us sitting together; it quickly turns to a frown when he sees the open suitcase. "Not ready yet? They won't hold the plane for you, my boy."

"No, of course not. I'm nearly done." He shoots me an anxious look and starts throwing in the rest of his things. With each one, I find a better placement for it, a way to fit more in.

Father clears his throat and clasps his hands before him, a sure sign that he's about to launch into a speech. "Now, Laertes, there are many things you need to keep in mind as you head out on this venture: be careful of what you say, and of what you do; be friendly, but do not be overfamiliar or vulgar; find some few friends who may be true and steady, but do not seek to be the friend of all, or you'll attract dullards and leeches and idiots of the worst sort; be cautious in seeking an argument or fight, but should one be necessary, come out on the right side of it; listen more than you speak; be the best judge of character of those you meet, but reserve your judgment; spend what you are given and have earned, let them see your station and accord you your worth, especially in France where the clothes very much make the man; do not borrow money, for you can have no need of that, but do not lend it either, or you'll find more friends than funds; but this, my boy, above all other things remember: to your own self be true, and it must follow that you cannot be false to any man."

Laertes' eyes glaze over halfway through, and he tends to his packing with a feverish nod to pretend that he's listening. He flips over the lid, tugs me to sit atop it, and struggles with the zipper and locks. It takes both of us, as well as some shifting within the case, to actually get it shut.

Father clears his throat again and hands Laertes a plastic bag stuffed with a credit card, some American money, and more euros than I think any of us would know what to do with at once. "Put that away and hurry down to the car; Reynaldo is waiting to take you to the airport, and there isn't much time to dawdle." Despite his brisk words, his eyes are misty as he embraces his son and firstborn tightly.

When he's finally released, Laertes gives me a more simple hug and a kiss on the cheek. "Remember what I said."

I resist the urge to roll my eyes. "Consider it locked in my memory, and you shall hold the key."

"What is this?"

Laertes hesitates at the door, flicks a glance between me and Father. I shake my head in subtle warning, but either he doesn't see it or his elder-brother-officiousness makes him ignore it. "Ophelia isn't as careful around Dane as she should be." And before Father can even register the full statement, my brother sprints down the hall with his suitcase dragging awkwardly behind him.

I should have just left the condoms in the bag for Reynaldo to discover and bring to Father.

I ease off Laertes' bed and walk towards the door, but Father's hand circles my arm just above the elbow to hold me back. He doesn't squeeze—yet—but having finally healed from the earlier bruises, I would much prefer not to win more so soon.

"Ophelia."

I sit on the edge of the bed and fold my hands in my lap.

Father paces before me, hands clasped behind his back. He doesn't say anything at first; this is the kind of thing he would really rather work up to. "I've noticed that Dane spends a great deal of time with you," he says eventually, "and Gertrude has mentioned several times how grateful she is that her son finds himself so calm in your presence. Now I ask you, Ophelia, and I expect the truth: what is between you and Dane?"

I take a deep breath to give myself time to sort through the welter of words available. What is the truth? What is between me and Dane?

I have no idea.

"He has, lately, expressed a decided preference for my company," I answer carefully. "He says I make him feel real."

"Real? And you believe him, do you?"

Sometimes I do. That isn't something I should say to my father when he has this look on his face. "I don't really know what to think."

"I will tell you exactly what to think: you are a child for having even considered these affections to be real. You must value yourself more dearly, Ophelia, or you'll be taken by the first hot-blooded young fool and left with a child, a disgrace not only to yourself but also to this family and to the Danemarks who have taken us in so completely."

"He says he needs me—"

"All he needs is his hand and a magazine."

"—and behaves most honorably towards that end!" I so rarely argue with Father, but Dane hasn't done anything I haven't allowed him to.

"He's a young man, and he'll behave as he needs to until you trust him enough to let him take what he wants. Ophelia . . ." He sighs and crouches down in front of me, his hands over mine in my lap. "Ophelia," he continues more softly, "I know how it feels to be your age, and I know how easily words come to those who want something so badly. These blazes give more light than heat, and they never last; you must not take them for fire. Dane is a good boy—I don't mean to imply that he isn't—but youth and foolishness go hand in hand, and you are both vulnerable.

"From this time forward, you will make every effort to avoid Dane without Gertrude or myself there to act as chaperone. You will not go to him just because he snaps his fingers or asks it of you; you are better than that, and you have a higher duty." He considers his edict for a moment, then shakes his head. "No, I can see we're well past avoidance. You will not be at all in Dane's company without his mother or myself there. Not at all, Ophelia, promise me."

He really looks nothing like either of his children. There are lonely threads of dark brown woven in with the thick mixture of white and grey atop his head and in his neatly trimmed beard, his eyes a middling brown with no particular shadows or warmth. He was handsome once—I have seen photos from a younger time—but while he has grown into dignity, the virtue of beauty has become worn with time.

Gertrude's words ring in my head, remind me of the possibility that there might not even be any blood between me and the man before me. I look and I look, searching for some physical sign to connect us, but even the shape of our faces, the structure of the bones, everything Laertes and I have physically, we have from our mother. Even pictures conspire to set our father apart.

But to this man, there has never been a question that I am his daughter, for better or worse. He loves me, however awkwardly he expresses it, and he cares about my well-being. This is important to him.

Dane asked for a promise.

Laertes asked for a promise.

Father asks for a promise.

A promise is a rope around the neck.

Little Ophelia, who's never been needed before, is suddenly needed in very different ways, pulled in very different directions. I've only ever had my own secrets to keep, and now everyone, it seems, is asking for a promise. I close my eyes, feel the weight of words on an unwilling tongue. "I'll try," I whisper.

Forgive me, Dane, but I have to try. This pain you've recently learned has been my father's companion longer than I've been alive. For all the heartache my mother's given him, I have to try.

CHAPTER 18

It's nearly eleven before I can sneak out of the house to join Horatio and Dane. Father kept me close after dinner—how much of that is nostalgia over Laertes' absence and how much is his concern over our earlier conversation is anyone's guess, but he's strangely reluctant to get pulled into yet another discussion of school policy with Claudius. Eventually, however, his need to make sure everything is ready for the return of the students intrudes and he retreats to his office and closes the door.

I break one promise to keep another, but I'll break that one too in a few hours, all my best intentions shattered around me.

I run across the school grounds to the light that burns alone in the midst of darkness. The gymnasium is locked, but that poses less of an obstacle than it should; those of us who live here year-round have a talent for acquiring keys we're not supposed to have. I pull my ring of keys from the pocket of my skirt, where it's been clicking against the glass tube of the syringe, and find the proper one for the gym.

The tiny lobby is dark and silent. I find the cool glass of the trophy cases and trail my fingers across them until I reach the wall. Through the creaking double doors, the main room is deserted, but light glows through a window on the far side. I cross carefully, hoping there's nothing strewn over the floor but reach the far door without trouble. The light, yellowed and uneven as it is, stings my eyes as I open the door to the weight room.

No matter how much it's scrubbed or aired out, the weight room is home to a perpetual funk of stale sweat, deodorant, and body wash, mixed with the lighter smells of sawdust and chalk. It wafts around me as I blink furiously, trying to adjust to the light. An unsteady series of thumps hovers in the air like a panicked heartbeat, accompanied by softer grunts of effort. When the stars clear from my eyes, I see Dane and Horatio at one of the hanging bags.

Boxing is another of Elsinore's treasured anachronisms. Other schools favor football or lacrosse, but Elsinore has always valued boxing—"the gentleman's sport"—above all else, even as the opportunities to compete with other schools dwindle every year.

It's usually Dane and Laertes on opposite sides of the bag, egging each other on through warm-ups and exercises. My brother is— or was, as he's gone now—on the boxing team, his thirst for competition, for winning, driving him towards several of the trophies in the lobby. Dane, though . . . Dane just wanted the skills. They partnered together in practice bouts, and Laertes never seemed to realize that Dane could have trounced him if he actually tried. Dane didn't need to win, and my brother needed something to be proud of, so Dane made him work for it and gave it to him when he thought he'd earned it.

But Laertes is gone, flying over the Atlantic, and Horatio stands in his place to hold the bag, wincing with each impact. Despite invitations and challenges from the other boys, he's never taken up boxing, choosing to swim and row and soak up as much sunlight as water until the cold drives him to the indoor pool. He closes his eyes against another strong punch, bracing his feet against the concrete floor.

Sweat tracks down Dane's bare back, muscles bunching and moving under the skin with each punch. They're both so involved with the bag that they don't hear me come up beside them until I clear my throat. Horatio loses his balance and clutches the bag to keep himself upright. Dane straightens, dragging his hand across his dripping forehead. "What took you so long?"

"Father." I take his hand and trace his swollen, callused knuckles and the blood that seeps in fine lines from the cracks in his skin. "Aren't you supposed to wear gloves?" I ask. "Or tape?"

"Yes, he is," Horatio sighs when Dane doesn't answer. He releases the bag with what I suspect is relief. "Go get cleaned up."

Dane stalks to the locker room without looking at either of us. The door slams violently in his wake. A minute later, the pipes squeal overhead.

I sit on the edge of one of the weight benches, legs crossed at the ankles, and watch Horatio press cautiously against his ribs. "Has he been like this all day?"

"Pretty much." He rubs a towel over his sweat-damp hair, and we sit in silence until Dane rejoins us, water stains making his black shirt cling to him.

Horatio flicks off the light, and together the three of us leave the gym and cross the wide path to the school proper. Keys jangle too loudly in the uneasy night, and then we're in the building, jogging through the deserted hallways and up the stairs to the attics, where Horatio pulls his keys from his pocket. The attics are ghost lands, populated with the cloth-draped relics of earlier times. Even the cleaning staff doesn't venture here, and the dust stands thick on every surface.

Dane yanks on the cord for the trapdoor in the roof, and a flimsy ladder unfolds to clatter against the floor. From time to time students have committed suicide off the widow's walk that prowls the perimeter of the mansion roof; each time, the Board talks of having the trapdoor sealed, the ladder removed, and each time they leave it as it is.

Horatio goes up first, and Dane motions for me to follow. The boys always sandwich me between them on stairs and ladders, I suppose to catch me if I should fall. Usually Dane would be making a crass comment about seeing up my skirt right about now, but he says nothing. His silence is a terrifying beginning to a night that cannot be anything but bad.

Within my skirt, the syringe smacks softly against my thigh.

I haven't decided what to do with it yet; part of me still hopes that the ghost won't make an appearance tonight, that Dane will think it all nonsense.

I've never been very good with hope, either.

When I reach the top of the ladder, Horatio pulls me up and sets me down out of the way. Dane climbs out by himself, and the boys close the trapdoor. There's almost nothing to mark it in the darkness, a single iron ring at the base of the shingles, but Horatio pulls a handkerchief from the back pocket of his worn jeans and knots it through the ring. I've never been up here, despite how much I've wanted to. They think Mama and I had an accident all those years ago in the lake; they've politely kept me from the widow's walk in case of another accident. It's unnecessary but sweet. But that small shred of protection seems to make them feel so much better that I've never tried to go against their wishes.

"Where was he?" Dane asks, and Horatio leads us around a corner of the roof to the stretch that overlooks the Headmaster's House. The lake stands to the left, the gardens a broad swath between water and house; straight ahead, beyond the house, blue-white lights flicker in the cemetery.

There are soft clicks behind me as the boys light up. I lean against the waist-high rail and look down into the gardens. Lamps burn at intervals, illumination in narrow pools. We're too far up to see if the pixies are out tonight, but beyond the reach of the lamps, glowing white forms weave idly through the hedges and the carefully tended boundaries of the paths. I frown and try to see them better. They're somewhat indistinct, and then I realize it's because all the features blend together in that pearly silver light, hair and skin and long translucent robes layered not quite to opacity.

The bean sidhe.

They dance in broad patterns through the gardens, eerie in their silence and their inhuman grace. Goose bumps carve down my spine. I've never seen them away from the cemetery before.

Before I even look to the lake, I know what I'll find: all of the morgens—not just Mama and Dahut, but all of them—lined up against the shore where they can see the gardens and the widow's walk, a breathless audience for whatever tragedy or farce will play at the midnight hour.

I used to think the bean sidhe were angels. If all the eyes of the fae are on the roof tonight, surely Heaven and Hell have their eyes here as well? But there's no sign of them if they do, only the desolate baying of the hounds that ride the Hunt.

We wait in silence for midnight. Laertes isn't here to fill the night with his nervous chatter, the only one who finds no comfort in the simple act of not speaking.

Horatio's voice shatters the stillness of anticipation. "Dane, look."

We turn to follow his shaking hand. On the far end of the walk, an ice-blue aurora slowly tightens into a man-shaped form, tall and broad, draped in professorial robes and an elegant suit. As he draws closer, we can see a tasseled mortarboard atop his dark hair, ribbons of silver through his neat beard. His strong face is written over in rage, the stern features replaced by an endless demand and fury.

My hand closes around the syringe in my pocket.

Dane stares with wide eyes. There's no question that this thing bears the shape of his father. Where in life he bore the plain gold ring that now sits on Dane's finger, there's a narrow stripe of pale flesh, so bright it's nearly an accusation. "It's him," he whispers. "It's really . . . Ophelia, tell me it's him!"

"It looks like him," I say repressively. I'm not sure he even hears. "Dane, appearances are never a guarantee."

"He was blessed and buried; what act could cause Heaven to reject him this way?"

"It's not about Heaven; it's that there's something to bind it here."

"Him."

"It," I say again. "It, Dane, we don't know for sure."

Dark, hollow eyes stare at me from that glowing face, then dismiss me to focus on Dane. A hand lifts from the folds of the robes and beckons.

"You want me to come closer?"

"Dane, no!" Horatio and I both speak, both reach to grab one of his elbows to keep him with us. Horatio shakes his head. "Dane, be reasonable. We're four stories up; what if it just wants to trick you over the edge?"

"Horatio, let me go."

I dig my fingers through his long sleeves, but I'm not strong enough to bruise his skin. "You can't go."

"Let me go."

A muffled curse stings Horatio's lips. "No."

"Damn you both, I'll make ghosts of *you* if you don't let me go!" he cries and wrenches away from us. He's panting, his chest rising and falling in sharp little gasps as if there isn't enough air in the world to fill the void inside him. "That may not be my father, but if it is and you keep me from him, I will never forgive you. I. Will. Go."

I'm the first one to look away, back to the morgens and the bean sidhe and their breathless anticipation. I can feel the heat between Dane and Horatio, the moment that burns and singes any who try to hold it. Then there's a sigh, and Horatio leans against the rail beside me. Neither of us watches as Dane's footsteps carry him away from us, towards the ghost at the far end of the walk.

"What do you see, Ophelia?" Horatio whispers and lights a fresh cigarette. The thin smoke drifts around us in a filmy wreath, bitter and sour and familiar.

"Too much." I glance to my left, where Dane and the ghost hover just within sight at the corner. I can't hear the words, but I can hear sound. Hamlet has found his voice and uses it now as a weapon against his son. "You're not going to Germany, are you?"

"What?"

"The study abroad." I turn my gaze back to him, to the face drawn tight with pain. "You're not going."

"No," he says slowly, "I'm not."

"You haven't told them that yet."

"No." He almost smiles, even as he takes a deep drag and

exhales the smoke in a sharp sigh. "How did you know?"

"Because you love him too much to leave him alone, especially to go someplace he wants to go."

The cigarette drops from his hands and tumbles down onto the stone balcony below. The tip glows red for a little while, then fades away. He reaches for the pack and his lighter, but his hands are shaking and he can't get a grip on either of them. "Ophelia . . ."

"But you'll never tell him."

This steadies him, because he knows me well enough to know that it's almost a promise. If he won't tell, I won't either. I listen more than I speak, a lesson Father would rather Laertes take to heart. "No, I'll never tell him."

"But you do love him."

He doesn't answer immediately. His eyes are fixed on his hands, strong and capable, the tanned skin dim in the moonlight. When the trembling stops, he pulls out a fresh cigarette and lights it. "Yes," he whispers. Every muscle in his body tightens with the word, like he's expecting a physical blow.

I reach across and take the cigarette. I rarely join them in smoking, but tonight there's something appealing about dragging poison into my lungs, something about the bitter taste in my tongue and throat that feels right.

With a breathless laugh, Horatio digs out yet another from the half-empty pack and makes the end burn cherry-red as he breathes in to light it. "I don't know if I'm attracted to boys," he says eventually, his voice even and earth-rich again. "I don't know if I'm attracted to boys and girls or to girls and Dane or maybe just Dane. But I do know Dane, and if I told him . . . I don't think he'd be scared by it. Others maybe, not Dane. But it would be . . . awkward because he doesn't feel that way about me. And he does feel that way about you."

"I'm sorry."

"I'm not." He switches the cigarette to his right hand and takes my free hand with his left. "I'm glad he has someone to care about, someone who cares about him the way you do. And I'm glad it's you, because I know you, and I know that you see *Dane*, not whatever else he might be."

"My father's forbidden me to be around Dane anymore."

"And you've decided?"

"At least for a little while, I think I have to. Not long, I hope, but Father . . ." I shiver at a sudden burst of laughter from the morgens. "Laertes is gone and besides the school, I'm all he has, and . . . I'm too much my mother's daughter."

"And Dane is too much a blend of both his parents."

It makes me smile to hear it that way, but it's true. He has so much of Hamlet in him, but he also has Gertrude's high-strung anxieties. I finish the cigarette and rub it out on the railing. When he's finished with his, Horatio takes them both and drops the stubs back into the pack to dispose of later.

My hand closes around the syringe in my pocket again, thumb rubbing against the clay bead that protects me from the needle. Dane and the ghost are still talking at the corner, both of them worked up, but most of their words don't carry the way they should in such an open space. "Promise" and "family" and "vengeance" float like whispers on the breeze, so faint I wonder if it's the wind speaking instead.

"You've seen the ghost before."

"Many times now."

"You didn't tell Dane."

"And you don't tell him you love him."

"Is it the same?" he asks with a faint smile.

"It is." I twine my fingers through the long silver chain and the ring that's too large for any of my fingers. "Love makes us liars, and we call it protection."

"Are you still lying?"

I hand him the syringe with its milky remnant of poison.

He turns it over in his hands, a puzzled frown marring his features. "What is this?"

"The reason the Headmaster is a ghost."

The breath rushes from his body as though he's been struck.

His hand closes around the glass so tightly I'm half afraid he'll shatter it, but I can't touch his clenched fist without the equal fear that he'll drop it. "Who?" he demands shakily.

"Does it matter?"

"Ophelia!"

"Claudius." I take the syringe back and slide it once more into my pocket. I wish I could give him this thing to carry, but Horatio will have enough burdens to bear after I walk away. For the first time in my life, I'll be the one walking away. "There's no proof. Except, perhaps, the word of a ghost, but while that might make for an excellent tale of blood and madness, there's no good to come of it in truth. There's no proof. Nothing to be done."

"And so no good in making it known," he finishes for me. He doesn't agree, exactly, but he knows me.

"If a heart attack was impossible to get over, how much more so murder?"

He swears and rakes a hand savagely through his hair. "So I should never have brought up the ghost?"

"You thought it was for the best."

The bean sidhe have stopped dancing. They're gathered now around the stone chaise, their hands linked as they stare up at the roof and the ghostly figure who lectures a boy all too flesh and blood.

"Besides," I add slowly, "I think he would have seen the ghost eventually anyway."

"You know things I don't."

"They're waiting." I can barely hear my own voice, scared and small and little more than a wisp of sound in breath. "Everything is just waiting to see what happens. They shouldn't care. We're mortal; we die all the time. But they're waiting."

"He's coming back."

We both straighten and put our backs to the rail, watch the haunted young man tread carefully across the widow's walk as if any step could send him plunging straight to Hell.

"We lie and call it protection, because the truth hurts so badly,"

I murmur. "Just once, I have to be a good daughter. Take care of him, Horatio."

He fixes me with a troubled gaze but has no chance to answer before Dane rejoins us, his dark eyes alight with a feverish glint. His face is pale but for two bright spots of color that burn high on his cheeks. "Well, hello."

"What did he say?"

Dane considers this a moment, his head cocked to one side as he studies both of us in turn. "I think not," he replies coolly. "I think you'd tell."

"You know I never would," retorts Horatio, his pride—or perhaps his love—stung by the accusation.

A small, bitter smile floats about Dane's lips. "And Ophelia is incapable of telling, so perhaps there is some truth to that. But you must swear to me, both of you, that you will never tell anyone what you've seen or heard tonight."

"I swear it," Horatio says immediately.

I just shrug. To swear, to promise, they're words, and words have loopholes. Intent means more than the vow. At least this promise I can keep.

The smile twists, deeper and stranger at once. His hands reach under his shirt for the crucifix on its plain silver chain. "Swear by the cross."

A sudden bellow rips through the night, and we all flinch. "Swear it!" The ghost stands still at the corner, black holes where his eyes should be, hands curled into fists at his side. "Swear it!"

With shaking hands, Horatio lifts the cross to his lips. "I swear it," he whispers.

Dane turns and lays the cool silver against my lips, the feet of the Savior digging into the tender skin. "Swear it, Ophelia." My lips shape the words against the metal. Something savage flashes across his face, and he doesn't even move the crucifix before his mouth crashes against mine. He tastes of toothpaste and tobacco and blood. The pendant's sharp edges bite into my lips, my tongue, before the crucifix falls away to swing against his chest with a smear of blood against the dark fabric of his shirt.

"This is . . ." Trembling, Horatio wipes away the fine beads of sweat from his brow. "This is unlike any . . ."

"There are more things in Heaven and Earth, Horatio, than are dreamt of in your philosophy." He suddenly seizes his friend's hand, grabs mine in a crushing grip. His skin burns with a fever no medicine will cure. "We have things to set right! But first . . . first we have to know. We have to have proof, even if it's only knowledge."

"Dane—"

"Don't be scared, either of you. I may act . . . I may . . ." He shakes his head and tries again. "I'll only be acting, I swear it, but you have to trust me. You can't let them know it's not real. Promise me!"

"We've already sworn," Horatio points out dryly.

Dane gives him a manic grin and laughs so loudly—so suddenly—the entire night seems caught in it. "So you have, my truest friends."

The bean sidhe drift back through the gardens to join the morgens at the edge of the lake. From the woods, dull shadows tramp from the trees, their shapes indistinct under the enormous basin they bear between them. They drop it to the damp earth with a heavy thud that echoes in the stillness like a muffled shot.

The morgens step up onto the shore as far as they can, just their toes still in the lake, and wring their hair out into the basin. Water splashes against the metal and slowly fills as they return to the depths and soak up more. Inch by inch, the basin fills. The morgens laugh as they go about their task, and softly—too softly to be called accompaniment—the bean sidhe begin to sing.

The grey shapes prove to be women dressed in tattered robes worn thin by time and repeated washings, their long legs flashing through rents and ragged edges. They look older than the bean sidhe, still peculiarly ageless in the way of all fae, but they wear the experience in their faces as so few faeries do. Their long grey hair is bound into sectioned braids that trail on the grass behind them.

147

They brace corrugated boards within the basin and position themselves around it.

And wait.

The bean nighe have come to Elsinore Academy.

Dane may never tell us what the ghost made him promise.

He doesn't have to.

The washerwomen wait to cleanse the blood of those soon to be slain.

Revenge, after all, is a very messy business.

PART III

CHAPTER 19

Dawn comes early in the summer. It's not even five before pale, pearly grey streaks across the sky from the east. It isn't dawn, not yet, but the sky slowly lightens to stretch a canvas for sunrise. We slip back through the trapdoor and the attics and the empty school, back to the house that trembles under the weight of something it doesn't even know to fear yet. All day long, the students will be arriving for the year ahead. The grounds that have been quiet all summer long will suddenly explode with noise, with laughter and shouts and, from the youngest ones, perhaps some tears as they cope with truly leaving home for the first time.

I catch Dane's hand as he starts to follow Horatio back into the house. "I need to talk to you," I whisper.

He looks surprised, and I wonder if I've ever said that to him before, if I've said it to anyone. Little Ophelia, the living ghost in the corner of the room, never needs to talk, she just listens and remembers and never tells anyone what she hears.

Still, he follows me to the lakeside, where no amount of shouting will reach the house, to the stand of willows that sprawls across a stretch of shore between the dock and the midpoint. Here, he set me on fire and crafted the sun that burns inside my chest to bear his fury. Here he collared me with silver and sapphire and aquamarine, and bruised me with his pain. Now it's my turn to do, to undo. I'll still bear the bruises, but this time I won't be the only one.

I open my mouth but don't know where to begin, and then he's kissing me, hard and consuming, and thought shatters beneath his touch. My back presses against one of the trees, a small knot digging painfully into my skin. He soothes the tiny scabs left behind by the bite of the crucifix, even as his hands trail over my body and light fire in their wake.

He laughs against my skin, his face buried in a mass of hair over my shoulder. "I like your way of talking, Ophelia."

A flush scalds my cheeks. For the first time, I wonder if there's a part of Father, a part of Laertes, that's right. The comfort he claims to need of me, if it takes only this form, he could get from nearly any girl in school, but they're not here yet and I've been here all along. Even the thought wounds; given voice, it might cripple.

"My father has forbidden me to see you."

The words fall flat, and for a terrifying, tremulous moment, they have no meaning.

Then the pain pulls across his face, and I know he's made them mean too much.

"You told him to jump in the lake, I hope."

I wince. Even in my most rebellious thoughts, I've never sought to remind him of how Mama died.

It's answer enough, though, because Dane spins away from me with a violent grace. His eyes flash with a fury that doesn't quite hide the hurt. "You said yes! How can you—how could you—you said yes!"

"He's my father."

"But you're your mother's daughter. How can he mean anything?"

Because he's the one who didn't walk away. But Dane thinks that long ago day in the lake was an accident, a tragedy, so there's nothing I can say to that. "Dane, he needs me to be a good daughter."

"You are a good daughter! Just as you are, you're a daughter any man could wish for!"

"No, I'm not," I whisper. "I try to be, but I never am. Not in the ways that matter. I *have* to try. I'm sorry."

"Don't be sorry, be here." Swift as a blink, he yanks my hand to his heart, flicks apart the top buttons of my blouse to press his other hand against my breast. "Be here, right here. Where you promised to be."

I swallow hard, at his words, at his touch, at his eyes on the ring still on its chain around my throat. Hours before Dane saw a ghost—before he swore to be a good son to a sundered soul—I promised my living, breathing father I'd be a good daughter. It's the same vow, the same cost; only the details differ. "I'm sorry."

"Ophelia, you promised me." He lets go of my hand, my palm still pressed against his chest, and traces his fingers down my sternum to the silver band. Goose bumps trail in his wake. "You promised me."

"I know," I whisper, "and I'm sorry."

"Stop saying you're sorry!" he snarls. His fingers curl around the ring. With his other hand still braced against my chest he yanks at the chain. It pulls me with it, choking me even as pain blooms from the clasp at the back of my neck. He lets go of me but pulls again, and I drop to my knees as the links on either side of the clasp finally give way. The ends dangle from his fist like strands of a whip. "Stop saying you're sorry."

Tears grip my chest in an iron band. The ring was such a little weight, but I can't breathe with it gone. His other hand shakes as he strokes the top of my head, and I lean against his knee, sobbing. Salt stings the tiny cuts on my lips, and I can taste the sour, copper tang of blood.

He moves away so suddenly that I pitch forward against the roots that tangle their way to the edge of the lake. "I need you," he whispers, the words like shards of glass. He says nothing else, just turns and walks away.

Always walking away.

The tears flood me, quake my body with waves of pain. The sun where my heart should be scalds my bones, my muscles, curls through my skin until I'm just a heap of blistered flesh, unrecognizable within the agony.

A cool hand passes over my hair in a damp streak, lightly lifts my face to trace the path of tears down my ravaged face. Mama sits on the tangle of roots, her feet still in the water, her night-purple hair plastered to her pale skin. "And Dahut and the strange lover in the red armor stole from the sleeping king the key to the city, and opened the gates," she murmurs. "The tide, swelled by the terrifying storm, rushed in through the gap in the bronze walls and swamped the city. The great bells of the soaring churches sang in the wind and the strength of the water. The ocean roared in triumph as it finally dragged the great city to the base of the bay and drowned its beautiful buildings, its elegant churches, the cathedrals that spoke more to the arrogance of man than the grace of God. Even had he the key in hand, the King himself could not have turned back the flood."

She gently pushes me to make me stretch out on the roots, cheek pillowed on one arm, and she strokes my hair into a great fan around me until I'm drowning in a spill of night. "You let Dane steal the key from you, Ophelia."

"I gave it to him," I whisper.

"That never mattered."

I gulp in shaky breaths, but the sobs don't stop. They tear at my lungs, make my muscles burn because my body is too weak to take this agony.

"There are less painful ways to drown than in tears."

But the tears aren't water; they're fire, the flares of a star that orbits the shattered pieces of my heart. You can't drown in fire.

You can only be consumed by it.

Then Father is kneeling beside me, his face ashy and fatigued, and I wonder if he's spent all night staring at the papers on his desk. "Ophelia?"

"I told him."

His hand hovers, awkward and uncertain, over my face, then lightly touches my tear-slick cheek. "I know it hurts," he says softly. "I'm sorry you have to feel this way, Ophelia, because I know you think you love him. But this is for the best."

Mama laughs derisively, a cruel sound that Father cannot hear, has never heard since her death. "As stars with trains of fire and dews of blood, disasters in the sun, and the moist star upon whose influence Neptune's empire stands was sick almost to doomsday with eclipse." Her voice is almost a song. "Even in the end of all things, when all omens shriek to what comes, men will be the fools their petty lives have scripted them to be. Pain is only for the best when it ends."

I close my eyes against her words, against the genuine concern that wars with relief in my father's face. I can feel her hand against my hair, my skin, my back, even as I hear him urge me to return to the house, to clean up and perhaps go to bed for a few hours. The roots dig into my skin, sure to leave bruises, and my elbow stings as particles cling to the bloody wound.

I deserve this.

This pain, this terror, this despair, this is mine to bear.

I promised Dane I would help him bear his grief.

And I walked away.

CHAPTER 20

It's a relief when classes start again. Surrounded by people, always with places to be or things to do, it's harder to drown in the endless weeping of the drowning sun in my chest. I'm a sophomore this year; I have no classes in common with Dane and Horatio, who are both seniors.

Dinner during the week is a haphazard affair at best. Those of us who live here year-round can choose to dine in the mansion with the other students or eat in the private dining room of Headmaster's House. Or if one is cowardly and weak, in Father's study with a tray and a pile of papers that need to be typed. Where other students have laptops and privacy, I have a father whose idea of parental controls involve his being in the room. Consumed with a million details, Father doesn't notice my self-imposed isolation. Or at least, I think he doesn't; he might choose to let me keep myself separate for a time, but I don't believe he could make that decision without comment. Whatever he does, whatever he decides, Father will always have a speech to make on the subject.

It would be easier if I could say that Dane hated me for walking away.

Sometimes I can say that. Sometimes I can feel his eyes on me in the halls, feel the glares that smoke and blaze between my shoulder blades as though with a single glance he could flay all the flesh from my body and leave it to rot. On those occasions, he passes by in sullen silence or even knocks the books from my hands for the simple pleasure of causing me pain.

Sometimes the only way to make a pain bearable is to make others feel it too.

But then there are the days where he acts as if nothing has changed, where he sits beside me at lunch and laces his fingers through mine, where he traps me in corners and kisses me until breath is just a faint memory with no meaning. The days where he drags me into hidden alcoves in the gardens we know so well and traces fire across my skin with hands and lips.

Then there are the days that set everyone to talking.

The third day of classes, Dane swept through the halls in tights; a long, sleeveless leather coat; a blouse with billowing sleeves; a long cape, all black edged in silver; and a gaudy gold crown perched lopsided on his sable hair. He answered all questions put to him quite solemnly, with no indication of a prank or a game or anything at all out of the ordinary.

The next day he spoke entirely in German—not just in the halls but in classes as well, speaking over the professors with rambling, disjointed monologues. Rumors filtered through the lower grades, but Horatio met me in the gardens that night and told me the truth of them. Some of it was poetry, he said, or bits of plays or even operas; and during their Latin test, he stood and delivered an impassioned recitation of large chunks of *The Communist Manifesto*.

He's had days where he can't seem to stop talking and days where he hasn't said a word. One night he walked into a bathroom of the girls' dormitory and set about his evening ritual like he didn't notice the thirteen-year-olds shrieking from the shower stalls. Another day he pretended to faint every time someone said his name; another day he assigned everyone the wrong names and genders; yet another day he threw such a violent fit in his literature class that the first-year professor broke down in tears.

Father and Claudius spent hours convincing the poor woman not to quit, finally offering her a raise and promising to cover part of her tuition should she decide to pursue a doctorate in education. They even offered her two weeks of paid vacation to recover her nerves, and it was still a near thing to make her stay.

Three weeks in, as I sit in Old Testament Studies with nineteen other girls, the door slams open. Our steely-haired professor—a born spinster if there is such a thing anymore—drops both chalk and eraser in a pale puff of dust and turns to stare.

It's Dane, of course, and my heart sinks at the sight of him.

His bare chest gleams with oil, a black bandana knotted around his neck like a bandit at rest. A black Stetson sits at an angle atop his dark hair, and his black jeans couldn't be tighter if they tried. A coil of rope rests in one hand, a lasso drooping from the other. He catches my eye and winks, tipping the Stetson in my direction. "Little filly," he drawls.

My face flames, and I look back at my notes amidst a chorus of whispers and growls.

"Mr. Danemark!"

He smiles at my scandalized professor and swings himself over the first row of desks. "Howdy, ma'am. Just checking the herds." He reaches my row and hops onto the desk behind me, knees to either side of me, and strokes my hair. "Easy there, filly."

"Mr. Danemark, I insist you leave my class this instant!"

He eyes her sourly, the lasso twirling slowly at his side. "Mene, Mene, Tekel u-Pharsin," he says softly.

You have been weighed in the balance and are found wanting.

My professor is unimpressed. Purple blotches spread rapidly across her narrow face as she stalks toward the call button for the intercom. "Mr. Danemark, leave my class at once, or I will be forced to take you before the Headmaster for your actions."

Probably not the best thing to say.

Dane leaps to his feet on the desk, and the lasso spins in a blur over our heads. "Time to cull the herd, beauties!" The rope flies forward, the loop dropping over the sputtering woman. When he pulls the slipknot tight, she falls to her knees and scrabbles against the floor as he yanks her inexorably closer. I could almost feel sorry for her. Dane jumps down and hauls her to her feet by the neck of her blouse. "Say good-bye now, ma'am."

"Mister—"

He seals his mouth to hers, and we all watch in horrified fascination as the colors spread down her neck. She swats at him ineffectually, but then his hands are flying, the rope whipping around, and suddenly she's back on the floor with her wrists and ankles tied together behind her back. When she opens her mouth to scream, he stuffs his bandana between her teeth.

And none of us move; none of us try to help.

I'm not sure which one we'd help if we weren't frozen.

Then it's out of my hands entirely because Dane grabs me, then Kelly Hunter beside me, and drags us out of our desks and out of the room, yelling so enthusiastically that every door in the hall pops open so heads can watch our skidding, drunken progress. He doesn't let go until we reach the auditorium and the stage, where he interrupts an Advanced Drama class to hurl us into the startled arms of Kelly's older brother Keith.

Thank God for Keith, who just holds us steady as Dane steals a fresh coil of rope from the lighting closet and races across the velvet-padded chairs and out the door again. Kelly giggles and breathlessly relates it all to her brother. I close my eyes against the tears that make the room swim before me.

How many people understand the writing on the wall?

There's no way to predict these unfathomable episodes, no apparent trigger or pattern to them. He might appear completely normal at breakfast but explode later in the day, or in the evening, after hours of bizarre behavior, he looks at any who might question him on it like they've gone insane. The incidents might be scattered with a few days between or strung so closely together that only the particulars prove that they're separate occurrences.

The performances are in no way limited to the mansion where classes are held. His frenzied antics continue in the Headmaster's House so long as there is even a single maid to serve witness to it. One morning I awake to the sound of Father locking my bedroom door; Horatio tells me later that Dane spent several hours wandering nude around the house. He half laughs through the entire story, but his hazel eyes are dark with concern. That same night, Dane bursts into his mother's room and waltzes her through the hall in her dressing gown, bellowing Wagner at the top of his lungs. Just as Gertrude's astonishment finally turns to laughter, he drops her hands and walks away with a scowl.

As long as he has an audience, he's performing, even if the act is to appear normal. There's a logic to his frenetic activity, a twisted course of thought that eludes me even as I know it should be obvious. That it is an act I'm certain. He warned us; he swore it would all be acting. I have to remind Horatio of this after Dane spends their calculus class fencing invisible foes with two pencils taped together. We know the behavior is forced. What we don't know is why.

Only around Horatio and me does the act drop away, but he doesn't discuss it with either of us. Somehow this play at madness is part of his arrangement with his father's ghost, a cog or a tool or a process. I'm grateful beyond words for Horatio's love for Dane, for the steady regard that seeks to support him no matter the chaos all around us. It's not a simple thing by any stretch of the imagination, but it yields a simple result: around Horatio, Dane can be real. He can put away the plots and the plans and allow himself to be exhausted by his grief and fury.

Claudius and Gertrude notice his antics, of course, but other than speaking of it in hushed voices when they think no one else is around, they don't do anything. Claudius' inaction is easy to understand, I think; to him, it must seem as though Dane is acting out purely to reflect poorly on his uncle as the new headmaster. After all, if he can't even control his nephew-stepson, how can he run an entire school? And it's not as though that line of reasoning would be out of character for a teenager. Claudius' lofty pretense that there's nothing going on makes sense to me.

Gertrude, on the other hand, presents a puzzle. She's clearly concerned for her son. Her blue eyes track his progress through a room, her hands fluttering helplessly at her breast whenever she witnesses one of his episodes. She's too aware of her reputation to weep in public, but some nights the soft sounds carry through the old walls of the house.

On those nights, Dane flees the second level and comes to me, his dark grey eyes haunted by a pain deeper than just the reflection of his mother's. Every time, I come face-to-face with the knowledge that I should turn him away. Father's edict hasn't changed. I made him a promise. And every time, I come face-to-face with the knowledge that I can't ever turn him away. I made Dane a promise, too. I'm a liar with every breath.

Whenever he runs away from the muted proof of the pain he causes his mother, I open the door and let him come in. Somewhere within my father is a remnant of the man seduced by a feral beauty half his age, the man who offered to walk away from the job and school he loves because he thought it was the right thing to do. Somewhere in that echo I think—I hope—is a piece that understands why I can't be a good daughter and close my door in the face of the pain that's become a living thing.

During the days, Dane vacillates between hating me for walking away and pretending that I never did. Both take a strength he can't find at night. When he comes to me for comfort, he's just the boy who's lost his father, who's losing his mother. Sometimes it's enough for him just to hold me, to fall asleep in my arms and know that I'll still be there when he wakes up in the morning.

Then there's the Dane who needs, whose teeth and hands summon bruises to my skin, whose lips crash against mine to capture the startled whimpers as his touch hovers between pleasure and pain. No matter which Dane comes to me in the night, I know the next morning I'll find a letter or small gift tucked into the basket of flowers that Jack sets by my door, and always a flower that hides words behind a meaning. Years ago, Gertrude gave me a book with all the meanings; it's gotten more use now than ever before. More than anything, those gifts show the Dane I know.

The Dane I miss.

As September passes into October, as his games grow more and more savage, he shows up at my door nearly every night. Horatio stays with him all through the days, and it makes me wonder if perhaps Dane is afraid to be alone. Like a music box wound too tightly, he seems constantly on the verge of flying apart. Sometimes I wish he'd confide his plans with us so we could help him. Other times, more selfish times, I'm glad he doesn't. Nearly two months he's been playing his deep-seated game, and so far as either Horatio or I can tell he's no closer to whatever he seeks. If it's proof he's looking for, he's chosen a very circuitous method of digging for it.

Dane performs and Claudius ignores, a stalemate that seems as though it may never end. One of them will lose his patience before too much longer, but I don't think any of us—even Dane—looks forward to that moment.

But there's a day, one single extraordinary day, when I don't have to worry about Dane or Hamlet or Claudius, don't have to dwell on the fact that Laertes hasn't written once since he left for France.

October 26 dawns cold and crisp, with a heavy, drifting blanket of clouds that promises an evening storm. The rain will be half frozen, I think. Summer surrendered early this year, and autumn stands poised to do the same. Color gradually leeches from everything, leaving school and grounds a study of soft blues and greys. When I leave my room for breakfast, there's a note from Father on the door excusing me from classes.

I'm sixteen today. Today is the day I was born and the day I died, the day Mama died, the day Father had to watch Hamlet decide which of us to try to save. Father couldn't swim, won't learn now, and Mama had weighed herself down while only holding me loose in her arms. I was easy for Hamlet to pull from the water, but to actually save me meant a choice. Save the girl? Or fight to pull out the woman and likely lose them both? I wonder, sometimes, if Father regrets that choice, if he would have been better off if Hamlet had left us both to the gleaming towers and delicate bells of the City of Ys. Every day on this year, Father excuses Laertes and me from classes and spends the long hours locked away in his study with a bottle of whiskey and a bottle of misery to discover which will empty faster.

Always the whiskey.

Laertes usually sticks to my side like a burr in my skirt, but he's thousands of miles away, and this year, this day, I can do whatever I want, go wherever I want.

Along with my usual basket of straggling hothouse violets and other flowers, Jack's left me an extra gift: a crown of roses, deep peach at their throat but rusting up the petals to a cinnamon at the edges. It looks faintly ridiculous with the uniform, all midnight and ice blue and perfect pleats, but I wear it anyway. Today is the one day no one will ask if I've taken my pills, where I can leave behind shoes and socks and feel the earth beneath my feet, where I can wear flowers in my hair and no one speaks of faeries or madness.

I retrieve a picnic basket and cold lunch from the maids and sway along the chain to the middle of the lake. Mama's already there waiting for me, her dainty feet dipped in the dark water. A matching crown sits atop her night-dark hair, thick locks pulled through the weave to anchor it in place. She laughs when she sees me and claps her hands like a child. Every year she spends this day on the island, like we did eight years ago before she cast us into the lake at sunset. This is the first time I've joined her there since that day.

"Is it sweet sixteen, Ophelia?" she asks with a kiss against my cheek.

"The day is young."

She just laughs again.

We spend the day together, just me and Mama on the island. She tells me stories of a hundred impossible things, and I count off how many of them I've seen. I dance around the circle of dead flowers as she waves her hands, and as the afternoon shifts to murky twilight, she whispers of old promises and a drowned city that waits patiently beneath the water. And once again, I tell her not yet. Not no—just not yet. My mother ran to the lake because she had so much emptiness only the water could fill. I don't have that emptiness, not yet.

That emptiness is called Dane, and he burns like a star in the void where my heart should be.

Thunder rattles the chain as I cross the lake. The clouds have darkened through the day. They surround me like the halo of an angel bound in Purgatory, vague bruises reflected from a black mirror. Clean blue skies, ice blue, remind me too much of Hamlet's funeral. This bruised world is where I belong.

With this early darkness, the cemetery is lit up with blue-white pillars that flicker in a way that has nothing to do with the wind tugging at my short skirt and long hair. The wind stings tears to my eyes, dries my lips until they crack and the taste of copper blooms on my tongue. The closer we come to All Hallows', the more restless the ghosts become. For most of them, it's the only day each year when they can leave their graves, see what's left of their families or loved ones. They itch to be gone, to see more, to do more, even those whose families have long since become dust in the ground. Time passes differently for ghosts, I think. The years don't mean what they should.

Nearly alone on the blessed side of the graveyard, Hamlet sits on the plinth of his massive headstone. The mottled grey marble gleams in his ghostly light, a dance of shadows across the darker veins of stone. A dark metal plaque affixed to the base proclaims his name and title; his dates of birth and death; and a graceful inscription in Latin that speaks to a life of duty, honor, and love. The right side is blank, waiting for Gertrude to join him one day. Atop the plinth, two tall angels in draping robes stand with their wings outstretched behind them, every feather carved in exquisite detail. The one guarding Hamlet's body holds a claymore with Hebrew words carved down the length of the blade; beside it, Gertrude's angel cups its hands to hold a dove poised for flight. The angels themselves are sexless, stone curls of hair over beautiful, androgynous faces, but there's something of Hamlet in the one holding the sword, something of his sternness and quiet pride in the strong serenity written into the marble.

This ghost, this Hamlet, is not quite the Hamlet I knew, but he is so much closer than the one that rages through the night and drips poisonous revenge into Dane's dreams. He greets me with a sad smile, a hand lifted not in a wave but in something more formal.

A little drunk with dancing and with Mama, I hop up next to him on the plinth, hissing as the cold stone stings the back of my thighs where the uniform skirt rides up. There's a perfect hollow between the feet of Gertrude's angel, just the right size to lean back against the angel's knees and not feel like I'm about to fall.

His smile grows slightly at the sight of the crown of roses, and becomes a little less sad. "Happy birthday, Ophelia."

"Thank you, sir."

We sit in silence for a long time, both of us staring up the hill to Headmaster's House and beyond that to the school. Lights blaze through the night, a spill of gold from scattered windows. Shadows weave across them from time to time as the people in a room cross before the glass. The school is full of life. Students gather for study groups or movie nights or forbidden parties, couples find private spaces or closets to grope and pant, the youngest ones race through the halls in complicated games that aren't beneath their dignity yet. Even Headmaster's House glows like a jewel in the moonlight; Claudius hosts yet another gathering with too much wine and laughter. I hope Father has found deep sleep within the whiskey bottle, or the sound of such merrymaking must be hell.

I'm rarely as good a daughter as he needs me to be, but I do love him. His pain cuts me, even when I'm not the one to cause it.

"Souls can sunder, Ophelia," whispers Hamlet. "In all our lessons of faith and doctrine, no mention was ever made of such a thing—that it isn't merely the heart that breaks."

"You are sorrow; he is rage."

"And yet, we are the same person. We exist simultaneously, in two different forms; yet we are both Hamlet, both pieces of the whole that was."

He looks so tired. This is the face of the Wild Hunt in the quiet moments, those breathless seconds where they slow to a walk and look to the greyhounds to see if they'll jump off. This is the weariness without hope of relief.

"Dane can't see you."

"I don't let myself be seen. Except by you," he adds with a familiar gleam in his dark eyes. It's fleeting, but the memory warns me despite the icy wind that shears through my skin to my bones. "It seems I have little choice in that regard."

"Have you thought that it might help him?"

"I have thought." His sigh trembles in a hackle-raising crack of thunder. A violent fork of lightning stabs the sky, so bright it leaves an echo against my eyelids. "I have thought and wondered and pondered, deliberated, debated, discussed . . . It seems I cannot help but turn it over in my mind and pray that my choice is the correct one, but the dead, Ophelia, have no business with the world of the living. You stand with a foot in either, but even you know to separate yourself on most occasions. Dane cannot be helped by seeing his father further destroyed in death."

"Dane will destroy himself for this revenge."

"My son made his promises."

And promises, once made, must be kept, and if later you regret them, you should have been more careful in making them. Dane will always keep his promises, and I . . . it seems as though I will always break mine.

In the moment of death, or perhaps the moment of awakening, all that was good and true about the fifth Hamlet Danemark sundered from all that was hurt and betrayed. The sorrow, the dignity, the compassion, centered on this tired shade beside me, who even now bows his head against the weight of grief and a fathomless pain.

"I'm sorry."

"We all are, or shall be." He reaches out as if to brush against the crown of roses, but his fingers pass through it; in their wake, the petals he's touched crack and wither.

The rain starts as I leave the cemetery, just a few scattered drops at first and then, without further warning, a deluge that stabs frigid knives into my skin. My hair, my clothing, clings to me, and I can feel the crown of roses slowly breaking apart under the onslaught.

The cold takes my breath away, such a sharp contrast to the blazing star of my heart, and I can't help but laugh. As I move along the path, my feet step in circles, in patterns, in a swaying dance that belongs around a corona of flowers back on the island.

In the lake, the bells pound and toll, swept by the storm that rages along the surface. They roll through my bones like thunder, like joy, and shriek against the night sky. On such a night, the gates were opened and the city drowned, but there are no more keys hidden away, nothing left to open, to drown.

"Ophelia!"

Everything has drowned already, and the water thrust away what it could not yet keep. We don't die a second time; we go home. When it's time. When what was borrowed has emptied away.

"Ophelia!"

All stars die. They burn and burn bright, and then, when they have consumed everything that can be offered, they fade and die and leave a black hole in their wake, a vast void, an emptiness of incalculable space.

"Ophelia!" A hand closes hard around my arm and yanks me against a firm chest; another hand smoothes along my cheek to lift my face.

Dane.

Water drips from the ends of his hair, traces in rivulets along the creases of the soaked black clothing he wears in place of his uniform. Knife-edged shadows skitter across the sharp lines of his face in a flash of lightning, illuminating dark grey eyes and a puzzled, uncertain smile.

"Dance with me."

"You didn't take your pills this morning," he murmurs, but there's no accusation there, only a kind of wonder I haven't heard from him in so long. "I can tell. Your eyes . . . your eyes are so alive."

"So dance with me."

He actually smiles, and in that moment he looks so much like his father the star burns brighter in my chest. We nearly glow in the darkness, pale pearls that gleam in bursts of light. His fingers, long and elegant—his mother's hands—trace my face, my lips. "You're nearly blue."

I've been blue before, when they dragged me from a lake that wanted to freeze us within its grasp.

Bending nearly in two, he catches me behind my knees and sweeps me off my feet. He cradles me against his chest, our breath mingling in a frosty cloud in the scant inches between us, and the rain slices the mud and grass from my bare feet. Laughter spills from my throat, and I lean back against his support, my arms spread wide to catch the frozen tears that fall from Heaven. The angels weep and the bean sidhe sing and for a moment they make nearly the same sound.

He carries me into the house, through the garden door and up the servants' stair to avoid the party. Water drips and pools behind us with every step. I shiver in the sudden loss, the sudden warmth. The dim lights hurt my eyes. Dane takes me straight to my room and closes the door with a soft, careful kick. He doesn't put me down until we're in my bathroom and in the standing shower.

There used to be a bathtub, but Father had it taken out before I was allowed to come home from the cold place, because he thought the tub was too much like the lake.

With a twist of his wrist, the water pours over us, sharp and cold at first, and we're back outside in the storm and the lightning, but then it warms and soothes, and the storm is only something to hear. He's still smiling though, like he's discovered something wonderful, and I twine a hand through his hair and pull his face down to mine so I can taste his joy.

He's startled—I've never kissed him before, always he's been the one to kiss, to start—but it's only a moment and then he's kissing me back, his hands tugging at our sopping clothing and dropping them to the tile with wet slaps of fabric. The hot water streaks across his skin with a pale flush, and I follow it with my hands and suddenly he groans and presses his weight against me, the crucifix digging into my shoulder.

My mother's laugh echoes in my ears, a sharp arrow that darts around the narrow space between my body and Dane's, and I follow its path until he sets his teeth into my neck to stifle his cry. He drops to his knees, his face pressed into my stomach, and as the water cools around us, the laughter recedes until there's nothing but the sharp sting of bruised and broken skin; his gasping breaths; and that beautiful, terrifying sense of wonder.

CHAPTER 21

The next morning, Father and I both take pills with our breakfast. There are pills at Dane's place setting but no Dane or Horatio. They're up on the widow's walk, where Dane has the portable microphone for the intercom system and greeted everyone at four o'clock with the strident cries of a rooster. And three hours later, he is still doing it because he's broken the lock to the control room so Claudius and Father can't get in there to turn off the system. Horatio, I think, is just there to make sure Dane doesn't do something stupid like jump off the railing.

It's Saturday, though, with no classes to distract anyone from the noise, and I think it's Claudius who'll break the stalemate. He grits his teeth even as he sips his tea, and every time a fresh peal comes through the speakers, his grip tightens so on the delicate porcelain cup that it trembles from the strain.

If Dane threw in a hyena laugh just to mix things up, I think the handle of the cup would break.

The fact that I wish he'd do it is proof enough to me that I shouldn't skip my pills twice in a row, and I dutifully swallow them one by one under Father's approving gaze.

Someone, probably Reynaldo, got him started on the aspirin last night. He has a headache, but he isn't actually hung over.

After breakfast, Father and Reynaldo retreat to Father's study. I drift after them for lack of anything better to do; it's a vague thought that perhaps I'll ask permission to use the computer. I don't have any papers that require it, but perhaps Father will let me search maps of Paris to see my brother's new haunts—not that I have any letters to tell me where those haunts might be.

Father has left the door open; neither man sits in the well-worn leather chairs around the broad desk. Reynaldo stands on the visitor's side of the wood, the edge level with his chest. He wears lifts in his shoes to try and disguise how short he is, but he doesn't know how to walk in them so he ends up hunched and waddling like a duck. That might be part of why he always looks like he's scowling even when he smiles.

After digging through the massive stacks of paper on the desk, Father hands him a large manila envelope. "There's money in there, in addition to what I've added to his card; make sure he gets those letters please. Perhaps our previous ones have gone astray."

He's sending Reynaldo to Paris?

I can't help but smile. Reynaldo has been Father's stooge nearly all my life, but I cannot be comfortable around the leering man. He is more careful in his expression when Laertes is here to glower at him, but these two months have been filled with lascivious looks and wicked smiles that make me very glad I have no skill at reading men's thoughts.

"Before you meet with my son, Reynaldo, I would have you do a few other things first."

"Sir?"

"I need you to inquire after his behavior," Father tells him, a sigh heavy in his voice. "Find out what other exchange students are there, where they tend to spend time outside of classes. He'll more likely spend time with them than with his French classmates. When you question them, you can freely say that you know his father and family, and thus know him. Am I making myself clear?"

"Perfectly."

I lean against the doorframe, mostly lost to the shadows of the hall.

"I want you to tell them wild stories, Reynaldo. Say that he's wild and half drunk, and whatever stories and lies you wish to add there. None, if you please, that will permanently tar his reputation or damage any useful contacts he may be making—nothing that will dishonor the Castellan name or the one who will be responsible for it when I am gone. We both know he is young and his hormones . . . in any case, assign to him whatever wild tumbles are popular to teenagers of his type."

Reynaldo shakes his head; he doesn't entirely see where Father is going with this. "Like gambling? Or . . ."

"If you wish, or fighting or drinking, swearing inappropriately, you may even go so far as to say he goes whoring if you wish."

"Sir!" A blush spreads across Reynaldo's olive skin. "Surely whoring would damage his reputation!"

"I think you misjudge the French." Father adjusts the rimless glasses on his nose. "At any rate, to say merely that he works his way through women is not such a scandal as to say he is addicted to it in some way or to imply that there is some perversion in his tastes. To have a healthy appetite for sex is a hallmark of youth. What you must do, Reynaldo, is spin these stories in such a way that they seem only a reflection of his sudden independence, not a general flaw of his character."

"Sir—"

"Why do I ask you to do this?"

Reynaldo sighs with relief. He doesn't like appearing stupid, doesn't like having to ask for explanations that Father is only too willing to give.

At length.

Interminable length.

"Yes, sir, I would know that, please. What you ask seems rather extraordinary."

"I want to know the truth of what my son is doing in Paris, Reynaldo." Father adjusts the glasses again, though they can hardly need it so soon, and sinks down into his chair. The leather bears worn patches on the back and arms where his weight has rubbed away the darker color. "Asking him for a report on his behaviors is unlikely to yield that result, but he must be doing quite a bit that he cannot manage even a single line of e-mail in all this time. So. Ask those he spends time with, but not in such a way that invites dishonesty. If you paint him with all these vices, and they agree with you—surely it must be true. But if they protest your descriptions, then they know him for a good boy. We will have the truth of it with Laertes none the wiser."

It isn't hard to imagine Reynaldo stalking along Parisian cafés in search of any friends Laertes may have made. The fact that he'll look ridiculous won't occur to him—he takes himself far too seriously for that—and for whatever tact he may employ, he has no idea that the other students will just tell my brother when next they see him. It's impossible not to relate that a strange American man, barely five feet tall, came to them and made all sorts of horrendous accusations against Laertes' character.

I press a hand against my mouth to hold back a giggle. He seriously expects to go up to a table of American teenagers and talk about "whoring"?

Father knows his duties as an administrator very well, but he knows far more about paper than people. Such a plan can't possibly work. It might even amuse them to string him along with even worse stories.

Dane would do that.

If even just one of those exchange students is like Dane, the others will follow his lead as he spins horror stories of sexual diseases and drugs and absinthe, as he tells a spellbound stooge of gambling dens where Laertes loses all his money to brawls. Add in a few rumors about unexplained corpses and Reynaldo might just die of joy at the prospect of sharing such awful tales.

I have to tell Dane and Horatio.

I'm actually at the front door before I catch myself. Whatever grace I gave myself yesterday, whatever gift of disobedience I gave myself to celebrate my birthday, ended when Dane left my room still with that look of wonder and joy in his eyes. It's one thing not to push him away when he comes to me; it's another thing entirely to seek him out away from Gertrude and Father.

Even when one is thousands of miles away, Father still feels like he has to know every detail about his children's lives. He has to take away the locks, the chances for privacy, for secrets, and yet . . .

I trace my hand along the curved pattern of teeth in the side of my neck, shiver at even this slight pressure against the bruised, fragile skin.

Father wants to know so much.

Or rather, he thinks he does.

Because if he actually knew, if he knew how Laertes spends his days and nights, knew that this semicircle of pain keeps the sun burning in my chest, there wouldn't be enough whiskey in the world to dull the pain.

CHAPTER 22

The rest of the morning and afternoon passes by as I lie on my bed, my hand over the bruise on my neck. I can feel my heartbeat through my fingertips with each rush of blood to the damaged skin. It throbs and stings beneath my touch like something alive in its own right.

When he finally managed to get to his feet again in the shower, Dane kissed me so sweetly the star scalded my breath, but then he wrapped himself in one of my towels and walked away. This morning he stood up on the widow's walk with a microphone and crowed for hours like a demented Peter Pan.

Peace doesn't last.

My door flies open and I flinch, start to sit up on the bed, but then Dane is there, pinning me to the mattress. Half the buttons of his black silk shirt are undone, the other half matched to the wrong hole, and his black slacks are unfastened and barely clinging to his narrow hips. His hair stands about his pale face in every direction. Wildness lives in his eyes, a frantic, manic gleam that's supposed to go away with the medication he probably hasn't been taking.

His chest rises and falls in short, sharp pants; his bleeding lips tremble with the force of each breath. He looks as though he's been loosed from Hell. His fingers dig into my wrists where he pins them to the bed. Pain blooms beneath his touch, sleepy and familiar.

He shifts his grip, still hard and strong, to hold my wrists with one hand. The other moves to my face.

"Dane . . ."

A finger presses softly against my lips, and I fall silent. His eyes follow the path of his fingers as he traces every line and curve of my face, like he would memorize it, or draw it, somehow immortalize it beyond his means. His touch carries down to my throat. He lingers at the bite, his breath warm and sharp against my ear. He pushes a thumb against the mark, and I bite my cheek against a cry of pain; his lips dig into mine, and the cry turns into a silent gasp.

He yanks my turtleneck up until he can press his lips where his class ring belongs and isn't. His cheek rests against my breast, my heart, the sun that spins and burns with his name written into the flares. His face softens, but his fingers close even harder against my wrists. A sudden, damp warmth trickles through the silk and lace of my bra, and I realize he must be crying. Silently, subtly, with nothing else but this kiss of tears to give it away.

He lifts his eyes to mine, the thin corona of grey nearly drowned by the pupils. "You took your pills this morning." His voice, rough and low, sends shivers down my spine.

"Yes."

"But you'll let me do this anyway." His hand moves down and I gasp, a too soft sound swallowed by his harsh kiss.

In the moment of death, or perhaps the moment of awakening, Hamlet's soul splintered. Three Hamlets: one the Headmaster that was, one that is sorrow, one that is rage.

Dane isn't dead, but he's splintered as well, fractured and shattered into so many different pieces that I never know which of them I'll see. There's a knot between my lungs, a solid force that allows no air to pass, and I writhe against his touch until the knot explodes with a breath that shapes his name.

Just as suddenly the breath is gone again, lost to the hand that closes now around my throat and squeezes gently. His fingers trace warm smears against my skin, readjust themselves over and over again as he slowly increases the pressure. "You'll let me do anything to you, Ophelia, even this. Why? Why do you let me do this?"

Black lights burst before my eyes with unexpected, dazzling colors. They're beautiful, but too soon they disappear into a growing darkness that spreads inward from the edges of my vision. It sweeps me away, floating on an endless ocean of weightlessness.

There's nothing here.

Not the salt of his tears against open wounds, not the way he carves his name into my body, not even the echo of the wonder. Laughter rushes in to fill the void, some of it my mother's, a euphoric cacophony that would cut and bleed if there was anything real.

The hands snatch away, and there's pressure on my mouth, air forced into my lungs. The darkness fades into a spill of light and color that makes no sense, and I mourn its loss as the world races to reclaim what was nearly stolen. His eyes wide, his face horror-struck, Dane stares at me. His hands tremble against the mattress on either side of my head.

"Ophelia," he chokes out, as though the hands had been a collar around *his* throat.

But I let him collar me now as I let him collar me with his ring, because sometimes it's a choice.

I take a deep breath and feel the muscles protest, feel the bruises that will form.

This is the Dane who made a reckless promise, who burns with the need to keep his word.

This is the Ophelia who broke her promises, who clings to a sputtering star to keep from drowning.

He rolls off the bed and backs away, still staring at me like I'm something new and terrifying, like I'm the ghost that plagues his promises. When I simply lie there and watch him, he risks a single step forward, brushes a fingertip against my swollen lips. "Doubt that the stars are fire," he whispers brokenly, "doubt that the sun moves, doubt Truth to be a liar, but never doubt that I love you."

With a hoarse, panicked cry, he hurls himself against the locked window.

A shriek rips from my throat as he collides painfully with the unyielding glass. He stands, shakes himself out, and starts to laugh hysterically. "Rapunzel in her tower," he gasps, backing towards the door. One foot in the hall, he strikes a dramatic pose, declaiming loudly for the entire house to hear. "Danae in her prison, Ariadne on her island, Jephthah's daughter in his stupid vow! Your father will protect you straight into misery and Hell!"

He darts back into the room, yanking my sweater back into place and cradling my face in trembling hands. "But what happens when the walls are breached?" he asks in a voice little more than a breath shared between us. Startled shouts and footsteps hammer up the first flight of stairs. "What happens when Zeus comes, when Theseus leaves? What happens . . ." He swallows hard, closes his eyes as his forehead leans against mine. "Ophelia, what happens when the promise is made?"

His face swims in a sheen of tears. When I try to answer, my voice is as shattered as the boy on his knees before me.

When a promise is made, it must be kept.

Or broken.

The footsteps reach the third floor, and Dane springs into the hall, crashing into Father and Reynaldo. Through the door, all I can see is a tangle of limbs. "Thank you for the string, dear lady!" Dane yells as he extricates himself. "When I leave you on that stinking rock, think well of me until your Dionysus finds you!"

Curled in the center of my bed, I bury my face in my knees and laugh until the tears come.

"Ophelia, are you—" Father struggles to gain his feet, one hand braced against the wall. "Reynaldo, quickly, go to the Headmaster and tell him—Ophelia, are you all right?"

I scrub my face with my hands and sit up. "I'm fine," I whisper, my throat tight and painful. "He scared me, that's all. I don't know—I just . . ."

Which role does Dane want me to play this? I'm not part of his game, not really, but by staging this scene in the house, by dragging Father and his stooge up the stairs, he's hauled me into the center ring. What is he trying to do?

I cross my arms against my stomach, clutch my elbows against the need to fly apart, to shatter. "He burst in and grabbed me, and he was just . . . spouting nonsense."

"We'll have to tell Claudius," murmurs Father. "This is . . . I knew he was out of balance with grief over his father, but I had no idea you meant so much to him. This cannot be anything less than the madness of love!"

Love is its own madness?

But then, I suppose it is, sweet and painful and consuming, a way to drown so deliciously that it doesn't even occur to you to gasp for air. I open my eyes and stare at the broken lock on the window.

"Passion can, at times, break our reason." Our? I look up at him, but he sees something impossibly far away. "I am sorry for it, Ophelia." He hesitates before touching my shoulder. "Are you all right? Did he hurt you?"

Even as we speak, bruises bloom in violent bursts of color against my skin.

But I let him do anything.

"No," I whisper. "He just scared me."

"Have you two argued recently? Any hard words?"

"You told me not to be around him without you or Gertrude present," I remind him. "I told him that before classes resumed. He was angry then and has been angry since, when he has not been sullen and silent or . . . about his antics," I continue carefully. "He's interrupted my classes a few times, but other than that, we've barely spoken in two months. Though . . ." I take a deep breath and pray again that I'm making the right choice. "He has left notes outside my door, which I've never answered."

"Which must have contributed to this . . ." He rubs a hand against his beard. "I thought this was just a passing attraction, that he was just trifling with you. God curse my jealousy! I thought him too young to form any sort of proper attachment." This time he doesn't hesitate before pulling me to him in a gentle and all too brief hug. "I need you to come with me to see Claudius. If there is a solution to Dane's behavior, he needs to be told before keeping this secret causes some greater harm."

The idea is enough to make me bite my swollen lip to keep from laughing. Claudius, the master of harmful secrets, will somehow amend this problem? He can't take away Dane's pain without losing everything he's won since the summer.

But Father's hand flattens against my back and gently propels me away from the window. "Come, Ophelia. And bring one of those notes."

And because I try to be a good daughter, despite all my failings, I follow.

CHAPTER 23

The Headmaster's office has a small waiting room attached to it, a place for parents to sit in comfort until the Headmaster is ready, and it's here Father leads me. I sink down into a chair by the door and flick off the lights while Father enters the office to arrange for a moment or two of Claudius' time. There are other voices inside, and I know Father won't interrupt them, but he'll hover until he's had his say.

Moonlight floods the room from the tall windows that march along one side. It casts shadows of purples and blues against the carpet and walls, stretches the furniture out of proportion, gleams against the metal curve of sconces and statuettes.

Without Father standing over me, I push back the sleeves of the dark violet sweater and inspect my wrists. I can see his fingers, his hands. Already the angry red fades to a soft purple. As time passes, the color will deepen, the pooled blood collected under the skin in damaged cells, individual microcosms whose walls have been breached by a storm of fury and drowned in a tide of blood.

If I close my eyes, will I hear the bells of all those lost cities resonating in my veins?

But this, this mass of marks and color, this souvenir of fury and loss, this is what I am.

I am a bruise in the moonlight, a fragile-skinned creature with shadows under my eyes, drowning in the whispers of night-purple hair. I am a living wound upon the soul.

I'm a ghost without the sense to leave the body to its eternal rest. I am a bruise, and Dane is the one who inflicts me.

The pain is there in the guilt in my father's eyes, in the horror of Dane's. He wields me as a weapon against himself, because I at least am a pain he understands. There isn't a thing in the world that can make sense of a murder, of the loss of a father, but a bruise . . . a bruise is such a simple thing to understand. It's science. It's fact.

It's me.

I tug the sleeves down to hide my wrists and turn the overhead lights back on.

The door opens and doesn't quite close, and shapes pass by me in the sudden brightness. It takes a moment to recognize Messrs. Voltemand and Cornelius, from Monticello Academy and Reggie Fortin's progressive education project. I suppose it makes sense that the Fortins wouldn't give up. What pretty words did Claudius send them away with this time? What empty promises of friendship?

Then I hear a sound that makes me sit up and pay attention to that sliver of open air between me and the office. It's the sound of a throat clearing, but it's delicate. Feminine.

Gertrude never goes into the Headmaster's office. The closest she ever went before was this room, to soothe nervous parents or comfort a child called to the house for whatever reason. She always said her work was outside of the office, that she had no business there, and yet there she is.

"Welcome, Mr. Rosencrantz, Mr. Guildenstern. Thank you very much for responding to our request, especially so quickly."

Rosencrantz? Guildenstern?

Why has Claudius brought the Toms back to Elsinore?

In their time at the Academy, Tom Rosencrantz and Tom Guildenstern were simply a pair, just Ros and Guil, or sometimes the Toms. They never had much use for me, and they didn't seem to enjoy spending time with Horatio or Laertes, but they'd put up with us to spend time with Dane.

In my nicer moments, I could call them awkward friends.

More realistically, I could acknowledge that they wanted the advantage of being friends with the Headmaster's son. Ros, nervous and fluttering, and Guil, with his endless flattery and smug over-confidence, they don't know Dane, either of them, and I think we were all privately relieved when they graduated two years ago.

Dane gets e-mails from them occasionally, usually stories of parties and conquests that sound half fabricated. They're supposed to be in college, learning business so they can one day step into their fathers' places.

I stand and silently swing the door the rest of the way open, leaning against the frame.

"You mentioned a mystery, Headmaster?"

That's Guil, always the first to speak, the first to barge in, with a nervous little laugh that follows everything he says even when it isn't a joke.

"Rumors being what they are, I know you've heard something of Dane's recent behavior," Claudius says grimly. Ice clinks against a glass, followed by the delicate chime of crystal and a splash. "We might well call it a transformation, for certainly he in no way re-sembles the boy he was. There must be something more than his father's death that has unhinged him, something more to create this behavior, but what that stress could be, I can't imagine. You two are his friends of long duration and know him well, so I would ask you a favor."

"A favor?" Guil scratches at his ear with a high-pitched titter. "What sort of favor?"

"I would ask that you stay with us awhile in one of the guest-houses and put your energies to spending time with him, to discov-ering just what afflicts him so we may find its cure."

Ice clinks again in the short pause; his throat works convul-sively to swallow.

"I am, of course, grateful that you have taken time from your courses to assist us in this and will be personally speaking with your dean to ensure that this doesn't speak against your academic records in any way."

Gertrude's heels tap on the hardwood floor of the office. "He has often spoken of you, even after your graduation," she lies gently. "I'm sure there are none to whom he is quite so attached."

Because it's the duty of a wife to assist her husband with judicious flattery where appropriate.

"If there is any way you can help us with this, we would not be remiss with our gratitude," she continues. "For your time, for your sacrifice, we wish to give you a living stipend while you're with us."

Ros coughs anxiously, a half-born sound that trails into a true cough and a gasp for breath. Gertrude discreetly hands him a handkerchief, and he thanks her with a weak smile. He's never sure of what he's saying, doesn't like to speak in front of people. "We owe a duty to the school; you could just—"

"But we are glad to assist in any way we can," Guil quickly says over him. Fabric rustles, followed by a muffled *ow*. "It's a privilege to give you any service you ask of us."

"Thank you, Rosencrantz and gentle Guildenstern."

"Thank you, Guildenstern and gentle Rosencrantz," Gertrude corrects Claudius with a wry laugh. "And if this does not come too soon upon your arrival, please, go and seek my son at once."

"God make our company healthful to him," Guil replies pompously.

Chairs scuffle and scrape against the floor. The two young men stand to stroll out of the room without even a glance in my direction. Ros gnaws on a fingernail, a muscle tic making his left eye twitch constantly. Coarse caramel hair curls tightly against his scalp and his skin, normally the color of milky coffee, has a sallow, unhealthy cast, like someone without enough fresh air. His clothing is just a little bit too big, always close to the right brands but not quite. Beside him, Guil's clothing is always just a little too tight, meant to complement a physique that he thinks is better than it is. He's darker than Ros, much darker, with a shaved head and a very narrow line of hair along his jaw that pretends to be a beard. A gold stud gleams in his left ear. They leave the door open behind them, and before they've even left the waiting room, Guil is already full of plans to make Dane spill all his secrets.

Poor Dane.

But Father's plan for Reynaldo and Laertes starts to make a little more sense. It still won't work, just as it won't work here, but Father and Claudius have broken their stalemates in very nearly the same way. Neither of them can ask their questions directly with any hope of an honest answer, so they call for others to do it for them.

There's nothing overtly malicious about what Claudius is doing; it could even spring from genuine concern. Certainly Gertrude seems relieved at the possibility of a breakthrough, of a cure.

But how can it help to bring in those who have only ever looked for the rewards of being connected to him? They don't know him; they don't know anything of what's happened this summer.

They don't know that by playing mad, he's becoming it.

Dane knows, though, or at least suspects. Perhaps he only fears. But he knows there's a strong possibility that his promises are forcing a disconnect between thought and reason, between reason and impulse.

I can see it in his eyes when he looks at my bruises.

I can hear it in how his voice trembles when he speaks of promises.

The Hamlet that Dane sees, the Hamlet he makes his promises to, is the ghost born of madness and rage and fury. That Hamlet is the one who was murdered; the Hamlet who sits with the angels is the one who died. But Dane doesn't know that, doesn't know there's more than one, and I can't tell him because it doesn't change the promises he's already made.

Because knowing he made his promises to the wrong one might make him shatter further.

Sometimes I tell myself that if I play at being a good daughter for long enough, I'll eventually become one. Like it's just a matter of practice. One day, after so many rehearsals and attempts, I'll just wake up and be the daughter my father wants to see. It's never worked, and I know it never will.

It wasn't the theory that was wrong, just the application.

The Dane that came to my room wasn't an act. He wasn't performing for anyone, couldn't have counted that I would scream and have to tell my father part of what happened.

He came to me because he's scared, because the madness he plays with becomes more and more a part of him, the part that singes my body to a tight point of pain and shatters me. The part that's scared the wonder he sees so rarely may not exist.

I never thought I would envy my own madness, but I wish I could give this breed to Dane. There's no pain in my mother's madness, only wonder. Whatever suffering comes from others, not from the madness.

But Dane . . .

Oh, Dane.

I cross my bruised wrists over my heart and push until the pain and the circling star become one. He gives me the pain he can't bear.

How much more pain will he find to give?

CHAPTER 24

My father clears his throat to finally claim his share of attention. "Headmaster, I know it's very late, but could I impose? I believe it will be worth any inconvenience."

"It's time for rounds; can this conversation be held while walking?"

"Ah . . . it can, if you so wish, but it might perhaps be best saved for a more private venue such as—"

"Excellent. Follow along, Polonius." Chair legs scrape against polished wood. "The exercise will do you good, confined behind a desk as you always are!" Claudius laughs at his own observation. After a moment, Gertrude's light, soft laugh weaves through in a delicate harmony.

It's a wife's duty to support her husband by laughing at his jokes, even when they aren't particularly funny.

Claudius walks past me without noticing me. I don't think he's ever looked directly at me. I don't think he's ever had a reason to. Gertrude smiles when she sees me, but the faint line of a concerned frown is permanently carved between her eyes these weeks past. Father gives me a concerned glance and closes his hand around my wrist as he passes, tugging me to my feet. His fingers press against the shadows of Dane's, and I bite my lip against the hiss that wants to snake through. Blood blossoms in a copper splash against my tongue, a reopened wound I don't remember receiving the first time around.

I obediently stumble along behind them until Gertrude frowns at my father and frees my wrist from his grasp. She tucks my hand into the crook of her elbow so we walk a few steps behind the men. We could be on a Sunday-after-Mass stroll, except Father and Claudius walk too briskly, too business like, men with things to do and places to be. Twice a week Claudius takes his turn at rounds with the professors, making a full circuit of the inside of the school to make sure everyone is where they're supposed to be. At this hour, everyone should be in their dormitories, though the common rooms and attached study spaces are still acceptable.

It isn't until we're actually in the school, our steps ringing on wood and tile, that Claudius seems to remember why he has three extra shadows. "Now, you were saying, Polonius?"

Father clears his throat, a little winded from the speed of our journey from the house. Perhaps Claudius was right, and he should leave his desk more often. "Brevity being the soul of wit, I will be brief: Dane is insane. Well, I call him insane, but to define true insanity, where there are so many breeds and variations, such distinctions as to render the term nearly incomprehensible, but yet, what can his behavior be but insane?"

Gertrude shakes her head with a fond half smile. "My dear Polonius, we are not all such complicated minds. Your words are lovely, but perhaps you could speak less artfully?"

"Madam, I swear I use no art at all!" he protests. If he were a chicken, all the feathers around his neck would be ruffled with his indignation. "He has succumbed to just such a breed of insanity, but it is one with a cause that I have recently—just this very evening—discovered. Ophelia, being an obedient daughter and a good girl, just gave me this." He pulls the crinkled note from his pocket and holds it up. The heavyweight cream paper was folded in smooth, flawless lines when I reluctantly gave it to him in my room, but like everything else about my father, it has become somewhat rumpled. Dane's writing, tall and precise, marches in uniform lines across the page. The letters used to be private, a way to circumvent the e-mail for which my father chose the password. He unfolds it, clears his throat again, and begins to read aloud. "'My dearest, loveliest Ophelia'—what a ridiculous greeting, that, a vile way to begin anything—'In a night of such interminable, unrelieved darkness, you are the one star in my Heaven, the only point of light and hope and goodness. The compass needle spins and spins with no direction for there is nothing to lay claim to it, nothing that pulls through the Earth to render direction, so I set my sights on you and follow you through the night, and only by gazing at you do I avoid the obstacles and terrors that plague every other path.'"

"Dane wrote this?" Gertrude asks with understandable amazement.

Claudius gives me a swift, penetrating look. "How did *your* daughter receive these letters?"

Father puffs up, his spine straight with the offense. I'm hardly hurt by the slight; Claudius is a man half blinded by glitter. Why would he notice a shadow? But there's Father, sputtering as he tries to find the right words, and I love him a little more for his indignation.

"Now, now, I mean no offense," Claudius soothes quickly, one hand extended in a placating gesture.

But it isn't enough to remove the fault entirely. Father tugs irritably at his unbuttoned blazer, an adjustment without discernible effect. "I would certainly hope so, but whatever you might think, as soon as I saw the heat of his feelings for her—as I perceived them, I must tell you that, before any word passed my daughter's lips—well, what might you think of me had I kept my silence or offered to ignore it in any fashion or even, God forbid, to have assisted it in some way! What might you think of me! But no, I bent immediately to the unpleasant, necessary task, and impressed upon my daughter the importance of severing this affection. 'Dane is a prince out of your star,' I told her. This must not be."

But Dane *is* the star, spinning and burning and keeping the lake at bay.

"I told her then that she was not to be around him without either myself or Gertrude present, that she should encourage him in no way, and as she is a good girl, she obeyed; she repelled his advances and kept her distance. As any young man rebuffed must, he fell into sadness, even into sulking, but where a young man who felt less might have soon returned to a customary lightness, Dane declined further into his present madness." Father seems pleased with the case he's pled.

Claudius leads us up a set of stairs and into the mathematics hall. In the dim night lighting, I can barely see the smirk that twists up his lips. "And you believe this?"

"It may be," says Gertrude, the words slow and reluctant. There's hope there, too, some fragile chance of an explanation to excuse her son's behavior. She reaches out to touch her husband's arm, light and delicate as a butterfly's wing. "He is very fond of Ophelia."

"And has there ever been a time, I would ask you now, that I have ever positively said a thing was so when it proved otherwise?" Father demands.

I look away to hide my smile. Poor Father, all prickly and unappreciated. Claudius is wise to know how important my father is to keeping the school running smoothly, but he hasn't yet learned how to keep him unruffled. Hamlet had a great deal of skill in that arena. I wonder if Father misses him or if it's the school he serves, regardless of who runs it. If you count when he was a student here, Claudius is his fourth headmaster.

The smirk abruptly vanishes; Claudius has realized his mistake. And yet, he is still not as careful as he should be. "Not that I know," he allows cautiously.

"Strike my head from my shoulders should I lie even by mistake. If circumstances will allow, I will find the truth of this no matter how it may be hidden."

"What do you propose?"

Now Father is in his element. Make a plan, implement it, something that should always be as easy as reciting steps off the blackboard. Paperwork always proceeds exactly as you expect it to. There's so much he's never learned about people.

"You know that Dane sometimes paces here in the school after hours, especially in the portraits hall."

"So he does," murmurs Gertrude, "for hours on end."

"We'll arrange for Ophelia to already be present, seemingly by herself, and we may observe the encounter for ourselves from the security office. If he does not love her, if this is not the reason for his disconsolate and bizarre behavior, you may expect my resignation to follow."

Father never offers to leave his job unless he is very, very certain he's right. It's his promise, his guarantee that what he says is the truth, and always that has played out like a check-mate seen from five moves away.

But he's wrong this time. Dane isn't mad for love of me. His madness comes from madness, from playing too close to a deadly truth until he can't discern the act from the fact.

And Father can't know. I could tell him now, tell all of them, and finally be free of this terrible truth. I could tell them about the poison, produce the syringe from the clothespress at the foot of the bed.

Gertrude and Father slip into easy and meaningless parental prattle—hormones and phases and other nonsense I can hardly bear. And I could silence them so easily. I could tell them how Claudius murdered his sleeping brother, stole from his corpse all life, love, and position. I could tell them of the ghost that mourns and the ghost that rages, could tell them that Dane lulls them into complacency, because what I've finally begun to understand is that madness allows for an appalling honesty.

Horatio once spent all night walking me around the gardens and grounds because honesty spilled from my lips in broken shards that cut too deeply. I'd let too many days pass without pills. I can't be disingenuous without the chemicals to teach me how to lie. It's the reason Father locks me away in the cold place until they can find the right balance of lies to make me question my truths, until they find the combinations that veil another world. I couldn't lie about why Mama took us into the lake that evening, couldn't conceal the promises she'd made.

And now Dane, too clever for the rest of us, for himself. This is why he plays his long, terrible game. When they finally believe he's mad, he can say things no one else could get away with, the things that aren't polite or fit for company. He can use his words as weapons and watch the truth bleed from their eyes.

If he can get that far.

For the first time, Claudius pins that cold stare on me and studies me from head to toe. His thoughts are uncharacteristically near the surface. Who is this creature? Who is she that Dane could ever lose himself in her? What game is she trying to play? "I think, Polonius, your plan may well be the right one."

I can object, but no one will listen. Not even Gertrude, who believes in the difference between the concerns of men and the duties of women. No one asks me if I'll do this thing, no one asks for my opinions, and no one will hear it even if I offer it.

The star burns in my chest. A little brighter. A little hotter. A little larger. It expands into my lungs with tongues of flame that scald my breath into nothingness, not even ash to mark that it once existed. Heat blazes behind my eyes, dries them out to keep the tears from forming. I am a ghost, a bruise, a whisper.

And now . . .

Claudius nods once, a sharp, decisive gesture. "We will try it."

. . . now I'm a blade that kisses with death on my lips.

CHAPTER 25

Sleep eludes me and I'm grateful for it, grateful for the dry and burning eyes that stare at the painted-over holes in my ceiling because the pain is so much easier than the dreams that await me. Every time I close my eyes, even for a moment, blood and blades battle against an endless spill of ice blue, cold blue, drowned skin blue. The star spins with a steady murmur of *danedanedanedanedane*, but the bells from the lake toll in a different rhythm; none of it matches the laughter of the morgens as they play through the dark, frigid waters that blaze with thousands of candles of a forgotten city.

When the morning comes, I look like I haven't slept, so Father lays the hoarseness of my voice to fatigue and not to the dark ring of bruises I hide beneath a turtleneck sweater. He accepts my silence through early Mass and even puts his hand to my shoulder several times through the service. From him, this is effusive affection indeed. I shouldn't be surprised, though. A headmaster gave his blessing to a plan *he* constructed, and Father does love a vote of confidence. Cheerful and oblivious, he can indulge in this expansive mood. He even gives Horatio a magnanimous smile when my friend asks to escort me back to Headmaster's House.

I know Dane doesn't tell Horatio everything that passes between us, but I've always thought he must say something. Now I know he does, because Horatio walks so slowly that the distance stretches easily between us and everyone else. When the others are out of sight, he stops on the path and turns to face me. His hazel eyes are darker than they should be. His hand trembles finely as he gestures to the neck of the sweater. "May I?"

I tug the fabric down without a word.

His breath hisses through his teeth, making me wonder how bad the bruises look. His fingertips gently brush against my throat. "I went to check on you, after he told me. You weren't there."

"Father."

"He saw?"

I shake my head and adjust the fabric so it conceals everything it should. "Something else. They're springing a trap, Horatio."

"I saw the Toms crossing to the south guesthouse last night."

Easier to nod than to speak. We resume our progress up the path, each step slow and carefully placed to give us as much time as possible. With each forward motion, the syringe sways in the pocket of my skirt to tap against my thigh. I clutched it through the night to help keep myself awake, the glass cold in my palm, and brought it down with me to church for the same purpose. The touch of it makes my skin crawl, pushes the exhaustion just a little farther away.

"Just the one trap?" he asks finally.

I shake my head again. The Toms are one trap; I am another.

I am the blade that sings silver in the moonlight.

"I don't think I've ever seen him so scared as last night."

"I could have pushed him away."

"Could you?"

No, of course not. The ability to speak the words is always there. It's the will that's lacking.

But he doesn't press me on it because he already knows the honest answer. He's heard the truths that taste of blood and tears.

"What happens if you let him go too far?" He puts an arm around my shoulders like the touch comforts him. "If he hurt you that badly, Ophelia . . . it would destroy him."

"I trust him."

"He doesn't trust himself." We stop outside the door for another moment of peace before all the games and the traps resume. He glances around, then presses a gentle kiss against my temple. "Promise me you won't let him choke you again."

"Horatio—"

"Please. It'll make me feel better, and it'll make Dane feel better. You bruise easily, Ophelia, we've always known that, so the marks on your wrists, on your arms . . . you have those pretty frequently. Don't let him put a hand to your throat again."

"He scared you last night."

He gives a short, humorless laugh. Autumn cold leeches the color from his skin. "I think he scared everyone last night, except you."

"And that scares you most of all."

"Yes." He sighs and a plume of grey trails from his chapped lips. It's unexpectedly lovely, like the words have an image, a shape. "Ophelia . . . I am never scared of you. But more and more, I'm scared for you."

An important distinction, and one I can understand. I wrap both my arms around one of his to borrow some of his warmth and bury my face in the thick knitted scarf with its panels of school colors. "He's in so much pain."

"It's one thing to help someone bear their pain. What he does to you . . ." His other hand rises to press so very gently against the bruises on one side of my neck. "This is unacceptable, no matter how much pain he's in, and even you know that. You cannot let him do this to you again."

"I promise."

"Thank you."

We stay outside until I start to shiver in my coat, goose bumps stabbing my skin through my tights. Weather like this usually makes me plead with Gertrude for at least one set of trousers because I freeze in the skirts, but she insists that it's inappropriate for women to wear them. I have no allowance, no money of my own to spend, so I can't even purchase them on my own. When my shivers grow obvious, Horatio turns away to open the door and hold it for me.

In the front hall, Dane sits on the fourth step of the staircase, all in black. I can hardly remember what he looks like in color. Black is all he's worn since his father's death, an entire wardrobe of grief and recrimination. He attended Mass that morning but left before the benediction; I wouldn't have expected him to come to the house. He's waiting for something, but I don't think it's us. He looks up when we enter, his eyes wide and horror-struck at the sight of me. I would offer him comfort, but I don't know that he would believe it from me.

But Horatio sits beside him and nudges his arm with an elbow. "She's fine, Dane. Promise."

"Ophelia?"

Shucking out of my coat, I sit to his other side and lean my head against his shoulder. "I'm fine," I whisper. "Promise."

"Would you lie to protect me, Ophelia?"

"Do you think I could?"

He doesn't answer. Because he doesn't know? Or because he doesn't think it needs to be said?

Horatio's stomach growls in the sudden silence. It startles a laugh out of all of us; just for a moment, we feel like we used to. "Is there a reason you haven't gone into breakfast yet?" he asks, the words distorted by a chuckle.

"Keith was supposed to meet me here, but he's late."

"Keith . . . Keith Hunter?"

"The one and only."

Horatio and I trade a look, identical expressions of confusion on our faces. Though he's a senior like the boys, Keith Hunter isn't someone they spend much time with. Theatre has never been one of the prize jewels of Elsinore Academy, and those who pursue it tend to keep to their own kind. There's something almost menacing about watching them slide in and out of character, their effortless falsehoods that feel so real. They don't rely solely on words to lie; they lie with everything they are.

Horatio licks his lips, wetting them to speak, and winces at the sting. I can see the question take shape on his lips, but before he can give it voice, the door opens again. All three of us look up. Dane's astonishment shakes his entire body.

"Toms!"

Gertrude asked them to find her son last night, to start immediately on their mission, but Dane's shock is real. Whatever they did last night, it didn't involve finding Dane. They shiver in clothing unsuited for the swiftly approaching winter. Guil's dark skin is ashy from the cold. Ros swallows hard and looks to his companion to take the lead.

"What are you two doing here?" Dane asks and lurches from the step to shake their hands. "Aren't you supposed to be off faking classes, deflowering freshmen, and making your parents thoroughly ashamed of you?"

"We're taking a break from all that; your uncle was kind enough to let us crash-land here for a few weeks."

"Flunked out already?"

"Recharging our batteries."

"Then what's new with you, that you need to be recharged?"

"Nothing at all, Dane; the world's grown honest!"

"Did the Rapture happen and I missed it?" laughs Dane. He looks so genuinely happy it makes my heart hurt. He grips both men by the shoulders, shares his smile between them. "But seriously. Why are you here?"

"We're here to see you, Dane," Guil tells him. He almost seems sincere until his hand rises to twirl the gold stud in his ear, a nervous habit he's had as long as I've known him. "I don't much like my old man, but I can't imagine losing him, and you and your pop . . . you two were close. You must be having a rough time."

His words do what his appearance did not. Dane's eyes narrow, study the men he calls friends. Ros sways back and forth, ever so slightly, shifting his weight between his feet. After a moment, Dane glances back over his shoulder and meets my eye.

I don't know what he sees in my face. Perhaps the dread that tracks the fidgets of the Toms. Perhaps the pain that comes from being forged into a blade. We learned in one of our history classes how swords are made, how they're softened and beaten and folded again and again and again until the shape is right and the red-hot steel plunged into water.

"Come on," he says too lightly, his eyes still on my face. "You were sent for."

"Dane—"

"Your faces are your own confession. Claudius and Mother sent for you."

"To do what?" Guil asks with a laugh. "What could they possibly—"

"That you must tell me." He turns back to them, but despite the mild smile, all the joy is gone from his body. Every muscle is written over in tension, a wound spring about to explode with violence. "But please. We have been friends for so long, and if we have meant anything to each other, if our friendship is as important to you as it is to me, then I beg you. Just tell me the truth: were you sent for or not?"

Ros gives a nervous little titter. "What are you saying?"

"I'm saying you need to tell me the Goddamn truth. Were you sent for?"

"Yes, Dane, we were sent for," Guil snaps. He rubs a hand over his closely shaven head. "Your mother and uncle were concerned; they thought . . . they thought you'd appreciate a visit. They made it possible for us to come."

"Oh, yes, I'm sure they were very concerned." Dane returns to his space between me and Horatio and leans back on his elbows on the step behind. It isn't just his voice; everything about him mocks them, from his casual pose to the half smile that teases about his lips. "Shall I tell you exactly what makes them so concerned?"

Claudius meant to spring a trap; now he's just given the cat new mice to torment.

Of course, cats have a way of eating the mice they play with. What that promises for the Toms probably doesn't bear thinking of.

197

"I have lately—though I have no idea why—left off all my normal hobbies," Dane continues. "Nothing's funny, nothing's light." Guil fidgets with his phone, and in one seamless motion, Dane snatches it from him. He launches the browser and types as he talks. "Everything is bleak and depressing, like the whole Earth is just sterile. And it should be an odd thing, right? Look around you, this beautiful place with as many lights as Heaven, as much gold as Midas' hall, but to my mind it's nothing but a foul pit of stench and disease." A page loads on the phone's screen, and Dane holds up a choice bit of pornography that makes Horatio close his eyes. Tapping the back of the phone for emphasis, he continues. "What a piece of work is man! How noble in reason, how infinite in ability, in form and motion how admirable, in action how like an angel, in understanding how like a god, and yet—so much value do we lay on dust. No, I have no delight in my fellow man." He glances at the screen. "Nor woman, either, though your smiles say differently."

His sour look makes them quickly swallow their leering laughter. Ros shakes his head so hard his neck pops. "We weren't thinking any such thing!"

"No?" Dane arches a dark eyebrow but otherwise doesn't change his disapproving study. "Why did you laugh then?"

"Well . . ." Ros gives his partner a panicked look, then forges ahead. "It's just that, well . . . if you have no delight in your fellow man, the theatre geeks won't get much thanks from you, and we bumped into Keith Hunter on our way here. He wanted us to tell you that he'd be late; his sister isn't feeling well so he's taking her to the nurse."

"But he's still intrigued by whatever you wanted to discuss," adds Guil, because he can't stand to not be part of a conversation.

Dane gives him a tight, feral smile. "I see my patience will be rewarded. How like my uncle I am after all."

Despite the well-concealed dismay on his face, Horatio can barely hold back a laugh. I bite my lip against the same impulse. Dane can be cruel when he puts his mind to it, but oh, what a wonder it is to watch him play.

There's a knock against the door, solid and confident.

Guil seizes upon the sound with relief. "That must be Keith."

Dane pushes gracefully to his feet. "Gentlemen, you are welcome again to Elsinore, but my uncle-father and aunt-mother have brought you here needlessly."

"How so?"

He actually grins at them, but there's something bitter and hateful beneath it. "I'm only mad north-north-west. When the wind is from the south, I know a hawk from a handsaw."

Dane unmutes Guil's phone just as the piece of work on the video reaches a very vocal climax, tossing the groaning device back to its owner.

Horatio loses the battle with his restraint and laughs softly into his hands to muffle the sound.

The knock sounds again, and this time my father appears from the door of the dining room, his mug of murky coffee still in hand. Guil tries frantically to kill the sound on his phone. "Five of you standing here, and none capable of answering the door?" he grumbles, but he shakes his head with an almost smile and crosses towards the main door.

Dane's eyes track his progress. "Look, Guil, and you too—that great baby you see there is not yet out of his diapers."

Ros and Guil have no particular love for my father; he can give them no advantage. Guil smirks and wedges his hands into too-tight pockets. "Perhaps he is just in them again. They do say old age is like a second childhood."

Father ignores him with grave dignity and pulls open the heavy door. It frames a young man of average height, his ashy blond hair slightly messy around his face. His brown eyes flick over each face in turn, identifying each person present. He's the type of boy you notice when you pass but don't look back over your shoulder to see again. Normally, at any rate. When he's in a role, it's impossible to look away from him.

Keith gives Father a polite nod. "Hello, Dean Castellan. Dane asked me to come up."

"Dane, you have a guest."

"Dane, you have a guest," Dane echoes. "O Jephthah, judge of Israel, what a treasure hadst thou!"

Horatio straightens abruptly, reaches behind Dane's knees to touch my shoulder.

But I recognize the allusion, as Father doesn't, as the Toms do not. But Jephthah . . . somehow it doesn't surprise me that Dane uses this name. He must feel a great connection with a man who made such a foolish vow.

Dane swore revenge.

Jephthah swore sacrifice.

Judges 11:31. Every girl, sophomore and up, would understand Dane.

For victory over the Ammonites, Jephthah swore to honor God with the burned sacrifice of the first person he saw upon returning home. The soldiers entered the town of Mizpah greeted by music, and drawn by the sound of tambourines, his daughter danced from the house in joy.

A vow is a vow, a promise, especially when made to God.

At Horatio's small sound of question, I look down and realize that my hand is pressed against my chest, fingertips over the star of my heart and palm over the place where two months has yet to take away the phantom feeling of Dane's class ring.

Because what Horatio may not remember—but I think Dane does—is that his daughter accepts that an oath must be fulfilled. His oath was foolish, given without thought to the consequences. Her love was real.

"A treasure?" echoes Father.

"A treasure beyond value: a beautiful daughter and no more, but he loved her exceedingly well."

Father's eyes snap to me, and I can see the triumph in them. He thinks this feeds his theory, that this proves him right.

"Aren't I right, old Jephthah?

"If you are intent on calling me such, then yes, I have a daughter I love exceedingly well."

"No, no, that doesn't follow!"

"Then what does?" Father asks with careful patience.

"Learn from the mockery that is your daughter's education. I hear it is the pinnacle of rudeness to so ignore any who've come so expressly to see me." He finally acknowledges Keith with a nod and a secretive smile. "Thank you for coming. Sit here in my place." He jumps up and pounds the space he left. "We have much to speak of."

"Um, Dane—"

"Surely you'll forgive me this one shred of business, Tom?" Dane asks Guil without looking away from Keith. He takes two steps down and turns as Keith drops casually between Horatio and me, but one step down. "I thought to present a show, a gift as it were, and there's no one better than you for such a thing."

"I wouldn't be here if I weren't already curious, Danemark. You needn't bait the trap any further."

Except the trap isn't for Keith. It's for the old man who watches with avid interest, for the pair of fools who have already missed the biggest clue they could hope for.

"A show, Dane?"

With a sudden burst of energy, Dane leaps down from the stairs and half lands across my father. The mug drops from startled hands and shatters on the tile, coffee spilling in a dark flood. "A show, old man, a show! A performance, a play, a wonderful confection!"

The syringe in my pocket is cold against my fingers, the clay bead rough but secure. I draw it out, hidden within the curve of my hand, and offer it to Keith. He just looks at me and I shrug, aware of Horatio's eyes on me as well. "You'll need it. For when he gets to the point. Don't let him see it, but . . . if I'm right . . . you'll need it for what he wants you to do."

"And how do you know what he wants me to do, little Ophelia?" he asks me, not entirely unkind.

"Did you know that Jephthah's daughter is never named?"

Keith doesn't understand; Horatio does. His eyes close against a physical wave of pain, his hand drops from my shoulder. He understands.

Father scowls at the mess and impatiently shoves away Dane's weight. "Ophelia, come away, this is no place for you right now, not without other ladies present. Go to your room; I'll bring you breakfast presently."

"Yes, Jephthah's daughter, go weep in the hills, for you shall never marry."

Keith looks up sharply, his entire body taut like a hunting dog on point. Now, only a little, he understands.

I leave my coat for the maids and walk up the stairs, Dane's laughter wrapping around to blister my skin.

CHAPTER 26

When Father brings me my breakfast, he brings also an admonishment to remain in my room until he comes for me. After all, the trap will yield nothing if Dane takes the bait before there are witnesses. He scolds me lightly for my company downstairs, but his mind is already on the scene to come and the expectation that his theory will be proven correct.

I so rarely find an appetite; his words and mood rob me of it entirely. The breakfast cools, untouched, on my nightstand as I change into something suited to skulking in a corner of the school waiting for Dane to stumble upon me. My skin itches from the turtleneck, a symptom of the cold outside, so I wind and knot a dark, filmy scarf around my neck to hide the bruises.

Sitting on the edge of the bed, I reach between the mattresses and remove the plastic bag of forgotten pills, missed days that number far more than they should. Guilt cradles the madness, but it won't keep me from adding today's pills to the mix. I can't take them without food, but eating will only make me nauseous and then neither food nor medications will stay down. There seems little point to making the attempt. I pry open the lid for Sunday and empty the contents into my hand.

Five pills. Five chemical wonders to blind me to the world.

Four, I suppose; I'm fairly sure one of them is actually birth control, to keep my hormones regular despite all the chemicals.

Not that Father would ever speak to me of something like birth control. Even Gertrude can't bring herself to discuss such things with me. It was Nurse Jacobson who had to teach me about various feminine products and what to expect. And it's Nurse Jacobson who silently keeps me stocked with such items as I require them. She once offered to buy me a private supply of them, but the thought of Reynaldo pawing through them looking for secrets made my stomach curdle.

Four little pills, and the question of normality and madness decided between them. If I took three or two or even just one would I be a little less mad? Not cut off entirely from the world I love and fear but sane enough that the wildness in my eyes would be gone?

I separate out the pink one, the one I'm almost positive is the contraceptive, and swallow it dry even as I spill the others into the bag. They clink against those of the other forgotten or skipped days. One of those days is my birthday, the one day I'm allowed to skip without guilt, but there are so many other days in there, a calendar of sorrow and seduction and rage.

Metal scrapes against the door, and panic leaps to throb in my battered throat. I shove the bag beneath me to hide it and scramble for a reason to send Father away even just for a few minutes.

But it isn't Father.

It's Dane.

He closes the door quietly behind him, pulls a wooden wedge from his pocket, and jams it between the wood and the carpet. It isn't a lock; it won't entirely keep anyone out, but it will slow them down. I should ask why, but I never ask Dane the questions that Polonius' daughter should. He shrugs out of his black blazer and tosses it across the hope chest at the foot of the bed. Metal flashes at the small of his back, but he faces me before I can see it properly.

"When it comes to your own safety, you would lie to me," he says quietly. He kneels down in front of me and sits back on his heels, his hands palm down on my thighs. I can see bruises and splits across his swollen knuckles, the blood-heavy darkness across one side of his hand that says he's broken something. How many hours has he spent punishing himself in the weight room, trying to exercise something that's too much a part of him to kill? "To protect me."

"Dane—"

"I need to see them."

I should argue. I should lie. I should tell him they're nothing, that they can barely be noticed.

I'm better at lying by omission.

My fingers unwind the loose knot at my collarbone and tug the scarf away until it slithers in a silken fall between my breasts to pool in my lap. My hair falls forward to follow it, to continue the masquerade as a whole person. My hands brush against his on the way to the hem of my sweater. I bunch it between my fingers, the cashmere soft and comforting, and slowly pull it over my head and down my arms.

Air hisses between his teeth, and he closes his eyes against a wave of pain that swamps over me. His hands slide up my hips, around my waist, and gently pull me off the bed until I sit across his thighs, our faces level with each other. Fingers continue their path up my spine, curve around my shoulder and down my arms until he can encircle my wrists and bring them up for his inspection. Dark grey eyes trace the marks of his pain, deepest where the delicate bones ground together beneath his grip.

His lips press against the damage, soft flares of pain in their wake. When he finishes with one hand, he places my palm flat against his heart, the beat erratic but strong, and moves to the other. Tears gleam in his eyes, splash against my skin, and these too he kisses away, every touch an apology.

A tendril of flame reaches out to him from the star in my heart, tries to connect to him, to share the warmth that keeps the lake at bay.

His hands brush against my face, slide into my hair to anchor it back from my face, tilt my head back, and he continues his apologies to the necklace that blooms around my throat. Each touch is slow and unhurried, stripped of the frenzy that so often jerks him away like a marionette with too many strings. All I can see is the scarred plaster of my ceiling where my fan used to be, so I close my eyes and blaze with his fire. Finally, his mouth finds mine, a caress as sweet and gentle as bathing my bruises in his tears.

When his hands brought me trembling too close to the dark abyss, he breathed air into my battered lungs. He takes it back from me now, shares it between us in a prayer too fragile for words, for thought. Stars are fire, fire as hungry as the cold, dark waters of the lake, and the oxygen burns away too quickly, leaves me gasping against his lips even though the brilliancy of that colored darkness is so delicious. Dane pulls away, rests his forehead against the edge of the mattress by my cheek.

"There's a question, Ophelia," he whispers against my ear.

"Only one?"

"Only one. Only ever one. A single question: to be or not to be?" He lifts his head away, one hand still woven through my hair, to meet my eyes. There's a deadly, feral intensity in his gaze, even as his voice turns over the words in the closest thing to calm he's known for so long. His other hand slides down my side, my leg, to rest against my knee. "Is it more worthy, more noble, to endure this chaotic hell or to stand ground against a sea of troubles and, by standing, end them?

"To die . . . but that's sleep, no more." His eyes plead for confirmation. "And by sleeping we end the heartache and the million wounds of the flesh that we inherit." His hands shake against my skin in a fine tremor, like a ballad's final notes reverberating on the harp strings. "Isn't that the best we could wish for? To die, to sleep; to sleep, to dream . . ." His hand clenches in my hair, pulling my head back, and he presses his lips against the ring of bruises on my throat. "But we suffer such terrors in life. The dreams that come in that sleep of death must give us pause, and that's what keeps us back, isn't it?

"Who would willingly bear the assault of time, the oppressor's wrong, the insult of pride, the injustice of law too slow and unwieldy, the offense of power and not integrity rising to success, and the constant contempt so often smeared on good men by those who are only ever less?" His words tumble over each, white-hot and too painful, blood spilling from wounds that should be invisible. "Who, when he might lay himself to rest with no more than . . ." His hand moves back up my leg, but this time there's a cold kiss of metal, a scrape of too-sharp edges. He lifts a gun between us, so close our lips brush against the steel. It's a small gun, meant for concealment, with the Danemark crest tooled into the handle. The flash of metal at the small of his back. "Who would tolerate all this?" His eyes beg an answer from me, but the hemorrhage can't be stopped. "Except we dread what comes after, that undiscovered country from which no traveler may ever return . . . No one, except you. You know, but the rest of us fear and let that fear chain us to cowardice and conscience and sap all hope of action from a moment too mired in thought to become action. But you, you traveled there, and you returned. Why would you ever want to return?"

The barrel, short and compact, drags an angry line down my jaw as he presses it into the hollow of my throat. His thumb clicks back the hammer, and suddenly my pulse thunders against the delicate skin, so violent I wonder it doesn't roll down the barrel in a ripple, a peal, a sound more than the rush of blood in my ears.

"You didn't even have to answer the question to find out." The gun moves away and presses now against his temple, his gaze never leaving mine. "What happens, Ophelia? At that moment when you cross the boundary, when you enter that new land and leave this pain and despair behind. Does something welcome you? All promises would be left behind, vengeance simply a missed opportunity, and is there ever truly a guarantee of being consigned to Hell? Can Hell truly be worse that this?

"Do you have any idea how lucky you were, Ophelia? To find that peace without any sacrifice?" He laughs despairingly, and the gun drops to the carpet. "I'd give anything just for a moment of that peace, death without cowardice or choice, a glorious accident that claims all guilt and burden. And your mother, how much luckier, to escape entirely these relentless coils and not be so roughly yanked back. Was she grateful, do you think? Did she understand how lucky she was that such an accident came her way?"

"It wasn't an accident."

The honesty shreds my lips, and I swallow hard against a mouth of dry fear and blood. He stares at me; his hands tighten against me in a spasmodic gesture that just as abruptly releases me for fear of bruising further, but the fire that burns in my chest has leapt into his eyes, his soul, to blaze like a beacon in an endless night.

"Say that again," he demands harshly.

There's so little breath, even less voice, but somehow the words find shape a second time. "It wasn't an accident."

"What happened?"

"Arrogance and love too blind built the City of Ys beneath the expanse of the tide," I whisper brokenly. Mama's voice bleeds into mine, the memory of her words shaping mine, but now, too, is the burn of Dane's kisses, of his touch that makes me yearn and blaze and *need*. "The King caused a great bronze wall to be built around the city to hold back all of Nature's power and fury, for the Princess Dahut loved the ocean. The night she took a stranger in red armor to her bed, a terrible storm, such as sailors name widow-makers, crashed against the walls, shook the city until every bell in the cathedrals tolled, and Dahut told the stranger not to fear, for the walls could only be breached by the key that lived around her father's neck.

"The stranger's lips traced poison into her skin; he kissed the words into her mind, until with a single thrust the idea became hers, planted in her need for the man in her bed, and she stole the key from the neck of her sleeping father. Together, Dahut and the stranger in red armor opened the gates at highest tide, and the storm-swollen waters swept in to drown all the city. But it waits."

"The city?"

"Beneath the lake. When it's quiet you can hear the bells of the cathedrals; and deep in the waters thousands of candles burn like a reflection of the heavens. Mama promised she'd take me there." My voice shakes against the memory of the cold place. I've been so good; I haven't told anyone, not since the first time, but now Dane's pain leeches the words from my skin and oh, God, I don't want to go back to the cold place, but he's here, right here, and I can't go anywhere but where he leads. "Dahut fled to the embrace of dozens, hundreds, of men because she had such a terrible emptiness the ocean waited to fill, and so did Mama. She promised. Such a beautiful city, sleeping beneath the waves and waiting for Paris to fall so it can rise again, such music from the bells that floats through the dark stillness, and she promised, so she took us into the water so we could go down and see the city. Because she promised." I close my eyes, immediately open them again because the lake is there in the darkness. "It wasn't an accident; it was a promise."

"A promise." His hands curl into fists in the coverlet, his entire face transformed by the fierce, terrible satisfaction that writes the features of a raging ghost into living flesh. One hand tears the plastic of the bag of pills, no longer hidden beneath me, and he drags it down between us. Wonder joins the fury, the dark joy. "She found the city, didn't she? When our fathers dragged you from the water, she went on without you and found it?"

I nod helplessly. For the first time, I understand why others are afraid of me, because this madness is so alien, so familiar.

So beautiful.

So heart-breakingly beautiful.

Or perhaps just heart-breaking.

"And when a storm shakes the school, you go out and dance in the rain," he breathes. His pulse races against his throat; his chest rises and falls in a sharp, jerky rhythm that's almost a pant. "Your mother's daughter."

His lips crash against mine, swallow the cry of pain at hearing the words spoken with such certainty, such truth. Such joy.

"And you promised her, didn't you, Ophelia?" he murmurs against my heated skin. "You promised her you'd see the city one day."

"She promised."

"And so did you!" He lurches to his feet, drags me up with him, and yanks me into the bathroom, the bag of pills still clutched in one hand. He spins me on the tile and slams the door behind us, trapping us in the small space. His manic laughter stokes the star in my chest until the flames sear away the bruises in my throat. "These pills are supposed to hide you from her promise, from your promise. Your father would make a liar of you, Ophelia, when our honor is the only thing we can claim as our own. You let him shape your world into lies."

"Dane!"

With a swift, sudden gesture, he upends the bag. Dozens, hundreds of pills pour into the porcelain bowl of the toilet, a pebbled river of white, blue, yellow, and pink. We both stare at them, at the ripples that bob across the disturbed surface of the water. Is this what he did with his? Threw them away against the temptation of taking them, of moderating the grief with chemicals? He takes my hand and thrusts it against the cold metal of the handle. "Don't let him, Ophelia."

His fingers tighten around mine, but don't press. He could so easily make me press the handle down; it wouldn't even take much to do it.

But he doesn't.

He just watches me, his hand warm against mine, and waits for me to make the decision.

Which, more than anything, makes me decide. Dane and Horatio are the only ones who respect my decisions, who give me the space to make them, even if I never say what they are. They don't make them for me and simply assume that I'll obey, that I'll follow along with no will and no mind as I so often do. Under Dane's steady regard, in light of his patience as he waits for me to make my own decision, I take a deep breath and shove my weight down against the steel handle.

Sound rattles around the small bathroom as the pills disappear in a swirl of water, accompanied by Dane's rich laughter. It takes several flushes for all of them to disappear.

Then there's nothing left, no trace of forgotten days or chemicals or the hope of being a good daughter.

Dane gently pushes me back against the door, leans against me until his warmth seeps through my skin to join the inferno in my heart. He fumbles at the back of his neck, and then he's kissing me, hot and sweet, and something snags in the fine hairs at the nape of my neck. A small weight settles between my breasts.

For a blinding, searing moment, everything is right.

When he pulls away, he presses his lips against my forehead, the top of my head.

His fingers tremble against a ring of silver studded with a dark sapphire and two rectangles of icy-blue aquamarine. I bring my hand over his, press against it until his fingers splay across my skin, the ring against his palm. I've felt this phantom weight for two months, this piece of me so violently torn away, this piece of Dane that costs no pain to bear.

"The play's the thing, Ophelia," he whispers against my temple. "The play's the thing."

I tilt my head back against the door and capture his haunted smile in a kiss. I'll never be a good daughter, never be what Father, what Laertes, needs me to be.

But I can be what Dane needs.

Just by being myself, no chemical lies, by being a night-dark bruise against moonlight skin, I can be what Dane needs.

Which means I can be what I need.

I can feel the toll of the bells in my bones.

PART IV

CHAPTER 27

Dane sprawls across my bed as he watches me pull my sweater back into place, his eyes following my hands as they drape and knot the scarf around my neck. The gun sits on the mattress beside him, all six bullets pulled from the chamber to puddle in a curve of the coverlet nearby. He picks at my cold breakfast, grimaces with each swallow of rubbery eggs and soggy toast, and I know he's only doing it to make it look as though I've eaten.

The slight pressure of his ring against my sternum feels right, like it belongs there and I've been incomplete in its absence. Even with the chain through it, the ring is too big for any of my fingers, but I try it on each one as I tell him of the traps his uncle sets for him. He's already figured out the one that involves the Toms, but there's another one yet to spring, and that weapon is me.

He laughs at that and pulls me to him on the bed to tease me breathless with kisses. He says he knows what he needs to do, that I need to trust him just a little longer. His fingers trace the bruises through my scarf when he tells me that there'll be a dinner tonight, a special one followed by a play, purely for the denizens of Head-master's House. This is why he sent for Keith—and why I gave Keith the syringe—but I don't ask him for details. After all, I'm part of the audience, part of the trap, and I'm a terrible liar.

One by one, he loads the bullets back into the chamber and tucks the gun into the back of his waistband. The gun's hidden entirely by his jacket. I should ask him why he even has it, but I don't. I'm not entirely sure I want to know. Whether he aims it at himself or his uncle, I don't want to know, don't want to wonder or fear or anticipate. He kisses me once more before he pulls the wooden wedge from under the door and leaves me with a delicate bouquet of primrose blossoms.

Eternal love, or so Gertrude's book tells me.

I open my Bible and composition book and arrange them across the bed to give an excuse for the rumpled covers. In another school it might be calculus or physics, something both challenging and useful, and chemistry and home economics wouldn't be nearly the same class. But I'm a sophomore girl at Elsinore Academy, so it's Old Testament Studies and only the math needed to manage household accounts. I can feel the ring against my skin with every breath, every motion. I've only just pulled out my current assignment when Father pushes open my door.

"It's time, Ophelia, come along."

Obediently, I slide off the bed and back into my heels to follow him into the hall.

"We've received an invitation for this evening, along with the Danemarks," he informs me. "It seems Dane wishes us to see a performance he's arranged, and the Headmaster has consented. To be active in something with other students, perhaps it will do him some good."

When did Dane get the clasp repaired?

It didn't occur to me to wonder at the moment he replaced the chain around my neck, but I remember the clasp breaking when he ripped it from me, the only time I have ever tried to walk away. He had to have gotten it repaired at some point and then wore the ring around his neck rather than on his finger where it belonged.

He was waiting for me.

Father's talking, but I can't hear him over the endless, joyous whisper of the star in my heart that murmurs Dane's name to dispel the darkness.

We walk away from the house, up into the school proper and

into the portrait hall. Father sits me gently on one of the padded benches beneath Iphigenia Danemark, the only headmistress we have ever had. She led the school while her husband fought in the First World War, then stepped aside when he returned, just a wife and hostess again. I meet her painted blue eyes and try to see if she ever regretted that, but it's only paint. Father presses a book into my hands. Claudius walks in, greets Father with a nod and me with a gimlet stare that would peel flesh from bone if I weren't so used to Dane.

I run my fingers over the gilt lettering on the leather cover. A prayer book?

"It will give you a reason to be off on your own," Father answers my unspoken question. "Certainly we often use the appearance of devotion and faith to hide deeper quandaries, so even the Devil may shape a prayer to go undetected."

Claudius winces.

"We will be in the security room," continues Father, oblivious as ever. "You have nothing to fear, Ophelia; we'll see everything on the cameras. We will resolve this in a short time."

"He's nearly here," Claudius reminds him. Without another word, they disappear behind the heavy navy blue tapestry picked out in silver, white, and ice blue.

There are four tapestries in the hall of portraits. Three of them conceal alcoves with comfortable benches, very popular with students for stealing some privacy with significant others. The fourth opens into a narrow hallway that leads directly to the security office. The hall of portraits is just off the main hall and the grand double doors that front the school, so they use this hall to respond quickly to any unauthorized guests at the front door. The red eyes of the cameras wink at me from the ceiling. Father and Claudius watch even now.

With one fingernail, I separate the gilt-edged, tissue-thin pages and let the book fall open across my lap. *Oh Merciful God, take pity on those souls who have no particular friends or intercessors to recommend them to Thee, who either through the negligence of those who are alive or through length of time are forgotten by their friends and by all. Spare them, O Lord, and remember Thine own mercy when others forget to appeal to it. Let not the souls which Thou hast created be parted from Thee, their Creator. May the souls of all the faithful departed, through the mercy of God, rest in peace. Amen.*

Dane's smile tugs at my lips, the smile that delights in irony and words and meanings, in inversions and subversions and sometimes even perversions, all the many angles and shadows and shades of words, words, words.

The prayer for the forgotten dead.

But Hamlet isn't forgotten, and Mama didn't stay dead. We name them in our prayers to work against the sins they accumulated in life, the faults left without expiation and absolution, but one's a morgen and one is split into two ghosts released from the cleansing flames of Purgatory, and the prayers do nothing for them.

Spare them, O Lord.

A shadow falls over the pages, and I look up to see Dane reading the words upside down. He meets my eyes and raises a questioning brow. Hidden from view by his body, I shrug delicately, and a fleeting smile flashes across his face.

"The fair Ophelia," he greets sardonically, his voice just loud enough to be picked up through the security mics without straining. He tucks a delicate cluster of love-lies-bleeding into one of the pins holding my hair back from my face. "Do you remember my sins in your prayers, nymph?"

I don't count his sins because I bear his pain. They're different tasks. And so far as my father knows, as far as Claudius knows, I haven't been alone with him in two months. "Hello, Dane," I reply, trying to be what anyone else would call normal. "How have you been?"

"I humbly thank you. Well."

Father has tucked a reminder into the book—between the last page and the back cover are several letters Dane wrote me that I had to turn over to Father. I rub my fingertips along the heavyweight paper, gather the letters into my hand. I hold them out, slightly to the side so they can point to the flashing light of the opposite camera. His eyes follow the progress, and he nods to show me that he understands. "I have letters of yours that I have wished to redeliver. Please, take them back."

"No, not I," he says lazily and backs three steps away. "I never gave you anything."

"You know right well you did, and with them, words so sweet as made the letters even more precious. But now the sweetness is gone, and so I ask you to take them back." I press my hand against my heart, my palm over the ring. One of the pages slices my lip and the taste of blood blooms on my tongue. "Rich gifts grow poor when givers prove unkind."

He grins at me, the expression hidden from our audience. I've known that grin for as long as I can remember: come and play. "Are you a virgin?"

"Dane!"

"Are you beautiful?"

"I don't know what you mean."

He snatches the letters from my hand and tosses them up into the air. The pages separate, float down like feathers from an angel's wings. "If you are both chaste and beautiful, you should admit no interaction between your chastity and your beauty."

"Could beauty have better interaction than with chastity?"

"The power of beauty will sooner transform chastity from what it is to a whore than the force of chastity can translate beauty into its likeness. It is easier to fall than to fly." He crouches before me, traces my face with one strong hand, and I want nothing more than to close my eyes and lean into a touch that has nothing to do with pain or sorrow, even if it is for a game. But there's an audience and a script I don't know and now isn't the time. "I did love you once."

I swallow hard. To hear such a word in a game . . . perhaps the pain is still here after all. "Indeed, you made me believe so."

"You should not have believed me; virtue cannot remove the corruption innate in us. I loved you not."

"The more deceived me," I whisper, and his fingers brush

against my bleeding lip in apology.

It's the only warning I have. He seizes me by my upper arms and yanks me from the bench, the prayer book dropping to the floor in a blasphemous heap, and spins me around. Just as suddenly he drops me atop the prayers, his chest rising and falling in sharp pants, my hair in a night-dark cloud around me.

"Go, Ophelia, go! Someplace clean, someplace honest, to a convent go! Why would you breed a race of sinners?" He drops to his hands and knees over me, his entire body trapping me in place, and his face hovers barely an inch from mine. His hands gently pin my wrists over my head, too gently to bruise or hurt. "I'm not much for virtue myself, and yet I could accuse myself of such things it would be better had my mother never borne me." He leans forward, kisses the words into my skin and the silk that hides the bruises. "I am very proud." He rolls his hips against mine and swallows my gasp with another kiss. "Revengeful." Another kiss. "Ambitious." A kiss. "I have more sins at my command than thoughts to put them in, imagination to give them shape, or time to perform them. What should men such as I do as we crawl between Heaven and Earth? We are absolute bastards; believe none of us."

He pushes away from me, rolls to his feet in a graceful surge, and paces wildly about the space. "Away to a women's college, Ophelia. It is the only place for beauty and uselessness to go hand in hand. Where is your father?"

I watch his progress through the space, still propped on my elbows. He knows exactly where my father is—what possible purpose can he have in including his audience? But he watches my face and expects an answer, so I stammer the first lie that comes to mind. "At . . . at the house, Dane. He's at the Headmaster's House."

"Then I hope all the doors shut and lock upon him, that he can play the fool nowhere but in his own house. Good-bye!" He leaps for the door, then slowly turns on one heel. He seems to look at me, but he watches the swiveling camera. With a swift pounce, he drags me to my feet and against the wall, my back pressed against the edge of the tapestry that hides the hall. "For love of her father,

218

Jephthah's daughter never married, but perhaps, for all his foolishness, your old man is no Jephthah, so if you should marry, I'll give you this plague for your dowry: even if you're as chaste as ice, as pure as snow, still you won't escape slander. Never marry, Ophelia. Farewell—or, if you should marry, marry a fool."

He leans into me, every line of his body defined against mine, and I bite my lip against a gasp. He enjoys this game. My father and his uncle are only a screen away, only the position of his body keeps the cameras from seeing every detail, but he slides his hand under my skirt anyway, his breath warm against my ear. "Marry a fool, because wise men know well enough what monsters you make of us. God gives you one face, and you make yourselves another; you dance and you sway; you nickname God's creatures and claim ignorance of all the ways you provoke and excite and tempt us."

Heat sears my chest with each movement of his hand, each gesture tied to the flares of flame that leap from the surface to reach the source of the pain and pleasure. "I'll have none of it, none of that which made me mad," he laughs. "I say we'll have no more of marriage! Those that are married already, all but one, shall live, but for all the rest, they must stay as they are."

He kisses me hard to swallow my cry, then abruptly shoves me to an ungainly heap on the tile. We both struggle for breath, staring hard at each other, and he lifts trembling fingers to his lips and sweeps them away in a sardonic salute. "Go, Ophelia."

Fire dances before my eyes so I can't even watch him leave. I fold in on myself, clutch my skirt about my legs, and feel the sun expand even further. Inch by inch, the star claims more of me, burns away the darkness and the emptiness that the lake waits to fill, but stars...they fade, they die, they collapse. They devour and they die and if all of me becomes this blaze of pain, what will be left of me when it's carried past its time?

I gasp for air, but the fire drowns me; panicked tears scald my cheeks. Even away from the lake I still drown, again and again I drown and die only to have the air forced back where it doesn't want to be.

"Ophelia!"

Hands grip my shoulders and I recoil, but they hold too tightly, fingers digging into my collarbones, more bruises to cover, to hide, until my entire body will be painted by them. Father pulls me against his chest, and I sob into his rumpled coat. I'm not even sure why the tears have come, but they choke me as surely as hands at my throat, with far more pain than Dane's touch has ever caused me. Father rocks me slowly, hesitantly, back and forth like a child.

Claudius stands over us, his hands clasped at the small of his back in that vaguely military stance he always adopts when his face is as blank as is ever possible to be. He shakes his head slowly, his emerald eyes hard and unforgiving. "Love?" He snorts eloquently. "If that was love, give me hatred; at least it's honest."

Honest!

"He's disturbed, certainly, but not mad. This behavior, his brooding and his antics . . . he's hiding something beneath it, something dangerous, and we must protect both his mother and this school from his troublemaking. This has gone on long enough."

"But, sir—"

"He'll go to England tomorrow. I have friends there, and perhaps the distance and new surroundings can expel this . . . *obsessive* eccentricity from his actions. His mother didn't wish him so far away, but she will understand this necessity, and I will place him in the hands of those who owe me a great deal."

"I . . ." Father smoothes a hand over my hair; it's shaking. But he wouldn't be Father if he weren't utterly convinced of his own rightness. "I think that shall do very well, sir, but I still believe these actions to stem from too much emotion unreturned. Be calm now, Ophelia," he murmurs and hesitantly kisses the top of my head. "You needn't relive any of it; the cameras showed us everything."

Not everything.

He swallows hard and turns back to Claudius." Sir, do as you please, of course, but if I may suggest—as a parent—after tonight's performance, let his mother speak to him alone and ask after the source of this grief. She has followed your wisdom all this time, but he is her son, and if he will speak to anyone, surely it will be to his mother? Of course we could not ask Gertrude to betray her son's confidences and of course there are no cameras in Gertrude's chambers." Something about Claudius' expression makes me less confident of that statement than my father. "But if you'll allow, I'll hide myself and bring to you all I overhear. Then, if you cannot come to the truth of it, send him to England or wherever you think best. But give him this last chance before you send him from the only home he has ever known."

Father speaks as though he's fond of Dane. Even more astonishing, I think he actually means it. Whatever his reasons for disapproving a match between me and Dane, he genuinely cares for the wounded boy he's watched over all his life, an affection held as closely and awkwardly as any feelings for Laertes and me.

Claudius nods sharply. "So be it."

"Come, Ophelia." Father urges me to my feet, then leaves me against the wall so he can scuttle around and collect the letters and the prayer book whose spine is now cracked and bent from its abuse. "We have hours yet before dinner; you can rest. Rest will do you wonders."

But before we can climb the stairs in the house, Claudius says he needs him in the office, and rather than my clean, sterile room, I flee to the greenhouse where even on a Sunday Jack works to keep the plants alive out of season. The violets struggle and try, but they're never strong within the glass house. I curl up in the warm, damp soil of their bed, let their elusive perfume conceal every other scent from me.

Jack doesn't say a word. He tucks a white tea rose behind my ear and covers me with a burlap sack in place of a blanket, then goes back to work.

The pixies never dance in the greenhouses. There are never any footprints, no glitter to light fires in the air.

I'm almost asleep when I feel hands gently lift me from the earth. Drugged by the peace of the plants caught between living and dying, I don't even struggle, just let the arms cradle me and turn my cheek against a shoulder. I take a deep breath, but all I can smell is the ghost of violets. A second pair of hands swipes a cold cloth across my face and legs where the soil clings. They brush the earth from my sweater and skirt, from my hair, and take care not to dislodge Jack's rose.

Dane and Horatio.

Safe in their care, I turn my face deeper into Dane's shoulder and let sleep claim me the rest of the way.

CHAPTER 28

One of the maids wakes me up hours later so I can shower. "A gift," she tells me quietly, nodding to the garment bag draped over one arm. "From young Master Danemark."

Dane bought me a dress?

I don't remember him and Horatio bringing me back to my room, placing me in my own bed, and the sense of displacement makes me briefly nauseous. The hot shower helps, even as it brings new bruises into stark relief. There's a particularly dark one where Father's thumb dug into my collarbone, darker than any of Dane's, darker even than my eyes in the mirror. When I leave the steam-filled bathroom, cold air stabs against my skin with a ripple of goose bumps in its wake.

The dress, out of its protective plastic and laid out across the neatened coverlet, makes me laugh. It's a beautiful creation, stiff plum silk with a delicate pattern of drifting cherry blossoms picked out in embroidered silver, cream, and pale blush pink, and though the knee-length skirt is wide and whispering against an underskirt, the top closes tightly around me, sleeveless with a high mandarin collar and silver cord fastenings.

He bought me a dress to hide the bruises.

And the class ring, back in its proper place against my breast-bone, but I'm fairly sure the bruises were his main concern.

A fresh basket sits on the floor outside my door, full of straggling hothouse violets. They're a pathetic bunch, limp and faded, like they never had the strength to bloom into their full color. A note from Jack, scribbled nearly illegibly across a scrap of paper, sits curled in the throat of the healthiest flower: these are the last. The last violets until spring thaws the earth to let him plant outside, because the violets never want to live caged within glass.

The impulse is born from the star of my heart or perhaps from the part of me that's my mother's daughter, but I sit at my vanity and knot the violets into a crown in my hair, twine the remainder through the length. So I wore my hair to Hamlet's funeral—the Headmaster loved violets—and Gertrude smiled to see them.

Will she smile now?

There's nearly a full week of pills in the compartmentalized box on my nightstand. Dane threw away all the forgets, the days past where I was a bad daughter to my father, but he forgot the pills I'm supposed to take in the future. The pills that get refilled, that my father thinks he checks.

Or perhaps he merely left the decision up to me.

I open the lid for each day and separate out the little pink pill, then empty the rest into my hand. It's almost more than I can hold, a tower of chemical lies in my palm. I could split them back into their days, replace them in their little boxes, a reminder of the obedience I owe my father. I could choose to take them, to keep my thoughts whole rather than leave them to splinter and crack down the seams.

Or I could be the person Dane needs.

The person my mother made her promises to.

The person who feels the lake, cold and empty, press against the blazing sun in my chest.

Before I can change my mind, I cross to the bathroom and drop the pills into the porcelain bowl. Ripples dance across the surface, distorted where they cross paths with each other.

If Father comes to check that I've taken my pills, he'll see that the rest of the week is gone. He'll know I'm not taking them.

He'll send me back to the cold place.

The star lodges in my throat, choking and painful, but it forces back the nausea that always accompanies the panic. Dane won't let him take me. Dane needs me.

And perhaps, after the scene he just witnessed—what he put me into—Father will forgive me this week with a few lectures.

There's a knock on the door, soft and polite, and I know who it is before I even get there to open it: Horatio. He wears his suit from the wedding, the shoulders not as loose as they were before, and I wonder how much he's grown in the past few months without my noticing. Physically, anyway; I can see from his eyes how much he's grown in other ways.

But he smiles and his eyes light up, despite the concern that still lurks in the deeper shadows of the rich greens and browns, and he kisses my cheek in greeting. "May I escort you to dinner?"

"Dane?"

"Finalizing a few things with Keith. And . . ." He shakes his head with a small sigh. "Well, plotting something else, anyway. He'll be in rare form this evening."

"Are we doing dinner up at the school?"

"No, here in the house, the play as well. They're performing in the parlor, I believe."

I take his arm and let him lead me down the hall to the grand stairs. "Do you think this will ever end?" I ask in a whisper. "Do you think we'll ever get our Dane back, without the games and the need and the mania?"

"They're a part of him; they always have been."

"But now they've consumed him."

"I don't know. For anything legal to happen, he has to provide a great deal of proof. And for anything illegal . . ."

"We might lose him."

"Exactly."

"But we can't exist in a stalemate forever."

"Can't we?" There's no joy in his face at this, no cleverness or delicate teasing. "You live in a kind of stalemate, Ophelia."

Not anymore. Now the pills are gone, and all the things they've kept at bay will come rushing in to fill the void.

Ros and Guil meet us at the bottom of the stairs. Ros gives us a jerky nod of acknowledgment, but Guil ignores us entirely. Without Dane to impress, we're not worth his attention. Father enters next, his suit still rumpled from the afternoon and his tie lopsided in its knot. He smiles to see me on Horatio's arm. He's always liked Horatio, admired him even. It takes a great deal of courage and strength and hard work to succeed as a scholarship student at Elsinore Academy, and Horatio has always risen to that task with grace and integrity.

In so many ways, Horatio really is the best of us, and I wonder if he won't pay the highest price for what Dane has drawn us all into. Those of us half drowned already don't fear the water, but for someone who has always sailed in sunlight . . . Horatio has no place in the darkness of pain and poison.

Gertrude joins us on Claudius' arm, elegant in a sapphire sheath and a collar of sapphires and diamonds that glitter fiercely in the light from the chandeliers. Dark pink marks mar the skin at the base of her neck where the heavy weight of the necklace digs into tender flesh, an unaccustomed weight that has her careful in how she moves her head. At her side, Claudius wears an ice-blue tie against a crisp white shirt and charcoal suit. The school crest gleams from the tie tack. It's less than subtle, especially when combined with the silver and sapphire of Gertrude, more suited to an official gathering with donors or the Board of Governors or even ambassadors from universities or other preparatory schools. For such a small dinner, it smacks more of defensiveness than of pride.

By the third time we've been called to the table, it's obvious that Dane doesn't intend to join us for the meal or at least doesn't intend to sit down with us. Claudius forces a smile onto his face—it doesn't reach his eyes, never reaches the emeralds that hide his thoughts—and leads us into the private dining room.

Glasses of wine sit at every place, even mine, and Father nods his permission. Horatio sits beside me, a buffer between me and the rest of the room. I haven't eaten today, and I know I should; the food looks and smells wonderful, and I'm aware of the hollow feeling in my stomach that will shortly turn to pain, but it all turns to ash in my mouth until chewing is a Herculean labor that makes me want to gag. If I could deafen myself in some manner, I might be able to eat, but I cannot close my ears to the conversation that robs me of all appetite.

For the first time, I think I know the edges of what hate feels like.

There's something shameless about the way Guil flatters Claudius. Something equally shameless about how Claudius just smiles and accepts it as his due. Ros fidgets and laughs nervously and knocks his glass so many times the tablecloth is stained purple in a wide swath around his place, as uncomfortable here as he is anywhere. Guil takes in the crystal and china and silver with an acquisitive eye.

"His father's business is hemorrhaging money in lawsuits," Horatio whispers. "They've been selling things off for a couple of years now to try to keep it quiet."

Which explains why his clothes look almost but not quite right for the company he keeps, like cheaper copies of the real thing. Which explains why he so desperately needs Claudius' gratitude.

Claudius still has his business ventures, however secretive he may keep them. Does Guil hope to be placed there? However lacking in subtlety his actions towards the school and Gertrude have been and are, Claudius is nearly inscrutable when it comes to his businesses. Even Dane doesn't know the names of them or what they do. Transport? Sales? Services? Claudius' fortune is vast, perhaps equal to Dane's inheritance from his father, but he never speaks to how he acquired it.

I think of the early morning phone calls, the friends in England who owe him a great deal, wonder if the hardness in his eyes came from business or if it was always there, and decide that Guil will be eaten alive if he tries to enter into such a contract.

The thought should fill me with remorse or at least give me a moment's pause, but instead it fills me with a feral sense of satisfaction.

Because Guil knows nothing of friendship.

He calls Dane his friend even as he reaches out blindly with the knife to stab anything he can manage to find, and he knows nothing of what it means to be a friend, to have a friend. Ros is at best a lackey, a nervous shadow that follows along where he's told and by simple virtue of his anxious bumbling makes Guil look better than he is. They arrived only last night and have barely even spoken to Dane, but already Guil speaks confidently of a cure, brags that their connection will yield the truth before there is even cause for further concern.

Gertrude latches on to his words, believes them because she needs to, but Claudius is amused by them and Guil doesn't see it. Claudius thinks Dane is simply acting out, being an ass because he can. For Gertrude's sake, he phrases it as an intercession, but he doesn't actually expect the Toms to achieve anything. He doesn't think he has anything to worry about. Thinks his secret is safe.

And the Toms are, as ever, clueless.

I push the food around on my plate even though I can sense Father's worried regard. Unobserved by any of the company, Horatio slips a bread plate from the table and sets it in my lap on top of my spread napkin. Then it's a game, to make the food vanish to the plate without anyone seeing it on the way down, and suddenly Father relaxes because he thinks I'm eating.

"Promise me you'll get some bread from the kitchen later," Horatio whispers.

"If there's a chance."

"If there isn't a chance, I'll bring it to you myself."

If Dane burns a star in my chest, what does he do to Horatio? Horatio, who loves me as a friend and loves Dane as so much more; Horatio, the best of us. Since that night on the widow's walk, he's had a Saint Anthony medal attached to his crucifix. The patron saint of lost things. How lost you have to be to fall under his purview. Does Horatio pray to Saint Anthony for our sakes? For the lost souls that wander around in their bodies because pain keeps stabbing in to keep the emptiness from crumpling in on itself?

When dessert comes, he starts a steady flow of words, a soothing waterfall of his rich voice and the love he has for his family as he relates the latest e-mails from his parents and siblings. His voice, soft and strong, drowns out the others, and I'm able to enjoy the white chocolate mousse and swirls of raspberry jam. For all that he almost never gets to see them, Horatio's love for his family is a palpable thing, a balm against bruises and knives and guns that wait to go off. He tells me of his sister's straight As, of the early college interest in her, of his father's offer of a better job that could mean his mother could go down to working only one job instead of three. He talks about the soccer scholarship that lets his brother on the school team, of the surprise funds sent by Gertrude that lets another sister look forward to a fashion internship in the city come the summer. By the time he's finished telling me of his youngest brother and his science fair volcano fiasco, I'm nearly in tears from laughter and all of my mousse has been eaten.

Father pays us half attention, and I can see the thoughts written plainly across his face, but he'd be disappointed if he knew the truth. I love Horatio, as he loves me, but it's a very different kind of love than what we both bear for Dane. Horatio's the better person, the better choice, would make a better boyfriend and better husband, but hearts want what they want, and ours both beat for Dane.

The sudden slam of the door opening makes Ros drop his glass again. This time, rather than simply sloshing, it hits the table at an angle near the curved base of the goblet and snaps neatly from the stem. Dane stands in the doorway in an elegant tuxedo, even the shirt black beneath the bow tie and cummerbund. A black scarf of softest wool hangs from around his neck, the fringed edges nearly to his knees, and a floor-length impresario cape swirls around him with the force of his entry. He even has a top hat perched atop his sable hair.

He surveys us all with a scowl that abruptly morphs into a manic grin. "Come, come!" he cries, clapping black-gloved hands. "You're all late! The show is ready to begin!"

"There you are, Dane," Claudius replies calmly. "How are you?"

"Excellent! I eat the chameleon's dish, air all promise-crammed. You cannot feed capons so."

The lines around Claudius' eyes deepen, but he knows if he appears less than mild, if he shows his perturbation, Dane wins this round. "That isn't an answer, Dane. Your words are not mine."

"No, nor mine now." He turns from his uncle to pin my father with a mocking smile. "Sir, I heard a most strange rumor; is it true you once performed in university?"

"That I did," answers Father, oblivious as ever that he is the source of anyone's amusement. "I was thought quite a good actor then."

"What did you perform?"

"*Julius Caesar*; Brutus killed me in the capitol."

"It was a brute part of him to have done so."

Horatio rolls his eyes and helps me slide my plate of hidden food to the floor.

"Well? Are you coming, or aren't you? The players wait upon our arrival!" He spins in a great circle, his cape swirling around him like a dervish's skirt, but there is nothing of prayer and meditation in his movement. He bounds from the room, singing "It's a Small World" in German and leaving us all staring after him.

Horatio sighs and shakes his head. "Exit, pursued by a bear," he mutters, and I laugh and accept his aid in standing. The others follow and together we enter the parlor that Horatio tells me has been locked all afternoon.

The small dais Claudius erects for gatherings has been extended into a stage two steps high that marks barely ten feet across, the ends hidden by hastily mounted curtains. Hothouse flowers cover the front and back of the space, perhaps three feet deep, and around the Hellene chaise that stands as the only furniture. Within the audience space, there are only three chairs, two of them nearly thrones side by side, the other more simple and placed slightly behind and to the left.

Horatio and I sink to the thick carpet to the right of the chairs. Ros and Guil hesitate, looking about for more seats, then reluctantly follow suit on the left. They aren't comfortable on the floor.

But then, Dane knows that. It's exactly why he's arranged it this way.

Gertrude sits in one of the quasi-thrones and pats the air to her open side. "Come, Dane, sit by me."

"No, good mother," he says shortly and drops to the carpet beside me. "Here's metal more attractive."

"The games I can handle; the puns may kill me," murmurs Horatio, and I bite back a smile.

On Gertrude's other side, Father nudges Claudius and whispers something, more proof for his theory, I think.

Plopping his hat atop Horatio's head, Dane sprawls out across me, his head pillowed on my thighs. "Lady, shall I lie in your lap?"

"No," I retort, aware of Father and Claudius watching.

But he doesn't move. "Do you think I meant country matters?"

"I think nothing."

"It's a fair thought to lie between maid's legs."

Heat floods my face, burning the skin like the star burns my breath. "You're merry tonight."

"Who, me?"

"Yes, you."

"What should a man do but be merry?" He grins at me, but the bite is still there in his tone, in his eyes. "After all, see how cheerfully my mother looks, and my father dead only these two hours."

A quick glance shows Gertrude's stricken expression, Claudius' anger slowly leaking past the congenial façade. "Not at all, it's been more than four months."

"So long? Oh heavens! Dead four months and not forgotten yet? Then there's hope a great man's memory may outlive his life by half a year." He settles himself more comfortably across my lap, one arm thrown over his head to drape across Horatio as well. "How like a hobbyhorse our pathetic little lives are, forgotten in the attics of other men's memories."

Gertrude's hand flutters at her chest in her distress, tears bright in her blue eyes. "Dane . . ."

"Hush, woman! The show!"
Above us, the lights of the chandelier dim.
The play's the thing, he said.
The show must go on.

CHAPTER 29

"Play with me, Ophelia," whispers Dane, voice hidden beneath the shuffle of Father and Claudius taking their seats. He laces his fingers through mine, places our joined hands against his chest. I can't feel his heartbeat through the layers of fabric, but I can feel the star spin where my own heart should be.

With the hand he hasn't claimed, I stroke Dane's hair back from his face. "So, what means this?" I ask lightly, for my own benefit as much as for the game he asked me to play.

"What, this? Miching mallecho! It means mischief."

A single light returns, fixed on a slightly nervous eighth-grade boy on the middle step.

"We'll know by this fellow," Dane says lazily. Unseen by those in the chairs or beyond, his other hand grips Horatio's with a white-knuckled grip. I can feel the tension in his body despite the seeming ease of his pose. "The players can never keep a secret. They'll tell us everything."

"And will he tell us what the play will show?"

"Or any show you care to give him. If you're not ashamed to show, he won't be ashamed to tell you what it means. Will you give him a show, Ophelia?"

Father makes a disapproving sound that brings a reluctant smile to my lips. "You are wicked and horrible, and I'm watching the play now."

The eighth grader—a fierce blush burning under the make-up—clears his throat and releases his lines all in a rush. "For your generosity and for your patience, we and our tragedy beg your careful listening." He races offstage, and I can hear a few of the younger actors giggling. But then, they've had less than a day to prepare this.

Dane shakes his head. "Is this a prologue or the inscription on a ring?"

"It is brief," I allow.

He brings our joined hands to his lips and places a lingering kiss against my palm. "As woman's love."

Piano music, soft and menacing, spills from behind one of the curtains, and Keith walks onto the stage with one of the sophomore girls on his arm. I should know her. I know we have classes together, but it's never seemed important to know the names of people I'll never truly know. They both wear elaborate crowns and fine costumes that wouldn't be out of place in the celebrity pages. They dance for a time to the music before he bends close and kisses her deeply, an embrace she returns with equal ardor. When he pulls away, he rests his head against the curve of her shoulder, a gesture somehow more intimate even than the kiss that preceded it.

Passing a hand over his face, the King lies down across the chaise, surrounded by the hothouse flowers.

Like Hamlet's favorite alcove of the garden.

The alcove where he died.

Oh, Dane.

In silence, in stillness, even in the costume of a king, Keith isn't someone you notice more than once, but as he takes a breath and swells his chest to speak, there's something mesmerizing about him. "Thirty years we've had together, thirty years of dreams and growth, of moons and suns and the endless cycle of the Earth beneath our feet. Thirty years, my dearest love, since the Church and our families united us in sacred bonds." He lifts her left hand and kisses the plain gold band there, a simple gesture that brings a worried smile to the Queen's face.

Gertrude's right hand twitches in her lap to cover the left; so Hamlet used to kiss her wedding band, grateful every day for the gift of their marriage.

The Queen touches his cheek lightly, draws his face to hers, and kisses him gently. "And I hope we have another thirty years, but I worry for you. You're so tired of late, so out of sorts and depressed." She gives a soft laugh and pats her hair, a dead-on imitation of Gertrude. "I know we women fear too much, as much as we love, and as thirty years have made my love great, so has my fear grown. What worries you so?"

"I must leave you, love, and shortly too. Everything in me grinds to a halt, and you shall live on in this fair world, and remarry—"

"Oh, do not say the rest! Such a thing must be blackest betrayal. In second husband, let me be only cursed: I will wed no second but that he kills the first."

"Well, that's a bitter gift to give yourself!" Dane laughs. Neither actor gives notice to his interruption.

"Second marriages have much of practicality to them," she continues, "of financial comfort, but nothing of love. If any second husband kisses me in bed, a second time it kills my first."

Claudius sighs and shifts in his chair. Gertrude angles towards him, an instinctive response, but her hands lay folded in her lap to conceal the ring that glitters even in poor light.

The King smoothes a hand over her hair beneath the crown and sinks down to sit on the edge of the chaise. "I know you believe what you say now, but what we would vow, we often break. Purpose is but the slave to memory, strong at first but with little stamina. The vows we would make to ourselves have little to keep them once the reason for them is gone, as many a man knows when he falls from fortune to disgrace and must see how his favorites desert him for greater gain. This is how our world works, so it is no strange thing for you to vow so fervently that you will not remarry. These thoughts will die when I am also dead."

She shakes her head stubbornly and lays her hand against his heart, taking a deep breath. "May the Earth give me no food, nor

Heaven light; may the days deny me all pleasure and the nights all rest; to desperation turn my trust and hope, as in a prison with no scope beyond its barren walls. May every curse follow me and give me lasting strife if, once I become a widow, I should ever be a wife."

"Oh, if she should break that now!" Dane laughs again, a manic sound that splinters the silence of the tiny audience. All but Horatio and I flinch. "A second time cursed, and by her own tongue both times."

"It's a heavy promise." The King sighs and passes a hand over his face. "Sweet, leave me here awhile. I am so very tired."

Kneeling down beside him in a waterfall of beaded silk, the Queen kisses his brow. "May sleep come quickly and gently, and let no misfortune ever come between us."

He's asleep nearly before she exits, his head propped on the high, single arm, one hand pressed against his heart.

Above the stage, someone—Keith and Dane, no doubt—has rigged a screen for a projected slide show of photos, all of Gertrude and Hamlet. They start in school, both in the uniforms that have barely changed, and progress inexorably to a wedding day where a scowling Claudius stands at his brother's side, to Dane's birth, moving through the years until the last photo, taken only a week before Hamlet's death. Gertrude gasps at the enlarged image of her portrait's gentle smile and closed eyes as a laughing Hamlet kisses her temple. Keith slumbers on.

Dane twists about in my lap until he's sprawled across both Horatio and I, chin in his hands, elbows digging into Horatio's thigh. "Madam," he directs towards his mother, "how do you like this play?"

"The lady protests too much, I think," she answers stiffly, but there's uncertainty there too.

Gertrude is not the cleverest of women.

"Oh, but she'll keep her word, of course!"

Claudius clears his throat, willing to speak now that the actors show no immediate sign of continuing. "What do you call this play?"

236

"*The Mousetrap.* Isn't it apt? It tells the story of a murder in Vienna. Gonzago is the Duke's name, his wife Baptista. You'll see. It's a bastard piece of work, but what of that? Where our souls are innocent, its darkness cannot touch us."

A new player enters and stops at the foot of the chaise, in clothes nearly as fine as the King's.

"That one is Lucianus, brother to the King."

"You're as good as a chorus, Dane."

He twists back around to grin at me, lays flat on his back again over our legs. "I could interpret between you and your love, if I could only see the puppets dallying."

"Yes, Dane, we're all astonished by your keen wit," I laugh.

Taking my hand, he brings it past his heart, past his stomach, and presses my palm hard against him. "It would cost you a groan to take off my edge."

"Still better and worse. You're a wretch."

"Better and worse? More the fool your husband. Come, murderer!" he yells suddenly at the stage. "Quit making those damnable faces and begin!"

The senior playing the poisoner isn't as good an actor as Keith; the barest smile twitches across his face before he can pull his character back around him like a shroud. "Evil thoughts, ready hands, waiting poison, the time is right. No one's here to see." From his waistcoat, he produces the syringe with its remnants of proof and holds it up for us to see in all clarity. "An instant death." He fakes removing the clay bead and pretends to inject the liquid behind the sleeping King's ear.

Dane twists back around so he can see his mother and uncle. "He poisons him in the garden for his estate," he announces disingenuously. "The story actually exists and is written in very choice Italian. If you wait but a moment, you can see how the murderer wins the love of Gonzago's wife."

"Look at Claudius," I whisper.

Claudius' chair falls back against the carpet with a dull thump, overturned by the violence with which he rises. He stares at the stage, at the picture still emblazoned above. His eyes glitter fiercely in a too-pale face. Every muscle is taut with tension, the stillness before the storm.

"Claudius?" murmurs Gertrude, stretching out a hand in concern. Not the one burdened with their marriage vows.

"Stop the play!" calls Father.

The boy playing Lucianus glances offstage, probably to the Queen as Keith is "dead" and won't break character, and holds his position.

"Turn the lights on!" Claudius croaks, and Father immediately calls for it to happen, but before anyone can get near the light switches, Claudius races from the room. After a moment of stunned silence, Father and Gertrude follow him, the Toms hot on their heels.

Dane watches them, all the mockery gone from his voice, his face. "So goes the wounded deer to weep. Some must watch while some must sleep, thus runs the world away." He sits up, worms his way between Horatio and me so he can face us both. A mask seems to slide away and his expression eases. "I think I deserve a permanent star on the walk for this performance."

"Perhaps an insert in the program."

"Not at all, this is worth an Oscar!"

"I'll write the Academy myself."

They're both trying too hard, but Dane can't keep it up. Keith stands to flip on the lights, drowning the projection, and Dane doesn't even blink. "It looks like Father's ghost was correct. Did you see it?"

Horatio takes a deep breath. We're on the edge of the precipice, the proof that Dane has been seeking for two months, and his words may well hurtle us over. "Yes, I did see."

"At the moment of poisoning?"

"Yes, Dane, I was watching."

The door opens again. Before the shapes can even enter, Dane has already fallen back into the character that's only half an act. "A show should have music, yes? Not just that dreary piano. Don't you have any recorders back there?"

Keith, still with the crown lopsided on his hair, smiles and tosses him a recorder. "From the wedding scene."

Guil clears his throat from the doorway, uncomfortable and angry and scared. Perhaps he's finally realized that the task he's promised won't be as easy as he thinks. "Dane, can I have a word with you?"

"A whole novel, if you like."

"The Headmaster—"

"Is dead. What of him?"

"The Headmaster has gone to his room, pissed as hell."

Behind him, Ros sways nervously on the balls of his feet, hands shoved so deep in his pockets that his belt strains to hold up his trousers.

Dane simply gives them a banal smile. "Is he drunk?"

"No, he's furious."

"Then tell it to a psychologist, not to me. If I were to tinker with his fury, it's entirely likely I'd stoke it instead."

That's true enough.

Keith tosses more recorders our way. I catch one and wet my lips with my tongue, aware of the way Dane watches the movement. I lift the mouthpiece and arrange my fingers over the holes, moving them in the memory of a song but don't give it air to give it voice.

"Dane, seriously, we need to talk."

"And we are talking, are we not?"

"Your mother is very upset, almost in tears, and she's sent me to you."

"And you are most welcome."

"This is not a joke, Dane!" snaps Guil. Ros shrinks back against the door. "Either give me the chance to tell you what your mother said or I'll simply leave now!"

"Sir, I cannot."

"Can't what?"

"Give you a chance. Chance, after all, is luck, and my wit's diseased, hardly a matter of luck and fortune, and therefore, no matter of chance. But convey such words as you wish to parrot, and perhaps I'll in some measure comprehend them. My mother, you say?"

Guil stares at him, confounded into momentary silence. Horatio's jaw trembles against the need to laugh.

But Guil wouldn't be Guil if he didn't barrel on obliviously, so even though he can't find words, he elbows Ros sharply. His shadow flinches violently, eyes wide and terrified, but he swallows hard and makes the effort. "You've baffled her, Dane. She can't understand your behavior at all."

"Oh, wonderful son that can so astonish his mother! But there's a sequel to your words, yes? Please, continue."

"She wants to speak with you in her room before you go to bed."

"And we would obey were she ten times our mother. Is there anything else?"

For the first time, I can see a trace of the Ros that might have been if Guil hadn't gotten a hold of him at such a young age and browbeat him into submission. His dark eyes study Dane miserably, and I think Ros might actually regard Dane as a friend in some way. But Ros doesn't have the strength to protect himself, much less anyone else. "We were friends once."

"And so we are still."

"Then why won't you tell us what's going on? You don't do yourself any favors by keeping your friends in the dark."

"Sir, I lack advancement."

"You'll be the next headmaster of the damn school," snaps Guil.

"Yes, the next, but while the grass grows . . ." He gives a crooked smile. "No, that doesn't quite work, does it? But you do take a backward way of approaching things. Why do such a thing, like to drive me into a trap?"

Guil is somewhat recovered, though still clueless. Dane warned them this morning, but they didn't understand then and they don't understand now. "We didn't want to offend you by being too direct."

"Well, that makes no sense at all. Will you play this pipe?" He holds the recorder out to Guil, flat across his palm, and pain flashes through his dark grey eyes.

Guil shakes his head. "I can't."

"I'm asking you."

"Believe me, I can't."

"Then I shall beg you."

"Dane, I don't know how!"

"It's as easy as lying," Dane says, voice taut as piano wire. "You put your fingers over these holes, breath into it, and it makes music. See, here are the holes."

"I can make a sound, yes, but not music. I don't have the skill."

"Then how unworthy a thing you make of me." Horatio and I stiffen and watch Dane as he stands and paces towards Guil with the recorder still in his hand. His tone is mild, but only a fool would take it that way.

Tom Guildenstern is many kinds of fool.

"After all, you would play upon me," Dane continues too calmly. "You would try to know my stops. You would pluck out the heart of my mystery. You would play me from my lowest note to the top of my range. And yet this, this simple thing of plastic, there is such excellent music and voice to be called from this tiny thing, and you cannot make it speak?" He lashes out suddenly, strikes Guil across the face so hard with the recorder that the plastic snaps in two. The mouthpiece falls a short distance away. "Do you think I am easier played upon than a pipe? Call me what instrument you will, *you cannot play me.*"

"Dane!"

"Hamlet."

"What?"

"I am Hamlet!" he cries, his entire body lost to a spasm of fury. He wrenches the cloak and scarf from his body and throws them aside in a dark cloud of fabric. The rest of the recorder smacks hard against the wall and leaves a long crack along the holes. "I am Hamlet, as my father and his father and his father before! Hamlet!"

Hamlet is a distinguished older gentleman who always has the time to smile for a homesick child, a father figure, a mentor whose pride in you means something wonderful and grand. Hamlet is a friend who sleeps beneath the earth, stone and flowers to weigh him down. Hamlet is the ghost who weeps in dreams for his son, so nearly a man, now left behind as a ghost among the living.

Dane is the boy, the joy and the sorrow, the highs and the spirals, the always friend who terrifies me—soothes me—with the sometimes something more. Dane is the dream and the wish and the longing, he is the known and familiar.

Hamlet is not the seething, poisonous pain that attacks the fine chairs with feet and an animal cry, but neither is he Dane. This is someone new, someone frightening and alluring. He isn't just lost in the darkness, he drowns in it. He isn't Dane; he isn't Hamlet.

What name do we give the pain? The fury? The grief? What name do we give the part that drowns and the part that dies? What do we call the fragments that remain?

Mine.

The star burns and blazes inside my chest, brighter and larger until the flames licks my stomach and arms. It sears my sight, deafens me to everything but the spinning whisper of *danedanedanedanedane.*

Father enters the room, stops short at the sight of Dane kicking apart the chairs, then makes the visible effort not to comment upon it. "Your mother would like to speak with you. Now."

Dane calms abruptly, though his chest still heaves from the exertion. He paces slowly to the door, until he's staring down into my father's face. "Do you see that cloud that's almost in the shape of a camel?"

We're inside and night has long since fallen, but I can see the thought in Father's face: play along. Keep him calm. He forces a smile and a small nod. "I do indeed, and it is very like a camel."

"I think it looks like a weasel."

Father's smile falters, but he still makes the attempt. "I . . . yes, its back is like a weasel."

"Or a whale?"

"Very like a whale."

I close my eyes so Father can't see the shame. Did he do this to me when I was younger, before he realized that I was never going to grow out of being my mother's daughter and he put me in the cold place, put me on the pills? Did he play along, just nod and smile as I talked of sorrow and rage that rode forever through the woods?

Did he sound so much like a fool?

"Then I'll see my mother in a bit. Now go, and take these idiots with you."

Father hesitates, but he says nothing further. Not to Dane, anyway, and not to me; he simply ushers the actors and the dumbfounded Toms out the door and closes it behind him.

"Dane—"

"Go, Horatio, please. If you love me, go."

I open my eyes in time to see the pain flash across Horatio's face. Does Dane know? Or does he use that word as friends do, with no idea of how much more it means to this boy who wounds himself to keep Dane safe from this ill-begotten promise? Horatio squeezes my shoulder, careful with his strength because he can't stand to add to my bruises. "Stay with him until he goes to his mother. Please."

I glance over at Dane, who inclines his head in barely perceptible agreement. "I will."

When the door clicks quietly shut, Dane just stares at me and the recorder still in my hand.

Wetting my lips, I bring the recorder back to my mouth and start to play.

And he laughs.

CHAPTER 30

Dane crouches next to me and watches my fingers move over the holes, watches the way my lips part for breath before pressing again against the mouthpiece of the recorder. "You're the only one with any right to play me and the only one who never tries," he murmurs.

I set the recorder to the side and use his shoulder to steady myself so I can stand. Pins and needles race up my legs after so long sitting, but he doesn't move until he's sure I have my balance. "And Horatio."

"That he has the right to play me? Or that he never tries?"

"You already know what I mean, Dane. There's no one else here to play with."

"Are you scared of me, Ophelia?"

"Sometimes," I whisper. "But most of the time, I'm scared for you."

"Horatio said that."

"He's better than either of us."

"I know." His fingers travel over my face, smear the shimmering powders around my eyes down onto my cheeks. "Play me, Ophelia. As only you can."

"I don't know how."

He gives me a crooked, mischievous smile, and for a moment he's just Dane, the Dane I knew, the Dane I miss. "You managed fairly well on your birthday." He laughs at the blush that blazes beneath his fingertips, kisses me softly. But the softness doesn't—can't—last, and then the need and the hunger and the desperation clutch me against his chest until the darkness dazzles my sight. "Come," he gasps, wrenching away. "Come with me."

I don't even bother to ask him where. It doesn't matter. I promised Horatio I'd stay with Dane until he went to his mother, and would have gone even without the promise simply because Dane asked it of me. Because I bear his pain, and where the heart goes, the pain must follow. Always.

The cold attacks us as soon as we step outside, and I shiver in the wrap that offers barely enough protection against an air-conditioned room. It does nothing against a night just shy of All Hallows' Eve, a night with a wind that swirls and stabs.

And sings.

The bean sidhe have begun to sing again, but it's a different song, a different sound. The death they announce hasn't happened yet, but in the way of faeries, they already know that it will happen.

But Dane can't hear them, so he doesn't pause in his mad race across the grounds to the garage down near the gatehouse. Cold air burns my lungs, and my heels skid across the gravel walks until we reach the paved drive. His hand is laced through mine, tugging me after him.

In the garage, he hangs my wrap on a hook on the wall but slides onto his bike without a helmet. When I reach for one, he makes a growl of impatience that has me backing away from the thing that could save my life. It's uncomfortable on the bike, my skirts bunched beneath me, but I hunch against his back and wrap my arms around his chest.

I can feel the hard metal of a gun against my stomach, the gun he's once again tucked into the back of his waistband.

The motorcycle roars to life, and we race from the garage, down what's left of the drive and past the sleepy guards in the gatehouse. They cry after us, but we're gone before they can even identify us, and Dane isn't the only boy in school with a bike and a girl.

There's a sort of thrill to terror, a frisson of feeling that races through you when any moment your life might end. In that moment, that split second, you've never felt more alive. We skid on the narrow curves and take them too tight, too fast, always on the verge of spilling off the bike onto the road with nothing but a bit of cloth between the asphalt and our skin. Wind whips my hair around us, a cloud of ink that blinds us, and he doesn't even slow.

He races in front of cars, cutting them off so abruptly the drivers have to yank aside to avoid hitting us. Curses muffled by thick windows follow our progress, accompanied by a cacophony of blaring horns. We zip through a red light and leave the loud crunch of metal behind us.

How many nights, in the hours between his frantic antics and his visit to me, has he ridden out like this, courting death just to feel alive in a world of ghosts and pain? How many nights has the gym not been enough distraction?

Red and blue lights flash behind us with an ululating siren that makes my heart stutter and stop. A squawky voice, deep and masculine, crackles over the police cruiser's speakers. "Pull over."

Dane ignores him.

The cruiser follows us through town, the orders growing stricter and stronger, and then a second cruiser swings off a side street to join the chase. Dane laughs and slows down just enough to ride between them, then zips forward through a red light and a line of cars that couldn't pull out of the way in time.

Ahead of us, the lights flash at the railroad track, warning us of the freight train about to pull through, but Dane gives them the same consideration he gives the police, and he crashes through the barricade. Wood splinters rake my arms. The conductor yanks on the whistle when he sees us.

We cross the tracks with inches to spare, the air alive behind us with the force of the train's passage. Even police can't go through a train.

There's no one to follow us now, no one to keep the thrill alive, but Dane doesn't slow. He races through sleepy neighborhoods, mostly full of older couples whose children have long since moved away and had children of their own, who went out to an early-bird dinner and now, barely pushing nine, are readying for bed.

We stop so abruptly my stomach lurches. I swallow hard against this new kind of nausea, my face buried between Dane's shaking shoulder blades. I can't tell if he's laughing or trying not to cry.

Silence presses in all around us, not just the absence of noise but the sort of silence that waits in the cathedrals at the bottom of the lake. When I'm sure my shaking is only from cold and no longer from fear, I slowly sit up and look around. We're actually in a building, a large gap behind us where double doors used to be, but not even fragments of the wood remain. Thick black soot streaks up the grey stone walls around gaps where fractions of stained glass windows still cling to the leaded frames. Holes gape in the colored panels of glass. Most of the roof is missing, letting in rippling pools of moonlight like quicksilver, and dead leaves litter the floor in a thick carpet. Here and there I can see signs of life, a bird's nest in the open cradle of a beam, the skeletons of small rodents tucked into the corners half buried under leaves. Behind the charred remains of what used to be an altar, a statue of the Christ weeps tears of soot, hands and feet blackened.

They said it was arson or a prank gone horribly wrong and never did figure out who caused it, but the church caught fire and blazed like a burning bush on a dark snowy night, so cold the water in the trucks wanted to freeze. We could see the conflagration from the school. Dane, Horatio, Laertes, and I huddled under a single blanket on the roof of the gymnasium and watched the flames dance and leap against the darkness, like angels made of flame that spun and twirled to the song of shattering glass and sirens.

They built a new church instead of repairing this one, left the carcass to rot until it became a ghost of stone and broken windows. Frost edges the leaves, our breath birthing clouds in the frigid air. Most of the pews are gone, burned away, but some pieces still stand, blackened and too thin, crisp like the skeleton of the altar.

This is what I'll be when the star stops burning, when the lake drowns the flames.

Tears sting my eyes, but I don't know if they're for me or for this pitiful remnant of a church.

Dane tugs awkwardly at me until he can get a grip on my waist, then twists me up and around until I can straddle his lap, our faces touching. My skirts spill around us, but my feet can't even touch the floor. He strokes the hair back from my face until it falls in a tangled mass of knots and violets down my back.

"After we took you back to your room, I was going to visit my father's grave," he whispers, "but I saw Claudius going into the church, so I followed him. He knelt down at the altar and clasped his hands and bowed his head, and I thought how easy it would be to end it all right there." His voice shakes, and there's a terrible intensity in his face. "They teach us how to shoot and call it education and physical exercise, so I could have stood at the back of the room, pulled the gun from my back, and known how to aim it, how to shoot it. I could have stood and watched the bullet bury itself right in his black, murdering heart. I promised to avenge my father, and that's all it would take. A single shot. A bullet. A death. I even had the gun in my hand and aimed almost perfectly. He never would have known what hit him. Dead before he even hit the floor."

"But you didn't," I murmur, unsure if words are what's needed from me right now. Words or silence, sometimes it's hard to tell, and I've never been good with words, not for other people.

"He was praying," he spits. "His entire face was screwed up like the words were poison on his tongue, and I wanted him to choke on his confession. I had my finger on the trigger and then I realized: if I kill him while he's at prayer, while his soul is in his communion with God, I send him straight to Heaven. My father, a good man, burns in Purgatory for sins he had no chance to confess. How would it be any sensible sort of vengeance to guarantee his murderer Heaven because I couldn't wait to take his life until he left a church?"

His hands grip my upper arms, drive the splinters deeper into my flesh, and I bite back a cry of pain. "It was a good reason not to kill him. Then. But what if I can't do it? What if every reason I've had for delay, my need for proof, my need to know I'm right, what if it's all just a way to hide my cowardice? Ophelia, what if I can't kill him? What happens if I can't do this?"

I have no words for him, but this time, I know it isn't what he needs. I can't tell him to kill Claudius. I can't tell him not to. All I can do is take my share of this pain too great for his body to hold.

"So many chances I've had to kill him, but I haven't done it, and now I'm not even sure I could. All my life I tried to make my father proud of me, did make him proud of me, but this one thing . . . the only thing he's ever truly asked of me . . . what if I can't do it?"

Only one of the ghosts has asked it of him. The other never would, never could. But that hardly means anything, not now.

His lips crash against mine, and his palms trail blood down my arms as he pulls me flush against him. His fingers fumble at the clothing between us, clumsy with the fear that threatens to devour him. The star burns and expands, and maybe this time it won't stop; it will just grow and grow, consume everything in its path, until all I am is the pain that Dane can't hold.

Laughter echoes against the ruined walls of the church, and I hear my mother's voice, Dahut's voice; the laughter is the song of the morgens, and they play and seduce and seek men to drown, men with emptiness where their hearts should be, men who claim to love when they only ever need and devour. We're born in blood, and we die in blood and oh!

Blood follows us every step of the way.

Blood and pain and sorrow and rage, all woven together into hands slick against my skin, a body that desperately tries to consume mine. The devil kissed poison into Dahut's skin, but Dane kisses pain into mine, traces love in blood until I shatter, floating lost on a storm-swollen sea of bells and laughter.

CHAPTER 31

"Ophelia!"

I open my eyes slowly to find Dane's panicked face inches from mine, his eyes wide with terror against a face that's far too pale even in the moonlight that spills from the missing sections of roof. When my eyes meet his, he crushes me against his chest, his entire body shaking.

"You have no . . . you just can't . . . you can't . . . Ophelia!"

Pain throbs everywhere we touch and mixed through the heavy scent I associate with my brother's room is the unmistakable smell of blood. It streaks my arms, his hands, my thighs, and my skin burns with every breath of contact, even where the frigid air curls between us.

"Why don't you ever stop me?" he demands, his voice as broken as the windows. There are holes in the words, just like the windows, pieces missing that finish the picture. "Damn you, Ophelia, why don't you ever stop me? You can't let me do this to you!"

Damp warmth seeps into my hair, and I reach up to touch his face, draw my fingers away to stare at them in wonder, at the clear pearls that glisten with salt and shame and fear on the ridges of my skin. "You're crying."

"You're the one good thing, but you'd let me destroy you. Don't let me, Ophelia, please don't let me. Everything else I think I could survive, but not if I destroy you. You can't . . . you can't let me. You just can't let me."

With every breath, the sun draws back into my chest. I shiver violently in the cold it leaves behind, until he tugs off his tuxedo jacket and slides my arms through the overlong sleeves. His hands move between us again, correcting, adjusting, fastening, but he doesn't move me to the back of the bike. He cradles me against his chest like I'm every precious thing, like I'm Pandora's box and all that's left within me is hope. He starts the bike.

We drive slowly around the outside of town, obeying every law and sign and light so as to attract no attention. He leaves the road a half mile from school and turns onto a narrow path worn mostly smooth by time and contact, a path that weaves into the woods and through the trees. Flashes of white and silver and grey streak through on either side of us, and the baying of hounds lights a fire in my blood. Those who watch the Wild Hunt as it passes can be driven mad.

If you're already mad?

There's only wonder.

Dane kills the bike as we pull up beside the plain chapel on grounds, the ghosts' blue-white pillars of flame within the fences, and part of his father's fractured soul watches us walk hand in hand up the path to Headmaster's House. Each step hurts, aches, but if I'm strong enough to bear his pain, I'm strong enough to bear my own. He walks me to my door and kisses me so softly I can barely feel it.

"Dane?"

He hesitates but finally drags his eyes up to my face like he's afraid of what he'll see there.

"I choose your pain. What you give me, you won't use to attack your mother, who waits to see you." Because hurting her hurts him as well, even when he's the one doing it.

"A choice."

"A choice." I lean forward to kiss him, gentle and slow, giving him all the forgiveness and love that keeps the lake at bay. "I love you, and the choice is mine to make."

Some of the fear—the pain—leaves his face, and he closes my door silently.

But for the spill of moonlight through the window, my room is dark. I can't see if the dress is ruined, don't want to see. I carefully pull it off and lay it over the hamper, study my ruined underwear before wrapping them in old homework and throwing them away. I don't want the bloodstains raising questions in the laundry. The water in the shower is only warm, not hot—a floor below me, I can hear the groan of pipes and know that Dane is cleaning up before he goes to see his mother—but it washes away the blood and the dead violets and some of the ache. Shivering in my towel, I flick on the light to dig the splinters from my skin with tweezers. They make a bloody pile on the edge of my sink, and then I have to wash my arms again before I can bind them in lengths of white gauze.

Tonight is a night to need comfort. From the chest at the foot of my bed, I dig out the few things of Mama's Father couldn't bear to throw away, the things he knew she would have wanted me to have. Her wedding dress is in there, carefully wrapped in layers of tissue, along with some of the ridiculous, beautifully old-fashioned gowns she wore whenever she was forced to appear at a formal occasion on Father's arm. I unwrap each gown and hang them up around the room. With each new yard of cloth, with each embroidered hem and jeweled bodice and set of stays, I get to retreat deeper into the fairy tale.

My nightgown is simple next to all the lovely gowns, white satin that shivers in the moonlight, soaked through where I brush the tangles out of my hair until it falls in a wet mass down my back and thighs.

I can feel the toll of the bells in my bones. There'll be no sleep this night, but it's too cold to cross the chain to the island in the center of the lake. Frost dances patterns across the surface of the water, not yet frozen, a delicate layer with the elegant, fractal geometry of a snowflake. I pull the coverlet from the bed and wrap it around me as I drag the chair from my vanity to the window.

The morgens gather at the edge of the lake, dancing in the shallows. They feel no cold, no pain, no sorrow. They haven't felt any of that in a very long time. Their pale skin glows in the moonlight, hair spinning around. Dahut's golden hair glitters, a bright beacon in the darkness.

Mama's a bruise, a shadow against the deep night. I can see her smile from here, her laughter still bouncing around the inside of my skull from the ruins of the church. Wreaths of dried flowers are the morgens' only adornments.

Beyond the shore, right at the edge of the gardens, the bean sidhe gather in their own dance, solemn and stately, a dance set to laments instead of laughter. Their long, silver-white hair flows down their backs, indistinguishable from the long robes that waft around them with every movement and breeze. Their mouths move with the shape of their songs, their sorrow a living force that guides the patterns of their feet in the dead grass.

Scattered clouds clear away, spilling a host of stars across the sky. They glitter like the diamonds at Gertrude's throat, the candles at the bottom of the lake. Moonlight expands, a flood across the grounds, and illuminates the bean nighe at the edge of the shoreline.

The grey-clad women in their tattered gowns cluster around their enormous basin, their grey hair in thick braids that twine down their backs to pool between their feet. One of them reaches into the ragged bag beside her and pulls out a piece of clothing she hands to the woman next to her. Piece by piece she hands the clothing out until everyone has one, then pulls out the last article for herself and holds it up to inspect it.

It's a dark blue blazer, the cuffs frayed slightly, the elbows creased from constantly being pushed back. One of the lapels refuses to lay flat even after she shakes it out, and the heavy wool is distinctly rumpled. She slaps it against the water in the basin, scrubs it against the corrugated board. The other women follow suit, and they all scrub in time to the morgens' laughter, to the bean sidhe's keening.

Tears burn my eyes as I watch them. They say the washerwomen launder the clothing and armor of those about to die in battle, and Dane is out to kill Claudius to keep his ill-considered promise to his father.

One of Hamlet's ghosts prowls between the back of the house and the gardens, a pillar of light the same ice blue as the lining of his casket, my dress at his wife's wedding, the blue that trims my uniforms and the tablecloths up at the school. Ice blue, cold blue.

Dead blue.

A gunshot cracks through the night.

My hands clutch my arms, but the splinters aren't there anymore. I can only squeeze against the echo of pain in the hopes that it will engender more, pain to keep me still, pain to keep me silent.

The bean sidhe sing louder, the cries feral and inhuman. The death they've been waiting for has happened, but there's no triumph there. They define greatness very differently than a human does. Someone important has died. It matters nothing if it's in truth someone good, only that it is, in some eyes, someone great.

I shouldn't mourn Claudius.

I don't mourn Claudius.

But still the tears come, blinding, choking, until I fall from the chair to huddle against the wall like I can hide from the fear and the grief that freezes my blood. The whirling spin of the star of my heart drowns out the laughter, drowns out even the song, until all I can hear is the endless whisper of *danedanedanedanedane* and the slap of wet cloth against the boards.

CHAPTER 32

Hands pull me gently from the floor by the window, hands that shake with fear and pain.

Dane.

I bury myself against his chest. Is there a star that burns there? What shape does his pain take within his own body, when it spins in an orb of flames in mine? He lifts me up and carries me to my bed, places me gently on the sheets. His hands shake, but there's such a terrible calm in his face.

Is it done? Is it finished?

But the star still burns. Perhaps it always will.

He peels away my blanket, my nightgown, and then his own clothing drops to a pile on the carpet. Everything in him trembles with tenderness. The lips that push air into my seared lungs. The fingers that linger against all the bruises that paint my skin.

Before, I was consumed, everything I am taken into him to fill the great and endless emptiness that freezes his soul. Now . . .

He kisses me dizzy, traces every inch of my skin as though he would memorize me. He seeks nothing from me, needs nothing from me. This is the Dane who watches me with wonder, who treasures me as more than the receptacle of his pain. This is the Dane who first gave me his ring, the Dane that kissed me for a crown of violets.

The Dane who loves me more than he hates Claudius.

He whispers the words against my skin, against every mark and bruise, every throbbing ache, and slowly the spinning star takes up his words, replacing his name with syllables that mean the same thing. *Iloveyouiloveyouimsorryiloveyouiloveyouimsorryiloveyou.*

The house is in an uproar beneath us, full of shouts and cries, but here in the room there's only Dane and the voice that dances and twirls where my heart used to be.

And then he's holding me against him, sweat slick on our bodies, clammy where the cold of the room gradually takes back its control, and our hearts race in time to the murmur. Just holding me. One finger traces the words against my spine, a tattoo without ink or pain but equal in permanence.

"They're going to send me away, Ophelia," he whispers against my temple. His arms tighten around me, pull me even closer.

Any closer and our skin would join.

"They're going to send me away to my own little cold place, only they choose to call it England. They'll send me to guardians, but they're friends of my uncle, and they guard only his concerns. I think he'll have them kill me."

Something's wrong. There's something there that's missing, or rather something there that shouldn't be, something extra, but his hands keep tracing promises against my skin and the thoughts scatter.

"He bought the tickets this afternoon. One for me, one each for the sheep he thinks to call collies."

The Toms.

"He wrote letters for them, letters with requests, letters with promises. I haven't read them yet, but I will, and then I'll know exactly what he's asking. But if I weren't here . . . he'd have Mother entirely to himself. Mother . . ." He swallows back the pain, takes deep breaths against the words that try to crack his voice. Then he kisses me, like I'm the balm that lets him speak. "For a moment, I thought she understood. I thought I finally got through to her about what she's doing. I thought she finally understood how wrong it was to marry her husband's brother, and so soon. Just for a moment . . .

and then Father came and she couldn't see him and it scared her so badly I don't think she'll ever understand."

He strokes my hair, still damp from the shower and now with sweat, until it spills around me on the coverlet and pillows, a night-purple spill against white fabric. "Who am I, Ophelia?"

Who is he?

He was born Hamlet Danemark VI, but he's only ever been Dane, and who is Dane, really? Dane is the boy, the young man, the sour tang of cigarettes and vodka on a warm summer night, the class ring that presses between us, imprinting our skin in equal measure. He's the kisses that leave me breathless, the pain that makes me burn. He's Gertrude's son, with a million fears and anxieties and nervous habits. He's Hamlet's son, with honor and promises and strength of character. However much he hates it, he's Claudius' nephew, the one who calculates and manipulates, who plans. He's the star who spins within my chest.

"Mine," I whisper. "You are mine."

A slow, astonished smile curves his lips, his dark grey eyes lit with wonder. "Yours."

And because it's the one thing that can give him joy, I say it again. "Mine."

And he kisses me so sweetly I don't care if I never breathe again.

"You should hate me, Ophelia. You should despise me and send me away for what I've done."

He's not the only one who's bruised me. At least Dane's pain is honest.

"When you find out . . . I don't want to lose your love."

"You never will."

"I will." The calm is fracturing. He kisses me again, fierce and demanding, needy, and I wonder if there will be such a thing as Ophelia anymore. He would devour me, make us one flesh, one body, one pain with a million shattered fragments. He can't lose what only exists within him. The star grows, expands, dazzles my eyes with points of light in colors that have never had names.

Then he's washing me, the wet cloth cool and soothing against inflamed skin, and the sweetness is back, the peace, the calm, the balance that lets him breathe around the solid knot of pain. He pulls his clothes back on and sits beside me on the bed, his hand stroking my hair, my face, lingering against my lips and the class ring that, more than the bruises, marks me as his.

His voice is as soft as his touch. "I love you, Ophelia. More than anything, more than my life. I love you beyond words, beyond my ability to express. Every good thing in me, however small anymore, is yours. And I'm sorry. I'm so sorry for what happens next."

"When they send you, you'll go."

"For now. You had to try to walk away to be a good daughter, and I didn't let you. I understand a little better now." He takes a deep breath, clasps my hand against his heart. "I'll come back, though. I swear I'll come back, and I'll make it up to you, everything I've done will be repaid in whatever way you ask. If you want my life, it's yours. And Horatio . . ."

"He loves you."

His eyes close against a flash of pain. "He's the best of us. And I'm a selfish beast who destroys the people I love the best. Whatever happens, Ophelia, he'll take care of you."

"Do I need to be taken care of, Dane?"

"Yes," he says simply. "You need someone to protect you from me."

"Horatio can't protect me from you."

"From everyone else, then." He bends down to kiss me, and now I know what good-bye tastes like. Like salt and blood and nightmares. Like the bottom of the lake. "All my love and every good thing."

"Mine."

"Yours."

He helps me back into my nightgown and finds my robe, then presses trembling lips against my forehead. No more words.

I sit up on my bed and watch him leave. The door closes behind him with a soft click, and there's something terribly final about the sound. He'll only be in England for a little while, but he'll be back. Unlike Laertes, he'll write—he'll remind me he loves me. He'll trace the words with ink instead of sweat and tears, but they'll be just as real as the letters that form in the flares that precede the growth of my sun.

An irate bellow roars over the furor below. It takes me a moment to place it, but when I do, the blood freezes in my veins, even as the star expands.

Claudius.

Dane missed.

But the bean nighe . . .

I belt the robe tighter around me and slide off the bed. Horatio will know what's going on. He'll tell me what Dane couldn't.

But who do the bean sidhe sing for?

CHAPTER 33

Horatio isn't in his room. I don't even have to knock on his door because the music that always plays through the night is silent. Every member of the household staff is out in the halls, searching through empty rooms and public rooms, most of them with robes or coats hastily thrown on over nightclothes. No one has time to tell little Ophelia what's going on. They glance at me as I approach or wince when I address them, and then they look away, back to whatever it is they're searching for. Some of the maids are crying, but they won't tell me why; they just apologize and keep to their task.

As I come down the staircase to the first floor, I see Dane walking between the Toms. They have him roughly by the arms as though they actually think they could hold him if he took it in his head to escape. He catches my eyes and gives a solemn nod.

They've tied his hands behind him.

They disappear into Claudius' study and slam the door. Heated voices filter through, but the words are indistinguishable. One of the under-gardeners draws me gently away from the door.

"Miss Ophelia, you should go back to your room for now," he says gravely. There's fear in his eyes, but not of me. Jack won't keep gardeners who fear me or my mother's legacy. It's the only way he's ever tried to protect me, the only way he thinks I need it. But this young man is afraid. "Please."

"What's going on?"

"Miss Ophelia, please."

My father's office is empty, but the lights are still on, the papers are still stacked neatly across his desk. He puts them away every night, gets them out every morning, but it's a tradition, a ritual, something that lets him put the work away so he can sleep at night without his thoughts tumbling over words and numbers and names.

In the kitchen, the cook sits by the old-fashioned hearth and weeps into her apron. She's an old woman who's worked here in the kitchen since she was my age, the only real home she's ever known, and she wails like a pale shade of the bean sidhe outside. Her entire body rocks with the force of it, a steady back and forth on the short stool, a ship rising and falling in the crests and troughs of a storm-swollen sea.

I want to back away from her pain, but the under-gardener is still behind me, trying to get me to return to my room, so I race through the kitchen to the outer door and into the edge of the gardens. Cold air slams against me, sears my lungs, such a slight difference between burning and freezing. The gravel path digs into my bare feet.

Jack paces back and forth in front of a stretch of burlap-covered roses. His overalls cover a threadbare sleep shirt, his heavy great coat thrown over. He hasn't even tied his boots or tucked them in; his bare feet slide inside them. His step is slow and painful, his arthritis plagued by the cold and the long day of work that's already passed.

"Jack!"

He shakes his head when he sees me, rubs a hand against the shiny bald spot on his crown. "So much death, Miss Ophelia," he mumbles. "Every year, every single year, never can keep anything alive."

"Jack, what is everyone looking for?"

"They're looking for death, Miss Ophelia, but it's everywhere." He sinks down onto a stone bench, his entire body bent with the effort, and buries his face in his gnarled, dirt-streaked hands. "So much death."

Fear is a stench within the house and gardens. I shouldn't be able to smell anything; the cold should burn everything away, but fear stings my nose and brings tears to my eyes. So much fear, the kind of fear that only ever walks with death, but even this fear didn't accompany Hamlet's death.

But Hamlet's death wasn't accompanied by a gunshot in the middle of the night.

So much fear.

It crawls down my spine, erases Dane's words from my skin, shifts the letters into something new, something foreign. I sprint across the gravel paths deeper into the gardens, but Jack doesn't even lift away from his hands to watch.

The flowers are draped in burlap to protect them from the cold, to let them sleep until spring and rebirth and Jack's careful attention, but it makes the gardens a barren waste of brown and grey and dead, dead brown. Only the hedges are dark green and glossy, the leaves sharp edged and spiny and waiting to stab.

I turn away from the paths, and my feet skid across the dead grass, the crisp blades already damp with forming frost. Moonlight glitters off the lake, a cloudless night with a whole host of diamonds in the sky to dance and shimmer against the thin rim of frost. The morgens dance and play beside the dock.

Except for Mama.

She stands as close to the shore as she can, only her heels still in the water, and watches the house and gardens. Her pale skin glows. She doesn't look away, but her hand extends to me as soon as I'm within range, and I cling to it against the fear. It's contagious, a plague that stretches out from the house to infect all it touches.

But morgens can't feel fear. They leave that behind with everything else, with the love and the sorrow and the pain and the anger. They just leave it behind.

I can't infect Mama with the fear I don't understand.

She takes a step back and pulls me with her, another step and another, and then my feet are in the frigid, dark waters of the lake and digging into the mud to keep from going farther. "I promised, Ophelia, and now more than ever you need me to keep that promise."

But there's still a star spinning through my blood, a star that fills my chest and stomach and stretches tongues of fire down my limbs and into my throat. Soon I'll open my mouth and the flames will take the shape of truth on my tongue, liquid glass that still shreds and tears with too much honesty. I'm not empty yet, so the lake has nothing to fill. I tug back against my mother's grip, and then Dahut joins in on her side, leaving the dance and the laughter to try to lead me into the lake and the city that waits beneath the waters.

"I can't, not yet," I tell them, beg them. "Not yet."

"Oh, Ophelia." And when my mother finally looks at me, I can see the ghost of the sorrow she left behind, the memory that once she knew how to feel it, the truth that she would feel it if she could. "Time isn't kind."

"Not yet."

"*Dona eis requiem,*" whispers my mother, and the words stab through me, make the fear worse. The thought takes breath, the breath takes shape into voice, the voice shapes into a prayer that stumbles from my mother's lips and ripples across the surface of the water.

I jerk away, nearly fall in my haste to scramble back onto the questionable safety of the grass, and she watches me with eyes that remember too much sorrow.

"Oh, Ophelia."

I keep backing away, and then my back fetches up against a great metal basin. The silver burns wherever it touches, flowers of frost blooming across its outer curves. The bean nighe study me with empty grey eyes, their bare arms buried in the sudsy water.

I've only ever spoken to the morgens before, and only because Mama is among them, but there's so much fear the very air reeks of it. I swallow hard and curl my hands against the rim, feel the frost that burns and blisters. "Whose clothes do you wash?"

"Ophelia, no!" cries Mama. She shakes her head, a great fountain of night-purple hair. "Do not ask anything of the washerwomen! They always answer!"

One of the women studies the dark blue blazer in her hands. Strands of grey hair—not silver, but a true grey like dull iron—stick to the sides of her face where her damp arms have brushed them from her eyes. She reaches out to one of the other women, who surrenders her scrap of cloth without a murmur and hands it to me.

It's a faded white, or it would be if blood hadn't splashed through folds in patterns like batik. Embroidered squares march haphazardly along the edges, the stitches lumpy and either too loose or too tight, the wandering borderline of silver thread showing where squares grew too tall or didn't grow enough. Silver and dark blue and ice blue—dead blue—and in one corner, curling initials where the thread didn't quite cover the thin marker beneath.

PCC.

My fingers throb with the memory of needles, of tearing away tiny flaps of skin as I accidentally stabbed myself again and again. I was barely six, but one of the maids patiently taught me how to sew, to embroider, and I made a handkerchief for

PCC.

Polonius Cassian Castellan.

Father.

The scrap of cloth drops back into the water, and I race away from the basin, from the bean nighe, from the morgens that dance in the lake and Mama who stands apart and watches me with eyes that want to be worried but can only summon the echo of concern.

Father was going to hide himself in Gertrude's room.

Father was going to listen to her conversation with Dane.

Father was there.

Father was . . .

I sprint into the gardens, so much fear, so much death, but I can't go back into the house, not the house that crawls with people grieving, people scared. A blue-white flicker dances before me and a hand extends, compassion and sorrow and patience.

Hamlet.

Not the Hamlet that prowls and paces and roars, not the Hamlet that rages or asks more than should ever be asked. This is the Hamlet who has only ever stayed in the cemetery, sitting against the angel that guards his grave and waiting for the long nights to end.

"This way, little one," he sighs.

I follow him around the bends and curves. He never hesitates at the branches and intersections, never stops or looks back to see if I'm still there.

There's no reason for me not to be.

I have nowhere else to go.

The star blisters my lungs, great gaping wounds that make it impossible to breathe.

Here he died.

Here he was murdered.

Here Jack found a syringe of milky-white poison.

Here Horatio spilled a secret.

Here Ophelia birthed a lie.

Here Dane . . .

Dane . . .

And Father . . .

Here Father lies, blood a brilliant blossom against his white dress shirt, dark against his rumpled navy blazer. Here the handkerchief, stained with blood from the bullet in his heart. Here the look of astonishment on his face, the realization that Dane was only ever partly playing mad, the shock that he was wrong.

Here the man the bean sidhe keen for, here the man whose clothes the bean nighe wash, here the man Mama would mourn if she could, for all that she hated the ties he bound her with. The man she would mourn for my sake.

Here Hamlet.
Here Father.
Here the endless scream that shreds my throat as it rips through the fear-drenched night.

PART V

CHAPTER 34

They won't tell me where he is.

They tore me from his body and locked me in my room, and they won't tell me where he is. The maids weep when they bring me food, and they weep when they take it away again. But they won't tell me where he is. Horatio would tell me if he knew, but he doesn't know, and they won't tell him, either.

They won't tell him about Dane either.

They won't tell me about Dane.

But Dane told me himself, off for his own little cold place, off to England with the Toms on either side, off to Claudius' friends and the chance he might die before he can return, but he promised.

He promised.

To come back.

To make this up.

Because when he made that promise, he'd just hidden my father's body in the gardens, positioned him where and how his own father had died, murdered just the same. Poison and bullets, it's just the shape of a thing, the form of the death, but the death is the same.

Because Dane pulled a gun, pulled a trigger.

But they won't tell me that either.

They won't tell me anything.

They lock me in my room and bring me food, and only Horatio tells me anything, but he knows so little.

It was an accident, he tells me.

Dane thought it was Claudius spying, he tells me.

Dane thought he'd finally kept his promise, he tells me.

But Dane already knew the truth: he destroys the people he loves the most.

Horatio comes in the morning with the maid and begs me to eat.

He comes at lunch and begs more.

He comes in the afternoon and walks me to the shower, tries to take me to the gardens, but they always tell him no and take me back to my room with no tub and no ceiling fan and a lock on the window.

He comes in the evening and then he's so tired and so close to tears that I eat with him, the food ash and stone in my mouth, and he holds back my hair when my stomach rebels.

I know I'm hurting him, but I don't know how to stop.

Dane never knows how to stop.

Mama cries my name from the lake, over and over, a clarion, a siren, and even though she can't feel, I think she still needs.

Needs to see that I'm all right.

But I'm not.

They lock me away and don't tell me anything, and Dane pulled a trigger and traced love into my skin.

Even now, the words tremble and sob and whisper in the star that blazes through every part of me *iloveyouiloveyouimsorryiloveyouiloveyouimsorryiloveyou.*

In the darkness, I can hear Claudius yell, hear Gertrude weep, hear Horatio turn up his music to drown it all. And then, while the music is still playing, he leaves his room and comes to mine, picks the lock on the door to come and sit beside me on the bed and hold me through the long night, because he promised Dane.

He would have done it anyway.

Because Horatio is the best of us.

And then he leaves to shower and change and comes back with the maid who brings breakfast, and that's the only way I know anything has changed.

Because nothing else does.

Jack lights a candle, but he doesn't know where to burn it, doesn't know where the body is so the soul can leave it and follow the flame up to wherever it goes. So he burns it in the gardens where the body was found and where it disappeared and sobs with great heaving gasps that wrack his entire body because there's just so much death in autumn and winter.

Because all the flowers are dead and dying.

Because he knows the hothouse flowers have only borrowed life, unnatural and out of season and never as strong.

Because everything dies.

All the pills are gone.

Dane threw them away, I threw them away, and the others are locked away in Father's office. Hidden away like the rest of him.

Horatio is so tired.

For his family, he keeps up with his classes, forces himself through the work and the tests and the applications.

For Dane, for me, he stays with me through the long nights when even the endless murmur of the star can't drown the keening lament from outside the walls.

He falls asleep stretched out on my bed, his face too pale with fatigue, and sometimes I can stay next to him and watch him and stroke his dark auburn hair and be grateful.

And sometimes I have to walk away, to find the door he's left open and wander through the halls as the ghost no one sees, no one talks to.

All my life I saw the ghosts, the only one who did.

And now Horatio is the only one who sees me.

We destroy the ones we love the best.

Father's bedroom is locked, and the boys never showed me how to pick locks. Horatio took all my keys for all the places we were never supposed to go. He asked and he begged, tears in his eyes, and I gave them willingly because there are so many accidents waiting to happen.

Not scared of me.

Not scared of what I could do.

But scared for me, and what might happen.

Even his eyes give me that distinction, give me that truth for comfort.

Because Horatio is the best of us.

Father's bedroom is locked, but his study isn't, so when Horatio falls into fitful sleep, I leave my room and walk through the halls and down the stairs to the room that Father spent so much time in. I sit in the heavy leather chair with the awkwardly shifted padding and trace my fingers over the worn, discolored patches. It matches his hands, his elbows, the back of his head, nearly in place with mine, because Laertes got Mama's height and I didn't, but Father didn't have it either, and we're so nearly the same size.

The papers are scattered across his desk, disrupted by people looking for something they didn't know how to find.

They won't tell me anything, but have they told Laertes?

Laertes, who hasn't written, hasn't called?

Laertes, who disappeared into Paris and may never come home?

Laertes, who maybe did what Mama never could and found a way to cut the ties that keep us held to Elsinore Academy?

I separate the papers into piles and tap them against the scratched surface of the desk to line up the edges of the pages. I don't know how to sort them, but I can stack them.

This is the room Father loved, the room that held everything he thought he was. The room he always came back to. The room he hid in. He buried himself in work and the school, but he was at his happiest here.

He loves—

Loved.

—his children, respects—

Respected.

—his duty towards us, and I know he *felt* a true affection towards us, however clumsily the expression might be, but we were accidents. We were the chaos in his life, our mother's legacy, her children far more than we were his.

My mother's daughter burns with the touch, with the kiss that's been banished to England.

My mother's daughter sees too much.

My mother's daughter remembers the lake and the promise and the emptiness that only Dane's star fills—the only things that keep me from the drowned city.

He trembled to give it voice, as though voicing it would make it real, but always the truth was there in his eyes: I am too much my mother's daughter.

And now I always will be.

"Ophelia, you know better than to disturb me while I'm working. Out of the chair now and back to your bed, be a good girl."

The papers drop from my grasp, spill over the worn wood of the desk. A blue-white flicker fills the room, and I slowly lift my eyes to the pale pillar that stands between the visitors' chairs on the other side.

There's a slightly darker glow against his rumpled shirt and coat where the blood flowed, the edge of the handkerchief sticking out of the chest pocket. His short hair is mussed, his beard needs a trim, and his face has such fond exasperation that, for a moment, I can almost believe that the color is just a trick of the moonlight.

But it isn't.

It can't be.

"Father . . ." I whisper, and he flaps his hands at me.

"To bed, Ophelia, now. I have a great deal of work to do."

"You're dead."

He takes a step back, one hand rising to adjust the reading glasses he isn't wearing. "That isn't funny, and the time for games is done."

The time for games will never be done.

Not until Claudius is dead.

Not until the rage of Hamlet finally sleeps.

Not until Dane keeps his promise.

Which promise?

The tears choke my throat, blind me to everything but a blue-white field of light, and I run away.

But I can never run far. I run up the stairs, up to my room, up to the bed where Horatio needs the sleep so badly, and shake him awake anyway, because he's the only one who sees me.

Who hears me.

"He's here," I sob, and even before his eyes open he's squeezing my hand to give me comfort. "Horatio, he's here—he shouldn't be here, but he is, and you have to tell them! You have to tell them because he shouldn't be here, but he is and he doesn't even know it; you have to tell them."

"Tell them what, Ophelia?" he asks, his voice still scratchy from sleep.

"Father! You have to tell them about Father!"

"What about your father, Ophelia?"

I can't force the words through the sorrow, but he holds me and strokes my hair and waits for the storm to pass, because he's always sure that it will. For Horatio, there are no gates to breach, no key to foolishly give away so the tide can enter. For him, the walls always stand and the storm always passes.

"Father's in his study," I manage finally. "He's in his study, and he doesn't know he's dead. You have to tell them so they can fix it."

"They can't fix it," he tells me gently. "They won't see him, and they won't know how to fix it. They can't fix it."

They can't fix anything.

They won't tell me where he is.

I squirm out of his grasp and back into the hall, down a single flight of stairs to the second level where the Danemarks live and throw myself against the door of Gertrude's private suite. My fists pound against the locked door until the skin cracks and bleeds, but there's no answer, even when I call and sob her name. One door down, Hamlet used to sleep, until he slept forever and his brother took his place, and though it was Claudius who started all this, who formed the first ghosts and set the stage for the second, I pound on his door too and beg and plead.

Horatio follows me and tries to pull me away, but he can't bring himself to bruise me, and he can't tear me away without gripping too hard and marking my skin, the only one who ever cares about the marks and scars he leaves behind and one of the few I would always forgive.

They won't tell me anything.

They won't even listen; they can't hear.

And despite the star, I can hear the murmur of the lake, feel its liquid whisper in my bones, a thin layer of darkness between water and flame.

CHAPTER 35

Through the days that follow, I try and I try and I try, but I can't find either Claudius or Gertrude. They leave a room before I can enter it, they lock a door with me on the other side. They won't see, they won't listen, they won't . . .

They won't anything.

And Father stays in his study, ghostly papers in his hands because he can't touch the real ones, but he doesn't realize that it's all awash in blue-white light. He never believed in the ghosts in life, and he doesn't believe in them in death. He doesn't believe in himself, in his own existence.

Restless in his years of service and his hidden grave, he returns to his office and his duties, nothing out of the ordinary. When dawn comes, he flickers away, back to Purgatory or nothingness or wherever, but when the sun sinks into the lake, earlier and earlier every day, he flickers back and goes about his tasks, creating them to fill the void left behind by his death.

I'm the only one who sees him; I can't let them lock me in anymore. Horatio kisses my cheek and leaves for classes—something that grasps at normal in this madness—and I reach for the heaviest book in my room: my Old Testament Studies text. It's a comforting weight in my hand, solid and familiar. I lift it over my head and bring it smashing down on the doorknob, again and again, until I hear a great crack in the wood. The knob sags in its carved hole, then drops down to the floor, and I can see through into the hall. The lock falls after it, a perfectly innocuous piece of metal on the thick carpet. My door drifts open and won't fully close, won't stay closed.

But they can't lock me in anymore, and with this small freedom I race downstairs to throw myself into the flood of people.

Gertrude and Claudius don't see me, but there are many others Claudius must see, and they in turn see me. Parents and members of the Board, students who want to know what's going on, who connect the crack of the gun in the middle of the night to Dane's absence, to Father's absence, to my absence. I don't know with what pretty words Claudius soothes their fears—as if such a thing can be soothed when it's a living force that prowls through the house and the dead gardens—but they come out of his office looking relieved or thoughtful or, for some, uncertain.

But they see me.

So I wait for the people to come out of Claudius' office, and I beg them to go back in and speak to Claudius again, to tell him of my father's ghost who comes to his office to work as he always did, to tell him that murdered souls can't rest easy. Faces melt into each other, time fracturing in strange ways. I reach for a woman's scarf in the late morning and find myself clutching a man's sleeve in the early afternoon. They both shake me off, those two and countless others.

They never go back inside.

Claudius never comes out when he knows I'm there.

And eventually, either Horatio or one of the under-gardeners or footmen comes to take me away again.

And now someone stands, at all times, outside my broken door.

Mama's dresses are still hung about my room, tapestries of embroidered cloth that make a brilliant spill against the sterile white walls. She hated the formal occasions, hated the expectations that were made of a school wife. She would have nothing to do with Gertrude's elegant sheaths and simple lines.

She wore the corsets of an earlier time, the yards and yards of

277

fabric that swept around her like a fountain. She needed less air in the stays, and then she went to the lake and didn't need air at all.

I pull one of the gowns from the wall, all plum silk and sheer black overlays, nearly the color of my hair, my eyes, my bruises. I fumble with the stays, with the laces that tighten around me like Dane's arms, that squeeze my ribs and waist and my hips. I can't tighten them all the way on my own, but I can get into the dress, with its drapes of jet beads and the black embroidery, black like the waters of the lake at night. It's too long for me, but I hold up the skirts and spin around and around and around until the skirts and my hair spin with me in a great spiral of ink, of night, of bruises against the air.

"Ophelia."

I stop spinning, but the air doesn't. It goes on without me, tugging at me until I fall, and strong hands have to catch me.

"I . . . I think I convinced Mrs. Danemark to see you." Horatio never calls her Gertrude, even though she gave him permission that third summer. "You'll have to come now, though." His eyes follow the lines of the dress and pain fills them, darkens them.

I take his hand and lead him out the open door, then let him take the lead because I have no idea where we're going. Gertrude will stand in one place, and maybe she'll finally see me, hear me; maybe I won't be the ghost my father is, that Hamlet is. He takes me to the parlor, but the stage is long gone, the chairs restored to their private clusters around the space, even the dainty little couches for the women that look as though they'll collapse if anyone sits on them.

Gertrude's eyes are red against her pale face, and strands of silver gleam at the roots of her hair. She's in her late forties, and for the first time she looks it, looks older, and Claudius' ring weighs down her hand.

She weeps at night because she can't weep where anyone might see her, and now she's too tired to hide the signs.

Horatio exhausts himself to take care of me.

She exhausts herself to take care of an image.

She isn't quite bright, isn't quite clever.

And now, worn and weary with her makeup painted on more thickly to try to conceal that, she isn't quite Gertrude.

"Where is the beauty of the Danemarks?"

Her right hand—the hand not weighed down by a ring too bright and gaudy—flutters anxiously at her chest. "How are you, Ophelia?"

"Your hand wouldn't pain you so were the right love upon it."

Her eyes widen, deepening the lines she's always hidden so well. "Whatever do you mean, sweet child?"

"He is dead and gone, lady. He is dead and gone, and at his head an angel guards and an angel weeps, all for a band of gold that broke in the face of the truth."

"Ophelia—"

"Black his shroud, and blue, ice blue, dead blue, the color of the school blue—"

"Claudius!" she cries with relief, and a shadow moves across the floor to take its place at her side. She clings to the hand that extends to her, clutches it against her cheek like a lost child. "Claudius, look, the poor child."

"Flowers covered him, clothed him head to toe, but flowers never grow on a grave without tears to nourish them. Where are your tears, lady? Why don't the flowers grow?"

Claudius stares, and for the first time since I've known him, his eyes aren't emeralds, aren't cold, hard stones that keep the thoughts behind the facets. He stares at me, and there's pain there, the pain that wasn't there when his brother died. He clears his throat uncomfortably, his hand shaking as he reaches out to touch my cheek. "How are you faring, lovely girl?"

"Lord, we know what we are, but know not what we may be!" Laughter spills too brightly from my lips, but how great a change this has wrought in him! He never saw me until he couldn't ignore me and now, how he calls me lovely and lets us see the humanity in his eyes, the humanity that comes at too great a cost and too late.

Far, far too late.

"But sometimes we don't even know what we are, and now a ghost sits in a worn leather chair and shuffles papers that don't exist. You have made a ghost of him who served you best."

Claudius bends down closer to his wife, passes a hand over her hair without mussing the arrangement. "How long has she been like this?"

"I don't know; I've only seen her just now."

They aren't going to listen.

"I can't help but weep to think that you've hidden him in the cold ground," I tell them quietly, "and yet my brother must know of it, if he knows of anything, and so your secrets bury us less deep than you suppose. Good night, lady. Good night, sweet lady."

Gertrude is not the cleverest of women, but she has always tried to do well by me.

Until now.

Such fools do our fears make of us.

CHAPTER 36

The driveway is full of cars, full of people who mill about in suits and talk over each other, full of students who watch their parents and their parents' lawyers with wide eyes or cynical smiles. I drift among them and pockets of silence burst around me; they stare after me.

Do they know my father's dead?

Do they know Dane pulled the trigger?

Do they know Claudius started it all?

But they don't know anything, that's why they're here, to demand the answers Claudius can't and won't give.

Horatio tugs gently at my elbow to lead me away from a clutch of former students and drapes his jacket over my naked shoulders. The grass is grey now, all the green leeched away by death and fear and frost, and it crunches beneath my bare feet. Away from the drive, away from the people, away from the house of ghosts and those who create them.

To the gardens.

But the gardens are also a world of ghosts, ghosts draped in burlap and stripped branches and dead plants that Jack mourns, each and every one, like a slain child.

Jack has never had children.

Every autumn, every winter, I think I understand why.

Because there's just so much death.

All through the fractured days and nights, the bean sidhe have sung for my father, but now it's a new song, gentle and deep and so sincere I wonder if I've ever heard them sing before. Their laments are a duty, but now they mourn, truly mourn, and their song kills the few plants still struggling to live. I tuck my arm through Horatio's and let him lead us along the paths, close my eyes so I can listen to the song that calls an answering sorrow from the star in my chest.

Death is an old friend at Elsinore Academy, a constant companion to the students whose parents want too much, give too little. It murmurs through their fears, through their desperations, through every test and grade and struggle, through every friendship and relationship, through every e-mail or phone call home, every visit that does or doesn't come. Death stalks among us, and sometimes we take it by the hand and let it lead us to a place where none of it is supposed to matter anymore.

And it doesn't matter.

It just doesn't go away.

It ties Hamlet even as it sunders him, ties him to the cemetery and the rage and a promise not yet fulfilled.

But it freed my mother, released her to the lake that had always waited to claim her, broke the chains of sorrow and fear and feeling until only the memory remains.

Dahut doesn't remember, or perhaps she never knew.

Perhaps she was only ever that terrible emptiness that waited to be filled by the storm-swollen tide. Perhaps the city and the walls and the gates were only ever delaying what always had to happen.

Mama will forget the echoes. In time. Eventually she'll forget even the memory of those feelings, won't be able to name them even in others.

The lament grows louder, and I open my eyes to see a bean sidhe before us on the path. She holds out a hand, not to take mine but to bring me closer of my own will, to follow her. I asked the bean nighe a question, and they gave me an answer; now the rest of the fae have no reason to ignore me. I broke the wall.

But perhaps I've always been one of them, because the bean sidhe simply holds out her hand until I tug against Horatio to follow her. He can't see her, can't hear her, but he studies my face and lets me change our direction without a word of argument. She stops outside the greenhouse, joins the line of silver-white women who can barely be seen in the gloomy grey light.

The glass is framed in steel and steel is iron, so they can't go any farther.

Before this, they've never seemed to want to.

The air inside the greenhouse is humid, each breath a weight in the lungs. Outside, the air is nothing but a cold knife that slices through. There's never really a way to breathe, to use the air for a way that makes sense rather than shaping it into meaningless words.

The flowers struggle, and some of them even bloom, but they're never as vibrant as their cousins outside, never as true. There's no truth in what's unnatural. There never is, can never be.

There's no truth in a ghost.

The roses bloom, their colors pale echoes, blush and peach and faded yellow, with never a chance to deepen, to become more. Their thorns are sharper, stronger, a defense against the artificial life. The heavy heads droop towards the soil.

Towards Jack.

"Oh, God," breathes Horatio and crosses himself.

I kneel down in soil still damp from the watering can at Jack's side. His eyes are closed, his mouth partially open, and he's fallen atop one of his arms, the hand over his heart. His left arm is swollen. Everything about him is still.

Horatio reaches past me to press two fingers deep into Jack's wrinkled neck, but we both know there'll be nothing to find. "We should call an ambulance."

There's no point. There's never a point. Mama was dead before they called. I was dead, but they yanked me back with bruises and breath long before the ambulance arrived. Hamlet was dead; Father was dead.

Jack is dead.

The ambulance never matters.

Petals drop from the roses, their edges curled and withering, and brush against Jack's leathery, sunbaked skin like kisses, like rain. Like tears.

I push against him until I can roll him onto his back in the bed of soil, fold his arms over his chest. His eyes are closed, so I close his mouth, his skin cool but not cold to the touch. Horatio doesn't run for help, doesn't pull out his phone; he just watches me as I neaten Jack's stringy white ponytail and the stained, patched overalls.

The roses weep for him, weep where I can't, because there are no more tears. The star burns away everything but the lake, and the lake never shares its water; it only ever takes, never gives. There are no tears.

I reach for the first knot of twine that binds the roses to the trellis. It's rough against my fingers, scratchy and tough and settled into its knots. Finally, it releases and I move to the next, thorns sipping from my skin as I move my hands through the plants.

Jack mourned each and every plant like a slain child, and they mourn him in return, weep for him in the way only plants can, by giving of themselves. Humans were never so generous. I weave the roses into a blanket over him, let them take the blood from my hands to make them strong so they can protect him from those who would try to take him away and make a ghost of him.

Others will hide his body without any of the rites, without the prayers to release the spirit, because that's what people here do: they create the ties that most are never strong enough to break.

There aren't enough roses.

His head and his torso are covered by the bower, but his legs stick out obscenely against the dark soil. Horatio clears his throat and steps forward with a rough burlap blanket, perhaps even the same one Jack used to cover me when I came to the violets for comfort.

He covers Jack's legs and tugs away one of the hydrangea globes from three beds over, places the mass of pale blue blossoms between the gnarled hands, surrounded by geraniums.

Perseverance and comfort, flowers to define the sum of a man.

For Jack, I think even Dahut will try to mourn, silent moments for the man who tended the flowers that twine through her golden hair.

The bean sidhe honor Jack; in their own way, they love him, the man who believed in them with every fiber of his being for all that he could never see them.

Horatio weeps, quietly and with dignity, and this is yet one more thing to batter him, to break him. Sorrows come not as spies but as armies, whole hosts that stand at the gates to tear down our defenses. He's so tired, so very tired. He surrenders to the tears that I can't find, and I move through the greenhouse, collecting the flowers and herbs that have no one to love them anymore, only tend them. Tending and caring are such different things. I pile them into my arms until I can't hold any more, my skirts dropped to drag through the soil at my feet.

The glass door swings open and ushers in a frosty gust of wind that trembles through the plants closest to it and frames one of the under-gardeners, the same one who stands so often at my door since I broke the lock. "Miss Ophelia, your brother is here."

I turn to Horatio, who mops at his face with his sleeve, and he gives me a weak smile and comes to my side. "Yes, we'll go see your brother," he tells me. "Honestly, did you expect something different?"

I didn't expect to have the chance.

I didn't think he'd come home.

I didn't think . . .

But then, the thoughts never stay even when they form, so perhaps I did think, and it flew away on sparrow's wings only to fall and fall and die.

There is so much death.

"Let's go see your brother," Horatio reminds me and steers me towards the door.

Arms full of death, I stumble forward.

CHAPTER 37

The under-gardener takes us back into the house and to the Headmaster's office. He leads us through the kitchen rather than the main door; the entire house hums with conversations and anger and excitement. Bits and pieces of the discussions float above the others, spare words like "irresponsible" and "deplorable" and "unconscionable." The under-gardener knocks politely on the door but calls through rather than open it. "Headmaster, Miss Ophelia and Mr. Tennant are here."

Locks scrape against the door before it opens. Gertrude has aged years since we left her in the parlor, years that show in the lines around her eyes and mouth, in the exhaustion that purses her lips into a thin line. She ushers us in, then closes and locks the door behind us, a lock and a door between them and the angry masses. The enemy at the gates.

Claudius' hands shake as he pours himself a glass of amber liquid. There's no clink of ice—he isn't wasting the space. He fills it to the brim and knocks it back; by the way his eyes are glazed, it isn't his first.

And Laertes . . .

He's so pale. Pale and worn, his deep blue eyes ravaged by tears. His entire body trembles with the force of his fury. I can't imagine they told him any more than they've told me, but someone has told him enough to put the picture together, someone has told him that

Dane pulled the trigger, that Claudius was the reason Father was even in the room. Someone has told him just enough to stoke his fury.

All in black, with his night-purple hair dull from travel, my brother almost looks like Dane. Only for a moment, from the corner of the eye, but the rage and the pain and the grief are all the same. His jaw is shaded with stubble, his face thinner than it was. Thinner, and older.

And stricken.

"Ophelia . . ." he whispers. "Ophelia, what's happened to you?"

I glance at Horatio, whose eyes flicker from my tangled hair, the fading ring of bruises at my neck, to the bruise-colored gown and armful of flowers.

"Have you been taking your pills?"

Pills, pills, always the pills. How long has it been since Dane threw them away? Less than a day between that and Father's death but how long since then? But what have pills to do with grief? With pain? What have pills to do with anything? The pills have nothing to do with Father's death. "They buried him in a secret grave, where even the flowers cannot reach to weep."

He touches my face, his hands shaking. "If you had all your wits and begged me to revenge, it couldn't be more moving than . . . than . . . this."

Revenge is sorrow waiting to weep.

Look where it got Dane.

Look where it got Father.

There are better things than revenge.

Flowers fall from my arms as I dig through the bundles and find one to press against his chest. "There's rosemary," I tell him, "that's for remembrance. You need to remember. And there, that's pansies. That's for thoughts."

Gertrude turns away, her face buried in a handkerchief.

"You're a lesson in madness, Ophelia, all your thoughts and re-membrances connected to that single fact."

"There's fennel for you and columbines. And rue—some for

you, and some for me." I tuck the flowers into his hair, into mine. "There's a daisy. I would give you some violets, but they all withered when . . ." The last basket of violets, knotted into my hair, washed out along with dirt and sweat to scatter along the tiles of my shower. Violets to a dinner, to a play, to a consummation that made the star blaze brighter than ever. "They withered, when our father died. *They* say he made a good end." I slant a glance towards Gertrude and Claudius; her shoulders shake as she weeps; he pours another drink. "They buried him in secret, not even a flower to mark his grave. Keep a murder silent like the grave and the body will vanish from thought as surely as from sight."

But he turns to Claudius and Gertrude, seeks an explanation from them because even now—now, of all times—he still won't listen to me. "Has she converted her grief to this . . . this . . . what is this?"

"Laertes . . ." Claudius sets the glass down hard on the desk and grips my brother's shoulder. He looks like he wants to step closer, bring Laertes closer, but he forebears. "Laertes, I know you have been rather . . . insulated from things here of late, but I promise to explain everything to you if you will only give me the chance. There is much to tell you, much to acquaint you with. Will you listen?"

I have no doubt Claudius will do just as he says: he will explain.

He will explain the poison into Laertes' ears as surely as he did his brother's.

"He isn't going to come back," I tell him, but Laertes doesn't even turn back to me. "He isn't going to come back. He is dead. Go to your own deathbed; he still won't come back. Revenge will not bring him back. He is gone."

Horatio takes the last flower from my hand and slowly, precisely, shreds it until a rain of petal pieces surround him like a circle of salt. "He's gone, Ophelia," he whispers, "but so is your brother."

Is he Father's son? Or Mama's?

Perhaps in this, he is Dane's friend more than anyone's son, a plague rather than an inheritance, a disease of revenge born of every ugly emotion with which death acquaints us.

The price of Dane's revenge is still mounting.

"Do you think you can eat something?" Horatio's face is thinner, his cheeks hollow. He's missed meals chasing after me, but he isn't used to pills that rob him of appetite, doesn't have a body that forgets to feel hungry.

I lace my fingers through his, silk from the too-long sleeves a soft layer between our skin, and give him a smile. "I can try."

The others don't even notice when we unlock the door and leave; Horatio deliberately leaves it open, and it's barely a moment before a group of parents charge past us to ram the gates. In the kitchen, I tell the cook I'm hungry, and she bursts into tears, gives me a quick hug that cracks my ribs and squeezes all the air from me. As she cooks, maids and footmen and under-gardeners drift in, a gradual cluster around the warmth of the massive hearth. She adds more food each time more enter.

The newest under-gardener, the butler's nephew who graduated high school only months before, is the last to enter, and then all the house and garden staff are gathered together, Horatio and I welcome in their midst. He pulls his hat off his head, ginger hair standing up in every direction and tears tracking down his face. "Jack's dead," he says simply. His eyes find me within the group and take in my shredded hands still streaked with blood and dirt. "He's with his roses."

Their grief is soft and gentle, a summer rain in the midst of so much raw pain. The cook passes around hot food and drinks and slowly, the stories start. Stories about Jack and his love for the gardens, his fondness for a good beer—or a bad beer—his ornery nature. Laughter joins the tears.

Then Horatio is smiling at me, and I look down to find my plate is empty. I don't remember eating, but his relief is so palpable that I smile in return, settle into his shoulder, and listen to this celebration of Jack's life.

There's so much death in this place, sudden and unexpected.

But there's joy, too, when the life was well-lived. There's comfort in the reporting.

Father has never had these kinds of friendships, never had this community to mourn and celebrate in equal measure. Laertes, Dane, Horatio, and I gathered together around an open grave with cigarettes and flasks and told stories of the Headmaster, to honor the man he was, and I think the staff gathered here to do the same.

No one speaks of Father. Another good man gone to his grave, yet no one gathers to celebrate him.

Even Laertes only speaks of revenge.

I want someone to speak of me someday.

Horatio's hand squeezes mine, and he leans over to kiss my cheek.

I think someone will. Someday.

CHAPTER 38

Laertes plots and plots and plots, with Claudius dripping poison in his ear like a malevolent fairy godfather. Every time my brother sees me, he looks newly stricken, and soon he doesn't see me at all. His eyes pass over me if I enter the room; his ears don't hear the words I speak.

So I stop trying.

Mama sees me, watches me, her eyes track my progress as I pace along the long curve of the lakeside. She laughed to see me in another of her gowns and told me how pretty I look, but there in her eyes I can see the echo of the worry she wants to feel. Dahut has had hundreds and hundreds of years to forget, but Mama's only had eight. Eight years since we died, since bruises and breath brought me back.

Father made a choice between us, and I've always wondered if he regretted it.

Now I'll never know.

Because though his ghost moves through his office with imaginary papers and conversations, though he smiles when first he sees me each night, it's still not something he'll speak about.

Mama watches but aside from that first observation each day, she doesn't say anything. Just the fact of her is enough to remind me of her promise. She waits to keep it, waits for the emptiness and the lake to rush in so she can take me away like she always said she would.

They've given up trying to keep me in my room. There's no point. Too many people have seen me, too many people know the carefully fractured pieces of truth that Claudius tries to spin and control.

Polonius is dead and Dane is gone and Ophelia's lost her wits.

Each morning, Horatio wakes up beside me, goes to shower and change clothes, and comes back with the maid that brings breakfast, and for his sake I choke the food down. When he leaves for classes, I come to the lake, because it's the one thing that still makes sense.

The only thing that ever did.

Always did.

A heavy wool blazer settles around my bare shoulders.

Classes must be out.

Horatio crouches down beside me, his balance off on the tangle of willow roots. He shivers in the cold without his coat, hunches his body against the fierce wind that slices through his thin dress shirt. "How you haven't come down sick is beyond me," he tells me, teeth chattering.

Because I have a star burning inside me. It burns hotter and brighter every day, tendrils of flame under my skin and on my tongue, too much truth in my eyes. I hold out my hands, the moonlight skin tinted blue from the cold I can't feel, and trace the veins that run like seams through the surface. Like cracks that will open up and spew forth streams of lava. "Do you know what a star does before it collapses?"

He shakes his head, eyes dark with worry. It's hard to remember how bright they can be, when he laughs, when he dances, because now even when he smiles he's worried.

"It expands," I whisper, and wait for the flames to show.

The star will expand until it consumes all of me, and then, when there's nothing left to consume, it will collapse into a hungry black void the lake will race to fill, a vessel without a bottom.

"I got a package today from Dane."

He holds it out to me, places it in my lap when my hands are too

292

stiff to take it without dropping. He chafes my hands between his to share his warmth, share his feeling, his usefulness. It's a plain box, but the markings aren't from England.

They're from Virginia.

Within, a slew of sealed envelopes bear ink across the front in Dane's careful cursive.

"He sent it from Monticello Academy."

Reggie Fortin's school. A model of what Elsinore could be without a Danemark as Headmaster.

"There's a letter in there for you."

The ink spells out different lengths, but the letters don't mean anything, have no connection to the letters of flame that spill through my veins and mingle *danedanedanedanedane* with *iloveyouiloveimsorryiloveyouiloveyouimsorryiloveyou*. His hands reach down into the box, sort through the envelopes until he can find the one that should have my name on it, but nothing about it looks familiar. I hold the letter against my chest, wonder if I can absorb the words this way instead.

"Who are the other letters for?"

"There's one for me, for Keith. For Laertes. For his mother and uncle. One for . . . one for Jack."

"Virginia is a long way from England."

"And not at all far from us," he sighs. "I haven't had a chance to read mine yet to find out why he's there and not in England. I just got the package before I came out here for you."

"Laertes won't read his."

"Sounds about right." He cradles my cheeks in his palms, and only then do I realize how cold I should feel, that his hands should burn my skin. "Will you come inside?"

"Not yet." I hold the box up to him when he would shift to sit beside me. "You have things to do."

"They can wait."

Can they?

After too long a moment, he sighs and takes the box back, pushes to his feet. "I'll come back for you in a little while, all right?

Unless you come in on your own."

"You're the best of us."

"Sometimes I wonder if that means as much as it should," he murmurs.

"Words never mean anything. Look beneath them."

He gives me a small, sad smile and leaves his coat around my shoulders as he walks back to Headmaster's House and its cacophony.

A small splash tickles my bare feet, and I look up to see Mama pulling herself from the water. She leaves one foot in, the closest she can ever come to leaving the lake. "You have things to do too, Ophelia. It's time and past."

"Not yet."

Because the sun is still a star and time is still moving too fast. Time slows at the event horizon, slows and slows and slows until maybe the actual point of destruction never comes. But the sun is still a star and the black hole hasn't been born yet.

She takes the heavy envelope from my hands, her fingers leaving damp spots that darken the paper, and slides a nail under the adhesive seal. When she unfolds the pages, a jumble of ink dances across the sheets, meaningless and incomprehensible.

"My Ophelia," she reads aloud, her voice soft with the compassion that's as much a memory as the fear and the mourning. "By now, you've learned the truth of what happened that night, or at least parts of it. As I spoke with my mother in her room, a voice cried out from within her closet. I thought it was Claudius—who else would hide in my mother's closet?—and before I could command my body to action, the gun was already in my hand and aimed and my finger against the trigger. The horror I felt upon finding it was your father . . . There are no words, Ophelia, for the horror or my grief. I hid him to buy the time to see you, to tell you, and then seeing you I couldn't find the words I should have spoken.

"I destroy that which I most love, and so all my destruction centers in you. You bear my pain, my grief, you take the bruises from my hands, and because of my love, you lose everything that can be held dear, and I am sorry for it, more sorry than you'll ever know.

"Tom Rosencrantz and Tom Guildenstern have long since reached England with the letters from my uncle in hand, letters which listed my name with a reminder of favors owed and a favor requested in response. He would have had me killed at the hands of his friends, in a foreign land where it cannot be connected to him, where by the time it filtered back to the parents and students of Elsinore Academy, it would have been just a tragic accident born of my own recklessness. Given my behavior over the past months, is there anyone there who would doubt it, save you and Horatio? Death would be no unwelcome thing, I think, but not now. Not yet.

"My promise was made foolishly, I know that. In life my father would never have asked such a thing of anyone; that he should ask it in death should have been enough to make me walk away with no oath made. But he is my father, even if his soul is sundered by the manner of his death, so perhaps I would have made the promise anyway. For his honor, for my honor, you again bear the price, a price beyond any reasonable measure. But the promise was made and must be kept, and I have much yet to do.

"I write this as a guest of Monticello Academy, a personal guest of Reggie Fortin, and I've been allowed to sit in the classrooms and witness firsthand the changes he wishes to introduce to Elsinore, and Ophelia . . . does it make me a disloyal son to think his changes would be no bad thing? The girls here speak of careers and achievements, things done in their own name, not of some unnamed, unknown future husband, and it's a daily race between the boys and girls for the highest ranks within the classes. They're happy, even with all the extra work, and I think so many of Elsinore's girls would feel the same way if they were only challenged in this manner. I've told Reggie some of what has occurred at Elsinore these months past—not all, surely not all—but some, and he has promised to continue his persistence. He reminds me a great deal of Horatio, whose heart will break when he opens an envelope and finds a will folded between the pages of a letter that can never say as much as it needs to, and the thought helps ease the pain.

"Soon after you read this, I will be on my way back to Elsinore to do what must be done to end these bloody games. That there will be more blood before they find their end I have no doubt, for death engenders death, like a plague that cripples us at our greatest strength. One way or another, promise kept or broken, this will end.

"And I hope to everything holy that you aren't there to witness it. For his family, for his future, Horatio must stay, because if he surrenders this what else will he have? But you, Ophelia, you have only the lake waiting for you there, and I can't abide the thought of you keeping your promise so soon. Your mother's promise, your promise, they're patient ones, ones that will abide until the time has come, and that time need not arrive anytime soon.

"Run away, Ophelia. Come here to Monticello, if you'd like, and Reggie will offer you sanctuary, but run away somewhere, far away from Elsinore and the bloody end that comes. Wherever you go, I'll find you if I should survive it, and even if I die to keep this wretched oath, Horatio will find you, take care of you. Just run away so none of this can bruise you anymore, so the rest of us on our paths to Hell cannot drag you down with us. You're an angel, Ophelia, the angel that bears my pain and every good thing about me, the only reason there is anything left of that goodness, and it is that in me that urges you—begs you—to run away. Escape the ending of this tragedy.

"Name me in your prayers, sweet angel, and someday, perhaps you can forgive me for all the ways I destroy you through our love. Yours ever, with all the love my twisted soul can offer, Dane."

Mama smoothes the creases from the pages and sets each one to float on the lake. The lake is hungry, so hungry, and it devours the paper and the ink and the words, so many words, words, words, not enough meaning that makes sense anymore.

And as the pages break into pieces, as the bonds between the words dissolve into disparate breaths and syllables, Mama laughs and watches them die.

CHAPTER 39

I could escape.

Statement or question? Dane seems so sure of it, but then he so often does. Dane lives in a world of certainties where even the worst torments might be escaped if one has the courage to take arms against them. He never woke in the middle of the night to his mother's soft kiss before she fled to that strange world beyond, my own undiscovered country. He never saw her eyes with her inevitable return, always a little more broken, a little more heartsick. A little more wild.

Of course, Mama also never had someone to run *to*, never had someone to make a place for her as Dane says Reggie Fortin would make for me. A place in a school that challenges the girls as much as the boys, a place where I could truly learn. Maybe even become.

Become what? Mama had to read me Dane's letter because the words on the page shattered. Monticello has strong girls who make names for themselves; I can't even make sense of my own name on a sheet of paper. Monticello has no place for my fragments.

I shrug off Horatio's blazer, peel out of Mama's fancy gown and leave it next to her on the shore. Delicate ice crystals, with little more substance than wishes, break against my bare legs as I step into the shallows of the lake. The cold shocks the breath from my body, but I take another step, then another, aware of Mama's hungry attention at my back. My slip soaks up the water, the stain and damp drifting above my waist, rising nearly to the murmuring star.

I could keep walking.

I could escape.

I can't tell anymore if they're the same thing. Maybe I never could. Could Dane?

I remember death. I remember the silence and the stillness, the absolute serenity. I remember that there was no fear, no dread of something after. This constant terror, this uncertainty, this unceasing pain didn't exist, but beyond the gates of Elsinore, they exist in abundance. Mama was so afraid, until she went into the lake and she wasn't. Barely an echo of memory remains anymore.

Somewhere in Virginia, there's a school of red brick and white plaster and marble, a school without a cemetery, without despair and death and every choking thing. There's a school with its arms open, willing to embrace a shattered girl, to do everything it can to keep her from breaking further.

The lake can never break a whole person.

It can only fill the empty ones.

Dane put a gun to his temple and asked a question, but he couldn't pull the trigger. The specter of dreams gave him pause. Fear is such a creeping thing, but it doesn't have to exist. Just a few steps . . .

I walk back to the shore, where Mama wordlessly helps me back into the dress, and I sit shivering next to her on the tangle of roots. Her hands move over my knotted hair, tying in bits of leaves and dried flowers from deconstructed crowns. She hums softly, a song I used to know, something about unfaithful knights and too-loyal damsels and tragic endings.

I don't want to be afraid anymore. I just don't know how to be less than afraid for Dane. *For* Dane, never *of* him. Never of him, never truly. There's a girl who could do as he asks, who could take action unfettered by pale thoughts, who could race out into the unknown and trust people to catch her, who could throw herself headfirst into life and forge an unbreakable name, an identity that stands on its own without fathers or brothers or loves who devour and shatter.

I've never been that girl.

When Mama slips gracefully back into the lake to rejoin the morgens, I listen to the whispers of the star in my veins and wait for Horatio to make me feel real again, even if it's only for a little while.

It isn't Horatio who comes back for me, though, but the youngest under-gardener. As he eyes my sodden gown with concern, he tells me that Horatio has been sent on an errand for the Headmaster, and I marvel that it was asked of him, that he went.

The under-gardener follows me into the house, and as I pass through the kitchen I can hear his half-formed protest meant to keep me there, but the cook touches his arm, tears in her eyes, and shakes her head, and he lets me go without argument.

Gertrude rushes past me when I reach the stairs, one hand clapped over her mouth and tears bright in her eyes, on her cheeks. Rushing away so no one can see her cry, because she doesn't realize we can hear her through the walls.

Skirts in hand to keep from stumbling on them, I retrace her steps to the Headmaster's study, the door still slightly ajar. My brother paces inside, his fury a living force within him that will not let him stand still.

I sink down into a fountain of fabric in the doorway, hands clasped in my lap, a little girl ready to hear her lessons and lies. So I used to sit as I listened to Mama's stories of bells beneath the waters or rage in the woods. So I used to sit as I listened to Father's insistence that there was no such thing.

"Laertes, you cannot simply announce in front of Gertrude that you intend to kill her son!" snaps Claudius. Crystal clinks against glass.

"Do not think you can talk me out of it."

"I have no intention of doing so." The astonishment is heavy in Laertes' silence, and Claudius knows to press his advantage. "The boy killed your father, and your desire for revenge is both natural and understandable. But you must *think*, Laertes! We do not live in a time of such lenient laws. Every death must be accounted for. You cannot go around proclaiming your intent to kill someone, especially not in front of that someone's mother! For all his faults, Dane is her son, and Gertrude loves him deeply. To hear you speak so causes her great pain, and I cannot have that."

"But—"

"If you are to achieve your aim, you must be more careful."

"You're serious about this."

"I am. To have Dane arrested, to have him tried and imprisoned . . . it would be a wound forever against the Danemark name, against this school. I love this school, Laertes, as your father loved this school and dedicated his life to its well-being. If you race ahead without thought or planning, you will bring this school to its knees."

For all his passion, my brother has never stopped to think what it actually means to kill someone. Claudius has.

He would have had friends in England do it for him, but now he has something better, something closer, something that cannot be placed upon him.

He has my brother.

Laertes, the biggest kind of fool, more than ever our father's son.

Claudius sighs and presses a glass into my brother's hand, a glass filled nearly to the brim with bourbon. "Drink this, Laertes, and sit down, and for love of all that's holy, listen to me. You can have your revenge, and I will assist you in it, but you must trust me, and you must listen to me."

"You would help me k—"

"I would help you avenge your father," Claudius corrects with a pained grimace. *Killing*, after all, is such an ugly word. "Dane will be back in a few days—"

Laertes cuts him off with a furious stream of words and the scrape of a chair against a hardwood floor. He's pacing again, lashing out against framed certificates and stacks of books and knick-knacks atop filing cabinets, a storm of destruction confined in such a narrow space. My brother the boxer.

301

"Laertes Castellan! Sit down!"

Claudius has never been a father, but he is a man used to giving orders that must be obeyed. Laertes sits before his body even registers the command.

"As I was saying," Claudius continues, his face and voice so very strained, "Dane will be back in a few days." He holds up a letter on heavy, familiar paper. "I've sent Mr. Tennant to escort him back from Virginia, but we have some time to make our plans. His return will give us the opportunity to do what needs to be done."

What needs to be done? Dane used those same words, minutes—hours—ago, days ago as he wrote the letter that sealed his promises in ink.

"Like what?"

"The first thing we must do is salvage the Danemark reputation. Elsinore Academy must be above reproach, so we must appear to welcome Dane back."

"Welcome—"

"Shut up," he says icily, and my brother sinks back into the chair, his protest dead on his lips. "We must *appear* to welcome him. Rumor is a plague, but there's no *proof* that Dane killed your father. Only what Gertrude saw, and we will not ask her to speak against her son."

"But—"

"Laertes, you will have your revenge, but unless you want to spend the rest of your life in prison for murder, you will help me in this! We must kill these rumors! And the swiftest, surest way to do this is for you to be the one who welcomes him back. After all, what son would knowingly embrace his father's killer? Whatever happened in that room, we call it an unfortunate accident and say that Dane ran because he was scared. We can make up an intruder if we have to, but we show the world that there's no ill will between the two of you."

"I'm not that good an actor," spits Laertes.

But Claudius chuckles, a menacing sound nearly lost to the splash of bourbon in his glass. "Your father thought you were a virgin; you lie well enough."

Blood rushes to my brother's faces, even as he gapes soundlessly.

"The Board of Governors is uneasy, and rightly so. We are going to reassure them." Claudius takes a long drink and sets his glass down with a heavy thunk against the desk. "We are going to give Dane a few days to settle back into his home. Then we are going to invite the Board and their wives for a dinner, where they will see you and Dane being friends. Lie to them half as well as you've lied to the girls in your bed, and we'll be well placed."

There's a small, traitorous part of me that admires Claudius' directness. He has my brother squirming in his seat, his reputation dependent on Claudius holding his silence in the matter. Between that knowledge and the offer of revenge, he has my brother firmly in his debt.

A debt is a promise.

And Hamlet taught us to keep our promises.

Laertes swallows hard and shoves his tangled hair out of his face. It never used to be so long; Father wouldn't allow it. "What then?" he asks hoarsely.

"As a cap to the evening, you and Dane will entertain our guests with a boxing match. An exhibition of sorts."

"A boxing match!" Laertes kicks the desk, but under Claudius' minatory glare, he stays in his seat. "So I give him a good beating, so what? He *killed* my *father!*"

"You've never had to wait for anything in your life, have you?" Claudius leans back in his leather-backed chair, a dangerous smile on his lips. Smiles are supposed to soften, to brighten, but Claudius' smile is like a razor slashed across the skin. He sips the spirits, replaces the glass exactly where it was. "The ring is where you'll have your revenge, but the beating is only the beginning."

"How?"

Leaning down, Claudius twists a key into a drawer of his desk and slides it open, rummaging briefly through its contents. "With these," he answers, laying the objects on the smooth wood.

I can't see the first from the floor in the doorway. Something metal that catches the light. But the second . . .

303

"Is that poison?"

Milky-white and semiopaque, clinging to the sides of the glass vial, and only half full.

Oh, Laertes, my stupid brother, can you really be such a fool? Do you really think he'll let you live to tell his part in this?

"Coat the knuckles in the poison and wear them inside your glove," instructs Claudius. "If you can deliver a few good blows, you'll open the skin and that's all this needs to work. A little goes a long way and will be less suspicious. Aim for his head, if you can. Boxing is a violent sport, you know. Aneurysms are an unfortunate consequence."

Laertes stares at the weapons on the desk. "What if it's . . . what if . . ." He closes his eyes, block them from sight, and tries again. "What if it's not enough?" he whispers.

Irritation flashes across Claudius' face, gone before my brother can open his eyes. "I intend to give each of you some wine for a toast before the match. Dane's will have a potent . . . additive."

Dane would never accept a glass from Claudius, and a heartbeat later, Laertes puts my thought into words.

"He will from his mother."

Will she know? Will she ever know or wonder? Does she wonder about her husband?

His hands shake so badly the glass rattles against the metal knuckles with their vicious points, but Laertes takes them anyway and slips them carefully into his pocket. "How will you get Dane to agree to all this? There's no prize, nothing to make it worth the risk."

"Ah, but there is a prize." That smile again. Goose bumps prickle along my spine. "One Dane cannot possibly resist."

"Which is?"

"Before I tell you, there is one condition to all this," he says firmly. "You must not speak of any of this. To anyone. As far as anyone outside this room is concerned, your father's death was a regrettable accident and you look forward to Dane's return. You absolutely cannot mention this to Gertrude; it would destroy her.

Though it must be done for the good of us all, I would spare her what pain I could."

The way he speaks, sometimes it's easy to believe he really loves her, that all these years it's been love alongside the jealousy that drives his actions. But such a love can only ever be poisoned, such a love can only ever bring about destruction and death, because such a love always wants the very thing it cannot have. It's the love that leaves a good man dead, that breaks a boy who loves his father.

"I promise," Laertes snaps. "What prize?"

Claudius turns his chair slightly, and suddenly he's looking right at me with that horrible smile. He's known I was here all along. "Your sister. With your father dead, Gertrude is now her legal guardian. If he comes back for anything, he'll come back for her."

Horatio isn't here, he's gone and isn't here, and I have no way to tell him now—now while I can keep the thoughts where they ought to be—the danger that Dane faces, that my brother faces. I can't write it because the letters and shapes lost their meaning, can't tell someone else because they won't believe me.

The star blazes down to my fingertips, fingers that trace the ring of bruises around my neck, my arms, the silver ring that keeps my soul tied to my body. It blazes and burns until there's no air, not even the memory of what it means to breathe.

Dane will die.

Laertes will follow.

And Horatio . . .

The best of us will shatter until there's nothing left.

There's just nothing left.

The star blazes and burns.

And dies.

CHAPTER 40

There's a terrible emptiness where my heart should be, where a star danced and twirled and whispered a name that meant so much more than my own.

Just a void, a void that spins and pulls and devours.

Consumes.

It tears the heat from my veins, destroys the tongues of flame.

There's no cold.

No ice.

Just . . . nothing.

Dane will die.

Laertes will die.

They'll both . . .

But the word doesn't mean anything, lost to the hungry void and the ring of dazzling darkness that surrounds it, grows with it. It used to mean something, but it doesn't anymore, the meaning gone along with the whispers and the murmurs and the words inked into my skin with sweat, tears, and kisses.

No one will escape.

The house reeks of death and fear.

Dane made a promise, but he'll die before he can keep it. A promise is a noose around the neck.

Laertes follows Claudius' gaze and sees me in the doorway, grabs me with bruising force and drags me up the stairs to my room. He's frantic, terrified of what he's about to do, but he'll do it anyway, because my brother is the biggest kind of fool. He tears Mama's gowns from the wall, tries to stuff them into the trunk, but there's too much fabric and too much memory, and it scalds his skin until he runs away.

Always running away.

Running away from the Hunt.

Running away from the stories.

Running away from Mama, from grief, from Elsinore.

Running away from me.

Because Laertes has always been scared of me.

Of me.

And that kind of fear never dies.

Mama's wedding dress spills from the trunk like a snowfall, a flag of surrender. I drop my dress to the floor, pull on the cloud of moonlight white. This dress tied Mama to Elsinore, to Father, to Laertes, and later to me, but I was the only one she could stand to be bound to, because I was the only one that understood that bonds didn't have to be cages. Because I was the one who could never walk away.

All my life, I've been a bruise against the world.

Now I'm a ghost.

No one ever sees the ghosts.

Should never.

No good can come of ghosts.

Dark has fallen, the clouds of an endless day of grey blown away. Blue-white flames flicker in the cemetery, the soil hard and frozen beneath my feet. The staff buried Jack beside my mother and decked their graves in the last of the hothouse flowers before they let the doors stay open, let the cold kill the plants that were never truly alive. Ghosts of flowers.

They didn't find my father.

But Jack's grave is dark like my mother's. There's no ghost to lament the loss of a life.

Jack's only regret was that he couldn't keep the flowers alive.

Ghosts can't help the flowers live.

Jack will never be a ghost.

But Hamlet is and Hamlet is and they watch me from their grave, solemn and weary. The rage still burns within one, but even he watches me with a terrible compassion, side by side with his better half, identical men whose faces have changed so much in death. They say nothing, just watch me pass through the graveyard, and when I look back over my shoulder from the wrought iron fence, they each lift a hand to me. One angel holds a sword, a terrible, patient justice, but the other clutches a dove rather than release it because it's terrified at the thought of empty hands. "Good night, child," they whisper together. "Sleep well."

But beyond the graveyard are the woods, deep and dark and far from silent, and the flashes of white and grey that no one ever sees. So many of the trees are skeletons now, their leaves a dead blanket beneath my feet, and they reach up to the sky with bony fingers that try to pray, and the wind whistles through their branches to give them voice like a death rattle.

And then the hounds bay, mournful and lost, the despair past the cry that human throats can give, and the Hunt approaches. They glow in the night with their borrowed faerie graces, a warning to those who fear madness. They ride and they ride and they ride, a journey without end, every moment praying for the journey to stop. They slow to a walk and then rein in, and the horses' heads droop with weariness. The men sit bowed and broken in their saddles, their eyes lost to a wildness and endlessness that human minds were never meant to bear, and the greyhounds across their laps bay and cry.

I lift my cupped hands and the nearest hound sniffs my palms cautiously, nuzzles into the unfamiliar touch. Its tail wags, ever so slightly, and then stops; his head drops back to the horse's withers and the eyes close with a great, heaving sigh.

I look up into the face that was once human, transformed by centuries of hopelessness. "I'm sorry," I whisper. "Not yet."

Maybe not ever.

The rider touches his hand to his heart, his lips, his forehead, extends it towards me in salute, and nudges his exhausted mount into motion. The others follow slowly, and then each step falls faster, harder against the frozen earth, and they're a blur of sorrow and rage in the harsh, frigid wind that stings tears into my eyes.

The woods aren't empty, overfull of despair that chokes and withers all it touches, but it drowns in the spinning void in my chest. A silver-white glow beckons me from the sleeping skeletons, and I follow the trail of the lament as it twists through the wind, follow it towards the weepers, the keeners, the sorrow singers, the wails of a night without stars.

They pull me into their circle, but my voice is suited to laughter, not to song, and through every note I can hear the endless, patient murmur of the lake in my bones, my veins, rushing into the void where my heart used to be. The bean sidhe kiss my cheeks and stroke my hair and re-form their circle behind me, their song soft and gentle and so full of love I would weep if I remembered how, but the lake never shares its water, never gives, only takes.

At the shore, the bean nighe nod from their silver basin, heaping bags of cloth between them. There's so much there, so much fabric soaked in blood and poison, so much death, but I asked them my question already, and the void doesn't care who else drowns within it. It's only ever hungry. They slap the clothes against the washboards, the suds clinging to their bare arms.

The morgens dance and laugh and play around the island, and Mama sits like a queen on its shore, the skeletal fronds of the willows still heavy with dried flower crowns around her. Her pale skin glows in the moonlight, surrounded by a wealth of night-purple hair and bruise-colored eyes, only the beginnings of the legacy she gave to me.

I could escape.

Not the way Dane wants—I'm as bound to Elsinore as my parents before me—but the way Mama does. She escaped and left the path open for me to follow.

Her wedding dress whispers secrets as I cross to the midpoint of the lake, to the frozen chain that leads to the island and the dance and the laughter. The chain sways when I step on it, and I sway with it, the edges of the skirts soaking up the dark water with every foot of progress. The metal burns my feet, so very cold, and delicate fractals break across the surface as the fabric and the skin drag across the ice that would try so hard to form.

Once upon a time there was a star that blazed within my chest and the heat suffused me, melted the ice that tried to form, but now there's a great, devouring nothingness in its place and the ice still can't form.

The lake is just as hungry.

Mama steadies me as I land upon the island, and my bones shake with the toll of the bells of the City of Ys. She pulls a wreath of dried roses from the weeping trees and places it carefully upon my head, twining tangled locks of hair through the weave to anchor it there. The bells toll and the bean sidhe sing and my feet move in their familiar pattern around the corona of dead flowers, skirts spinning and twirling like the star that used to dance and murmur.

There's a city that waits and waits and waits beneath the lake, where thousands of candles burn like stars in the night sky and the bells toll the hours in dozens of cathedrals to float through the darkness and stillness and silence. There's a city that drowned and now it waits, waits for another to fall so it may rise, but it gave away a key and the tide came in.

The morgens dance, but Mama doesn't, she just floats a short distance away and watches me with my eyes. I reach out to her, and our fingers barely touch, she's too far away, farther even than the dried crowns that hover over the rippling surface that reflects back a million billion stars and galaxies, a million billion points of other pains. I stretch and then I'm falling and she catches me, the lake catches me and cradles me and whispers *mine*, and in the terrible emptiness there's an echoing cry of *minemineminemineminemine*.

"Welcome home, Ophelia," murmurs my mother, and water soaks through a million secrets and carries me deeper into the darkness, but there, in the distance, thousands of candles burn, candles in windows and streets and the hands of women who laugh and dance and play and left fear and grief far behind.

Sound rushes to my head, a throbbing, panicked beat, an iron band across my chest, but Mama takes my hand and leads me closer to the lights that flicker and weave, and the sound bursts with a great cry.

The rest is silence.

ACKNOWLEDGMENTS

Quite simply, this book would not be in your hands right now without the chances extended to me by the fabulous Sandy Lu, Agent Extraordinaire, and my brilliant editor, Andrew Karre, who was honestly in favor of putting in *more puns*. They took a risk on me, and not only are they a joy to work with, but they took my words and helped me craft them into something so much better. I will be forever grateful to both of them and to the amazing teams at L. Perkins Agency and Carolrhoda Lab. A huge thank-you goes to my family. They've put up with any number of quirks and neuroses over the years (like walking into a room only to realize I'm talking out loud to my characters) and have always been relentlessly supportive, even when I didn't feel like I was accomplishing anything. With silly cakes and clipped-out articles, ridiculous over-the-top story ideas and mocking sales strategies just to make me laugh, they've been there every step of the way.

Thank you to the crew at work, not just for being excited for me but also for listening to me prattle on about everything. Also to those at the Archer Road CFA—aka my Writing Cave—for babysitting the girl writing novels in the corner and keeping me well supplied with caffeine and enthusiasm. Veronica, Christine, and Margaret were my first readers in this, so huge thanks for their feedback, especially Veronica, who listened to me endlessly on every neurotic worry and project detail for the last eight years and is probably the only one who'll ever understand why family trees crack me up. Older gratitude goes to the Ros and Guil gang: Betty-Jane, JD, and Jeff. We drove everyone else (and one another) crazy, but our endless debates and questions are really the genesis of this book, especially the Wine and Laundry Night discussions with Jeff that sparked a lifelong fascination with Ophelia.

I think all modern writers owe a huge debt to their teachers, but there are a few I'd like to mention by name: Dr. Robert Carroll, who saw promise in a ten-year-old's awful stories and cheered me on long after I was out of his classroom; Tammy Meyers, who taught me how closely writing and drama are linked; Anne Shaughnessy, who had us in stitches with Falstaff and Hal and in awe with *As You Like It*, our first realization that Shakespeare was allowed to be *fun*; Robert Wentzlaff, who not only gave me a chance but also taught me so much about dreams and achieving them; Ted Lewis, who taught me that novels and plays spring from the same impulse; and Dr. John Omlor, my honors thesis adviser, who was the first person to tell me to Do Something with my writing. From all of you I learned more than I can possibly say, and I'm forever in your debt.

Every day I am awed and humbled by the amazing YA community, the genuine fellowship that exists among authors, readers, bloggers, and aspirants. The advice, enthusiasm, and support, the no-holds-barred cheering for everyone's accomplishments, the open arms with which they welcome everyone transforms a nerve-racking time into something wondrous. A particular shout-out goes to Tessa Gratton, who's always ready with a hugely inappropriate (i.e. *awesome*) *Hamlet* joke—the Bard, I think, would be proud.

And finally, to you, because readers are the ones who make all of this possible. Thank you.

ABOUT THE AUTHOR

Dot Hutchison has worked in retail, taught at a Boy Scout camp, and fought in human combat chessboards, but she's most grateful that she can finally call writing work. When not immersed in the worlds-between-pages, she can frequently be found dancing around like an idiot, tracing stories in the stars, or waiting for storms to roll in from the ocean. She currently lives in Florida. This is her debut novel. Visit her online at ww.dothutchison.com.